Dear Josephine

The Steep Climes Quartet:
Book Two

The Steep Climes Quartet, Book One: *Kill Well*
The Steep Climes Quartet, Book Two: *Dear Josephine*
The Steep Climes Quartet, Book Three: *Over Brooklyn Hills*
The Steep Climes Quartet, Book Four: *Farm to Me*

Dear Josephine
[The Steep Climes Quartet, Book Two]
© David R. Guenette, 2025

ISBN 979-8-9885055-3-2
LCCN 2025905291

CMTI Publishing
21 Corashire Road
New Marlborough, MA 01230
www.cmtipublishing.com

What reviewers and readers are saying about *Kill Well*, The Steep Climes Quartet: Book One

Murder is another dire effect of climate change in Guenette's labyrinthine thriller. This first installment of the author's Steep Climes series envisions a near future in which catastrophic heat, droughts, and floods are fraying society, hobbling the economy, and nurturing deadly conspiracies…. Even global-warming deniers will enjoy the resulting page-turner. Despite overdone soapboxing, vivid characters and hardboiled writing make this an entertaining suspenser.
— Kirkus Reviews

Set in a near future where the DSM 7 includes a diagnosis of "climate anxiety," [Kill Well,] the first entry in The Steep Climes Quartet, Guenette's pointedly realistic thriller series, opens with a bang… A pointedly realistic thriller of murder, the fossil fuel industry, and climate activism.
— BookLife Reviews

Introspective and solemn, Kill Well *by David Guenette is a story of murder and danger, written by an author with a beautiful grasp of the English language, and an obviously deep, powerful, and intense passion for the harsh and shocking realities of climate change. There is everything to be said about an author who can turn that much knowledge into a thriller that often catches the reader off guard with its stunning realism.*
— Independent Book Review

Kill Well *is a smart, taut thriller that grabs you on the first page and keeps you guessing all the way to the suspenseful conclusion. David Guenette knows a lot about hacking and corporate skullduggery, and he knows a lot about people too.*
— Tom Perrotta is author of *Election* and *Little Children*, both of which were made into critically acclaimed, Academy Award-nominated films, and for *Little Children* he received an Academy Award nomination for Best Adapted Screenplay. His novels *The Leftovers* and *Mrs. Fletcher* have been adapted into TV series on HBO. His most recent novel is *Tracy Flick Can't Win*.

David Guenette manages to show that the climate crisis is already affecting our energy and food bills and intensifying the drama of local politics. Kill Well is a fun ride but uncomfortable, too, as we get another way to think about where we're heading all too quickly.
— Karen Christensen, CEO and Publisher, Berkshire Publishing Company and author of *Eco Living, The Green Home,* and *Home Ecology* (book and Substack newsletter)

No drowned worlds or climate-ravaged zombies, but a solid story with compelling characters that leaves you thinking that you haven't been thinking nearly enough about climate change. I can't wait until the next book in this series hits.
    —Larry D. Gussin, Gussin Climate Action Fund at The Sierra Club Foundation

Climate change is not something that is happening independent of people's lives, but rather is already part of each of our lives. Kill Well *helps you see that, and, like a magic trick, gives a poignant, entertaining, and funny read along the way.*
    —Winslow Eliot, author of ten novels, including *Bright Face of Danger, Heaven Falls, The Happiness Cure,* and *A Perfect Gem*

Kill Well *is more than just a suspenseful murder thriller. It combines the reality of climate change and climate activism, the potential devious tactics that the fossil fuel industry has at its disposal, and how difficult it is to exist without surveillance tracking you.*
    —Amazon Review

This is a terrific book and the first of its kind that I've read. It deftly combines a page-turning thriller with the dangers of climate change and the dark forces behind it, all the while giving us rich characters that you either care about greatly or strongly loathe…. One of the things I love is that there's plenty of climate change consequences, but experienced the way most of us experience these, which is in the background, lurking, and so easily put out of mind. This tension between real danger and our lack of recognition of it reflects the plot's progress that likewise moves unthinkingly through self-centered interactions, but all with the punch you want in an entertaining read.
    —Amazon Review

The detective story is gripping and unfolds in the context of dark corporate forces working to maintain the corporate status quo. Guenette gets us inside the heads of his characters, even into the minds of evildoers. The balance between the ordinary Main Street concerns and the bigger picture takes surprising twists and turns.
    —Amazon Review

It is amazing how David Guenette is able to blend emotions, anxieties of ordinary people who besides facing the challenges of everyday life, live at a time when drastic changes the environment will be very soon real and frightening. Yet, the language of the novel is so down to earth and friendly that makes the reading of this breathtakingly seductive.
    —Amazon Review

Contents

What changed in the United States with Hurricane Katrina was a feeling that we have entered a period of consequences.

Al Gore

Dear Josephine

The Steep Climes Quartet: Book Two

David Guenette

CMTI Publishing, New Marlborough, MA, USA

Chapter 1: Hear Noothink, See Nootink

He doesn't mind waiting in the dark.

In fact, I like it, William McPherson tells himself, although his telling himself this yet again, in what is likely the fifth or sixth time by his count since getting into position nearly thirteen hours before, suggests otherwise.

It is late March, 2029, and that it is 2029 seems barely possible, as if the turn of this century couldn't be more than just a few years old, but his sense of time has altered radically since he decided on his mission.

He's sorry that he hadn't been ready for the Ides of March. He likes the idea of the date for killing this first target, but he likes even more getting all the preparation done, and he simply hadn't felt ready, and this has him now thinking of his new life.

His old dread is gone, the dread of heading into work, the dread of all those endless conversations with his wife, some complaint or other he'd never understood, some formless criticism. But now he mainly feels excitement, although there is dread, sure, but it is an excited form of dread, a worry about getting caught, but that's why he spends so much time reducing that likelihood. It is a puzzle, exciting like a good puzzle, the sort of feeling that reminds him of how he had felt in his early career when he was doing interesting things and figuring out solutions, finding the best processes, but that had all disappeared over the years, substituted by his sense of simply grinding things out, like what the marriage had come to, too, a seemingly endless grind, day after day of growing dread, any hour, any week like any other, a deadening blur.

He's pushed back into the foliage near the front entrance, behind a cascade of what he is pretty sure is wisteria, pressed back into the boxwood, or whatever exactly the evergreen is that forms the long hedge. Tight up against the hedge is a high iron fence. Behind the fence is a stone terrace right off the side the house, and a tennis court is somewhere a good hundred feet or more from the side of the house.

House, he snorts, thinking about how big the place is, *a goddamn mansion, a goddamn palace.*

He's been snuggled into the boxwood since before dawn.

The urine bladder strapped to his left leg feels dangerously full. The Texas catheter feels loose.

He resists the urge to move to look at his phone, but he knows quite well the movement would be a waste of effort since his phone is turned off and in a foil sleeve.

Not to mention stupid, he tells himself. He's been ping free for two days.

Keeping the private residence's motion detectors and the video cameras off the whole time, he knows, is not a good plan, with resets being one thing and a full-on and long-running shutdown quite another. He'd done his homework, spending many hours combing corners of the dark web for schematics and tutorials, and the reboot signal device is one of the results.

Thinking about this, he reaches down, knees slowly bending, so his gloved hand can brush the top of the knapsack that sits at his feet, pushed into the boxwood. He's tested out the blind spot for this front corner area's motion detector, but limiting his movement is still a sensible precaution.

He's wearing a dark green coverall, plus cheap synthetic work gloves, mechanic gloves that anyone can buy anywhere, not that he'll leave anything behind. The coverall is loose fitting, does a good job reading as shadow, and with the cap, the gloves, the tucked and black duct-taped cuffs, there is little chance leaving much in the way of forensic traces of himself.

He knows he's got to be good at this.

Goddamn right, he tells himself as he moves slowly back to lean fully up against the crinkled branches and tiny dark green leaves, his weight now largely resting on the dark foliage compressed against the iron fence. The dense branches of the hedge feel like a spring, and he feels ready to shift fully forward at a moment's notice, ready to step through past the wisteria toward the top of the driveway circle.

The hardest part is the waiting.

But he remains excited. His new life is a mission, and he can sometimes wonder how long it has been since he'd felt alive, not feeling kicked, stepped on, suffocated.

He takes a deep breath.

He is standing, pushed back into the deep and ancient boxwood hedge, the trailing big vines of wisteria providing more coverage, and the gloom of the darkling evening coming on in this late-March day adds to his sense he is invisible. From behind the thick bare wisteria vines he can partly see the front of the driveway circle where he is sure the target will park. He's sure the target will go up the stone steps, pause to dig out his keys, and work the lock open.

He's managed to nap in short stretches, leaning this way into the hedge, knowing his driveway-approach telltale will vibrate and sound if anyone turns off the country road to drive up the long driveway toward the house. He knows the fastest the target has ever gone from car and through the front door is eleven seconds, and the target seemed in a hurry that one time. Most of the recordings capturing the target getting out of his car are more like half a minute or a bit more if the target reaches back in for a briefcase or small travel bag. In one of his surveillance videos, the target retrieved a takeaway bag from the Chinese restaurant the target passes when staying at his country place.

He waits. He knows there's a small shed behind the hedge and the iron fence that is tucked behind where he waits at the front corner of the main house structure. He feels like he knows so many things about this property, about the target's habits, about the net worth and assets of this target he's researched so deeply.

He still too often disbelieves that there are people like the target, that there are so many of them, *goddamn world-eaters*, and he starts to see he's letting himself get upset, so he does his breathing exercises.

He doesn't want to get caught, of course, but he has done so much so that he won't, not with all the work, all the time and attention he's expended thinking through how to do it, how to start on his list pulled from the Fortune 400, the list of targets that he aims to kill.

He waits in the gathering dark.

He'd like to know how the shed gets used, what the purpose is of this small structure behind the hedge, but it doesn't really matter.

Probably tennis stuff, he guesses.

It doesn't matter. He has thoroughly surveyed the property, using a stealthy drone preprogrammed and operating without a radio or Wi-Fi signal, grid-programmed and running dark at night when the house is unoccupied.

He's previously retrieved the video camera he placed in a tree branch of one of the trees that form the wood's edge on the other side of the road opposite the long driveway's start. The camera's placement provided clear line of sight to the front of the house, and even though the camera was a far way off, the lens and resolution were still good enough for his surveillance needs, and the many days of video have been streamed and carefully reviewed.

All without any trace or anyone's notice of anything, he is confident. He is pleased with this system he's been developing and refining.

Earlier thermal scans showed him the house remains at

heating and lighting levels that should only happen when someone is home, although even then, this itself would be a huge energy expense.

Got it, flaunt it, is what he thinks. *Assholes.*

The full structure amounts to nearly 11,000 square feet, he's figured, and that isn't counting the several outbuildings. He knows the target comes here infrequently, but more this time of year when the target's in the city for the annual meetings, a busy time with many other meetings scheduled.

The house gets used by the target during this time, and the target almost never brings anyone back, as best as he has determined. There are no full-time servants and no active security staff, but everything is digital with on-call drive-by security checks a person could set his watch to.

He now knows this schedule well. He's seen the checks come by twice today, with one more to go, but he'll be long gone by then.

Idiot, the waiting man thinks, judging the target. *The arrogance, the presumption.* The waiting man snorts in the dark, then starts, seeing a brief glint of headlights through distant trees further down the small country road.

It's him, the waiting man tells himself. He has to fight against his excitement and struggles to keep his breathing even.

The telltale vibrates as the car turns into the driveway, heading toward the house.

In the hedge by the corner of the house where the ancient wisteria vines run up naked onto the stone façade front portico, the man slowly moves his hand to the black knapsack, draws it up slow-motion and painstakingly slowly, slings one shoulder strap over his head, settling the knapsack, its top open, so it's midway down his chest, the contents easily available.

He reaches in and locates the reset switch box by feel, hand grasping it, thumb over the button.

The car pulling up is a Tesla, the newest luxury model,

as he learned when doing background on the target, a small complication in that it uses a biometric locking system.

I got to hand it to myself, the man says, somewhat embarrassed by the joke, but also liking it. Still holding the switch box, the man shifts slightly and gently touches the back of his hand against the top of the bolt cutter, which was vertically placed with care on one side of the knapsack so it can be easily drawn when needed. Then the man is back to concentrating on the car's approach.

The target always swings leftward into the circle and is doing this once again.

The man lowers his face and the dark cap visor and the dark overalls create a blending shadow as the car's headlights sweep over the boxwood hedge and wisteria vines for the briefest of moments, and then the car stops, shuts down.

Showtime.

The man presses the switch that triggers a reboot and system check of the house security systems, taking the security system and the cameras offline for almost a minute.

The man lets go of the switch box and shifts his hand inside the knapsack to wrap around the pistol grip. The Tesla's driver door whines open and the target is climbing out, so the man steps out from the hedge and gently and carefully teases the pistol from the knapsack and raises it, walking closer to the target. The target is turning back to get something from the car, and as the target straightens back up, the dark-covered man sees the Chinese takeaway bag, and then the target is reaching into his suit coat pocket for *the keys*. The man steps toward the target and squeezes the trigger, the first-round dead center in the target's forehead.

The man fires two more rounds into the target's center mass.

The target is still falling as the man's strides bring him close up.

He lowers the knapsack, dumps the gun in, and grabs the bolt cutter. It takes a moment to pull the target's right arm clear and another brief moment to finger the man's semi-clenched hand and placing the bolt cutter carefully at the base of the target's thumb, cutting between the thumb joint, through the tendon and skin. He picks up the thumb, then picks up the keys with the car dongle. He grabs his knapsack and steps over the body to the Tesla's still-up door, which is a timing bonus, he realizes.

Perfect, didn't think that through.

He rummages for the signal block and flips it on and tosses it onto the passenger seat. There will be no outgoing signals, no wi-fi, or cellular, or satellite as long as the signal blocker is on. The car is effectively air-gapped.

He settles himself in the Tesla, presses the door close paddle, and places the thumb to the ignition. The panel blazes with LEDs and a gentle voice chimes, "Welcome, Mycroft," which confuses the man for a moment since this is not the target's name, but he mostly concentrates on ensuring the car is set for manual control before he eases down the driveway, glancing only once in the rearview mirror.

The dead body is still slumped on the gravel drive, and the man figures he still has about a quarter of a minute to spare.

Mycroft?

Now on the road heading toward the covered place where he left the old gas car he stole earlier, the man finds himself puzzling about the use of that name by the car's system.

And then it clicks, Mycroft, Sherlock Holmes's older, smarter brother, the man behind His Majesty's Secret Service.

The man snorts, almost a laugh.

"And that's why we kill the rich," he says, not caring if the car hears him. He'll digitally wipe the car when he gets to the other one. He knows where the CPU and memory is, and he has a brick-maker in the other car, the first of two switch vehicles he's using. The degausser is too heavy to have brought with him.

He pats the rosewood trim embedded in the safety foam plastic dash surround.

"*I hear noothink, I see nootink,*" he says, his effort at the fake German accent of a long-ago television series Sergeant Schultz giving way to the adrenaline shaking and giggling that is coming on as he drives away.

Chapter 2: Timed Life

Sixty-four-year-old Davin understands life is a series of decisions.

Life is a series of fucking decisions, he thinks. He is in a dour mood.

He's been thinking about fucking—*well, who doesn't?* he asks himself—but this contemplation is specific in its quality since he has recently signed up for Match.com, tired of being alone, unhappy with the longing he's often felt even before the divorce, now more than six years back. His connection with Gwen had been waning for some time, although he had thought of that then as some sort of phase on her part, himself no doubt contributing, but the sort of thing that could happen in any marriage.

But it has been a long while now since he has been with a woman, and he's missing such contact, although his feelings seem more mixed every time he checks his online dating service.

He likes women, always has. He loves women, although he'd never digressed when married, not even on those few opportunities over the years, mostly when away at some tech conference or another, although he was never all that sure those were real advances made toward him since he'd been so uptight about remaining faithful. Now he wonders, yet again, if he missed more such invitations, or if maybe it was all made up, each of those few events imagined, not real.

"No one ever said I was bright," he says out loud, in his home office, sitting in front of his laptop, looking back at the browser screen showing off his *Matches of the Day*. He has his elbows on the desk surface, his hands over his face. Then he pushes his hands through his thinning gray hair and sits back up with a groan.

"Jesus," he says, clicking past yet another profile that confuses him. It's another photo of an unattractive woman, or a picture anyway so poorly considered in its unflattering light, or lack of focus, or the unintended absurdity of the setting. These images could sometimes make him laugh out loud. More often, though, it gets him wondering whether a woman in such a profile picture is conflicted about dating, or if she's simply unaware or unthinking, without any sort of intelligence of how the profile picture would make her come across.

The photo he clicks through next is actually clear and well-lit, and the woman attractive enough, but a mirror selfie no doubt. She stands in front of a tall house plant that seems, in the photograph, to be growing up out of the top of her head.

"I am told I'm wise beyond my years" is the first line in a brief profile text for the next screen, below the photo of a woman who looks okay, possibly quite attractive, but the image quality is dark and the subject is mid-ground.

Jesus, who says that? She should definitely list the names of each person who told her this, he thinks.

Another writes, "Í enjoy life and living life." He has seen variations on this theme, but this always throws him.

"I am pretty new to online dating, so here goes!" another profile starts, in a common style that he thinks of as getting a running start.

He clicks through, pressing the Skip button again and again, at times with only the briefest of glances. Some of the profile photographs lead him look at the additional images one or another woman has posted, and sometimes he finds himself putting a story of sorts together, but even in his fictions he can't shake his unease about the apparent ambiguities and contradictory impulses so many of the images or the text really communicate, whether fumbled along or absurdly cheerful. He is not without mercy or compassion, he thinks, and he often finds himself wondering just exactly how his profile comes across, including, perhaps, to some of these very women.

Davin lets out another long sigh and wonders if he might be projecting.

The very next profile offers only two photographs, and the profile image is of a woman holding a small boy. She looks good, but the second image is more of a close-up and is a bit startling.

And not in a good way, he can't help thinking.

He skims the scant text and sees the mention of a young teenage boy, so it must be the profile picture is a good decade or more old, and the second, the close-up, is more contemporary, but also more unflattering.

It's not like I'm not heavier than I should be or have a full head of hair, Davin tells himself, although some part of him remains convinced he might be at least somewhat good-looking enough.

He shakes his head and skips on to the next *Match of the Day*.

His profile parameters are set for his own age, more or less, with the youngest age selected for fifty-five years and the oldest at sixty-five years, one year older than his age when he signed up five months earlier. He's been active on the site only recently, however, because after he set his profile and photos to public status, he let the account lie fallow for nearly a month. He's still surprised by this paralysis, his feeling overwhelmed with something of a mix of anxiety, angst, and remorse. He'd sat with that mix of feelings, wrestling with some sense of guilt, and more than once he had had to remind himself Gwen left, not he, and he had been a good husband in most ways at least, neither wife beater nor drunkard, nor gambler, nor addict, nor layabout.

He had argued that the marriage should continue.

Even after the past few years, he remains unsure,

exactly, of why Gwen left, although these days he is less keen on this species of speculation. Yes, their interests had diverged, and she'd grown anxious about the resources they might have for retirement as he was spending more time in his studio making sculpture, and she was interested in retiring sooner rather than later and traveling too. The idea of early retirement still seems to Davin to run counter to the economic facts in front of him, and the concept of travel remains something only nominally of interest. He likes travel well enough, he believes, although possibly only when he gets to the destination. But travel is hardly a priority, unlike his artwork. And air travel is too good at raising the carbon dumping load of each and every traveler, so there's that too.

And the price of airfares these days, he reminds himself.

The biggest cause of the divorce, Davin has long suspected, is that Gwen came to see their ongoing marriage more and more as a burden. They'd both been unprepared to refocus on the other as partners, lovers, or pretty much anything beyond that of parents to the same children who were no longer children and long out on their own. He had seen this as something they could rectify, but she'd seen everything as too late.

Go figure, he says to himself.

These days, he thinks less and less about the divorce, but his finally looking to get back to dating has reinvigorated his confusion. What he still most struggles with is that he was judged not valuable, not wanted, period, full stop.

And now, *I want a woman!* he shouts inside his head, repeating the line from the old movie, *Amarcord*, by Fellini, a film Davin watches every few years, especially liking the scene of the crazy uncle up in the tree, shouting his desire to the world.

It occurs to him he could come up with some sort of clue about this scene, some sort of simple allusion, place it prominently into his profile, and only answer the indications of interest from women who can decipher the reference. The thought of it makes him laugh, but then he lets out another sigh, realizing the woman would have to interpret the allusion positively.

Fuck me, he tells himself, but he's not really angry or frustrated by the process he pursues. He's really more confused than anything else.

And he's feeling generally confused these days. He is confused about the professional work he's doing and increasingly so ever since he first cold-called Alicia, back in her *Berkshire Record* days. The work with *South County Interactive*, an undertaking just getting underway as the divorce was being finalized, has been a boon in many ways, admittedly. Helping Alicia Soares figure out how to build a local online paper's backend provided some focus for him and some income too, albeit modest in the first year or two. Back then, post-divorce, it had been his opening the house to housemates that had proved the difference economically. He hadn't had to sell the place.

Over these last several years there have been a lot of changes. There was the pandemic, of course, and the divorce, but there have also been the ongoing jumps in living costs, including, just recently, a doubling of his already expensive house insurance premium. One situation that has remained unchanging is the same brown water. His house probably goes through hundreds of dollars for filters each year, not that he wants to add up the actual total in case the cost is even higher. The town keeps talking about buying out the private water company serving Housatonic that seems unable or unwilling to successfully address the problems of ancient pipes that periodically turn the water brown. It would be good to be tied into the Great Barrington water system, but there haven't yet been enough votes at the town meeting for this to move ahead.

And then Trump had been reelected in 2024, and this had felt like another hard blow. The economy seemed okay, if not great, before that election, but that absurdity of an administration's economic policies had produced a recession that's been running like a low-grade fever, the economic stress no one seems to want to name. With a new administration taking office a few months back, there is probably little for the government to do that will change economic health, at least in the short term. The cost of power still runs high, taxes are up, and food costs remain unstable, dependent on increasingly undependable weather.

He thinks about his house insurance again, a fresh wound still, having just paid the premium. *More than doubled*, he again tells himself. He knows there have been the hard rains, those so-called hundred-year storms that are showing up most years, and even though he's spent a good bit of money improving the swales and gutter drain redirects, the recent on-site inspection by the underwriters remained unmoved in his assessment of high risk because the house is built into a slope, the backside of the second floor at grade.

I still have my studio, he tells himself, impressed this space has remained dry, considering three sides of it are built mostly below grade. There have been some minor water problems in the form of a bit of seepage, but no real damage. The studio was built like a bunker, and he designed it and took the lead in the construction, even driving an excavator at one point in the process. The space is pretty cool, he's always thought, but then it should be considering the cost even with him doing much of the work.

One half of the studio's roof is under the stone terrace, a nice green roof that helps define the terrace outside the second-floor living room, with the other half of the studio roof a four-foot framed bump up that provides fourteen-foot ceiling clearance on that side and small windows to bring more light in. Only the south wall of the studio is open to the cut driveway that leads past the studio's big windows on its way up to the back parking area.

But thinking of his studio reminds him of how little he's been using the studio and of the relatively few art pieces he's worked on since the divorce.

Yeah, big fucking deal, he tells himself, and the familiar despair of who he is and what he really wants to do floats up again in his thoughts, but the feeling is so familiar he's long ago learned to ignore it, largely. He knows it's unlikely he'll have any more time in the studio for the foreseeable future, considering the expansion of *South County Interactive* into the bigger *Berkshire Interactive* has been ever more demanding. Even now he should be working on the new version of the self-erecting site backend through which advertisements and calendar entries are placed by the companies and organizations themselves.

Self-erecting, he tells himself. He has always gotten a bit of a juvenile kick out of the term, but he finds this more technical and less admittedly funny these days, and then his sardonic mind comes to the rescue as he tells himself, *time to get laid*, and he gets back to the task of reviewing the *Matches of the Day*.

He certainly wants to have sex, but what he hopes for far more than the mechanics of intercourse is connection and the comfort of intimacy. He longs for the touch and presence of a woman's body, the sense of desiring and being desired, and to relax with another person, deeply, simply. He has long been missing the company of a woman but is also surprised by the force of this longing, half suspecting it shouldn't be the case, not at his age, but he's been shocked by the power of this need and so had signed up with the venerable dating service.

And now he's amazed by what he's been seeing.

And then with a laugh he thinks that maybe Alicia could be interested in his writing a regular column on dating over sixty. It isn't such a bad idea considering the older demographic slant of Berkshire County. Still, he's quite sure he wouldn't want to write it and thinking this reminds him of some writing he has to do. He's accepted an assignment about gauging local support for state renewable energy permitting reforms that have percolated down to town-level zoning changes. There's been some local resistance to permitting some recent clean energy projects.

The article is almost due.

He's thinking about including a pending permit for a project that is literally close to home, with the power lines that run behind his property targeted for load capacity buildout. He can claim a NIMBY standing, not that he opposes the project. Still, this could make a good angle for the story, because these lines and the proposed new construction are behind 400 feet of conservation woods that hide the lines from the back of his property.

But he decides to stay on target, even though his recurring dips into the Match.com profiles are like some odd emotional carnival ride, bouncing among amusement, horror, disgust, hope, and depression far too often. Davin figures a solid half of the profiles present glaring shortcomings, and the balance of the profiles coming up for his matches range from the marginal to the mediocre to the boring. Although there have been some profiles he's acted on, he remains surprised at the rarity. To date, there's the one woman he has plans to meet at a cocktail bar up in Pittsfield, although their schedules seem to fight against the prospect.

There are times, especially when the wave of physical desire flares, when he thinks he should try Tinder or one of the other hook-up services, but his judgment remains clear enough to keep from doing it, despite coming back to the idea periodically.

Also, he isn't sure Tinder is still a thing.

Monkey boy seeks monkey girl, is the tagline he thinks he'd use were he to go on Tinder. Or maybe *I want a woman,* he now thinks, which makes him think he's about due for another viewing of *Amarcord,* although he considers holding off until the right date night, should that ever occur. It would be interesting to see how the woman reacts to that scene of the insane uncle paroled by the asylum for a day outing with the family, and climbing a tree, calling out again and again, refusing to come down.

Gwen never cared for that movie.

Monkey boy seeks monkey girl, he repeats to himself, but he knows it's not just about sex. He knows he is longing for the sense of intimacy he had with Gwen for so many years and even with some of his various girlfriends in his college years.

It is the sex too, he thinks.

But mainly, he considers, he's lonely.

Barkis is willing, he tells himself, and then he is self-conscious, surprised at the oddity of his thoughts.

Thank god for a liberal arts education.

He is willing, but the search has been frustrating and often absurd. Although he's been on Match.com for several months, it all still seems new and puzzling to him, and his now more or less daily review of matches most often paralyzes him.

He closes the Match.com browser tab, once again disappointed.

Still, he has made some progress. Two weeks before he messaged a woman, and they'd been chatting by telephone and they have finally gotten their schedules in sync, so the rendezvous in Pittsfield is a go. This seems like a good sign, and he is pretty sure he could get lucky.

Get lucky, jesus. I'm like a goddam teenager, he scolds. *Listen to yourself.*

Chapter 3: The Gray Lady

This morning Alicia is stealing a bit of time in her office on one of her indulgences, which is reading the print copy of the Gray Lady herself, *The New York Times*, the only newspaper she regularly reads this way. The *Guardian*—her other news go-to—is only available in the States online but otherwise might offer some competition. Her encounter with newsprint and smudging ink is one of her daily requirements, a special pleasure in holding the *Times* in her hands, even with the smaller compact sheet size the paper switched to recently. With her background in the business, Alicia knows well that "compact size" is the same as tabloid, but of course the Old Gray Lady is far too grand to go with "tabloid." She shakes the sheets out, following up the front-page story about China's threats to withdraw investment money from overseas if the countries carrying its investments aren't meeting the recently signed UN carbon reduction numbers.

The usual hypocrisy, she concludes. She figures the threat is mainly more likely aimed toward the US, which still has a lot of its debt owned by China, despite the China economy collapse two years back when a good chunk of the debt was called home to prop up the downturn.

Reading on, she sees there is a counter story of sorts in the form of yet another US accusation of China for its continuing use of coal.

As usual, these aren't the only climate stories on the front page. There is a below-the-fold headline about the extended weather trend in Pakistan that is forecast to keep the heat wave growing with a subtitle referencing the heat waves that lasted the better part of the season in the Midwest some years back.

She looks up as Deidre steps through the front door to the office.

"Hey," she says, directing a nod toward Deidre. Her lover makes her way across the front room in what was once the shared waiting room for a small group of nutritionists or herbalists before Alicia rented the space to meet the needs of the expanded *Berkshire Interactive*.

Deidre steps into her office and around the desk to lean down and kiss Alicia's cheek, although Alicia's in her work head, and it takes her a moment to realize Deidre meant to land a real kiss. She feels annoyed, but she's unsure whether this is about her own clumsiness or Deidre's interruption.

"Thought I'd drop by to say hi since you were out this morning so early," Deidre tells her, and Alicia nods.

"I know, early meetings with one of the investors," Alicia says. "Guy's in London at the moment, so…"

Deidre sits on the corner of the desk and looks at her. "We don't get to spend much time together these days."

Alicia quickly checks to gauge Deidre's mood but relaxes because Deidre seems relaxed, with her dark hair and those gorgeous red lips, and those lips are smiling. Although when Alicia looks closer, these wonderful lips seem a bit chapped, actually.

"Ok," Deidre says, jumping up. "I better run back to the store," and with that she bends over and kisses Alicia on the mouth, a lingering gentle kiss, Deidre's hand lightly holding Alicia's chin.

Deidre turns to walk toward the door.

"Hey," Alicia says, and Deidre turns back around. "I know I've been busy, you know" — she waves vaguely with her hand — "all this, the work to get investors' interested, the right ones…" and she trails off.

Deidre, with her lovely eyes, simply nods and then says to Alicia, "They're saying tomorrow is going to be hot, maybe all week."

Alicia just nods.

"I was hoping we could start back up with the walking, but..." Deidre shrugs.

She is so cute, Alicia can't help thinking, but all she does is shrug. The smile on her face feels tight.

"I'll try to get home early," she tells Deidre, but now it's Deidre's turn to grimace.

"Oh, right, your shift at Farm Table," she responds. She wishes Deidre wasn't waiting tables, but Deidre insists on paying her own way and has repeatedly told her it's important she work. Alicia admires her for this, although that admiration is mixed with annoyance because the store position hardly pays minimum, and she also doesn't like that Deidre is a server, although she knows Deidre likes many of the people she works with.

She really hates Deidre's server job, and she thinks, maybe, that's why she can never keep the schedule in her head.

Deidre cups her hand and waves again, that funny thing she does that makes Alicia think of the British royal wave, and then she is walking out the door.

Beautiful, she can't help thinking, watching Deidre disappear through the entrance, but then she shakes her head, trying to get back to business, which at this moment would be finishing reading the paper.

She skims another below-the-fold story—with just the small headline and starter paragraph—continues the coverage of what's become known on social media as the "Trial of the Trainees." A number of activists going to last month's NYC climate march sponsored by an umbrella coalition of climate organizations are charged with assault after they physically frog-marched some young men off the train during the station stop at New Rochelle, with some punches flying. Those removed, whom the defense referred to as "the so-called victims," were a group of young men who took advantage of the free ride into the city for what they admitted was harassing those going to the march.

She shuffles the paper to get to page B-11 where the article continues and finds herself chuckling over the latest courtroom quote about "defensible dope slaps" raised by the defense team. There's been plenty of social media commentary about all this, and the discovery phase has produced evidence that the rowdies were set to task, by all appearances anyway, by a mid-management employee of the recently formed Super Pac, "Americans for Real Debate."

But then the issue of a PAC's alleged involvement has her thinking about the oil divestiture murder story from a couple of years ago, a story for which she'd had an exclusive, but a story that had petered out, stonewalled and blocked and double-talked into standstill by corporate lawyers and a well-heeled PAC.

Well, a little more than three years, she tells herself after running the math in her head.

Still, that story broke on *South County Interactive*, and the fees generated and the publicity were a big boost and got her thinking more seriously about advancing her franchise scheme to set up other online local newspapers. Those early plans had morphed into *Berkshire Interactive*, with Davin arguing the strong metadata design would allow readers to customize for their locality interests.

Not to mention the specificity of ad targeting, Alicia tells herself. *Gold Stars for everyone.*

She shakes the paper folded, and with a quick extra fold tucks *The New York Times* under some technical sales material Davin had brought in recently.

She's got piles of work ahead of her.

Lately she's been wondering about becoming a gray lady herself, but so far, her roots are keeping their color.

Chapter 4: The Metaphysical Budget

To Davin these days, it is certainly looking like he's a newspaper man, or an occasional online publishing writer, and *de facto* System Architect, one *Berkshire Interactive* role folding into all these other roles. For quite a while now he's been back to using his half-worn expertise in digital media but is afraid Alicia's business expansion plans for *Berkshire Interactive* will entirely consume his life. He long ago learned he gets satisfaction in helping others build something and working with Alicia—for Alicia—falls solidly into this category. But this is also a problem for him, especially since he knows he has consistently proved to be very bad at limiting the time he gives to any such undertaking.

Still, sitting out on the back terrace at the patio table with a cup of coffee in good weather feels quite pleasant and he doesn't want to ruin the feeling. The sun is well above the big still-not-dead ash on the southern property line, and it's not quite nine o'clock. He's already put in a better part of two hours on *Berkshire Interactive* work and has stepped out to enjoy his last cup of the day.

A hot spell, weird for this early in May, is supposed to settle in tonight or tomorrow, and for a while.

Look at me, I'm as happy as a kitten up a tree, he silently sings, the line an intentional misquote, one that has long served as one of his inner anthems, but one that for him carries both amusement and reprobation.

A lot of people his age are retired or thinking seriously about it, but at sixty-four, retirement isn't even a consideration, and the last calculations he's made sees his reaching seventy years of age before the earliest opportunity to retire.

If things go well, he tells himself. *Or at least okay.*

He knows by many standards things are going fine, not least in that he owns his house and he's been steadily chipping away at the mortgage. He's able to carry his various expenses, although the margin is never comfortable. To improve the margin, he's recently decided to add a fourth house share, but now even the third house share needs refilling, with Deidre leaving.

She'd told him earlier in the week that she's giving up her room, and he can't fault her. She's barely used it for months, or even well over a year. She'd more or less moved in with Alicia quite some time ago.

His thinking is that his second-floor office, a two-room suite, could be made over into the fourth house share's room. It's quite a nice office, but he knows the rearrangement of the space will be compelling for the right person and he'll be able to charge a premium for it. He'll post notices about the availability, knowing there likely will be many inquiries. The market for housing is tighter than ever.

Too damn tight, Davin thinks. He knows this creates hardships, but he also knows it works for him.

His phone rings, and he drags it over the small patio table he's sitting at and swipes *accept*, seeing it's from his son, Jimmy.

"Hello, buddy boy," he says, but he's worried something may be wrong. Jimmy rarely calls, mostly relying on text, although even that is rare. He's already emailed Jimmy and Cynthia back, telling them he'll go to the march with them, so maybe this call is to get the logistics of the visit better set.

"Daddo," Jimmy says, "some exciting news for you." Then Jimmy starts a sneezing run and during the fit, Davin wonders for a moment if maybe Cynthia is pregnant.

"I've just been offered a new job at NoNolo, taking on their whole IT," is what he tells Davin.

Davin tells him that's great but then tells him he's got no idea who or what NoNolo is.

"It's the outfit that does the legal clearinghouse thing, and provides support for the climate court cases," Jimmy tells him, and then the penny drops.

"Oh yeah, yeah," Davin responds. He finds the news very interesting. "Those are the guys providing coordinating data and legal resources to the uh, the suits, the uh..." He pauses, knowing he's read about the organization over the last couple of years, but he's never read closely. Something to do with various State cases or class action suits against oil companies. It strikes him these seem to have been going on for ages.

Jimmy confirms what he recalls, telling him a few of the major class action suits against various fossil fuel giants are going into court soon. "There's a couple of court dates set already?" he seems to be asking Davin until Davin understands it's just Jimmy thinking his father is something of a moron, probably, and trying to be kind.

Jimmy then continues, telling him this is a major bump in job responsibility, "although who knows if I would've landed the position without her getting Carbon's End coming through with a rec."

A recommendation, Davin realizes Jimmy means, from the big climate change organization, Climate Progress, that Cynthia works for, in one of their spin-offs. He got to know this organization three years earlier when the whole thing with Cynthia had to be untangled after her boss was murdered. She'd been on a trip with the guy, and she'd worked at the oil divestiture operation, a different Climate Progress spin-off.

He'd interviewed a number of the Climate Progress people for that article and the follow-on book he'd written about that experience. He got to know Morales, the founder, although he can't think of the guy's first name, for the life of him. He decides to look the name up instead of trying to recall it, so he can listen to Jimmy.

"Not moving, are you?" he asks his son, although he's pretty sure NoNolo is based in Boston.

"A lot of the work is remote, different staff in different places. There's a guy up in Anchorage," Jimmy tells him.

"No, no moving," he adds.

"Hey, what's the forecast in Boston anyway?" Davin asks, and Jimmy tells him another record for the time of year but not likely to stay so hot for more than two or three days, which is what he himself has just read for the Berkshires this morning. He asks a few more questions, and it does sound to him like this is a big career move.

"As you might imagine, Cyn is thrilled," Jimmy tells him, and Davin asks after her. He can hear, he thinks, some complaint in Jimmy's replies about her being in Middlebury a lot, but when Davin asks, Jimmy tells him things are going great and then the two of them are going over the plan for the visit and he asks Jimmy a few other questions, but as is typical of his son, there's not a lot more information forthcoming. He says goodbye after congratulating him again.

He stands, feels the heat of the day already building, and picks up the now empty coffee mug and heads to his office to get some more work done. But once he's seated at his desk, he's turning to look around at the space he's thinking of turning into another house-share bedroom, now second-guessing the idea.

This space had been his and Gwen's office space, and then his office alone, and he's starting to understand he's loath to surrender it despite having already started to box some files to move up to the third floor.

That new office would be in the finished south half of the attic space, a bit tight on headroom but big enough for an office.

I'll never have to leave my bedroom, he thinks, since that half of the attic space is gained through stairs in his bedroom.

With Deidre now officially going, Marsha will be the oldest active house sharer. She's up in what had been his son's bedroom growing up. That room became Jimmy's bedroom again for a brief time after Jimmy's retreat from Chicago some three years back, post-college, with the stranger Cynthia, in tow. Davin had known Jimmy's return home was a reluctant one, coming after Jimmy's layoff and then that awful heat wave that set records for the upper Midwest. Jimmy was home for a bit more than two months before moving to Boston, a good IT position in hand.

The room on the other side of the hall back then was taken by Chaplin, the very first house share, a young fellow Davin had to acknowledge worked out well—friendly, quiet, and willing to work on the property, especially the garden, when rent was short. But now Chaplin has been gone almost a year, part of a large concern installing solar fields, working as an itinerant panelman, an American Climate Corps guy.

Good on him, Davin thinks, remembering how hard the kid could work and how hard it had been for him to scrounge up enough construction labor in what continues to be a recession job market locally. Solar jobs these days are more common, if maybe not yet plentiful, but the companies doing this work go all over.

Chaplin's house share replacement is a young guy about the age Chaplin was when he became the first house sharer, and like Chaplin the replacement is a product of the regional high school. His name is Danny Trefault, but he likes to go by *The Turk*, or *Turk*, for reasons unknown to Davin, and Davin has a distinct lack of motivation to discover the answer. The kid is good enough, been there long enough, and on time with the rent, but not nearly as good as Chaplin otherwise, although Davin is willing to consider his view of Chaplin may be burnished a bit by nostalgia.

Although Chaplin almost never used the third-floor

bathroom, he finds himself thinking, mulling over an irritating aspect of house sharing. Turk and Marsha are supposed to use the second-floor bathroom off the second-floor library room, leaving the third-floor one for Davin's use only, but Turk interprets that directive as optional, and he has pretty bad aim with his piss.

He swivels back to his desk, waking his computer, but he's still thinking about what he should do. He knows the addition of a fourth house share in this office space on the second floor will likely make Turk's use of the third-floor bathroom— *my bathroom!* – more permissible, even sensible.

Davin twists a bit to look at the window to his right that holds an air conditioner already.

Turk's bedroom window has an air-conditioning unit.

Chaplin never demanded an air conditioner, although Davin knows the hot and hotter summers are even more the norm these days. Turk, however, was quite vocal about the hot nights and quite unwilling to go along with just using the window fans Davin had provided, although it was more a matter of Turk wanting to keep his bedroom door shut, which made the whole-house ventilation scheme ineffective. But then again, Davin isn't crazy about his bedroom door remaining open either.

In the end, he'd bought a slew of units, mostly because he'd also found window fans insufficient for cooling many summer nights. The Airbnb apartment has had an air conditioner for years, but he had resisted for the rest of the house, holding out with window and whole-house fans and sunscreen shades and judicious curtain closing habits, but by the time Turk was in his first summer as house share, Davin was ready to concede, and he added a big air conditioner to the first-floor dining room to make the kitchen bearable in the summer. He also added a high-volume unit in the north end window of the second-floor living room and one for his second-floor office that was only slightly bigger than the bedroom units, but then again the south-facing office got a lot of light. The smallest unit is for

Deidre's small bedroom on the northern end of the second floor.

Now ex-Deidre's bedroom, he reminds himself.

And too, there's one air conditioner unit for each of the three third-floor bedrooms.

He mentally tallies the number of window units now in place, and after he remembers to include the one in his own bedroom, the count is eight in total. He keeps all these units in the windows year round, but during the winter months they're covered with a clever hack in the form of a framed-out insulated soft fabric box, and with the magnetic connectors these have proved pretty effective in stopping air leakage. He just removed these covers for the season yesterday, and apparently not a minute too soon.

Of course, the electricity bill goes up appreciably during the hot spells and this year, early in the spring, he finally had to raise the rents. He makes sure he keeps the room costs competitive, although the rent fee is moderate only relative to what some others charge. Marsha and he have an arrangement where she helps with the Airbnb, getting a part of the Airbnb fees for each time she turns the apartment, cleaning it and putting things in shape for the next guest, although sometimes Davin does this too when she can't or when she simply doesn't want to.

She does like working in the garden and asks for no rent reduction for it, although this clearly helps keep her own grocery bills down, including by canning a lot of the harvest. Still, he's getting the bargain there, even if he had to buy a chest freezer the year before. With the small second fridge in the pantry for the house sharers, the only space he has for the freezer comes from taking out the leaves of the dining table so the small freezer has enough room to fit against the wall of the dining room where, when it's not being raided or packed, is used as a side table with a nice tablecloth over it.

A buffet, that's the word, Davin tells himself.

Marsha is something of an oddball and a bit rough

around the edges, he thinks, but she's working out well enough. She does have a small motorcycle she rides during the good weather and takes the bus in the bad weather and the winter, but in bad weather she mostly goes out only to her job at the Steiner high school in Stockbridge or to visit her mom. Marsha spends a lot of time at Ramsdell Library, but that she walks to, maybe ten minutes on foot on the north end of Main Street.

Main Street, Housatonic, A Village of Great Barrington, Trademark, he more or less automatically thinks. He loves that joke.

The weather is nice, and he's seen that her bike is gone, so she's no doubt at work or up in Pittsfield for a night or two. He'll text to check when she's coming back because there are new Airbnb guests due soon.

Marsha doesn't complain about much, at least much other than Turk, but Turk is often at his girlfriend's place, or at least that's Davin's theory, not that he's bothered to test it. Marsha goes to stay with her mother a couple of nights a week, her mother in some independent living facility in Pittsfield, or at least he's pretty sure, although it might be in Dalton.

The three house sharers make it so there's enough money coming in, and he isn't so paycheck-to-paycheck these days. Things have also improved financially over the last few years as his work has expanded for *South County Interactive – well*, Berkshire Interactive, *now*, Davin corrects himself. It's true his workload there has increased, with something of a modest income expansion to accompany the added responsibilities at the online newspaper for which, originally, he'd intended only to help the publisher select the right software platform.

The work now includes writing and some editing, too, more than occasionally, since the publication has taken off with something of a bang. Alicia and he sometimes still talk about his exclusive on the backstory of the murder of a fossil fuel divestiture activist in the deserts of Southeast

California, although on his part he's pretty sure his contribution to that conversation is largely his whining about how sales for the book that grew from that initial big article never materialized, nor had anything come from talk about television rights.

He knows why of course. The problem was the investigation mostly failed to lead to indictments even if the circumstantial evidence was titillatingly pointing to the probable involvement of one of the major fossil fuel-backed PACs, including one directly associated with the Koch Brothers. But the PAC proved more than well-enough funded to resist and deflect subpoenas and in countless ways insisted there was no connection, no involvement, and the investigation simply petered out, and so the book sales petered out, too.

The acquisition of a key oil services company went through, despite the divestiture interest of a major investment firm that could have scuttled the acquisition, which might have denied or delayed the pipeline project. That pending divestiture deal was thought to be the likely motive for the murder, but in the end, all was deemed conjecture.

Pretty convincing conjecture, Davin thinks, and hardly for the first time.

He still gets quarterly royalty checks, although the sales are now more trickle than flood and, really, had never been much of a flood.

Sales of *Death by Divestiture* helped him cut the mortgage down by a little better than half, but the real problem with the book was that the story was unsatisfying with no villain or evil corporation to take the fall, no rich cabal fingered, and somewhere still out there is the guy who had dressed in the uniform of the San Bernardino County Sheriff Department, who had stopped Joe Craigson's car, shot him in the face, tried to make it look like the assistant, Cynthia, did it, perhaps in a jealous fit, a lover's quarrel.

Even while the hoped-for royalties kept dropping,

other costs had kept climbing. Last winter's extended Polar Express hurt his savings, the price of heating oil for the big house jumping and jumping again, with fuel costs no longer being offset by the savings from the energy-efficiency improvements done during his long work on the house rebuild, and not by a long shot at that. The house's size and configuration make mini-split conversations impractical, with too many needed to make either economic or installation sense, even with the tax credit benefits.

But his thinking about the book has him thinking about Jimmy and Cynthia, and that makes him smile. He'll have to figure out a way to visit them more often, since the upcoming visit for the march is only overnight. He misses them, as much as their being around had been difficult in some ways.

He picks up his coffee mug, hoping for a last swallow that isn't there.

His chronic worry is whether he'll get back to the studio more, finish up two ambitious pieces, something the work with *Berkshire Interactive* seems unlikely to permit in any form other than tiny sporadic moments.

Is that okay, really? Davin asks himself. Can he do the *Berkshire Interactive* work for a while, maybe full out, and get on a better financial footing, then cut back, create a better balance, constrain the hours at *BI* to leave more for the studio? He has no idea, really, if this will ever be possible for him. But he does know this question will be asked again and again.

And then his video-call app chirps. It's Alicia, and he knows she'll be looking for that assignment he'd promised.

Chapter 5: These Are Not the Droids You're Looking For

McPherson has to admit the Tesla had been a very nice car indeed, at least after he'd calmed down, and tossing the target's thumb deep into the woods at the side of the road had been a good start to slowing his anxiety. He hadn't driven the Tesla for long, just to his secondary pick-up car. He's been back in his Ford Transit for quite a while and with each passing day and every bump in the road his regard for the comfort of the Tesla grows. The Transit is the high-ceiling model, the hybrid gas/electric version that still has pretty lousy mileage and is expensive to drive because of the cost of gasoline, but there are a million Transits out here, this newest version of the once-ubiquitous Econoline.

But I pay no rent, he tells himself, a frequent quip he makes, mostly when filling up the gas tank. He casts a glance into the back of the extended body, still proud of his build-out, including the little hiding places. The overstuffed recliner that is anchored to the floor also serves as his bed. There is some cabinetry and drawers, and the layout works, and is space efficient, and everything is in its place. He is particularly proud of the cassette toilet that has a slide out auto-close tray, and there's a handle for carrying it into restrooms where he can simply dump it into a toilet. No smell, not really, at least in the van, with the slight negative pressure fan rig and external venting in the enclosing commode surround. He still likes thinking about his various designs and tweaks of this space.

He feels like he's always thinking. Always thinking, he knows, is key. Planning and patience are his rules of operation. Drive safely, always signal, always full stop and count to three. Keep the van clean. Have a story. Use cash.

He has a laptop he uses for planning and research, and any and all necessary records and his writings too. This laptop is unlinked, the Wi-Fi and Bluetooth disabled. He uses public libraries for online work, downloading content he might need from one of their public computers by using a thumb drive. *Sneakernet*, he remembers, an old term, but then he's fifty-eight years old and had been a precocious PC nut in his youth and a network administrator and systems architect for much of his professional life until the big layoffs after DotCom. The start-up he'd signed on with disappeared in an instant and after that he'd only had sporadic tech jobs for a while, before getting what had turned out to be his final position.

But that was fine, as things turned out.

He now has time for his mission.

DotCom had been his wake-up call, but he didn't really analyze the key problem until years after, although by the time the market collapsed because of subprime securitization in 2008, he already had some better understanding of what was going on.

But his mission really crystalized only after his brother's death and the unexpected windfall that came his way through the settlement with the drug company. The influx of money had been entirely unexpected, just like the surprise of the tainted drug that was supposed to cure his brother of his particularly aggressive lymphoma, but which instead killed his brother and a bunch of others too. His brother, without him knowing, had named him beneficiary of his estate and that would have been nothing more than an odd joke considering how his brother had lived. His brother had been more often unemployed than not, and as the years went by, even when employed, the work was marginal.

The class action suit had changed that.

No one could have anticipated, the man tells himself, echoing the defense, the sort of shitty, stupid, whiney cowardice that was far too common these days in politicians, individuals, and corporations. The pharmaceutical giant had been so arrogant as to think they could skate free, arguing his brother and the other victims of Batch A-065-FG were simply unlucky anomalies, but the internal memos found on discovery were damning, including interdepartmental discussions about QA department responsibilities and failures. There had been plenty of blame to go around, including corporate efforts to cut costs by shifting their sourcing to overseas labs with the aim to further improve their already absurdly strong margins.

Well, fuck them, a typical refrain in his mind whenever he thinks about what happened.

After the lawyers who drove the class-action suit took their lion's share, he still had nearly two million in award.

The pharmaceutical's CEO is on his mission list, although he'll get to that target, this second of his special targets, only if he keeps at it long enough. As a relative of one of the victims he'd probably get flagged as a possible suspect if he acts too soon.

Though going after the executive he blames for everything that has happened to him — *The Fucking Business Genius* — is another special risk. It's who he wants to kill first, and so bad that he can taste it. But he has to wait for enough other target claims to cloud the chance of any connection. He worries he'll have to wait too long. But he's got to be patient, he tells himself.

And always thinking.

He hadn't any inkling of his mission, even after his divorce when he tried to help his brother by letting him stay at his apartment, a stay that ended up being almost two years, a tenancy that started even before his brother took ill and died because of the stupid negligence and greed of the shareholders. He hadn't known he knew he had something that needed doing, not until later, but he knows now.

The idolatry of shareholders.

His brother, in those two years he stayed at the apartment, had not worked at all, and he'd often felt angry at his brother and certainly frustrated. But he knew his brother was off-kilter somehow, had known this for years, and off-kilter increasingly so, or so it had seemed to him. While living with him, his brother's conspiracy theories came and went with intense bouts of online research, and there were all those hours when his brother would corner him, but he had learned how to cut short those rants. But as the months passed, he also glimpsed that there was intelligence behind his brother's complaints and critiques, some more tentative, perhaps, but some built on solid argument and strong evidence. There had been one argument in particular that came to fascinate him, and his brother, seeing this, turned more attention toward that issue. What had especially surprised him was the state of income inequality, even though he had paid enough attention to know the topic was often talked about, but in his workaday world there had been more pressing calls on his attention.

The year before the divorce had been a tough one at his work, his hard efforts focused on incorporating a different logistic back-end platform into his company's architecture to enfold his company's recent acquisition's assets. It had been a difficult slog and had occurred during the difficult time when Mary Beth was on her way out, and then there was the period of lawyering up, and the property settlement, and everything else.

It had been a hard time and it had gotten harder. Two days after the signed divorce decree he had come into work to find the company had itself been acquired. All that while he was still settling into his new apartment, and his brother was already crashing there, an unintended housemate.

With his company's acquisition, he could see his previous efforts conforming system architectures were largely pointless since the directive from his new bosses was for him and his two departmental colleagues to report for a temporary contract assignment to help port the back-end databases into the acquiring corporation's architecture.

It was the old *plus ça change, plus c'est la même chose*.

Maybe it had been the change in employment status, his full-time benefits largely dropped, and maybe it was the uncertain term of the contract work, but he had felt an existential exhaustion doing this type of work after the previous difficult slog. Perhaps it was his sense of the near impossibility of the task of developing any practical methodology for the port.

The reasons didn't matter why he had grown angry.

It may have been how quickly his role became irrelevant when the new corporation's AI system was brought into play and shocked him with the machine-learning platform effectiveness in managing the port. He had felt a fool for not keeping current—his expectations of what such AI systems could do outdated and ill-informed. Even the work he could have done to map and prepare the conflicting data set architectures of the two distinct platforms had already been done. The new corporation provided methodology from a previously acquired smaller competitor that used the same platform of his now acquired company.

He had felt unmoored, useless. It may have been the collapse of his marriage, along with the collapse of his comfortable, illusory life. He might have been generally unhappy, but he'd been economically stable, until, within a two-year span, his status as a married man was gone and his identity as a productive member of society morphed into a mediocre bachelor pad, a temporary contract position under threat, and his brother as roommate, and then that disturbing scramble for money to cover costs beyond his unemployment benefits.

Back then, he couldn't help but follow, now from the sidelines, any and all news of the new corporation's financial situation. What he saw had only made him angrier. The corporation had quickly emerged as one of the business media's golden stories, stock surging and the CEO an extremely well compensated darling held up for all to see how businesses succeed, the face of the new competitive corporation. He couldn't help but look at how he'd been treated, the old vested stock buy-in he had thought such a clever move, but his confidence in his previous company proved wrong when it was all cash-tendered at a much lower price than he would ever have guessed. With the stock market's erratic behavior, even his pension conversion into IRA looked bad for the retirement plans he had long harbored. His expectation of where he would be in a decade or so had shattered. Even the home sale giving him and his ex-wife each a chunk of money after the big credit line was paid off proved inadequate, eaten up by the added costs of COBRA insurance and rent and the weak performance of his mutual funds and his modest unemployment benefits.

He blamed his difficult situation on the new corporation model of monopolistic consolidation where the carrying cost shifted even further to the bottom ninety percent of his fellow citizens.

The rich should pay, have to pay.

His final contract expired just as his brother was diagnosed, and his life became focused on helping his brother get care. His brother appreciated this help in his own peculiar way, noticing he was becoming more focused on the issue of income inequality and his brother had thought sharing information on the subject was fair payment for his room and board and other help, paying it all back by becoming his tutor.

He laughs. "And now the student becomes the master," he says out loud, driving down old Interstate 60, just south of Evansville.

He takes the old routes, highways without E-ZPass and

the cameras. The smaller roads transverse long distances with much less security apparatus along the way.

He stops for fuel, always self-serve, always paying in advance with cash and with his duck bill cap pulled low, but not, he hopes, suspiciously low.

Running silent, he tells himself, a constant refrain.

He's heading toward Louisville, to just outside the city, to surveil the horse farm owned by the CEO he'd briefly worked for. He's got a few more targets he'll get to before he does this one, but he wants to spread out the planning. This one is special, but he understands he needs patience, and that time must pass to avoid suspicion, and caution must be his by-word.

The radio is on, low, but something about the weather catches his ear, and he reaches for the volume knob and hears a hurricane is forming, at least a precursor tropical storm, down near the Tropic of Cancer, west by northwest of Guyana, farther out, but the right conditions for something big.

"We're still debating revising the period of hurricane season, and this one, if it develops beyond tropical storm or depression, will be the earliest of the year, earliest on record," the NOAA person being interviewed says. "Alma on June 9, 1966, currently holds that record, but stronger storms, including last year's Matilda, a Cat 3, which was at the end of June, are more and more likely to develop earlier and earlier."

Today is May 8.

The NOAA man says something about the odd few days of weather, including New England fixed in a hot spell, and then is talking about something called Clausius-Clapeyron-A correlates, which means absolutely nothing to McPherson, right along with a string of other acronyms getting spouted, and the reporter is asking another question, but he, focused on the radio, is startled by a loud sharp bleat of a siren and lights flashing on behind him.

He jabs the radio button off and pulls over, using turn

signals.

The police car pulls in behind him.

"What the fuck," he says, annoyed, but he's calm, or calm enough.

There's no way... he thinks, but he pushes this thought away and instead does a lightening review of his procedures and the implementation processes more than a month back, his cleaning of the Tesla, his bleach spray, the bricking electromagnet, and then he wonders if he'd screwed up his second killing, the old money from Connecticut, a hedge funder who liked to play a lot of golf, and that had been a long-distance shot, *an hole in one.*

It is possible that he'd left some trace from the house where he'd stole the rifle, but he'd dumped the rifle right away.

That second killing had been clean, too, he is sure. He's dismissing the feeling as just a panic response.

He lowers his window and then turns off the ignition while the cop, a local, approaches.

He looks like he's twelve, he can't help thinking, and then he wonders if the cop seems annoyed the window is already down.

He wanted to rap on it, he can't help thinking.

"Yes, officer," he says.

"License, registration," the cop says, eyes curious, darting around toward the back part of the van and what he can see from the driver-side window of the inside.

He retrieves the registration from behind the passenger-side visor.

"Is there a problem?" he asks as he picks up his wallet from the center console, pulling out his license, turning back to the cop, handing him the requested material.

"Taillight," the young cop says.

"Oh jeez," he says. "I just got that fixed, just fixed, two days ago, dealership in Springfield."

The cop says nothing.

"Well, not much of a fix, I guess," the man adds.

The young cop doesn't seem to be listening. He's craning his head, trying to look past the man, into the interior. "You live in this thing?" the cop asks.

"Yup, built it out myself, after I retired," he tells the young cop. "You want to take a look?"

"No, that's okay," the cop says, although he thinks the cop really would like to take a closer look. Instead, the cop asks, "What were you doing in Springfield?"

"I'm doing a tour of the presidential libraries, there's the Lincoln one, Springfield, not a National Archives Library, but Lincoln, right?"

"Huh," the young cop says. His eyes keep glancing into the back.

"Huh," the young cop says again, looking again at the license before handing it and the registration back. "That sounds interesting."

McPherson is pretty sure the young cop doesn't find the idea of driving all around the country going to presidential libraries all that interesting, but he knows this makes an excellent cover story, especially since he actually goes through the trouble of visiting these libraries when he's at all close.

"All right, Mr. McPherson," the young cop says, a slight thump at the base of the open window. "Get that light fixed, right?"

"Refixed," William McPherson says, shaking his head.

"I hear you," the cop says, but he's already stepping away, and then he's got his hands up on each side of his face, pressed in close to the big side window, taking a look.

He steps back and thumps the side of the van again. "Be safe," the young cop says, turning back toward his patrol car where the lights are still flashing.

McPherson waits for the cop to shut down his flashing lights and pull out before he puts on his turn signal and pulls out too.

"These are not the droids you're looking for," he says quietly.

Chapter 6: Alicia Soares Scores
a Jeannie Louise

One of the nice things about running a newspaper is you get to meet people.

Well, Alicia thinks, *that is at least often a nice thing about running a newspaper.*

Today, she is over at *Orion Magazine*, wearing, as has become habitual, both her publisher hat and her editor one. She has long heard about *Orion*, which has offices in Great Barrington. She'd not, however, been curious enough to push through the tasks and meetings and ad calls that seem never to end, so she remained for far too long only vaguely aware the publication was something she should check out. But standing in the Co-Op checkout line just about two weeks back with her $2.99 naval orange, her greenhouse grown salad mix, box of mint tea, and the two sheep cheeses that are among her indulgences, she noticed the Co-Op had copies of the current issue of *Orion Magazine* near the registers, and she added a copy to her sundries without further thought.

And then, of course, she lost track of the issue for several days until she spied it on her office credenza in a rather shaky sloping pile of papers and folders and noticed only because the magazine had covered up the brochure for the Omega Institute Spring programs she'd been looking for. She gingerly retrieved both the brochure and the copy of the magazine, quite pleased she was able to reform the stack's integrity well enough to have it remain freestanding.

That was three days ago.

It is only this morning that Alicia looks at the copy of *Orion* and then goes online to read about the publication. Alicia likes what she reads, and by the time she has read the original mission statement — *It is Orion's fundamental conviction that humans are morally responsible for the world in which we live, and that the individual comes to sense this responsibility as he or she develops a personal bond with nature* — she is calling the office number listed on the masthead for the publisher, who more or less immediately asks her over, and here she is, two hours later, having a moderately pleasant chat with him and seeing he is well aware of her own efforts post-*Record* and her seemingly unstoppable march toward expanding across the tri-state area.

What Alicia wants to talk about is one of his contributors, Jeannie Louise Smith, who writes infrequently for the magazine on climate issues, but in-depth, and who, if her information is right, lives right in Great Barrington.

Don't you know the prophet hath no honor in his own land, is his line, and Alicia quickly understands the publisher appears to be angling for some sort of co-op effort that might help *Orion* get a little more subscription action locally. But she is now only half listening to what sounds like the publisher's rush of hope for free advertising. She has little tolerance for the way this guy discusses matters, preferring simpler, open conversation and less implication, so she takes a strategic break by going to the restroom, which, when she enters, is far dingier than she would have liked.

After dutifully washing her hands, she can't help noticing the recycled brown paper towels sloppily piled on top of the toilet tank. The paper towels fall apart just about as enthusiastically as they refuse to absorb water.

A quick glance at herself in the mirror over the bathroom's sink presents a woman with all the professionalism and dignity she can muster given her youngish looks and her tendency to blow herself a kiss whenever she looks at herself, which may be a strange thing for a forty-year-old to do, as this has occasionally occurred to her.

When she does this, however, she thinks her lips look ever poutier, and then this has her thinking about Deidre, her girlfriend.

Alicia loves Deidre's lips.

My young girlfriend, she finds herself thinking. She still wonders how it is she has a girlfriend, and it can still be a surprise even that Deidre has more or less lived with her for the last year. Alicia remains bewildered by it all and especially the force of the attraction. Deidre is sweet, and the sex is fantastic, although thinking about this, she sees it has been a while since they've made love, and thinking about this arouses her, but she finds herself shutting that line of thinking down.

Business first.

But it seems easier said than done for some reason she can't quite grapple with. She is finding herself thinking back to that first night she met Deidre, and that night still makes her smile. Something had happened that was entirely new to her, a rise of some intensity of feeling entirely foreign to her, but this had proved irresistible, unfathomable, insistent, unavoidable. There, in Deidre's bedroom, in the middle of a cocktail party at Davin's odd house, she had found herself lost in kissing this younger woman with a dizzying and overwhelming drive that also seemed like relief, a foundational and excited shift that felt like coming home. Not that it was like any home she'd ever known, or anything that had ever happened before, not really.

She realizes with a cresting disappointment that Deidre is at Farm Table again tonight.

She clears her throat and she's back to checking herself in the mirror, putting on her business face, and such thoughts and twinges of emotion are being pushed aside as she opens the door. She marches out back to the publisher, intent on getting handed off to the editor, who, in the form of editorial director, turns out to be the publisher too.

Alicia takes charge.

"Can I get Jeannie Smith's contact information?" Alicia blurts, well aware of the clumsy segue on her part but unable to spend another moment with this person who clearly seems a bit of a passive-aggressive nincompoop. Also, she's pretty sure the smile she presents is morphing into a kind of manic craze, complete with popping eyes under violently raised eyebrows about to start cramping from the effort.

From the doorway, surprising her, a small darkly dressed girl with a jagged, pink-streaked haircut and full-sleeve tattoos speaks. What the girl is saying delights Alicia, which is that Jeannie Smith is hoping to have a word with the editorial director, and Alicia takes this opportunity to say she'd love a few minutes with the writer she has just finished asking after, if that's all right, which it is, of course, or so she willfully infers, and then she's down the stairs, reaching a hand out to Jeannie Louise and asking her along to grab a coffee.

Chapter 7: Davin Gets Gas

Cynthia doesn't email often, so of course Davin, sitting at his desk in his office, has to go right to that email, especially because she hasn't bothered to put anything in the subject line, which he finds annoying. He's easily annoyed about lots of things when it comes to communicating with the younger crowd.

Cynthia emailing him is a very rare event, and he's almost nervous about opening it. He hasn't seen much of the two lovebirds since Jimmy raided his old left-behind items. Jimmy's been good about texting, although still not in the frequency of texts, but then Davin knows that he himself is not so great calling, or for that matter emailing, and less so yet texting.

His son almost never uses email at all, and most of the contact is via text, although Jimmy has pushed periodically for alternative messaging platforms, with *WhereU* the latest, a video chat that has all sorts of file management transfer capabilities and voice messaging of various ilk and operating systems integrations, but Davin keeps sticking with the ancient *WhatsApp*, to Jimmy's chagrin.

And the way punctuation gets used, or those weird abbreviations that require Davin to bring up a glossary search are other maddening habits. *Laugh fucking out loud* is the typical way Davin sounds out *LOL*.

Fortunately, neither Cynthia nor Jimmy use much in the way of emoticons with him. He's more than once gone on a rant about emoticons and he is sure they remember his declaration, repeated, he has no doubt far too many times in tantrum-like outbursts. He clearly remembers his assertion on that first occasion, and all too likely any number of other times, that it was his intent to keep his Purgatory sentence low by never ever using an emoticon, which had struck Jimmy and Cynthia as funny, fortunately, at least that first time. They, at least, seem happy enough to not lead him into temptation, keeping their own use of emoticons in check.

Thinking about this makes him laugh. He likes the Purgatory-sentence-reduction joke.

He reads Cynthia's email, and the lack of any personal information beyond the "Hey Davin" greeting strikes him as the likely result of a cut and paste, probably from the outreach campaign her organization is doing, since the message body I mainly a list of political action points regarding some new methane legislation.

Methane, methane, methane, he recites. It seems like this is suddenly the topic everywhere. He notes that there's a deadline, which is in three weeks, which makes him check on today's date, May 9, which is what he thought it must be, but he's always glad when he sees that he's keeping track.

The new freelancer Alicia's just brought on was talking about methane just yesterday when he'd gone by the office for a quick chat with Alicia about adding some new metrics for ad sales. The back-end platform service they use at *Berkshire Interactive* was touting the new features as AI, although he knows that just about any complex set of algorithms gets that moniker these days.

Calling something—*everything!*—AI is another of his pet peeves.

Davin rereads the email from Cynthia, and there's nothing to suggest whether she's at her Vermont apartment working on-site for the climate program she's been at for the last three years, or if she might be in Boston with Jimmy, working remotely.

He prints out the email, intending to do what the email asks, which is to call or write his US rep and his two senators, telling them to support the new bill she references.

He swivels to grab the printed email from the printer tray and then swivels back to highlight the deadline, and then he stands up and pins the printed sheet to the cork strip to the left of the office door that leads out to the landing and stairway down into the dining room and kitchen. He stays in the open doorway for a moment or two, listening for any sounds of activity upstairs, but he's pretty sure neither Marsha nor Turk is in.

For a guy who thinks he's doing the right thing opening his house to share with others, with housing so expensive, he finds it funny he delights in having the place empty. The Airbnb apartment on the north side of the first floor is empty at the moment too, although there is a couple coming in for three nights sometime later in the day. He takes a moment to think if the apartment is all set and ready, and then he settles back at his desk and checks the Sent Mail folder, double-checking he's sent out the detailed directions for the guests.

It's one of those bright, even sparkling, May days outside, the sun flooding in full on now that it's almost noon. He hates feeling stuck inside on a day like this, the kind of day when the temperature is normal. The recently threatened hot spell wasn't as bad as the forecasts had presented, although scrambling to keep the young garden watered was uncomfortable for a couple of days, but the temperatures had fallen back to normal soon enough.

He goes back to his inbox, but there are no other pressing emails, so he shifts to his Google News feed, and there's yet another big story about a massive methane leak, apparently the issue *de jour*, it seems.

Methane seems to be giving everybody gas, he tells himself, a little pleased at his joke.

He starts in on the news article and there's nothing funny about it. He scans the related headlines from other news sources, and they all seem to be some version of *Worst Ever*. The article he clicks on from the *Times* describes a fracking site blowout that has dumped the equivalent of the entire EU's annual methane emissions, and the wells involved are still liberally leaking methane.

Assholes, emerges as his main reaction.

He keeps reading and finds a link to a story about the previous worst leak from back in 2018, a reference he thinks he remembers, but he checks it and he's wrong, or at least it all seems like news to him. The linked story is about an Armstrong County, Pennsylvania, site run by a subsidiary of ExxonMobil. The article appeared in *The Washington Post* toward the end of 2019, the story emerging only after publication of a study by a team of American and Dutch scientists in the *Proceedings of the National Academy of Science* that reported on satellite data quantifying the blowout that had lasted for twenty days.

The tally was methane emissions that exceeded all but three European nations over an entire year.

And now we have a winner, he tells himself, clicking back to today's story. He knows methane is eighty times more potent than carbon dioxide over the same twenty-year period.

Not so funny, he tells himself.

He returns to the linked 2019 article, which includes a quote from one of the scientists. "We derive a methane emission rate of 120 ± 32 metric tons per hour. This hourly emission rate is twice that of the widely reported Aliso Canyon event in California in 2015."

The 2015 California story rings a bell, at least vaguely, and he thinks he remembers the story making the news then as the largest known accidental methane leak in the United States, having lasted for over four months, but he has absolutely no recollection of this even worse 2019 blowout. He wonders how many similar leaks and blowouts have occurred and how he could have missed such news. For someone who likes to think of himself as climate change conscious, he finds his lack of awareness about all these massive methane leaks disturbing.

This newest one is even worse than the Aliso Canyon

incident.

It isn't that he's unaware of the methane problem. He remembers an article some time ago, and he suspects it must be from *The New York Times*, that there are thousands of decommissioned wells of oil or natural gas that continue to leak methane.

Zombies, that's what those wells are called, and he's impressed he remembers this, but then he starts to doubt he is remembering it right, so he looks for the old article, and sure enough, up comes the title "These Zombies Threaten the Whole Planet." He reads the deck of the piece and sees he has wildly misremembered the number of wells. The deck reads, *Canada's oil patch has nearly 100,000 suspended wells, neither active nor capped, and they're a worrying source of planet-warming methane.*

He does a quick search on the number of used-up wells in the United States and finds estimates ranging from 330,000 to over 800,000.

His eyebrows rise.

He goes back to today's *The New York Times* article and pages down to the "More on Methane" list at the bottom. There are nearly two dozen other methane-related articles that have been published in the *Times*. The list includes links to articles about the current legislative effort to regulate methane wells and about the satellites now in place for tracking leaks, but he then scans an article on all the loopholes for regulating gas wells that had been included in the first Inflation Reduction Act, when restrictions on enforcement made the regulation toothless for all but the biggest leaks and larger producers.

He knows natural gas production has kept growing at least as far back as the Ukraine-Russia war, when the EU lost the Russia LNG feeds and suffered through a tough winter before the States and Mideast built enough infrastructure to substitute supplies, and that had boosted domestic production aimed at export.

That spike in natural gas production has kept growing,

despite all the climate rhetoric.

He shakes his head. *Profits before People*, he recalls from some old slogan.

Even these many years after the negotiated peace between Russia and Ukraine, natural gas is still high-priced in the States, although still more so for the European markets and many other spots across the globe. He understands some of the increase of natural gas being used is replacing coal-fired power plants, but the continually growing demand for electricity and the as-yet only half-built grid upgrades means the natural gas power plants continue to flourish.

He should be working on the backgrounder for the article he's writing — *trying to write*, he admits to himself — for *Berkshire Interactive*. The article is on the local permitting reforms, typically requiring changes in local zoning codes and for permitting process streamlining, and he also has plans to write a proposal for Jeannie Louise Smith, his new colleague who is supposed to be writing stories for *BI* about localized climate change consequences, as best he understands her assignments. Alicia has asked him to get Jeannie Louise Smith on board and up and running.

Unfortunately, Smith seems busy enough these days with her actual work as a sought-after commentator and analyst on the politics and policy effects of climate change efforts, and he knows her ongoing involvement with the online newspaper could prove unrealistic given the current workload she described when she met him late yesterday for a cocktail at one of the Railroad Street bars.

Jesus, that cocktail was mediocre, he recalls.

He will be suggesting to her that she cover a new study by the Berkshire Regional Planning Commission on renovating or reestablishing dams in the Housatonic River at long-established points of effective hydrology, including one of the best sites right down at the old mills he can see from his house. The other part of the BRPC study is on climate change remediation for flood control where a number of old mill ponds can be expanded to act as storm water collectors. He is particularly enamored of this article concept after finding a great book, now at hand, published by a local author some years back, and which recounts the history of industry in the upper Housatonic River. The number of existing or once-existing dam sites Davin had found shockingly high.

But he doesn't want to be working on the permitting article, which will include attending the regional planning board meeting in Pittsfield later in the day. He is at present not even enamored of the dam article proposal.

What he wants to do is work in the studio or be outside, enjoying the light, getting things done in the garden.

His email pings, bringing his eyes back to his browser.

Another email from Cynthia, and this one has a word in the subject line, "visit," and he gets to put off what he should be doing for yet another moment, reading that she and Jimmy would love a visit at their Boston place should he like to join them for the March on Methane, which is scheduled for next month on the Boston Common.

He tries to be politically active and is a dues-paying member of a number of climate groups, including the one where Cynthia is associate director, MEAT, or at least he thinks that's the name. He knows that her group, a spin-off of Climate Progress, has a lot to do with methane and farming and anti-meat consumption. She is clearly a true believer in not eating meat, at least if her reaction the last time they'd been up is a good enough indicator. He'd proposed using his beat-up old Weber for grilling some burgers, and her reaction had been so strong that these days, those rare times he eats meat, it's like he's a kid sneaking a cigarette.

MMEAT, that's the name, the acronym, he now remembers, along with recalling how annoyed Cynthia got when he made that comment about her organization having a stutter.

He'll have to look up what MMEAT stands for,

although he's sure the *A* is for agriculture and one of the *M*'s is methane.

He'll do the petition signing and the emails to his rep and senators right now.

Another procrastination, he tells himself.

He'll join them on the march. He'll be glad to go, he's sure, and all the climate actions are important, but it all seems yet another thing commandeering his attention.

All this is giving me gas, he tells himself.

He doesn't even bother to groan.

Chapter 8: The News Storm

Jeannie Louise loves her desk, although it isn't really a desk, of course, but a large old dining room table in her apartment's large front room. The table's length is impressive, too, with all the extra leaves she'd put in, stiffened with a couple lengths of long angle iron she carefully drilled and screwed under the leaves and table. She'd used screws of optimal length, just short of piercing the table surface, but sunk into enough wood to hold tight. The table has a dark mahogany veneer in good condition and solid carved legs in a Queen Anne style. Twice a year she'll clear the entire top for a good cleaning and then a solid polishing. That biannual exercise includes having to relearn to not toss a book or magazine or stack of reports too vigorously on to the surface because the new polish causes a lot skidding, papers fluttering to the floor.

Jeannie, although entering her seventy-first-year this coming fall, still often hears the old childhood nicknames and taunts in her head. *Jeesey Louise*, *Cheesy Louisey*, *Jeeser*, and the other variants roll around as if she has nothing better to do, although she's paid enough attention to this phenomenon to have figured out that a trigger these days is putting her name to an article or blog post, and considering she's doing this quite a bit of late, she's growing to like the nickname chorus that can singsong along throughout her day.

She can even admit to herself — at least now and then — that she's been feeling pretty good. There certainly are more aches and pains, and her somewhat stooped posture brings her gray hair forward enough she's been thinking more seriously about cutting it even shorter. She can afford to go to a stylist these days, not that she does. She's been experiencing better reception of her climate blog and picking up more freelance article work and even showing up increasingly on climate change conference meetings and panels. She's aware of the irony of her feeling good about her work, given that her subject focus is depressing, but this just makes her grin as the voices ramp up in a series of *Cheesie Louisie's* as she clicks on the "Publish" button.

She immediately goes to her own site to see how her latest post looks, despite having previewed it repeatedly as she'd worked through different aspects of the post.

"Jeese Louise," she says quietly, nodding as she scans the now-public post titled, "You're All Wet, I'm Dry: Public Policy Misses Again in the West." This post, like a number of other recent ones, nearly writes itself, drawn as it is from her own freelance articles and using more of the research she always undertakes for such pieces. She loves being able to put her research to use in these larger in-depth pieces on the blog, since this means she can ignore the word- and page-count restrictions most of her print and online outlets impose. More detailed versions of her freelance assignments are almost a compulsion for her because word limits of her freelance assignments guarantee that the work lacks the details and utility she's after.

She mostly writes about complicated matters and minute specifics that intersect climate change and political policy. That her blog, *RE: CC*, has gotten a lot more traffic over the last two years gratifies her. She sees this as confirmation that there are people who still read longform and still want to understand complex issues. However, her blog remains without a good sponsor even now, and her *bitbites* version doesn't produce much in the way of remuneration, even though her paid subscribers count keeps growing. The value she derives from her blog is mainly indirect, helping her get into expensive conferences for free by running their promotional co-op banner ads or through the increasing numbers of panel invitations. These days she only infrequently has to explain who she is and what she wants when requesting interviews or public budgets or government and NGO whitepapers and reports, and this feels like an incalculable benefit.

She sometimes finds herself wondering why anyone would read her writings, considering how much climate change content is out there already, but she has this reaction mainly after she's force-fed herself a big plate of climate news that is her daily habit. Her near-constant submergence in all the specialty blogs, NGO reports, activist groups sites, and scientific journals sometimes feels like cognitive dissonance when contrasted with the mainstream media's shallow coverage about climate consequences.

Her current frustration, here in the second week of May, is the lack of acknowledgement that events like the current Pakistani heat wave or the newest entanglements of the sub-Saharan conflicts have something to do with the bigger climate picture. The latest war news out of Africa, where more US troops and drones are getting involved, is just her latest example of the media's failure to cover climate as part of a larger news story.

On the other hand, she knows that climate change is big in the stories about the Carbon Reduction Act, a signature legislative effort of the new Democratic administration, already in debate on the floor of the Senate, already out of committee, already approved by the House. She always takes care not to call CRA a carbon tax, although most of her colleagues do. The CRA's passage will require a huge effort politically, even with the progressive gains in the White House and Congress, and she remains convinced this bill may not pass, even with the countless petitions, several record-breaking climate marches, and many other smaller ones, and, too, innumerable arrests. Talk about the then-unnamed CRA started after the midterm election shifts that helped moderate the congressional gridlock.

She knows the CRA is good news and that the law will make a difference, but she also knows that the likely compromises needed to gain the sufficient votes will create structural problems. As it stands now, the CRA grants and tax credits subsidies that will help offset costs for lower income people are scheduled to get smaller over the next two years and the result will be that for most people energy prices are going to climb as the CRA's scheduled regressive tax-like stepped cost-offset reductions take effect. She knows this is likely to undercut public support and is likely to hurt the climate change incumbents and candidates in the next election or two.

Or longer, even, she tells herself. Sometimes it all feels rather hopeless.

As it stands now, the CRA's individual, family, and small business cost offset credits have a sunset provision, so cost offsetting will entirely disappear by 2032. The most likely outcome, barring a change in the bill, is the costs of the utilities' buildout of renewables and the infrastructure needed to give people access to carbon-free electricity eventually will be fully passed along to rate payers. As she's previously written, the CRA as currently structured is a one-step-forward-one-step-back situation, but she is grateful for even imperfect progress.

She balances such gratitude with caution though, since she understands that while the nation may be emerging from the on-again/off-again recessions, there are still plenty of conflicting agendas loose upon the land. She follows politics closely because tracking climate change means tracking energy markets, which means tracking politics and the legislation that affects climate change and energy markets. And politics means ongoing US force engagements in the Mideast and Africa, and those conflicts too contribute to rising prices for fossil fuel products. The country, she understands all too well, has been at war somewhere or another since Bush went into Iraq in 2002.

Well, conflict, anyway, she corrects herself.

Other energy price pressures abound too. With COP15, the UN Climate Change Conference that took place in Paris finally bearing fruit in 2022 after Trump's 2020 defeat. The Inflation Reduction Act in Biden's early presidency helped put the country back on track, but the emphasis with IRA was on the size of tax credits and rebates, but tax credits mean there's earned income to offset and people have to spend money to receive the rebates. There's been an ongoing pushback to buy-in because of such up-front costs, and then there was all the IRA resistance in Trump's second term, although the 2028 Democratic administration has already reversed those claw-back efforts. Too many Republicans in key states had significant economic benefits from IRA, and so chose to do little more than pass largely symbolic legislation that left IRA mostly untouched. Fortunately, for the most part, climate change progress, typically at the state and municipal levels, mostly weathered the dark days of the previous four years.

Still, Trump and his fellow trumpers had made the past four years an uncomfortable, often maddening time for climate progress.

Fortunately for her, most people can't afford the time and effort required to understand the complexities at play, and even for her, all the power struggles can seem an ongoing Noh play, and quite hard for her to analyze and report all the subtleties. But she likes this complexity and it's perfectly fine for her because this is her bread and butter, and her own work has finally been paying off. She'd started a retirement account only last year, and she's been putting more into it than she originally planned. Still, except for better bourbon, she's largely kept her expenses and lifestyle the same.

In the past several months since the inauguration, not only has the long-bandied-about CRA been swiftly and confidently advancing in Congress, but there's a nascent Sea Wall Act showing up in a subcommittee of Energy and Commerce, and that has the potential to be a giant infrastructure fund aimed at climate resiliency. Where the funds might come from remains unresolved at this early stage, and she's well aware the current progress, modest as it may be, is mostly the result of more good old horse-trading and the traditional tactics, especially in the House, where votes are bought with promised money for congressional members' districts and states. She knows that there will be a lot more horse-trading with that legislation as it moves forward.

If it moves forward, she cautions herself.

Her view is that the Senate remains the tougher challenge, even with the Democrats and Independents picking up two more seats to help make climate- and job-related legislation more likely, but the Senate is now the part of the legislative branch that slows things down.

Well, has been for quite a while, she thinks.

That old chestnut about this being the role intended by the Founders for the Senate is still a popular meme, but she's convinced the main cause for delays and inaction is simple. Big money can be more effectively applied in concentration there, and big money is still pouring out of the fossil fuel industry these days.

Like crude from the broken bow of Exxon Valdez, she considers, pleased with the line. She wants to work in the line somewhere, although she wonders if anyone still knows the historic allusion. That thought makes her feel her age.

What she does know is that despite all the complexity in the politics and economic conditions, *it's the stupid oil*. The root causes of climate change are easy to identify, if harder to explain in ways that circumvent most people's reluctance to consider their own culpability. *The Age of Burning* is what she figures this time will be called by the historians of the future when enough time has passed for the last several hundred years to be more clearly seen for what it is.

Clearly seen, she repeats to herself, because that is funny, at least sardonically, considering smog, and the fabled London coal miasma, the particulate a silent but powerful grim reaper, and so many other health hazards across the decades and centuries and even now. Last year it was Delhi with car-free days and other strict measures imposed to keep death rates down. Two years back it was Beijing recording the worst air quality ever experienced, and for almost three months combustion vehicles were kept out of the city core and electricity was shuttled from more distant coal plants, the two proximate plants usually feeding the city shut down until the pollution cleared.

Combustion Era, she intones, trying it out and feeling the name fits all too well.

The frenzied shoveling of coal and oil and gas into the world's machinery, all of which has at its core the white-arc'ed light of the blazing furnace.

Hmmm, not bad, she thinks, and she's back at the keyboard starting another of her note pages, a log of ideas she keeps open in Word.

It isn't the Industrial Revolution, she types, *as much as it is the Burning Time, when what we've long thought of as progress has actually been the conflagration of the world.*

Jeeze Louise, she thinks, teasing herself. *It's a wonder anyone can see anything in this world for all its metaphoric smoke.*

She doesn't bother typing in this last thought. She knows she tends to lean towards being too arch.

She stands and tries stretching straight and tall, but her slight frame and modest height enjoy only a few spine pops and a clearer sensation of the tight neck and shoulder she tends to get when sitting at the keyboard and moving the mouse about for long periods. She thinks of her body with disappointment, but what she tries not to think about is how little she uses her body, always planning to exercise but hardly ever getting to it.

Well, she has been busy and she is pleased with the blog's growing readership because it has helped her build freelance assignments, both in terms of the numbers of such jobs and the increasingly better outlets that typically provide better fees. She still writes long pieces on climate change for *Orion Magazine*, which has its office in Great Barrington and is one of the reasons for her ending up in the Berkshires, but she'd be on welfare if she tried to live off what that magazine pays her. Not that she's well-off by any means, but she gets by with a nice sunny apartment—at least when it isn't pouring again, like today—and an old Toyota Camry hybrid, and a couple of vices, including her study of great bourbons and ryes.

Jeannie would like to have a small glass, an indulgence she often allows to celebrate the finishing of an assignment, but since it's only midmorning, she'll wait. She's got a lot of email to get to, including her follow-up interview request with Senator Jenkins, Republican of West Virginia, the Senate's power forward for coal, whose office earlier declined to speak with Jeannie.

Which is stupid, she thinks, but no interview is hardly a deal-breaker if the senator doesn't bite. She already has a working title or two. *Progress on Coal: Tout de Suite or Tout Soot?* is one. Another is *What Good Comes out of Coal States: Bourbon and Wry?*

She recognizes her approach to titles is something of a bad habit, but she often can't resist.

She also knows she's got some research ahead of her because wise-ass title or not, she always takes pains to get the information and data right. She sits back down and straightens herself out in front of her keyboard and monitor, intent to get back to work, but her thoughts remain focused on one of the CRA's worst amendments submitted by Jenkins and allowed for vote, and she sometimes surprises herself about how angry she is about the political necessity of the compromise. The CRA amendment exempted US coal exports to countries that aren't signatories to the latest UN climate agreement, which means that some third world countries and even several largely developed nations, including Pakistan, can still buy a lot of American coal, thanks to Jenkins and his ilk.

She looks up at the free-standing whiteboard to the side

of her big table, one of those full-sized ones that makes her think of the old-fashioned blackboards, except it's the other side that's showing, a full corkboard to which many pieces of paper, notes, tear sheets, and bits of scrap with phone numbers or email or whitepaper web addresses or report titles scribbled. The corkboard regularly gives up its secrets, with her taking an hour every couple of days going through and putting the content into her project management spreadsheet and her various notes documents. This spreadsheet is where she keeps her to-do items, story commitments, and anything else she has to remember.

She sighs. The clutter of the corkboard tells her its harvest is long overdue, but she simply can't do it. Instead, she can't help herself and looks at her news feeds, even knowing this won't aid her growing disorganization.

The heat wave that struck Pakistan is still one of the big stories on the feed. The stuck weather system is much worse than the one in 2018. Not only is this year's Pakistan heat wave the worst to date, but it has started nearly a month earlier than the record 2018 heat wave, and as the old record falls, death counts rise. Just like 2018, widespread electrical grid crashes keep occurring, and Jeannie believes yet more ministerial heads are likely to roll.

Pakistan has been suffering through sequences of heat waves and floods, and though her grasp on the larger climate system factors responsible is weak, she knows it is something to do with changes in the South Indian monsoon cycles. Pakistan's series of disasters puts the country in the lead as most screwed over by climate change for 2029, although the year has another half and more to go.

Not that the sort of disasters Pakistan has excessively suffered from are limited to foreign countries. If new patterns still hold in the West and Midwest US, there's a good likelihood of much hotter and drier weather that could badly affect a lot of the commodity crop plantings. She just might, in some future piece, use those conditions to bring the point home that food cost projections are already being raised.

If the good lord's willing… and the corn don't croak, she tells herself.

She looks up off to the right at the black-and-white image of the current Pakistani heatwave she'd printed out and pinned to the corkboard. The image, a screen grab from an earlier story, is a mid-ground perspective of the long row of wrapped tiny bodies of children dead from heatstroke. Among all the bodies, it was the single little foot free of the wrapped shroud that first drew her eye. This had happened three weeks earlier, but she has stopped looking for a while, really looking, until now, her attention drawn to it once again.

And then Jeannie Louise shakes her head.

Think Locally, Act Globally, she tells herself, although she then thinks maybe she's got that wrong, but her thought is interrupted by the chime of new email. This one is from her NOAA subscription with the subject field reading, "Mid-Tropic Atlantic Water Temperature Increases Accelerate Formations of Mass-Scale Depressions."

She's keeping the email closed at the moment. She's got to get things organized.

Jeannie Louise reaches for a small wooden box near the back edge of the table and pulls it toward her, flipping open the lid with practiced ease. She takes out a prescription bottle, holds it up to the dull light from the windows, and gives it a shake, then pops off the top and eases out a small white pill.

She won't add *pick up more Adderall* to her to-do list up on the board because that's something she never forgets.

Chapter 9: Cosmological Colic

The rain is gone. Today the sun is shining, the air is fresh, and there's just a slightly sticky warmth to it.

Another day in paradise, Davin finds himself thinking, once again sitting out on the terrace off the second floor living room with his usual midmorning coffee break.

But it doesn't feel anything at all like paradise for him since he's in yet another one of his funks, and he knows it isn't the slight hangover headache. It is a different sort of hangover, one he's all too familiar with, where he's dogged by conflicting perceptions of something so basic as his sense of self. Of course, he knows who he is, but he's still too often easily victim of confusing who he is with what he does. Sitting in the sun, his thoughts are flipping through his roles, a mix of emotions bounding with every role he recites, and that mix of feelings includes anger and confusion and obstinance, right along with substrata of longing and despair.

Artist, journalist, builder, landlord, farmer, he recites.

Digital platform whatever, he reminds himself. *Ex-husband.*

And then, out of nowhere, *Dead.*

This last thought comes up a bit too frequently for his liking. He knows he's worked on correcting such thinking over the years, including a run of cognitive therapy some years back, but his thinking about death, some half-wish to be dead, this is never far off.

Jesus, ain't I the cheerful one this morning, Davin chides, and he gets up off the wood-and-iron bench where he's been looking out at his property and eastward through the trees, beyond which is the west-facing side of Monument Mountain.

He starts walking the property, moving slowly out toward the big garden fence.

The sky is crystalline blue.

He should be feeling good.

"Fuck you," he says to himself at a normal speaking voice.

Davin can guess where some of the harshness he too often feels comes from, although after so many years he knows his religious upbringing is more just accent than cause. He had taken Catholicism seriously as a kid, even as an infant in all probability, probably on a molecular level, for reasons a therapist might possibly be hired to ferret out.

Or an exorcist, Davin then thinks with some amusement.

A touchstone for Davin's thinking this morning and so many other times, too, is an early vivid memory of Confession, one taking place not long after his First Communion, the Baltimore Catechism still fresh then, no doubt.

Because of his birth month, he was the youngest in that year's cohort.

He's retold this story enough times through his years of therapy that it has become shiny with humor. *Do not pass Go. Do not collect $200,* the reflexive voice in his head chimes in whenever he thinks of his six-year-old self heading back toward the family car after the Saturday afternoon ritual of Confession. His six-year-old had been pondering the state of his grace and that he was theretofore to be counted among the apostolic hoard, right? But in this presumed post-Confession grace, as he approached the sidewalk, he had found himself wishing for a car to careen into him, thus sending him to heaven. But in that flash of imagined relief he, the young boy, had transmuted this desire into the terror that such thinking was a form of suicide, a sin of thought, and it occurred to his early self this would bar him from the embrace of Jesus, surely.

Six decades later, Davin can be amused by the burnished memory, but even so, he can also feel yet again that moment and the tone of his confusion and his sense that easily extended to form the question, *Why bother?*

He should be feeling good this morning. The night before he'd hosted a small cocktail party, and the rain had cleared just in time. The party was ostensibly to welcome the new *Berkshire Interactive* contributor, but he likes to have cocktail parties, reasons or not. He likes the opportunity to enjoy a well-made drink and to introduce others to that experience.

The party, which was small, had been enjoyable, but Jeannie Louise Smith had been something of a Johnny-one-note, talking about the developing storm he'd seen referenced in his news feed just this morning, some sort of storm system that could be big. Fortunately, she had allowed Davin to distract her with his liquor shelf set up in the library, in what he calls his bar.

She knows her bourbon, that's for sure, he considers, and he finds that interesting.

And it had been nice to see Deidre, his now officially former house sharer, who has already in fact long been living with Alicia, even if she'd moved out of her room here far later than he would have supposed. He finds he already misses her, not that he ever saw much of her, and not that they ever had all that much to say to each other, but she had been one of the early house sharers, and polite, responsible, and for the last couple of years or so Alicia's girlfriend, although he knows the relationship may have started up quite a bit before then.

He scoffs at himself. *I'm already missing the rent.*

He's been spending the last few days, as Alicia has asked him to, looking at Smith's climate change blogs and other writings, and in the process he has fallen down an odd rabbit hole in his effort to gain a clearer sense of Smith's world.

The large numbers of writers on the topic was enough of a surprise, but the taxonomy of writers on climate change turns out to be the bigger surprise. Those spouting the technology optimist views are understandable, and of course, he's read enough to see that some such writers are fervidly positive or even Pollyannaish. There are those writers who take their time—like Jeannie Louise Smith—to explain complex issues of politics, economics, and science, and for all the dread contained within, such writing can feel good and even hopeful.

His upset is many with the category of climate writers he has learned are called *Doomers*. The worst of these are found in long-form posts on the platform *bitbites,* the micropayment content platform, one of several in the new crop of long-form social media that had absorbed *Medium* and a few similar older channels. According to some of these writers, renewables are a fool's errand, and for others it's the amount of fossil fuel needed to bring on full green electrification that would further and irreversibly drown the world in greenhouse gases, everything too little and too late. But the most macabre view among Doomers is that nothing meaningful can be done to slow or reverse the full collapse of mankind's tenure on earth, and that it makes no sense to even try since forces beyond the human scale of understanding—geologic timeframes, or even cosmological ones—make such human efforts silly.

After reading so much of this viewpoint, a line occurred to him that made him laugh: *Don't bother making your bed, for the sun will go supernova.*

But the joke hasn't kept him from the downward slide he's been caught in, and this had nearly ruined last night's party and lingers on still.

And now, midmorning, looking at the vegetable garden and the healthy set of the young shoots turning into tiny plants, Davin's still halfway stuck in the Doomer shadow and fighting his already pre-existing tendency toward depression.

He has done a lot of work in his adult years to understand and place into perspective those early habits of thoughts and feelings that are, fundamentally, a species of nihilism, but humor has always been in his *armamentarium,* and he long ago took up the Paul Valéry quote, *Only a fool thinks a man cannot joke and be serious*, although some time back he checked this attribution but couldn't find it.

But jesus, this fucking climate shit, he tells himself, still trying to shake the lingering effect triggered by the unexpected posts and essays on *bitbites*. Then again, he has always had to contend with the thought, *Well, if you're going to end up dead, why then not now?*

But he knows these sorts of thoughts are just artifacts of depression, and he knows he has counters to such thinking, including an answer that entails love in various ways and manners, including the connection he'd had with Gwen, although the five years of divorce makes that a less than clear argument, especially on some days.

His children, the two of them, daughter and son, are both adults and out of the house and out of the area, the daughter married and Jimmy in a relationship with Cynthia, and his connection to his kids remains strong, or kind of, anyway. Another comfort is his large group of old, dear friends, known one to the other over decades, most going back to college days, and survivors of marriages and children and career changes, not to mention of varying levels of success, the celebrants of pensions and 401(k)s, some not so much as others. It's just that he doesn't get to see them, singly or as a group, very often. In the early years out here, with the small apartment on the north half of the first floor that's now the Airbnb rental, they'd host their visiting friends, but being out in Western Massachusetts has had its bad side for visits in recent years, especially since Covid and then the divorce, and then with the house sharers and the Airbnb that make for there being no room at the inn.

He knows, too, his impulse toward art is another crucial element of his mental health. He takes joy in the experience and the perception of beauty, and the act of creation in his studio often effectively serves as a counter to his tenacious resignation unto utter obliteration.

Well, lah dee dah, he thinks.

He laughs, reflecting on his six-year-old very serious self, these days a comforting and positive memory as much as not, but negative thoughts and feelings are still part and parcel of a typical day within his head, alongside the minor mental cuts and scrapes of any day, as are the more quotidian feelings of delight, or despair, anger or joy, like everyone else, or so he has to imagine, each and every one with the whirling kaleidoscope of all such feelings.

He opens the garden gate and moves among the young shoots and new growth, liking what he sees.

Planting is an act of hope, he's read somewhere.

On the other hand, Marsha, who loves to garden here, has been bugging him about last year's garden having gotten too much sun and heat damage, and she's been arguing he'll need to buy and install sunscreens. He's not happy about it, knowing the size of the garden will make this an expensive proposition. But he also knows the summers can get that hot, a problem for some vegetable plants more than others, but a problem for anyone and everyone working under the sun too. There's the added benefit of the sunscreens offering some protection against hard rain and even hail, the special fabric suspended above helping to prevent the watery beatdowns becoming more common in the growing season.

Since Marsha joined the household, they've been eating well from the garden, but now there's another item to add on the expense side of the garden spreadsheet he's been keeping for the last three summers, and to date the math doesn't look good.

Not at all, he admits, but with something like a smile.

Chapter 10: And I Helped Too!

Gerald Greene is supposed to be on vacation, enjoying the pleasant Aegean breeze.

Global Warming, he tells himself. *What's wrong with things being nice and warm?*

It's an old joke, but then, his think tank, his Kehoe Institute, has long been hard at work keeping the facts confused about climate change. Writing climate denial reports to create and support the perception there are many people, scientists, experts, *thought leaders*, who quite sensibly believe that man-caused climate change is just a theory. This work has paid well, but he knows that the days of climate denialism and obfuscation are done.

He looks up from his laptop, gazing through the mesh curtain and out beyond the deck, the azure Caribbean of his typical three-week annual vacation replaced by the less turquoise Mediterranean.

He'd been planning a stay in St. John, at the private home he's become quite fond of sub-leasing, the vacation residence of a different pal of his, a corporate board member of the largest American fossil fuel company. Unfortunately, the unsettled Atlantic weather pattern is already throwing early storm system warnings and he's been proved right in making the switch. The storm system has developed into an early and growing hurricane heading west, and it doesn't matter that St. John looks to be spared because any big storm reduces travel options, and he's been through one hurricane in St. John and that was one more than he has ever wanted to experience.

This is the second time he's been here at the private resort on Patmos, where the small house overlooks the Aegean Sea. The weather is perfect, the air rich with the smell of the sea and the dry herbaceous Greek landscape. He typically wouldn't be inside, on his laptop. He's on vacation.

Except, of course, it turns out he's not. There's work to be done.

He doesn't like feeling nervous, or on his back foot. There's this new development that he's got to ride herd on.

He'd planned to be on Patmos another two weeks and then some, but he's flying back early because the *Powers that Be* are entirely unhappy with the latest problem. Because of the developing storm it's already too late to fly commercial, and he'll have to wait for air traffic reshuffling to settle down, which will likely be no longer than a day or two.

Or three.

Travel hassle isn't his biggest problem, nor is cutting his stay short.

No, his biggest problem is *that fucking report.* Out now less than two days, there's a report put out by some group of academics that names individuals active in the climate denial business, including some of Kehoe's own best contractors, which have made them radioactive.

And useless.

This report, he knows, is just the cherry on top, the nail in the coffin, *the last fucking straw* in his growing acceptance that climate denial messaging has become dangerously exposed, never mind grown inefficacious.

Efficacious. He loves that word.

He is almost two days late in seeing the report, having been en route, and, well, he'd been less than diligent about checking emails or looking at his phone, more interested in just settling in and enjoying the luxury of the exclusive resort.

This report is a kick in the ass for him. He's gone through it and it is in the main a textual analysis of a very large collection of climate denial writings, with the actual writers identified, giving lie to the big author names listed.

Greene sits up from the slouch he's been slowly collapsing into, an idea sending him up and out of his chair to grab his cell phone off the side table, thumbing through to the number he seeks.

"Yeah, Gerald Greene," he says, and after listening for a moment, he laughs.

"Yeah, fuck me, right? It will have to handled, it will be handled," he says, but the man, one of the middling oil business billionaires, is saying something.

He listens, nodding his head, murmuring assent here and there during the man's monologue on the other side of the line.

"Exactly," Greene says after the man stops talking. "Time to bring this up a notch, first thing a press release to reframe—" but the man starts talking again.

"Yeah," says Greene, "the problem is I'm stuck here because of the hurricane, I've checked and already flights are piling up, does the storm even have a name yet?"

Josephine is what the man tells him.

Greene does the math and realizes the first letter of the storm's name means there have been nine tropical storm systems or depressions that have previously developed.

"Right," he says after waiting out another run of talk by the man on the other end of the phone. "Well, weather, she is a wacky bitch for sure."

He asks the man about getting a flight back on one of the man's own jets.

"You want to come along for the ride, there's plenty we can talk about," Greene tells him.

Listening, Greene laughs. "Got it, sure, but how about Roberts, he still your Special Operations man?" and he is again quiet, listening to the man on the other end of the phone.

"Great," Greene says. "I'll jump to Athens, have Roberts text me terminal and time, and thanks."

The sort of things he'll want to talk about are best never

put on paper, and now he'll have the whole flight back to chat up Roberts on the scope of his thinking. He trusts Roberts as much as he trusts anyone. Roberts had been the one to vet Lobinsky for him.

He makes the necessary plans to get to Athens, and he'll be out of the resort within two hours' time.

He does his best work when pressed, and there's nothing like a general panic for inspiration. They'll do the usual re-framing, and see how good the report really is, and he makes a note to get his Director of Research to look into who's behind the big reveal. This report is by some group of academics called The Library.

Not Library, he catches himself. *The Laundry. Fucking ridiculous name.*

He's feeling unhappy. He's annoyed at having to cut short his bit of luxury island time, although the private jet solution is some compensation.

He looks at the kitchen counter and sees a draft by one of his best contractors, brought along because he hadn't gotten back to his man before leaving, and he'd reviewed it on the flight out, but otherwise has simply ignored it since, or until the email about *The Laundry* report, at any rate. The work sitting on the counter is just another of the sort of messaging on climate change that has been a waning action for years, but this recent exposé is killing any possible utility for the draft paper from this contractor, useless now that this contractor has been identified as the real author. His contractor is only one so named, one among most other key contractors hired by Kehoe and countless other entities, these contractors who are the real sources of so much of what has come from the mouths of politicians and business leaders and other thought leaders of the fossil fuel industry position.

Thought leaders. He's always hated that term, but maybe because he has long seen through the curtain. He knows how the sausage is made, and that puts him off the final product, which is the manipulation of language toward specific ends, mercenary ends.

Thought leaders, jesus, he tells himself again.

He's been very good at doing what he does, and maintaining a clear-eyed view is an essential skill and knowing what is now useless is another. Even more important, of course, is knowing what needs to be done and doing it, and all without any direct or traceable *quid pro quo* to the clients. There's not even any official client status, just undisclosed funders and their needs, and if one is paying attention no one has to say what they need. For years, part of what's needed for his funders is sand thrown in the gears of climate change actions, but that's just been the easy work. There's been far more difficult work too, undertakings that have more specific and direct consequences, and this thought leads to his thinking about Lobinsky. He'll wait to talk to Lobinky until he's stateside, when using the burner will be much less risky. If his newest thoughts find interest, there will be more hard work ahead for his operative.

He looks at his Tag Heuer chronograph and sees that he's got time to email the contractor and tell him the bad news, although he is confident the guy already knows that the recent exposé has named him, and being smart, knows there will be such an email on the way.

Greene understands what the bigger problem is. It's that the argument countering the validity of man-made climate change has played out. It's that climate denial, despite the ever-increasingly sophisticated de-bunking techniques, the social media tropes and memes, and all the money poured into PR efforts and astroturfing, have now become rearguard at best, and at worst, pretty much entirely useless.

He should know, since he's been an instigator of such tactics for years.

It hasn't helped that one of the most recent efforts—*at least not one of ours*, he thinks, thankful for that small consolation—was laughed down when a senator referenced the particular article during the continuing resolution debates. Literally laughed out of the room, in fact, with the late-night clowns having a field day.

He wonders how the just-released exposé will play in the media. He'll spend the flight back getting that picture.

He knows that he has reason to worry. Taking the lid off, identifying all his own go-to people and a lot of others too, that's bad enough, but the name of Kehoe Institute itself has shown up in the newly release report by *The Laundry*, right along with several like-minded organizations. One of his big worries is that the exposé might make it easier for others to uncover the financial connections among the institutions and contractors and thus the connections among the institutions and the clients.

He's done well and the Kehoe Institute has provided some of the very best work of its kind, words generated specifically to be placed in the mouths of others and immortalized in the *Congressional Record* and well-known publications and network interviews and news shows. The days when the mainstream press, open to a fair and balanced approach, would so easily fall into the thrall of such work, those days were already numbered, and increasingly these days denial commentary mainly shows up in fringe and useless publications. Even the best of the Kehoe-bought *bon mots* are now only uttered in the talks and speeches of ever more irrelevant politicians and pseudoscience mouthpieces. He's already known this work of ghosting articles and meta-studies and speeches was becoming less and less effective over these last several years. The debate is over, of course, because it's hard to argue against the facts.

Those pesky fucking facts, he says to himself.

The facts and his opponents who wield them have been making steady progress despite the money that has long been thrown against them, and that money has already been shifting to campaign donations and other forms of direct lobbying to influence key politicians. But even campaign contributions aren't buying what they used to.

Despite this latest revelation and the grind of responding to it, he's already getting excited about the new strategy he wants to implement, which will be to focus on the economic pain of climate change efforts.

For the common man, he adds, with a sniff.

All he has to do is get some of his clients excited about his strategy. His new take, still forming, will be that the fossil fuel industry's problem is the wrong arguments are being used, which is why he's going to pitch a renewed focus on economic issues to counter the climate change momentum. What's needed, he'll be reasoning, are detailed explanations of how the renewable energy transition hurts regular people with job loss, higher costs, tax increases. He will have facts and statistics on his side, at least if only the short-term is the only term considered, he knows.

But that is one of the magic tricks, isn't it? he reminds himself.

There are sectors of the economy, after all, that have remained moribund, resulting in unemployment jumping from the historically low levels after the jobs rebound post-Covid ran its course. The spending from The Inflation Reduction Act remains slower than the climate boosters expected, although at best the main contribution to the spending slowdown on the part of last administration was problems in workforce training and delays in permitting big projects that continue to tap the brakes. Even still, the growing transition to renewables is causing slowdowns in the fossil fuel sector, with negative effects on that sector rippling outward.

Negative effects, especially for my clients, he considers, but puts a pin in that angle for the moment.

He can make the cost argument based on government reports, although even here he'll have to cherry-pick and emphasize older reports because the latest modestly better employment trends aren't really much help to his argument, nor are some of the latest leading indicators.

There's some potential danger from the economic hits

on the fossil fuel sector that have already seen some of his patrons cut back on his work, but the core, the several dozen people of extreme wealth who have long funded PACs and think tanks, they're still there, still fighting the good fight, although now mainly trying to save their deregulation efforts and avoiding bigger taxes on carbon, but there's growing worry about losing fossil fuel subsidies too. He is sure the economics argument aimed at cost increases and negative monetary impacts will provide good leverage on several fronts, and, fortunately, fossil fuel subsidies can be easily spun as pocketbook issues.

Hmm, he thinks. *Let's try "pickpocket issues."*

There's plenty of opportunity, too, on the culture war front, it being easy to blame the *elites* for imposing their own self-serving *better ideas* on everyday folks, *ideas that cost others money.*

He knows hikes in gasoline prices have a long record of triggering public discontent, and public discontent always hurts the party in power. A well-timed oil production cutback might help, if he can get enough agreement on that.

He admits that he should have been pushing this economic argument from the start and he's annoyed at his reactive stance to what clearly has to be counted as a significant victory by his opponents. The climate change planners have been smart. He has to be smarter. He has to be more ruthless.

He'll put together some proposals advocating attacking climate change efforts on economic grounds, and with so many climate programs long underway, and much more likely soon, the national deficit is still staggeringly big and interest rates are still high. It can be easy enough to paint climate change efforts as job-killing and cost-raising and putting names and faces on the blame works best.

He is getting angrier with himself that he hasn't shifted until now, and now only after the climate-changers have forced his hand.

The fucking academics! He flashes in anger, but he calms

himself immediately, puzzling out how best to counter the exposé. He can admire the analysis work, surprised by its effectiveness since he has always thought the various contractors were quite thorough in their efforts to change styles, adopt voices, vary approaches. But the natural language algorithms are too good these days, apparently.

I'll have to find my own Big Data Daddy, he tells himself, although he's a bit perplexed as to how exactly he can do that, but he'll start by getting one of the contributing PACs to bankroll time on Google or OpenAI, or the new Korean platform, whatever it is called now, and he figures he can bring someone on board who is happy for the work. It will take some searching though, because the big data folks he knows are all from research institutions at universities, and he's long been *persona non grata* in that world.

To accuse the other side of that which you are guilty, this tactic has proved out again and again over the decades. And now he will be proposing to do just that, highlighting the climate change thought leaders as puppets of the elites and reveal who is saying what for whom, and why.

Or at least the reasons we'll ascribe.

He feels his sense of control is starting to return. The real meat, he knows, is to redirect the climate issue into household anxieties.

It is the economy, stupid.

His angle of attack will be to show there are really only a few people behind this energy transition argument, and a bunch of elites at that, and they aren't telling their fellow citizens the real consequences of what they argue, and they are getting rich lying, and everyone else is getting poorer, paying taxes, higher prices.

He'll make it a household economics issue.

It's all about money and power.

He loves it.

Money and power, he repeats.

He'll turn the spotlight on the motivations and mechanisms of the climate movement experts and their own best rhetoricians. He's going to argue the value of revealing where climate change people get their money and showing where that climate change money is being spent, and who gets what, and highlight the climate change shills and their puppet masters. It is simply fair play, he'll tell Roberts, using him as a sounding board. They'll take the lid off the climate change industry too.

He'll spend the time in Athens on some initial notes, even though he will have to scramble, and if Roberts or his boss doesn't get interested, Greene will easily find others enchanted by his scheme for countering the accusations being leveled at the climate-denial industrial complex. The kicker is to tie the climate change industrial complex to the accusation of hurting the common man's pocketbook, showing the elites benefiting at the common man's expense.

The common man, he repeats.

It is a strange phrase, but he knows it's a useful phrase, especially when you have names and faces of those earning a good living by making earning a living harder for the many, for the common man.

I'm heading back, baby, he tells himself.

He's excited.

And I'm helping, too.

Chapter 11: Gray Swan Song

Jeannie Louise is working at her desk on a piece for *The New York Times Sunday Magazine,* excited to be playing in the biggest leagues finally, but she can't really get herself to concentrate. She's supposed to be writing about the western drought, the dropping levels of snowpacks, now more or less vanquished in many areas, and one major consequence of the drought is the higher costs of food production.

Drink another cup of coffee, she tells herself, but she's been trying to drink less coffee since she's developed something of an acid stomach, although that might be her seventy-one years, not the coffee. She brushes her gray frizzing hair back, always surprised when it escapes the hairband that is supposed to keep the short mass in check.

Before she'd started in on the research for her *NYT* topic, she hadn't known that already by 2015 the snowpacks set a 500-year low record, and except for 2016's *El Niño* rains and then the freak atmospheric rivers and snows several years later, a new low water record keeps getting set. She's learned that most climate scientists don't see the drought being the new steady state exactly, but none she's talked to or has read see things going back to what everyone once thought as normal. Keeping track of all the facts and figures presented by the topic of climate change is, she knows, an unending and impossible task, even for someone like her who follows the science as closely as she does. She doubts even the leading climate scientists feel all that confident in their grasp of what is happening in any particular detail or other.

Nobody is likely smart enough, she considers, and not for the first time. Her eyes light on the several towers of paper, reports, and scientific journals she tends to collect in her work, work she first and foremost thinks of as reading and thinking and analyzing. The piles are on the far long edge of her desk across from her, and most of the piles are barely in her reach from where she sits across the width of the table.

This far edge of the desk, with its series of stacks, sidles up against the back of a sofa she knows has seen better days, but strategic placement of a couple of throws cover the worst of wear. Over the years she's come to accept the benefits of breaking from her reading and writing, stretching out on the couch for a catnap.

She's feeling one come on even now, but the late-morning sun still falls on the front of the house, the shut curtains set aglow with the light. The apartment is on the second floor of a house located on Cottage Street, up in the north end of town, and she's grown used to the traffic noise that seeps in from Route 7 running parallel to Cottage. Route 7 is a large block northward, but still close enough to hear the traffic as it starts and stops as cars and trucks make their way over Brown Bridge where, with a traffic light, Route 7 changes with a sharp turn left from Stockbridge Road to become Main Street, Great Barrington.

After six years here, she's gotten inured to the traffic sounds. Weird weather, on the other hand, is still something that has the capacity to surprise and shock her.

Some windows are open for the air, but mostly on the front south face. Air is being drawn through by one sizable window fan in a window on the north side at the back of the kitchen, the air flow pillowing the curtains away from the front window screens. There's an air conditioner in one of the front windows. She heaved up into place last week, but she always waits a bit too long to do this, somehow always surprised by how hot days can show up so early. But today, there's no need to turn it on. Today, the weather is beautiful in her part of the country.

There are a couple of chairs in the room from the dining table set, and each seat is occupied, one by a stack of LPs she'd picked up from a local listing at a great price, almost nothing, really, and probably the guy had picked them up at the dump.

Transfer station, she corrects herself. *So much more fancy.*

The town of Alford was reputed to still have good pickings, she'd once been told.

The other dining chair is near the front door and in between the window with the still air conditioner and the other two windows, and this chair holds a paper shopping bag stuffed with old clothes she's been planning on giving to Goodwill, although that is a plan made quite some time ago, she now realizes. Tucked up against this chair is a big cardboard box, one side a bit crushed in, with more such old clothes, and next to that is an old coffee table she uses as the base for her turntable, and receiver.

Jeannie Louise often sits back from her work to look over the space, and she's been known to push herself in a twirl or two in her expensive office chair as she does so.

At this moment, her eyes rest on her old Cerwin-Vega speakers from the 1970s, when that company was among the best makers of speakers. The speakers, each tucked toward their own front corners of the room, sound warm by today's digital standards, but that is very much to her liking. She's been busy in the last two decades keeping the speakers in good condition, including the occasional recaulking of the big woofer cones whose foam edge connectors tend to degrade and fail over time, but an easy fix using a carefully applied silicon bead. She'd researched this repair after pricing out replacement woofers, and even though she could swing such new woofers these days, her habits of modest spending remain. She knows anyone looking closely can see the cherry veneer of the big speaker cabinets has been reglued here and there where pieces have chipped off, but she keeps the finish looking good, waxing the cabinetry when she redoes her desk surface.

She's thinking about putting on some music and lying down on the couch. She's finding herself with mixed feelings about Alicia's pitch that she should map her expertise in the politics, money, and consequences of climate change to something that reflects more local issues such as the impact on weather.

Impact, that almost derailed any further discussion, although Jeannie Louise managed to keep her reaction to the usage under control during the conversation.

You are impacted.

Jeannie Louise has long banned the use of the word "impact" from her writing—along with "paradigm," "task," "utilize," and other words that have earned their place on her ban list. *Impact* joined that list when a nurse friend of hers, going back years now, described how "impacted" is used clinically to describe severe constipation.

Consequence, effect, result, aftermath, upshot, importance, significance, value, moment, import, concern, magnitude. All good climate change words.

It's not the beautiful weather outside that's keeping her from working, either, and her trouble concentrating on her present assignment isn't about the work itself. She's distracted by the tabs she's been checking for the last couple of hours, and she cycles through all four tabs yet again, including Weather.com and a national network news channel that is just one of the many such organizations to have gone to live coverage in the last hour. The other two tabs are the National Hurricane Center out of NOAA.gov and her Twitter feed.

Twitter, X, and one or two other names that service had gone through, restructuring and adding new business models and ownership changes, and the name that seems to finally stick is back to Twitter, although it is a nonprofit company now, some sort of quasi-public utility anyway.

The situation she is distracted by is that much of Florida

is getting swept by an off-the-scale hurricane named Josephine that continues to pick up strength. It was declared a hurricane only three days back, and the storm system then turned westward in the Atlantic, gaining more strength from overly warm waters just south of Bermuda, and the force of the hurricane keeps growing.

Josephine is already dropping its rain on southern Florida, but the bigger danger now is the Category 5 winds whipping the unfortunately timed high tide into a huge storm surge of a size that has been only theoretical before today. Here it is, the fabled Gray Swan storm, and hitting about the most vulnerable land possible. If the storm surge hits as it looks likely in the next hour or so, pretty much everything from Delray Beach south through Miami is going to be underwater. Evacuations are underway, but late, because Miami had been forecast for only a glancing blow, but the storm's unexpected and sudden shift now has Miami as Ground Zero. There's a frenzied last-minute effort to make sure large parts of the city are emptied, along with Kendall and Homestead and the rest of Biscayne Bay, but all such earlier efforts had been focused on areas more to the south.

She is transfixed by the live coverage. Everyone in the country, she would guess, is likely glued to the live reports.

After watching the coverage for some time, she'd realized there is a complete absence of the traditional wind-whipped reporter horsing around in driving rain, and that strikes Jeannie Louise as notable, given such scenes have long been part of the storm reporting canon. Instead, the news is focused on evacuation efforts. Concern and anxiety have invaded the tone of the anchors.

She now settles back on The Weather Channel, but she periodically checks in on another couple just-tabbed news networks. She well remembers Katrina, and the latest hit on New Orleans just last year almost as bad. That storm had helped start planning on the Sea Wall Act that is now, after the recent election, in early committees. She follows the proposed bill closely. She knows it's still far from a vote, but even in its current state she can predict that New Orleans may be largely left out, no potential benefits need apply. Fair or not, this is in part being blamed on the Louisiana Republican Governor and that state's congressional delegation's failure to discuss any compromise on their own earlier position withholding funding for the city's proposed resiliency projects, and pundits are predicting a shift of red-state votes in the next Bayou State election. But for New Orleans, she knows, it isn't just the politics. Even Congress seems likely to understand there are cities that can't be protected, not on any practical basis anyway.

And now here's Miami in the crosshairs.

Red state, blue state, wet state. And yet there are still clowns like Jenkins questioning climate change effects, which enrages her since she and anybody with the ability to read and think knows there are plenty of opportunities for coal states to shift industrial focus and develop new jobs.

If only I were emperor, she thinks, not for the first time.

Her phone rings.

It's Davin.

"So, you make any progress on Alicia's offer," he asks her, with nothing in the way of an actual greeting. "Sorry," he adds, "I'm just going through my list and Alicia has asked that I check in, she's eager, yeah, eager is right, with you coming on board."

"Um, thanks?" Jeannie Louise says.

"So," he says.

She doesn't quite know what to say. She loves the idea and the fees seem okay, and she knows it won't be hard to apply her knowledge of climate change to the local area, and she even thinks this work might be fun, at least a bit. The problem is she's already swamped, and she's been wondering if there is really any chance she'll have the bandwidth, and today, with the storm unfolding, she's having difficulty getting anything at all done.

"Yeah, this is something I really want to do," she tells

him, "but my biggest worry is I may be too busy, and it's a matter of priorities."

He tells her there can be plenty of flexibility in terms of deadlines and schedules, that this shouldn't worry her, but she is doubtful he understands how much more work she's been getting.

"I'm really pretty swamped," she repeats and then tells him about *The New York Times* assignment she has due, and then names a couple of other assignments for outlets she's sure he recognizes.

"Yeah, that's great, fantastic, but we'll figure out how to fit in your pieces for us, like there's no real time pressures," he tells her. He then adds, "Well, mainly, let's talk about what looks possible. What I know is that Alicia seems pretty gung-ho to have you doing your thing for us."

"That's very nice to hear," she tells him.

"Yeah, yeah, I'm excited too, not saying elsewise. I think these will be nice ongoing features, glad to have them, but why don't you look at your calendar and give me some rough sense of when you can do the first one, and we'll take it from there?"

She finds herself telling him what she's said to Alicia, which is that she is very interested and it's just a matter of time, and she promises to get back to him as soon as she can.

"Yeah, sure, great," Davin replies.

"You watching the storm, Josephine? It's huge," she asks, and Davin tells her that he's seen the news, and then he says goodbye, the call done. It seems clear to her that he's not on top of the latest developments.

She puts down her phone and wonders if she's getting a weird vibe from Davin, but she just pushes the phone away.

Glancing back to her monitor, she sees the network's live coverage is still focused on evacuation efforts.

She's speculating if her current assignment on the western drought might be pushed to a later issue anyway with all the Josephine coverage more likely to take center stage. She switches tabs to NBC, one of the Big Three, but now a multi-caster network using air, cable, and the Web in equal measure to reach viewers live. She stays with NBC for a while because the broadcast seems a bit less hysterical than most of the others. The NBC death index is already up to 324 and counting as news of one of the hurricane monitoring planes going down is reported. Already added are the occupants of a school bus full of nursing home evacuees that's been swept off a beachfront road by an early errant wave, and several boats and ships and crews are considered lost, including a small cruise ship, crewed but without passengers, that had been trying to make it out of the storm area. There are other unlucky victims already up on the board as well, including a surprisingly high number of candidates for the Darwin Awards, sightseeing the strong weather and getting a far too real close-up look.

There should be a separate index for these idiots, Jeannie thinks, but she knows any of these fools have family and friends, and a high number of the Darwin sweepstakes nominees probably thought they were being careful, and certainly no one really believes such a storm could or would ever happen, could be this off-the-scale, not really.

"Ah, yes, here we go," says Jeannie Louise, noticing a new alert that sends a wave of deep dread through her. St. Lucie Nuclear Power Complex, a.k.a. FPL Energy Encounter, is the subject of the crawling chyron, and the problem is the facility is built on the landside of Hutchinson Island, Port St. Lucie, thirty miles or so from Jupiter. That town is now being projected as the northernmost city in the full landfall zone, maybe just to be grazed by the storm, but also still possibly in the direct path.

St. Lucie Nuclear Power Complex has twin nuclear plants that use ocean water for cooling. It looks like the major storm surge is racing northwest in a direction just right to fill the channel between Hutchinson and the mainland. The nuclear plant is at an elevation of some seventeen feet above normal sea level, or whatever counts for that, these days.

She does a quick Google search that leads to a Huffington Post article from 2014, titled, "How Rising Seas Could Sink Nuclear Plants on the East Coast." The article, she sees, was published as a Hurricane Sandy follow-up.

She feels sick.

She turns her attention back to NBC and sees evacuation is underway in Port St. Lucie. By all accounts the late evacuation is going well, which she figures is due to the in-place plans and drills the NRC has long required. It should also help that Port St. Lucie is an additional twenty to thirty minutes ahead of the main storm surge. And then there is Brunswick Steam Electric Plant, in Southport, North Carolina, another nuclear plant. This one at nineteen feet above sea level but probably far enough north to miss the biggest surges.

Building nuclear power plants in potential storm surge areas should never have happened.

We are all morons, she tells herself.

She's surprised the network's coverage of the nuclear plant issue is so in-depth, but this confuses her only for a moment before she realizes they must have already had coverage prepared on this issue, but for Turkey Point Nuclear Generating Station in Homestead, another twin-unit facility also only seventeen feet above sea level. With the storm's path shifting northward, she can guess some news producer is simply repurposing a lot of the Homestead material to St. Lucie.

Wasn't Homestead in the news for Hurricane Andrew, maybe? Jeannie asks herself, wondering how Turkey Point did in that lesser storm, and she makes a mental note to look this up later.

She sees that the death count is up over 400 as Josephine is starting to swamp South Miami and the Miami waterfront. The storm surges are predicted to peak at over thirty feet at high tide with driving wind and rain.

According to the newscasters, the full storm surge is

still almost an hour away.

Art Deco Meets Josephine, she can't help composing as a headline, all the while wondering how well-built those hotels and condominiums are. She's pessimistic. Wasn't there an oceanside high-rise apartment collapse some years ago, and that hadn't required a mega-storm.

She is now flashing from one tab to another and another, going from one video clip of real-time destruction to another, to another, until she stops and mutes the audio.

She sits in stunned silence.

They're screwed, she thinks.

She's not one to use coarse language, but it seems appropriate.

We're fucked, she corrects herself.

Chapter 12: Love for Sale

It's more than a week since Josephine dissipated up toward Greenland.

Deidre knows that times are strange for everyone, with what has happened on Florida's Gold Coast, with the unprecedented numbers of dead and the scope of physical destruction on a whole new scale. The latest count is one hundred forty-seven thousand confirmed or presumed dead or missing, and from these there are the multitude of pictures of victims pulled, most likely from social media. The parades of images seem endless in number, face after face, in newspapers, on television, and across the Web.

Those-Who-Have-Died Portraits, is how she is now thinking of this.

The incessant photographs of the dead are a widely shared event.

She has only sadness for the lives lost and for those they've left behind, or she had felt this way, anyway, until this morning, when, suddenly, it's become all too much. The result for her, as of this morning, is her desire to never look at even one more such photograph.

She's looking at the morning news on the too-large TV that almost overwhelms the antique bureau, which is one of two similar bureaus in her own bedroom in Alicia's house. Deidre is still impressed with the room, although she's a bit embarrassed by this reaction since she's been in residence, for all intents and purposes, quite some time. It shouldn't seem so unreal at this point, she considers.

The room, in addition to a queen bed with matching

headboard and two nightstands, is replete with a pretty slipper chair, a side table with a straight chair, and a walk-in closet that is close enough in size to a bedroom or two she slept in growing up.

She's gotten into the habit post-Josephine of having the news on as she gets ready for work. The TV has many subscription networks, another thing she never had before. But as she watches today, what she notices is how the media pundits and cultural experts are transmuting the Josephine story into their own story, discussing their feelings about the continual postings and galleries of the dead and missing.

It's the way she's feeling today, but it seems wrong to her for them to make their own emotions the story of the hour. Unfortunately, the current babbling this morning is more meta-news than real news, the anchors reporting on the question of publishing more death pictures. If the program currently running was a call-in show, she could tell them how she feels overwhelmed by the portraits, too, but what she'd rather point out is the self-centeredness of today's live segment. It seems like the entire infotainment industry is again caught up in its habit of feeding on itself.

More eyeballs!

She grabs the remote and stabs off the TV.

In the sudden silence she finds herself wondering if there are any gods with multiple sets of eyes in the pantheons across the various cultures, like Shiva with the many arms, and she has a thought that strikes her as funny. The irony would be for her to find such a multi-eyed picture and post it as a meme with the caption: *More eyeballs!*

But with such a thought, Deidre understands that she's feeling less amused and more feeling overwhelmed.

She feels overwhelmed by the non-stop coverage of the recent disaster that had started with the forecasting of Josephine, and then the tracking of the storm's hunger for lives, and then the whole aftermath coverage, and it all seems to have been going on for months, even if it's been barely a week.

Such publicizing—*celebrating*—of grief suddenly seems unseemly to her. It embarrasses her. She'd like to go on a news fast, but she can also appreciate there's some odd sense of comfort in joining the many tens or hundreds of millions of others still watching, and she considers it might be some bad thing, her wanting a break from it all, knowing there are many thousands and thousands of lives disrupted, even lost. And then there are the unparalleled challenges that lie ahead, of course.

Maybe the problem is she can't help.

But she can't help it. It is all too much.

Alicia seems to be doing well with the storm, with her online newspaper thing, *Berkshire Interactive,* contributing its share to Deidre's sense of haunt. Not that they've talked much about the business or even how each of them feels about the storm and its aftermath.

What do we talk about? Deidre wonders.

That question bothers her.

A lot is bothering her, she admits to herself. The storm is hard to grasp, the numbers dead, displaced, the property damage. She's bothered, too, by the fact that all this remains too strong a pull on her attention.

Like watching the proverbial car crash in slow motion, she tells herself.

As best she can tell, most everyone she knows seems to be taking comfort in these personal stories, these portraits, or at least these stories are getting talked about a lot. Alicia has been publishing names and photographs of those dead from Josephine who have some connection to the Berkshires, people who have died or gone missing in the storm's path of destruction, like the young woman from her high school, who was in college at Brown Mackie, and who is still missing. There is the story of the former professor at Simon's Rock who just last year took a position at Innova College, reported as dead, swept off Jungle Island causeway, the speculation now reported as having died on his way to get his elderly mother in Miami Beach, who lived or lives—as yet unknown—in the Edwards Apartments, on a top floor.

Deidre knows of Edwards Apartments only because of Alicia's obsession with the locally related rollcall of death-by-Josephine. Deidre now knows that Edwards Apartments was built in the 1950s, was on the backside of the beachfront block at the corner of 10th Street and Ocean Court, all this according to Google Maps with its shockingly close-up 3D street images replicated right there in *Berkshire Interactive*. The other night Deidre found Alicia still up late in front of her home computer screens with this Google Maps intersection side by side with some of the first drone survey videos, and the contrast of the before and after images was shocking with all the debris and broken buildings, but Edwards apartment building was still identifiable and appeared mostly intact. The next day, *Berkshire Interactive* had run the drone image, a freeze-frame of the apartment building.

Josephine-related television programming is still nearly nonstop on the major broadcast and cable news channels even now. Starting a couple of days ago, a new kind of feature started to show up in several different forms depending on the sources, featuring detailed and high-resolution simulations reenacting Josephine's attack on Miami and the Gold Coast.

Already there'd been some pushback from viewers because of the special effects.

CGI, right? she wonders. *AI, must be*, she thinks.

The images are so realistic, it's disturbing to watch.

The ongoing coverage makes sense, she concedes, since Josephine has highlighted the need for additional classes of storm, as Category 5 seems too weak a rating with the winds so high, clocked at 203 miles per hour, toppling 1969's Camille's 190 miles per hour, which was the highest speed previously recorded for a hurricane. The massive power of storm's driving high winds was bad enough, but these factors were amplified by high tide and the approach from the southeast. The storm surge had manifested as an eighteen-foot-high wall of water washing over Miami Port on Dodge Island, making its purported barrier value moot. And now this is getting virtually replayed, pretty much on the hour. She already knows an absurd amount about Josephine and its aftermath, but all this blathering and the audio-visual teaching aids keep rolling.

She is struck by the idea of making a Trivial Pursuit pack on the subject.

She too often now feels like she wants to giggle.

Or maybe that's hysteria, Deidre wonders yet again. *Or black humor.*

The surge drowned Miami Port, pushing many hundreds of shipping containers before it, bouncing these objects and lesser objects such as cars, trucks, and chunks of buildings over McCarthy Causeway and into and over the artificial residential Islands of Stan, Palm, and Hibiscus, and in the process pushing most of those residential structures into Biscayne Bay. Still increasing volumes of water spilled over across Miami Beach before combining with the back surge coming in through Haulover Park.

She thinks she could close her eyes and replay the simulations she's seen over and over again. She can see the surge water crossing Route 1, extending well to the north of Miami and as far inland as Ives Estates and Pembroke Park, sweeping over sections of Interstate 95. The surge effect fell as far north as Pompano Beach, well past Fort Lauderdale-Hollywood International Airport. She has a visceral sense of the wind damage too, although she's still unclear what damage was caused by the surge rather than the wind. What she does know is the massive volume of rainfall, twenty-two inches in some isolated pockets, was a major contributor to destructive flooding across a much wider area.

She doesn't want to know this much about what Josephine has wrought, and now at least her morning job at Crystals is back on, the shop reopening three days after the Gold Coast destruction, due to the owner's general distress and specific supply chain problems. At Farm Table, the restaurant where she shifts three nights a week, cover numbers are way down except for bar patronage, and the net effect has been to turn the dining tables into bar extensions and the corners and secluded spaces into spots for drinking.

Mostly, though, the customers seem stunned, like everyone else.

There'd been only one big scene made by a very inebriated man who, as it became known, had an ex-wife and kids down there, and his raging and physical feints were met with a gentleness she would not have ever expected, the bartender, helped by the owner and the large dishwasher who emerged from the back of the house, enveloped the man with restraining arms, and helped carry the raging man off to a side room, holding him till calm returned, the owner, afterward, periodically checking in on the man passed out on the floor and placed in the safety position, a tablecloth folded for a pillow under his head and a basin and glass of water within reach.

That had happened three nights ago.

She's wanted to share this story with Alicia, but Alicia's been busy with *Berkshire Interactive*, and even busier than usual. Deidre has not anticipated this state of affairs somehow, although she has a dawning understanding about her obtuseness about the pressures Alicia still faces, and this makes her feel bad, like she is a selfish person, although she knows herself well enough not to take this too much to heart.

I've just been missing her a lot already, she tells herself. But it also feels like she's been missing Alicia for a long time, too, even when they're in the same room.

Berkshire Interactive has an updating list of remembrances and short eulogies for those lost and known in the local area, and those being honored range from second cousins and grown children of half-remembered old friends or departed parents, and the odd ex-boss or two.

Among the reader-submitted stories of such memories is that of a flight attendant who once helped a Berkshire resident through an attack of claustrophobia on a long-ago flight, and there are two Berkshire County college kids who were at their respective schools in the affected areas, and an additional one counted among the dead. Deidre has had to look up the name of that classmate—from a year after her at Monument Mountain—in the online yearbook. The photograph and name hadn't registered, not at first, and it had taken a dive into Facebook to bring the memory of this person into focus.

The actor and musician Kevin Bacon, who lives just south of the Berkshire border in Connecticut's Northwest Corner, has been among the many posters on the *BI* forums, and one of the more frequent ones at that, and which has started taking on the shine of the surreal, a least to her. Davin, her former landlord and Alicia's colleague, brought some helpful perspective in an editorial about the remembrance postings. Titled "Zero Degrees of Separation," this had just been posted yesterday. Pretty much a tearjerker, or at least that had been her reaction, but a helpful tonic, too, in its way.

The Florida area of destruction seems never-ending and she feels she's been repeating *Death toll, death toll, death toll* in her mind constantly, or something like that anyway, a feeling of it, at least. There are plenty of instances when Deidre doesn't think about Josephine, but unfortunately many of those other instances are instead filled with worry about Alicia and their relationship.

She's been seeing less and less of Alicia in recent weeks—*months?*—with Alicia's pleas about being too busy coming more frequently, even well before Josephine. Deidre believes this change in Alicia has a lot to do with Alicia talking with potential investors interested in her expansion plans. Alicia had already been busy enough between keeping *BI* moving forward, selling ads, and otherwise making the current effort look as good as possible, but this has all gotten worse, with Alicia up late many evenings preparing the presentation decks for meetings with this investor or another of several earlier prospects.

What Alicia once called *Just-in-Time Learning*.

Deidre had heard this expression again just two nights back when she returned mid-evening from an early close at Farm Table and missing Alicia had proved too much not to try for some connection. And try she did, but Alicia seems always full out with one task or another, barely taking the time to tell Deidre she is too busy to talk, too busy figuring out another part of the proposed enterprise of expansion, and unfortunately there hasn't been much in the way of any other sort of contact for some time.

The biggest worry Deidre has about Alicia, the one she tries not to admit, has nothing to do with Alicia's business efforts. It also is not that she doesn't love her, at least in some way, but that she may be hung up on the *lesbian-thing*, as Alicia herself has called it, those rare times, now months back, when Alicia and she would talk about such things. It doesn't have much of anything to do with Alicia being older because she's not that much older than Deidre, some dozen or so years, but she's come to think that Alicia is fundamentally ambivalent about being in a sexual relationship with a woman. Deidre has been making an effort not to take this personally. *The effort isn't working*, she tells herself, feeling the hint of a sob form. She's intent on pushing this back down. She's just feeling dramatic.

She needs to head out to work soon, but she decides she'll finish her own morning dressing and removes what clothing she has so far put on.

This morning, like most others these days, she knows Alicia is up early again, already well-immersed in the demands of her day, sitting at her desk in her home office, looking at one of her monitors or already on the phone, or typing away furiously.

Deidre, naked, comes up behind her and sees Alicia is glancing down at some papers. From behind the office chair,

Deidre wraps her arms around the already showered and dressed Alicia, only to be shrugged off like a pest, and she quickly retreats. She is dressed and is out the door with hardly a pause to say goodbye, which she figures won't be much of a problem for the absorbed Alicia.

But outside, Deidre sits in her old car and cries, and there she is for almost ten minutes before pulling herself together, arguing with herself about the causes and sources of Alicia's behavior.

Not that Deidre understands herself all too well, she's sure, and not that she's had scores of love affairs or knows what it's like to be in a long-term relationship or married. She's known she is attracted only to women at least as far back as high school. She knows, too, that this is all new for Alicia, but she also knows that Alicia has much more relationship experience, including a traditional marriage.

And widowhood, too, she reminds herself.

She find herself wondering if Alicia is really only longing for the end to a loneliness Alicia probably doesn't even know she feels.

We are all strange creatures, she reminds herself.

Pulling out of the driveway she thinks about her love for Alicia and her growing despair about it, and it's all mixing with grief that seems tied to every current instance of hurt and isolation in the world.

She tries not to weep again.

Chapter 13: Davin News Hounded

*F*ucking *Katrinization*, Davin thinks, angry because he's been struggling to cut back on the time he is spending reading too much about the storm, the relief efforts, the rebuilding issues. Even though he has plenty to do for *BI*, he still spends far too much time on the aftermath of Josephine.

He just wants to retreat away from it all again, the last week and more in the studio a nice antidote, but he's let things pile up and he's back at his work.

Paying work.

Which means, of course, that he's right back into the Josephine-fix. He is confident he's not alone in this. In most of his phone calls and emails with his friends, and invariably at the post office or supermarket or liquor store, Josephine is still part of every conversation. It strikes him that everyone has become an expert on what has happened, and what needs to happen, and who needs to be blamed, criticized, or offered sympathy. He knows the storm surge and record-breaking strong winds and downpours swept transportation infrastructure away and housing, and stores, distribution centers, hospitals, and schools. All along the Miami coast area, infrastructure is either destroyed outright or severely compromised. It all looks like a war zone.

He's having another pissed-off morning, the day almost half gone already and the progress he promised himself he'd make before lunch already lost. He's behind on his BI work because he'd found himself retreating to the studio for much of the past week. He suspects that this has helped him from pulling his own head off, trying to step away from all the terrible reports and updates and developments post-Josephine, losing himself in the sculpture he'd been too long away from.

He's been trying to build a mountain groundswell of what must be a hundred old keys, maybe even two hundred, to be shaped into a wave inside the mixed-wood box. He'd tried different approaches, including some missteps with hot glue, a terrible mess that had taken more time to clean up and rectify, but his building an armature and affixing soft modeling clay has been working out, with enough keys built on top in this substrate to make it all appear a singular mass. The exterior of the piece is a vertical amalgam of cherry wood and beat-up reclaimed wood, including some old plaster lathing he's long had on hand from his house renovation work, and melding the disparate material is a challenge he believes he's overcome. The base skirt, made from an assortment of painted and partly sanded old wood scraps is ready for short cabriole legs of cherry wood, but these haven't shown up yet from the North Carolina company he buys such items from.

He considers that the shipping delays everyone is experiencing because of Josephine has a good side, but his stealing time in the studio has put him behind his other work.

He's back in his office, but what he's doing now isn't helping with his to-do list because he keeps switching tabs on his browser to look at news and updates. It's been almost a month since the storm hit, yet he still doesn't seem able to help himself.

It feels like Stockholm syndrome, he tells himself.

He shakes his head, sighs.

He's been trying to revise the editorial calendar for *Berkshire Interactive*, yet another task he's accidently suggested himself into, arguing that all the Josephine attention has made the existing scheduling of stories and articles in the pipeline so off-track as to be useless. How this has fallen to him to correct is a good question, but when Alicia asks for help, he tends to say *yes*.

He simply shouldn't have raised the issue.

Asshole, he tells himself, a frequent self-directed accusation.

Davin is pretty sure he's once again gotten caught up in his tendency to overcommit, something he is all too familiar with from his earlier professional work, the work he moved out to Housatonic to leave behind, *Mr. Digital Content Fuckwad*, he tells himself, although another part of his mind is trying to calm down, knowing that letting himself get worked up leads to no good.

He takes a few long breaths. He picks up his thermos hoping there's still some coffee left, although of course he knows there's none, having checked this a while before.

It isn't like he is unhappy about being an expert, and what he's pulled off for *Berkshire Interactive* and the build-out of the backend that promotes local coverage has delighted Alicia and it has been a solid delivery. He's always been happy to play the know-it-all, and this is something he can't seem to resist. Even when he was in Cambridge, and even though he didn't much care for public speaking, he still took pride in his various conference presentations back at the height of his consulting work. But he learned over time the professional work could be brutal, at least for him, because he was always anxious he'd fall behind in the fast-changing, always evolving business, and always worried he'd experience some sort of humiliation moment, and usually there'd been some sort of anxiety while talking to a client, he nervous that unbeknownst to him the subject matter at hand had just been superseded by a new technology or business development, and he was the last one to know.

Like, duh.

He regularly tried to comfort himself in those days with the advice he'd gotten from a colleague early on when everyone was trying to figure out digital content. "You just have to stay twenty-four hours ahead of your client," his colleague had said, and indeed those were words to live by but never as much comfort as he wanted them to be. Of course he came to understand some years later he tended toward an impractically broad scope of his subject matter and that overly inclusive purview made taking any time off at all feel like he was falling behind.

On the other hand, this wide scope of practice helped build the consulting business, and for a while he had a small shop with three other professionals under him. Plus, for a time, there was admin support in the form of a young woman who was, by her own claims, quite well-versed in Microsoft Office, although it had been left to Davin to teach her what little he knew about Excel, and accounts and receivables required such frequent intercessions on his part he'd concluded it was more efficient to do this himself.

And cheaper too, he considers, thinking about the young woman, the first person he ever fired.

Firing people had gotten easier after that, and in a year's span, he'd gotten rid of the rest of his junior partners and only worked on bigger projects when he could team up with other independent consultants he liked working with and who could be assigned their own separate and distinct responsibilities. These virtual teams often worked well, and he knew he'd been frequently lucky, although it is those rarer virtual teams that broke down that are the ones Davin now most clearly remembers.

And now, in addition to working on his *BI* platform duties, it feels like he's spending his time obsessed with this storm, which means he's gotten backed up in his growing *BI* writing and editing duties, and all this is doing is keeping him from working in his studio.

Well, I need the eggs, he jokes, but this is a tired joke.

What he doesn't need, he is quite sure, is to be so distracted and triggered by Josephine and every little wind blow after, like Hurricane Leona, which came just two-and-a-half weeks after Josephine. Unlike 2011's Irene, which had set some records for destruction in the Northeast and caused some serious flooding in parts of Vermont, or the storm with no name in 2023 that killed several people with floods in western and central New England, Leona generally suffered unto New England only modest sorts of flooding and some power outages and trees limbs thrown about. In Housatonic and Berkshire County generally, just the small Taconic Mountains range away from Leona's Hudson River storm track, people and property were largely untouched, even though along the Hudson there was some bad flooding and wind damage. All the battening down was rather anticlimactic, although the lack of damage in the Berkshires was entirely welcomed for all that.

Like everyone else, Davin had become a rather close reader of the news and social media feeds in the days after Josephine, a habit that's continued for a full week, and then for him anyway, two weeks, and then three weeks and more, excepting, to some degree, his time spent in retreat to the studio. The news about the aftermath grew more reliable over time, and much more of the reporting is now accurate and detailed, but even nearly a month post-Josephine, things remain hectic and frantic, not to mention rather terrifying for anyone with any imagination and any heart at all.

And if that's not enough, there are maniacs running around killing rich people, he tells himself. That news had been blowing up, although Josephine had relegated those stories to back pages for a while.

Everyone he knows, and very much including himself, still seems exhausted. All the talk about Josephine being caused by climate change doesn't help, and as far as he's concerned, it just makes him feel worse. There's one meme making the rounds he finds terrifying for some reason, and it isn't the picture of Josephine's destruction close-up at street level that frightens him but the text accompanying the image: *Plus ça climate change, plus c'est un autre chose.*

People around the county and the Northeast have been

trying to get back to business as best they can, but reports of the Florida devastation continue to dominate the news cycles, although the final death toll has been concluded at a little over 35,300, give or take a thousand of those still listed as missing sometimes still being checked off the list that once numbered well over the 100,000 mark, even while any and all of the early feel-good reports of rescued survivors have long ceased.

The property damage assessment is over $1.7 trillion if full rebuilding is to be undertaken. Congress still acts stunned—*or maybe just stupid*, he can't stop himself from thinking—even while at the administration's direction, several key federal agencies are going full out, joined by aid organizations from a number of states. The National Guard from states as far away as Illinois, Maine, and Colorado are deployed along with many more from the neighboring southeastern states that had quickly put their Guards in place.

In the affected areas, both cholera and typhus had made appearances in the first full week after Josephine's rampage, but the outbreaks were contained and quickly stopped, to the relief of everyone. And now here he is, reading up on the recent reports of the emergence of Dengue fever in lower Florida, and just this morning there's more news about an uptick in Zika virus cases in Florida along with other parts of the Gulf coast largely unaffected by the various storms.

Fucking sub-Africa shit, was his first thought when hearing the Dengue reports a day or two before, although this thought embarrasses him, violating his sense of himself as a good liberal fellow, and he's self-conscious about it all over again as he recalls his misstep.

No racist here, ma'am, nothing to see here, move along, he tells himself.

On the other hand, he can't help but notice the majority of inhabitants of the current tent cities are black and Hispanic. And poor, he's also noted, but he realizes that circumstances in which these storm refugees find themselves would make anyone look poor. The pictures make him think about those old Depression-era documentary photographs, hopeless expressions minus the cakes of dust.

He reads a lot in the news about emergency relief, but he's also been noticing growing talk about the budget deficit, too. The causes for the deficit that most often get highlighted are the old Trump tax cuts and the follow-on pandemic's economic stimulus by Biden, and the newer tax cuts that managed to get passed in 2025. On top of the deficit issue there's been plenty of budget worries from the recession-like swings in the national economy. But now there's this new complication in national politics, which is how to pay for what Josephine has wrought.

It isn't even four full weeks out from Josephine's path of destruction and there are more stories every day about the high numbers of noninsured properties, and for those with coverage the expectation of severe insurance payout limitations. An editorial he skimmed just this morning in the *NYT* is arguing insurance payout limitations are unavoidable, and he spent some time studying an infographic presenting gross assets of the top five reinsurers mapped against the projected claims. He has only a vague sense of the arcane world of reinsurers, with Lloyd's as his example in mind, but he was surprised to see Lloyd's ranked sixth in size, and all the other bigger companies are entirely new to him. It's still too early to have an accurate picture of claim totals, the editorial mentioned, but after studying the illustration and rereading the editorial, his takeaway is there is indeed a significant gap between assets and calls on liabilities.

Previous liabilities on insurance companies over the last few years ranging from out in the western states where the fire seasons seem endless to storm-prone areas in the southeast, have driven insurers from some states or have seen premiums go much, much higher. Florida has long been a case study on this problem, he's read. In 2022, in the face of private insurers abandoning Florida, the state had passed legislation requiring flood insurance, but the policies are available only through the state-run insurer of last resort, Citizens Property Insurance Corp. There is also the National Flood Insurance Program managed by FEMA, but neither program has great coverage and CPIC, according to the news, is already *de facto* insolvent.

And Miami, a major American city, is largely gone.

After clean water, food, and sanitation, the most pressing problem remains shelter. There's the massive logistical response required to address the basic needs of a significant part of the nearly seven million people who were calling the Southeast Florida coast home. Demand for action from the displaced has been building, with some big protests, but civil order remains overall, although violent flares still crop up with regularity, including four early attacks by storm victims on some of the initial relief efforts. How long calm will last is something he wonders about with the storm's victims growing increasingly anxious with the immense and ever-looming housing problems becoming clearer, even if the overall scope of the problem remains barely imaginable.

He finds, at any rate, that this is certainly hard for him to grasp.

He knows he can't actually imagine what it's like for the homeless, or the hungry, the sick, thirsty, or injured, although his comprehension grows with each passing day and each hard-luck story. The hotels and motels throughout the rest of the state and adjacent states have become the first line for housing, but the term *Tarp Down* has already gained purchase as the indicator of the housing problem and the growing frustration with the general sense of the slow pace of aid. The phrase fits, given the sight of blue plastic tarps emerging as the major visual element of the area surrounding the hardest destruction. Not that there aren't plenty of affecting images beyond those of the miles and miles of tarp-covered wrecks of houses.

Tarp Down. Davin likes the phrase, he thinks it clever, with just the right touch of irony with its connotation that authorities are slow in their actions. There are several other choice phrases gaining currency, including *Katrinarized.* *FEMAnistas* is another, and *Gold Refugees.* Another term that had first appeared in a widely reposted social media meme of two photographic images side-by-side, one from post-Katrina and the other from post-Josephine. The Katrina photo showed water-damaged houses he guesses were probably in the Ninth Ward, but the Josephine image is of a huge swath of structures broken and bulldozed into jumbled mounds to make an endless-looking dune of the splintered remains of office buildings, stores, and homes alike.

The caption read *Gold Standard.*

Like a lot of what he's been noticing on social media, it's hard for him to determine with any confidence the tone of this meme, and perhaps this one was meant to be sympathetic, but he's more prone to see this as an attempt at a joke or maybe a reaction to the ceaseless media storm and the endless images of the large ribbons of land rushed by the surging seas. An ugly tone is on the rise with more and more reports of comments and acts that push past the early waves of sympathy. Most of this negativity and criticism is aimed at the perceived slow pace of the relief efforts, but he has also noted there is growing resentment regarding the displaced, too. The news of the massive civilian displacement and destruction is no longer something out of the subcontinent, and thus so easily ignored, or in Sahara's Niger, Chad, or Sudan, or the chronic migrations pushing out of Central America in response to chronic heat or drought.

There is growing frustration overall. He fears a revitalized tribalism could all-too-easily emerge when too many people compete for far too few resources. But most Americans still seem to believe that despite the unimaginable scope of destruction Josephine has wrought, the nation is still fortunate to have so many resources to mitigate the disaster.

More in theory, perhaps, he has to wonder, seeing the growing ugliness, especially in social media. There have even been these growing news stories about a group of wackos killing rich people.

This shit is why I should be ignoring the news, Davin scolds.

But he can't help himself, and there's uplifting news too. The United Nations, European Union, and The People's Republic of China have sent at least token aid, but it looks like more might come of this, although it will probably be months, he assumes, before the *whats* and *whens* of any substantive international aid will be known. So far, the progressives in Congress are holding their fire on the past unwillingness of the Florida delegation to sufficiently fund emergency agencies for disasters that had occurred elsewhere in the nation, and the remnants of MAGA Republicans are holding their tongues about One-Worlders and other conspiracies.

Fingers crossed, he thinks.

The talking heads are already predicting Josephine will show up in the next mid-term election, with some pundits claiming a full shift in Congress will go to the Democrats, although there is a contrarian view that the gains the Democrats have made in the last two — the mid-terms of 2026 and the presidential election of 2028 — could be largely reversed.

Again, he thinks. *As if 2024 wasn't a bad enough kick in the teeth.*

Davin has also been following the stories about several organizations seeking to apply the lessons learned from the so-called sharing economy as the scale of the disaster settles into the nation's understanding and as the immediate life-threatening problems are resolving. One example is Airbnb, which has offered to work with government agencies to pair up storm victims in need of housing with those Airbnb hosts who can provide housing. What Airbnb has already done is clone its back-office infrastructure and add a modified front end to help streamline the matchups, in what they've named Americabnb.

Davin takes some quiet pride that Airbnb has stepped up in this way, but he also knows he is ambivalent about participating. He's telling himself his worry is income, but he wonders if there's more to his discomfort with getting involved.

Fuck me, he tells himself.

He knows he'll need to decide about opening up the rental apartment on the first floor to those hit hard by Josephine.

Fuck me, he tells himself. *I shouldn't watch the news.*

Chapter 14: Paneled Rooms, Impaneled Plans

The man on the couch knows Gerald Greene loves his position as executive director of the Kehoe Institute, loves that he is a player, a bigwig. The man knows Greene makes the effort to look like he doesn't enjoy all this too much, but still, the man thinks Greene thinks of himself as *pretty hot shit*.

But Joey Lobinski knows pretty much exactly how hot shit Greene is, which is not really all that hot.

Although there's plenty of shit, he can't help thinking.

He knows that even Greene knows he's not the king, nor among the ranks of princes, just, really, an advisor to them.

The term *courtier* rises in Lobinski's thoughts.

The two men are alone in the richly appointed office of the executive director of the Kehoe Institute, and Lobinski watches Greene heave himself out of an armchair that is plush with an indigo chintz fabric, a grunt issuing as he rises, placing the nearly empty glass of bourbon with a light thump on the low rosewood coffee table. Lobinski remains seated on the brass-tacked dark leather couch opposite from where Greene had been sitting, his feet still are up on the coffee table, his head thrown back against the top of the couch, and now he closes his eyes, but then he opens them, picking his head up, eyes following Greene as he moves toward the massive carved mahogany desk a half dozen feet distant from the couch and the two indigo armchairs.

Behind the desk is an expanse of brownstone-trimmed fireplace, and hanging over the mantel is a portrait of a horse. The only object on the mantel is an empty glass vase. There are some brass pieces on the moderately cluttered desk surface along with two modest stacks of printed material. Otherwise, there is just a monitor and keyboard and a telephone unit, all with their attendant cables writhing off the right side of the desk.

Greene is settling himself, half sitting, half leaning on the desk's front edge, moving a brass piece, a horse to the side.

What is it with rich people and horses? Lobinski wonders.

"Well," Greene says to him, even while twisting to move something on the desk surface behind him before turning back to face the couch, and Lobinski knows this guy loves this room, his office with the dark walls moderately well-polished and the bookcases ornamented with books and objects, and on the walls the brass-framed photographs of the man with industry titans and politicians.

"Well," Greene says again, and Lobinski is now sitting forward on the couch, half-turned to look at the man leaning on the desk.

"We're thinking the KTR—Kill the Rich, the stuff in the news—that thing gives us cover," Greene says, "and it would be a shame to not take advantage, seems only fair."

Lobinski nods.

He knows Greene will get to the details eventually and turns back to the coffee table, picks up the decanter, pours himself another small glass of bourbon, takes a sip, and turns back to look at Greene.

Jesus, that's fine whiskey, he thinks, though still wishing it was scotch.

Greene starts back in. "Congress is not going to turn this next mid-term—I mean, the Senate—done deal according to most. We've been spending like crazy on the polls, the campaigns, the analysis, hell, we can read the writing on the wall as well as the fucking *Times*."

No shit, Sherlock, Lobinski says to himself. He resists the urge to look back at the decanter. He has promised himself he'll remain professional. He likes the money he makes. He's always been a go-getter, a fighter, but this all still feels like something new, different. He always likes a challenge, but this has the feeling of something more desperate.

Unhinged? he wonders.

"Can we get to the point?" he says, surprising himself a bit.

The other man loosens his tie, steps forward, and picks up his own heavy glass, and then walks backward to the desk, leans again, and empties the last of his drink. He frowns, putting the glass down on the wood surface and then is fishing around for something to put under the glass and ends up grabbing at the top of one pile, pulling what looks like a report of some kind, paper in a plastic sleeve. He settles the glass down on that.

Jesus, Lobinski thinks.

Greene starts speaking again. "McAllster, he's not going up for another term."

"McAllster," Lobinski says. "The *Fracker* himself."

Greene leans forward. "Yup. Yeah. He's just one of too many, and the message is getting out there, our people are quitting, leaving, or —"

"—turning," Lobinski says.

Greene nods, but with a show of annoyance.

Lobinski knows quite well Greene doesn't like to be interrupted, especially by people who work for him.

But then he also knows the man leaning on his desk is talking to Joey Lobinski. He's smart, and Greene has to know this because he had to be at least competent to get through the Special Forces training, and then there's his service record and his private sector work for Whitestar. He knows Greene knows all about him because Greene had him vetted. And Greene knows this viscerally now by the work he's already done for him.

Work done for *The Gang,* actually. *The Gang* being

Greene's favorite personal shorthand for the people like Senator McAllster works for, that Greene works for.

That I work for, right?

Lobinski doesn't have any sure knowledge of the individuals, although some, at least, he's pretty sure he can guess, and there are others, not really the core, but public figures like McAllster and a few others he could point to in the Senate and a bunch of the House, too, but he would say that they work with *The Gang*, not a part of *the Gang*. He'd go even further, that those would-be acolytes in the House have seen their relevance to *The Gang* fade as the House moves to further secure its progressive stances, this last election basically confirming the shift.

And now the Senate is up for grabs, beyond filibuster in all likelihood.

"So *Kill the Rich*, that news what's been in the papers, what 'do unto others'?" says Lobinski, and he stands, seeing Greene pull the sleeved report from under his glass and then leaning forward to hand the paper in the sleeve to him.

He opens the plastic sleeve and pulls out the thin plain folder, opens it, scans the cover page, then flips through the several sheets. The content is all plain text, no masthead, on cheap office printer paper.

"Hmmm," is all he says. He starts to put the folder back into the sleeve, but Greene tells him he wants the sleeve back.

"Huh," Lobinski says, handing the empty plastic sleeve back. "Full forensics protocol," he says, maybe to Greene, maybe to himself.

"Now there's a smart guy," says Greene.

He says nothing, simply nodding as he turns, striding to the office door, pulling the right one open, then he is out and about his business.

Chapter 15: March Madness

This morning, coming in early, is just the second time Davin has been by Jimmy's new apartment. The apartment is in a brownstone in Back Bay, up on the top floor, which causes him to be a bit winded by the time he makes the climb. Today is the first time he'd seen the place after it's been set up, although he had been there before to lend a hand when his son moved in. He likes the look of the place more now that there's actual furniture, and tasteful, too, he thinks, if mostly used. He's pretty sure this domestic touch is Cynthia's hand, although he could be wrong. The view from the front windows is out over Commonwealth Avenue, and it is a through-apartment with the back windows in the kitchen offering a glimpse of the Charles River and parts of Cambridge. Jimmy's small office has a day bed, so it should be comfortable for his overnight stay.

He's not in the apartment now, though, and he's not feeling comfortable, and at least part of that is being in the middle of a crowd, and a rowdy and spirited crowd at that. Davin hasn't been to a big march for years, although he declines to count up the actual years past. He feels Cynthia, especially, might just feel embarrassed for him if he would report the truth.

Rambunctious is the word that comes to mind as he takes in the crowd, which makes him laugh.

"A rambunctious crowd, yeah?" he says to Jimmy and Cynthia.

Cynthia shakes her head with a slight smile.

He's happy she's a good-looking woman. He knows this may only reveal his shallow self, but he's glad for Jimmy, and he thinks they make a nice match. He likes her, although for some reason he tends to feel a bit nervous around her. He remains reluctant to ask too many questions about her and Jimmy's relationship and wonders if this may be because of what came out during the investigation, three years ago, when she'd ended up in Housatonic, at his house.

He'd found out that she'd been in a sexual relationship with her boss, that guy who got shot on his way to an oil divestiture meeting, the start of the trouble Cynthia had found herself in, a person of interest in the murder, text messages pointing to her. She had run and ended up at his house in Housatonic. Even though he's written a book about the whole thing, he's still sometimes shocked, even these years later. He doesn't like the idea she'd had an affair with her married boss, but he's done a thorough job keeping that to himself, and he usually thinks it's not germane to what's happened since. He tries not to judge, not that he's always manages to avoid it, but at least he keeps silent on the matter, and besides, the two of them seem good together, and he knows Jimmy's happy.

Jimmy, at six foot seven inches, towers over Cynthia, who has to be a good foot shorter.

Davin gets jostled, and turning he sees a young man shrugging, a grin and a hand held up, which he takes as some form of apology, and Davin nods and turns back around. They are in the middle of the crowd, toward the right edge of it on the Tremont Street side of Boston Common, and the weather is nice enough, and warm enough, and the threat of rain has seemingly decided to be an empty one, the sky blue and nearly cloudless above him. Davin's a bit sorry he's overdressed and thinks about taking off his fleece and wrapping it around his waist, but everyone is so close in he decides to just keep it on.

Jimmy, like the vast majority of marchers, is dressed in cargo shorts and t-shirt, although there are plenty of others even more lightly garbed, including a few young women he has trouble not looking at, but he keeps his glances to a minimum.

I don't get out much, he tells himself, and laughs. He sees Jimmy look at him.

The event has a festive feel to it, although the PA system is lousy and with his sixty-four-year-old hearing he makes out the words being spoken only sporadically. It's never about the speeches anyway, he tells himself, but he still tries to understand what's being said. The frequent waves of cheering and clapping and whistling make this almost impossible.

He asks Jimmy how long the program is, but he has to ask again more specifically. "How many speakers are there, total," he says, but Jimmy just shrugs.

Cynthia though, checks her phone and pushes it in front of him where he takes in a mass of tiny text of what he assumes is the speaker list, but he doesn't have his reading glasses, and with the jostling of the crowd, trying to keep the phone steady makes it seem like reading in the car.

"Thanks," he says to her with a nod.

Jimmy, with his height, may be able to see the stage over the heads of the crowd, but all Davin can see are the backs of other marchers and the swaying forest of signs and placards.

He almost says *Great seats!* but stops himself in time.

God, he hates crowds, he hates jostling and being pushed and manhandled, and he clearly has the wrong attitude for this sort of thing, but it is a nice day and he's hanging with Jimmy and Cynthia and it's all a good cause, whatever exactly the march is for.

Climate something. He meant to look more closely at the website for the event but hadn't quite gotten around to it, but he recalls there's something about the methane legislation coming up for a vote.

"Go Red Sox," he shouts to Jimmy, who laughs, but Cynthia just shakes her head.

"Is this the line for the men's room?" he says to Jimmy, who laughs again.

But Davin is now sorry he's made the joke, because magically he now needs to piss, and suddenly the volume of the speakers seem to blossom higher into cheering, and with a jolt the crowd starts surging forward, the marching part re-commencing with horns and whistles and a wide range of hooting and singing going on.

He thinks he's right about the march going down Tremont and across City Hall Plaza on to Congress Street, with the end point, he thinks, maybe the Rose Kennedy Greenway, although now he's wondering if they're heading across to Fort Point Channel and the Federal Courthouse.

He's wearing good walking shoes.

Cynthia has checked her phone several times and now reports it's a good turnout.

He smiles at her. These days he's a big fan of hers, however nervous he can sometimes still feel around her. He's impressed how she's built a life doing what is important work, he's sure, although one reason why he can be a bit—*what, tense?*—around her is the whole *no-meat* stance, and he realizes he might just be feeling guilty.

He's recently cooked a nice grilled steak dinner for himself. He mostly doesn't eat meat, but, well, he still does sometimes.

They're trudging along, and he recognizes the curved façade of Circle Plaza with the old Beaux Arts state courthouse that is mostly hidden behind the garish 1960s architecture, and the crowd is thinning as it marches, spreading along the city streets and across the big City Hall Plaza infamous for its inhospitable windswept chill during Boston winters. He's looking at the City Hall, the top of it anyway, and there's a burst of static from the loudspeakers and then some sort of phrase being repeated over the PA system and the crowd slows and starts packing tighter again, and it sounds like speeches starting back up.

I really should have looked at the itinerary, he scolds

himself.

"Why are we stopping?" Jimmy asks Cynthia, who looks at her phone and shrugs.

Davin finally makes it out what is being said.

No one is safe, he's pretty sure he hears as it cycles through several more times, and the crowd's murmuring is rising, and then he makes out that the message is changing, a loop, he thinks, a recording that he finally makes out is repeating that people should move away from the John F. Kennedy Federal Building Parking Garage, wherever the hell that is.

Please move away from the JFK Parking Garage, Please move away from the JFK Parking Garage, repeats the message again and again, and then there's an emergency tone going off on everyone's cell phones, including his own, and the message starts mixing in *no one is safe* with the message to move away, and there's a schematic that has appeared on his phone showing the garage location relative to some locations he knows, including where they are at the moment on City Hall Plaza, and there is a growing cacophony of sirens and the message is being carried on thousands of tiny cell phone speakers, and there is a countdown on the phone screen.

Jimmy is saying something about hijacking the EAS, and Davin is asking what he means.

Jimmy is in the middle of trying to explain Common Alerting Protocol when the countdown ends, and not just ends, but ends with a bang, and that bang is mirrored by the jump of bodies reacting to the sound and to the now-blossoming ball of flame on the top level of what Davin now knows is the John F. Kennedy Federal Building Parking Garage, and the crowd becomes a back-surging wave, people losing their footing, people tripping over each other, there are shouts and screams, and when Davin looks up at Jimmy, he sees his son's arms surrounding Cynthia, his back to the swirling crowd as he envelopes her, a look on his son's face he hasn't fully resolved before Davin goes flying, knocked into the rush of people scrambling past.

Chapter 16: The ImAbomber, Baby

William McPherson is standing on the side of an access road that leads into the forest that stretches around him. It's a risk having set up here, but a manageable one. From the look of the grassy road at his feet there isn't active traffic, at least not recently, and undergrowth is thick, so there's no chance of being seen from the county road where he has pulled off. He's not far in, and if someone comes by, it could be hard to explain what he's doing there, but he's chosen this spot because there's a small clearing for the van. If by some slim chance someone comes upon him, he'll mention the road was unmarked, no *No Trespass* or *Private*, and he thought it was a state park, which it almost is, being adjacent to a state forest.

No *No Trespass* sign, at least now since he's detached just such a sign and flung it deeper into the woods.

Gotta love the multitool, he tells himself.

He's enjoying himself. He's enjoying the weather, the sun filtering through the trees as the day wanes.

He does his stretches, still stiff from the driving and sitting in front of various computers, *all over this land,* he silently sings as he stretches. *If I had a hammer* becomes his refrain, and then *Walk softly and carry a big hammer,* he says to himself, arms out from the shoulders, elbows bent, twisting his waist one way, then the other.

The small clearing is pretty much what it looked like from Google Satellite. He'd spent time looking for a good spot in the public library two towns ago, and the time was well-spent.

Just a little woodsy time, officer, a tiny break before heading back into the city.

Unlikely there will be need, he thinks, but if confronted, this is nothing a sincere apology won't fix.

Fuck it, I'm white, he tells himself.

He's got one of his Wi-Fi connected motion alarms set so he can keep an eye on the turn-off from the road but dialed down in sensitivity so deer or wind-swayed branch leaves won't set it off. The alarm should trigger only for a vehicle, he's pretty sure.

Maybe a moose.

An approach is unlikely, in any case, but just in case, he will want a heads-up.

He likes quiet for planning, but planning means there'll be material, maps, and devices out at any given time for prep.

He climbs up into the van's back, sitting on the fully upright recliner, laptop in front of him at the pull-down table.

He is again looking over the digital copy of this year's *Forbes 400 Richest Americans*.

He notes with satisfaction he's taken care of two on the list, although his third and most recent target had dropped from this year's Forbes list and for a brief moment he had worried whether he should have killed that target, and then that thinking makes him snort.

You can take the boy out of the middle class, he tells himself, *but you can't take the middle class out of the boy.*

Being dropped from the Forbes list doesn't make the target poor. The target was plenty rich enough to earn the kill.

He can think of himself as Unabomber 2.0, not because he thinks of Theodore "Ted" John Kaczynski as a hero, or role model, but because he has expended a lot of thought about how Kaczynski was caught.

Well, he corrects himself, *how he didn't get caught too.*

As for himself getting caught, there likely aren't any people with whom he has remained close, nor has he posted anything about his mission, ever, on social media. There really isn't any family who would likely recognize the manifesto language.

And, of course, my brother is dead.

Thinking about his brother makes him laugh. Now there was Unabomber material. Those conspiracies, the theories, the world out of balance, and he's sure his brother would have made a more likely candidate than him. His brother may have been right on the main points, but McPherson knows his brother would have lacked the focus on the prime problem, which is The One-Percenters are a cancer, the systems of the world corrupted to their advantage. Anyone who is anyone in economic theory knows, from Karl Marx on, that unfettered capitalism will concentrate more capital for those with capital. Regulations could level the playing field, progressive taxation could help, and ending estate tax exemptions makes sense, but such regulations have fallen far too short for far too long.

Money buys what money wants, more money, he tells himself, a favorite refrain of his.

At some point amid his brother's rants and monologues he had come to see income inequality as the symptom, and later he had arrived at a way he could address the larger problem. His solution is simple: kill in great numbers those absurdly immorally rich individuals, and this made for a target-rich environment.

Death to the World-eaters, he thinks, winding himself up with his typical mix of excitement and anxiety that he's barely aware has something akin to sexual excitement.

He does know what he can do himself will be at best modest in any practical effect. He understands that as one person he will never get nearly enough of the obvious targets. There are even whole families, tribes unto themselves, and corporations too, sitting on tens and hundreds of billions in cash reserves and endless equity. He knows he can't wipe them all out, but what he can do is bring the issue of vast inequality and the corruption of the world itself into greater relief and help more people wake up. He can claim a platform in the public sphere even while unsettling the world-eaters. Killing the rich is the right symbolism, a cleansing rite.

He also knows he simply may be shouting into the wind, but he considers, too, that what he's undertaking is right, this he is convinced of, even while he knows the revenge fantasy he nurses is a precious driver of his actions. The comfort of that fantasy can sometimes be the only thing that calms him from the terror that can fling him halfway out of his slumber, heart racing, or even when he is doing his work, this can run up a wave of anxiety that can still his breath. But his thoughts of the careless slights and the destruction that happened to his life at the hands of wealth could happen only if the perpetrators don't—*Won't!*—see people, and this answer has become his essential nourishment, the salve that can bring sleep. He has never felt this way before, so sure, not even when he was young, back when he just went along like everyone else.

He knows everyone thinks no one can do anything, or anything much. He knows that it's hard to perceive the abstract nature of the myriad details, the perpetuating schemes, the tax breaks, the lobbying, the false narrative that addressing the problem of income inequality would break the machine that drives the world. All this, he knows, is hard to describe and define, and any specific examples easily countered. And there is the problem too, perhaps hard-wired in everyone, of the fear of losing what one has managed to grasp for oneself to people with even less. He's come to see this belief is deeply indoctrinated, this *Us-versus-Them* mentality that works so well. The problem is people are too easily manipulated.

Us versus Them, he scoffs. *Half right, just the wrong Thems.* His targets are the right *Them*, and if he does this right, the message will grow.

He's not worried about someone reading the declarations he's sent out after each target completion and recognizing the writing is his. He's taken pains to avoid one style. He knows he'll probably not fool specialists in language modeling and analysis in the long run, but after he works on writing in a different style, he runs the text through a Google Translate into a different language and then back out into English, and he's been quite happy with how much change is made to style and word choice. He is hardly sure he himself would be able recognize the altered texts as his. He's also been sure to never post the claims at the places where he's taken targets. He posted the first two target completions two weeks apart, from different libraries, through an open-source de-tracer server he is less sure would work than he'd like, but even if the trace was to be made, and even if someone was sent out to interview library staff, such an effort wouldn't be successful. Between the disguises and his fast in/fast out discipline, it's unlikely his presence makes much of an impression, if any.

Hopefully, anyway, he tells himself.

Mr. Ninja, he says to himself.

He's quite pleased with the Google Translate trick, especially as it helps make it seem like there are different posters, a group, at movement, even. He wants *Kill the Rich* to be seen as the actions of many, and it's important these actions seem to be coming from different places and different individuals around the country.

Well, they are from different places, he thinks, considering his crazy amount of driving.

The message contained in the postings took a while to figure out, and then there is the style misdirects. Even the various taglines are slanted to suggest a secret army.

Kill the Rich, an army rising for economic justice, is what closes each post, now numbering three, the latest released just days ago. The posts are brief and have their different statements about income inequality, along with the details of target name, place of action, and method of execution.

There are news stories about what he is doing. In a couple of weeks, if all goes well, there will be a couple more posts.

And then the *asshole* gets his due.

He's not deluded. He knows he'll get caught at some point, no matter his caution and despite all his planning, because things out of his control will happen. But he also knows he'll probably have time to accomplish the personal work, which is to kill the CEO, the media darling, Mr. Monopoly, Mr. Consolidator, *that son of a bitch*.

The bonus kill would be the Big Pharma CEO, and who says it can't be personal when trying to save the world is as personal as it gets. He's aware this attitude may prove his undoing, but he can put such considerations aside, mostly.

Double your pleasure, double your fun, he thinks to himself, a hint of the jingle music behind the words.

But he needs to concentrate on his recon now, and so he's up and opening a panel that forms the side of the small kitchenette structure and starts to unpack his new drone.

There's still light enough for the close-up flybys, but he'll keep the drone up past the fall of dark when the infrared works better, and he'll come in close to the cabin structure, and the other building, and will leisurely send the drone down the long driveway, checking for surveillance signals.

Cabin! McPherson scoffs. *Yeah, right.*

Chapter 17: Ready Match Set

Davin is up in his bedroom, lying on the bed he's made not an hour ago, coffee sloshing a bit in his stomach teasing acid reflux, but he's ignoring that. His head and shoulders are up on a couple of pillows, his hands behind his head, and it occurs to him that maybe he should kick his shoes off, but his thoughts about the night before are what he's really thinking about.

The date went well, although the woman, Gloria, decided they'd go out to eat, but they'd been back at her place afterward, talking, sitting on her living room couch, talking and then kissing, and then making out. He'd been worried about the garlic from his Clams Casino, the appetizer he ordered in lieu of an entrée, not wanting to feel too heavy, his excitement putting off his appetite, his nervousness leaving a few clams on the plate.

The conversation during the meal was nice, even quite enjoyable, and he likes her. He had the story about the climate march he went on with Jimmy and Cynthia, and of course, the bombing, the whole No One is Safe angle, which had made national news. She seemed impressed by his climate change acumen, not that he doesn't feel a bit of imposter syndrome, but he thinks he was on his game, and witty, appearing well-read, informed, smart.

Of course I was okay, he tells himself, annoyed at the doubt and second-guessing he's experiencing after his fitful sleep.

It went great, he tells himself.

The kissing had grown vigorous, he paying attention to

cues from the woman, but it hadn't taken much attention.

She had known, from the first conversation over drinks some weeks before that Davin was just getting back to dating, that he'd not been with any woman other than his wife for the decades of their marriage, and during last night's dinner she volunteered she'd been out of the game for a while herself, divorced for seven years, the last relationship two years back, one she dismissed with a curt shrug. And then she had changed the subject to sexual health, noting she just had a checkup with a clean bill of health.

Davin had tried to be prepared for the subject after a number of friends he'd spoken to about his projected dating efforts raised the issue, but he nonetheless felt a blush coming on and ventured a peek over the plates and glasses and the oil candle's dull illumination of their restaurant table and saw her looking directly at him, and then she made a face and as a result he did too, and they laughed.

The first stirrings of an erection was the other result.

Gloria is attractive, well put together, neither tall nor short with a few extra pounds, less than he carries.

They declined to consider dessert. They had split the check.

Back at her place, he found himself kissing her, feeling the rise of passion, his hands traveling up her sides, pulling her close, siding her breast through her heavy knit sweater vest, her hand moving along his thigh until she could feel his erection, and then they sat back, laughing.

All hands on deck, Davin thinks with a bit of a smile.

He'd asked if she too was thinking of high school as he was feeling like he was over the girl's parents' house, making out, half expecting a parent to walk in.

That confused her.

"I'm a bit self-conscious," he tried to explain and asked for her patience.

She nodded and stood, bringing him up with her. Nodding again, seeming shy herself, she told him she understood, that it must be strange, and then she stepped away still holding his forearm. She smiled, telling him she'd be gentle, and he drew her back into his arms, both of them laughing into more serious kissing, and she stepped away, still holding his arm, leading him to her bedroom.

Davin, lying on his bed this morning, is remembering the night before, play-by-play.

He is still surprised by the calmness and directness he demonstrated standing by the side of her bed, whatever nervousness now well in check, it seemed.

They both began to undress, his steady hands unbuttoning his shirt, stopping to point out the yellowing bruise he'd gotten at the march, during the panic, from a young woman who had kicked him solidly as she tripped over him in those moments of the crowd rushing wildly.

He was undoing his pants as he watched her sit to remove her shoes, then her skirt, standing to slip the fabric down her thighs, a quick glance up at him, a face, a smile.

He, lying on his bed this morning looking at the ceiling strafed with morning light, is pretty sure he had been grinning.

Gloria had pushed herself back on the bed, the length of her along the side, her head resting on pillows, her blouse still on, watching Davin as he pulled his boxers past the erection, standing naked before her, but for his socks.

"Hey," he'd said to her then. "Nothing more ridiculous than a naked man with his socks on." And she said something, but he didn't catch it, bending down, clumsily peeling them off. She was looking at him, and then said something about *men and their erection dances*, but she was smiling, and Davin was leaning over unbuttoning her blouse, revealing a thick underwire bra covering small breasts.

Small breasts, she said, but Davin told her he liked small breasts, big breasts did little for him. He then rolled her enough toward him to get to the hooks behind, drawing his hand across the skin of her back and shoulders. With a bit of fumbling, he unlatched the bra and pulled it away, her rolling back and shrugging the left shoulder strap free, and then she settled on her elbow and arm, looking at him.

He stood back, looking at her naked form and told Gloria she had lovely breasts. He'd felt present, glad to be there, excited, of course, but some part of him, a whisper, was a bit surprised by how he was feeling so present, confident.

Davin, in the morning sun that floods his bedroom, this day after, recalls that moment, and how he nodded toward her to move over. He sat not quite fully on the bed as she moved and twisted toward her to run his hand over her flesh, gently, lightly, as if a blind man, and his reach followed her legs to her feet. He held the left foot with one hand, his other hand moving lightly down her abdomen, lightly over her pudendum, which was free from pubic hair, a surprise to him. His left hand traveled up, mid-thigh, and he told her a shaved woman was new for him. She explained Brazilian wax, this was how she kept herself she told him as he stepped his knees over between her legs, the two looking into each other's face. Then he moved downward, kissing her breasts, her abdomen, her hips and upper thighs, her inner thighs, and she was relaxing and murmuring. He asked if he could *eat her*, and she gently slapped the top of his head while saying, "Sure," and Davin scooted further back, his legs off the foot of the bed, his lips, his tongue whispering up her thigh.

That went well, he thinks, staring up at the ceiling.

Gloria started with a gasp and then moaned as his tongue found the favorite spots, the right rhythms and movements, and the cries were distinct, a guide, and he would withdraw from the heat, his own slobber, her wetness, and gently kiss her thighs, her low belly, and then come back to her.

He remains unclear about whether she had climaxed then, but he is sure this had been a pleasure for both, but it was what followed that still bothers him.

Well, all's well that ends well, he tells himself.

He had brought up his legs, kneeling upright between her legs, and then descended to kiss her belly, moving up slowly toward her breasts, kissing around the nipples and then gently sucking at the nipples, and then moving farther up until they were kissing, tongues darting, and he could feel her reach for him, guiding his erection into her wetness, and his entry was shocking, her vagina so different from what he'd been familiar, a distinct curving upward, a delight, yes, and the heat, and then he was hit with a wave of feeling, and he rocked backward and then half stumbled off the bed, trying to control his breathing. The air felt absent, his head felt light, his erection dying, his heart felt— *what?* – something, something intense, a weight, his mind, his body, inert.

He stood by the side of the bed, his eyes on Gloria, the beauty of her before him, her body, her look toward him open with a slight smiling question, and his erection returned. He climbed back between her legs and reentered her, her wet had diminished slightly but was back in a moment, and he was holding her face in his hands, looking at her, his elbows out taking his weight, but she kept her eyes closed as he thrust into her. The pace grew faster, and he had to slow for some moments, but he began to thrust again, her moans a pitching note, and they were both gasping. His erection grew harder yet and seemed to expand in her, in her heat, and he began to groan. He thrust once more and emptied into her, and then a half thrust more, and the heat of his semen seemed dangerous, like burning, his shudders kept going, and he finally grew still, until he was worried that his weight was uncomfortable and he'd flipped to his side and reached for the tissue box on the night table behind him, plucking out a handful and handing her some.

A few moments later he'd propped his head on his elbow and looked at her before collapsing back down, her hand resting on his hip. They both grew cold, and after clumsy maneuvering they managed to push back the duvet and blanket and slide their way into the sheets, pulling up the blankets, holding each other, eyes closed, breathing slowing.

He was up after an hour or so of mixed talk and quiet between them, and dressed, and then was in his car headed for his own bed.

By all means a successful first real date, he knows, but what bothers him this morning is the recollection of that feeling when first fucking her, the power of it, the feeling of being overwhelmed. It had been like he was thrown back from her rather than just a step or two, and he now knows what it was, had been.

Grief.

He'd not expected such a reaction and this morning he remains surprised by the appearance of such strong grief. He had thought in the years past the divorce he was doing well processing the grief of the collapse of the marriage. He'd let the years move on, steady as he could be in his reflections and considerations, and in his discussions with his on-again-off-again therapist, and his talking to friends.

Surprise! he tells himself this morning.

"Jesus, no fucking kidding," he says into the room. But this morning he remains haunted by the feeling he'd experienced, although this starts to make sense as he mulls it over. It was the first time he's made love to a woman other than his wife since the decades with Gwen, a life built around that person, no longer there, gone.

Still, he knows he'd just as soon not experience that sort of feeling the next time he has sex with this woman, although he's pretty sure the lapse went unnoticed by her, or at least not remarked upon.

Of course it was weird, he tells himself.

But they have another date, dinner at his house with the likelihood of Gloria staying the night, that likely being her expectation, anyway. The idea of seeing her again begins to stir him, but he is all business and swings his legs onto the floor.

Time to get to work.

Let that be the end of that, he says to himself about the burst of grief the night before, and he says out loud, "Jesus, no fuck," as he starts down the stairs to make some more coffee before reascending to work in his office.

And there's a faint echo, for some time, *let that be the end of that.*

Chapter 18: Click Tock Glock

This target will be easy in some ways, McPherson tells himself, and he's confident his surveillance has helped him pick the best spot. The big challenge is the target most likely won't be alone.

He's in the target's woods, and they're real woods even though this place is not far from St. Cloud where the target's company has its headquarters. He's in a part of the woods far from the driveway entry and not too close to the residence. In the falling light he pulls clothing items from the duffel bag he has dropped at his feet. He starts changing but when he pulls off his pants, he feels a bit uneasy about it for a moment, but it's just a flare of modesty acting up, and he laughs at his reaction. If someone is watching, there'd be bigger problems than being caught without his pants.

This target is the founder of one of the leading financial services, one of the worldwide giants, but more important for McPherson is the target's sexual predilections, which is what is likely to complicate matters for tonight's action, but he has come up with a way that makes this work for him. Or ought to, anyway, he keeps reassuring himself, thinking of the plan for tonight being a departure from his normal approach.

That thought makes him laugh.

Normal.

He knows there is nothing normal about what he is undertaking, but he also knows that nothing about the times he's living through is normal.

And the rich asshole is hardly normal, not only because the target's among the One-Percenters but because the target is some sort of goddam pervert, and that is common enough knowledge, at least if you do your homework. In the course of his research on this target, he came across some old press, and the more he looked the more he found, even if most of what showed up was vague enough to miss, the target's PR machine no doubt at work. But you can't erase court records, not anyway if they were leaked before the lawyers got them sealed, and what these records showed was the target's taste for sex workers.

This had come to light in an old civil complaint by a major pension fund that had huge investments handled by the target's financial service company, and the charge of failure of fiduciary responsibility was raised following significant—even catastrophic—losses from investments managed on the pension fund's behalf. During this suit, and for one brief moment, the accusations of lavish spending and inattention by the target, then president of the company, referenced his frequent use of prostitutes, and the story caught some of the gossip outlets. One tabloid ran the title *Hookers and Hangars* at the time, and it wasn't the facts about the target's airplane collection that were disputed. In the end nothing came from the suit, and the target's PR managed the story, positioning him as a playboy, subbing *girlfriends* for *escorts*.

But McPherson is dogged, a point of pride. He has been operating under the assumption that any would-be revelations about the target's proclivity for prostitutes were well controlled because there was plenty of money to keep things quiet, or the high-end escorts knew better than to talk, or reporters knew better than try to pursue the angle, or all the above, as he'd concluded. He just kept on digging.

The target's vanity will be his undoing, he hopes.

The first operational information was from a profile in *Robb Report*, a luxury lifestyle magazine, and it had been something of a coup to find the magazine available digitally through the public library he'd used a couple of weeks back, stopping as needed on his long drive up to Minnesota.

The *Robb Report* article had mentioned another story about the target's several *quote-unquote cabins,* as the writer had put it, and this had led him to a publication called *Wealth Collection Magazine.* He uncovered the specific issue in a digital archive on a Russian server dedicated to rights-cracked content, one site of many he's found to be of great use, even if these sites were short-lived, appearing and then disappearing, only to resurface again, newly named, on different servers pointed to by constantly updating lists that were easily found on the Dark Web.

That magazine had done a piece titled *Cabins Fever,* which showcased the target's residential properties tucked into various corners of the country, and there were plentiful photographs, including some of exteriors and grounds. While addresses weren't provided, the Minnesota county where he is now was mentioned, and that county's border turned out to be only twelve miles from the target's headquarters. At another library, he did an online property value search for Benton County, which narrowed down his search parameters even more. Some time spent with Google Satellite revealed the most likely match based on what he'd gleamed from the *Wealth Collection Magazine* photographs, and he'd found the property that seemed the most probable, one with a long swimming pool in the right position relative to several structures.

The property was held by a trust with a confident association with the target.

After that, all he needed to do was make a simple telephone call to main reception at the St. Cloud headquarters, made from a burner, to inquire about where to send important documents for the target, and the answer confirmed the target was at the company headquarters.

Easy-peasy, he thinks as he waits in the dusk.

The so-called cabin farther up the long unpaved driveway has good external security cameras. There are also active personnel, although merely domestic services or security he could not determine. The main structure is at the end of the lengthy narrow access way, a private unpaved road essentially, close to a mile long. He'd determined this distance from his own drone reconnaissance, although he'd not exactly measured since there was no reason to do so.

The man loves his privacy, he tells himself again.

He is standing far enough back from the driveway to be invisible. He looks around and takes in trees as far as he can see in the growing dimness of the closing summer day.

Some weeks previously, and many miles ago, he'd spent a couple of productive days surveilling a horse farm near Lexington, the effort made easier with the purchase of a stealth drone, one that used a directional relay so he could just live stream the feed and alter position or switch sensor modes on the fly. But then he drove a thousand miles, give or take, to Minnesota, with only one more target dispatched en route before putting this new drone to work. The drone is quiet and has great maneuverability and lots of new sensor packages, one of this year's new models, purchased for cash at a tech flea market. The preprogramming work he had to do with his previous model had been tiresome, and sometimes he would end up missing some angle or observation and have to do it all again.

I'm getting good at this, he tells himself as he once again goes over his plan. The setup for this target has taken a lot of time, including how to get better schedule information on the target and his whereabouts. The research and reconnoitering he's done for this target has been difficult, and he'd come close to dropping it once or twice, but he knows he has a stubborn streak.

Plugging away, he thinks, repeating one of his old man's favorite saws.

Keep plugging away.

The schedule recon itself had taken a lot of time and effort. Over the seventeen days he's been in state, he has learned the target uses a car service in town, is picked up in the morning at his town residence and dropped back at night, sometimes late, but the first Friday-evening surveillance saw the man dropped off on the early side, and soon after the garage door at the base of the target's in-town residence crawled open and a black Land Rover emerged.

What he had come to learn is that after work was done, the target typically drove his own car, if heading up to this so-called cabin, that is.

That surveillance had been a tricky spot for him. He was at risk of drawing undue attention to himself sitting for hours at a stretch in a rental up the street, but worse yet was that the plan required a tracker be placed on the vehicle, and accessing the target's secure garage was out of the question.

He'd have to do it on the fly, he had concluded.

The following Friday he was back on the target's street, and when the Land Rover emerged, he got out of the rental with a bag of groceries and an aluminum crutch, the kind with a forearm brace, and stepped into the street to cross with the Land Rover approaching.

He was dressed in a thrift store suit, feigning a swinging gate he hoped suggested cerebral palsy steps, although he had to wonder if it might come across as more *Ministry of Funny Walks*. In the middle of the street he shifted the paper grocery bag so the tear he had carefully made spilled the contents out onto the street with the Land Rover coming up on him, stopping.

The rolling grapefruit and apples did their job, one resting against the front right tire.

He hadn't expected the target to put the car in park and get out to help.

"Hey, let me give you a hand," the target had said, bending down and retrieving two cans of soup, then handing them to him.

He'd simply put them in his suit jacket side pockets, and a flush was rushing over him, sweat breaking out, rising panic from the unexpected close contact, but it had then occurred to him a crippled guy dropping groceries, being helped, might be embarrassed or flustered.

He swung-gaited to the front tire and bent over to pick up the grapefruit while his other hand grasped the tracking device between his palm and the crutch handle.

The wheel well was all plastic shield.

He then dropped to his knees.

"Huh," he said loudly enough. "There's a can of soup under here."

The target said something in reply, but he couldn't make it out, focusing on finding solid metal frame anywhere within easy reach, the device magnetically clicking on quite satisfactorily.

He grunted himself up, using the crutch, and turned, and there was the target close by. He looked at the man. The target looked like a regular guy. That was the closest he'd ever been to a live target, and it was a bit unnerving.

Unnervingly close.

Well, except for cutting off a goddamn thumb, he reminds himself, but then that target, his very first, was no longer alive.

The target looked to be around his own age.

The target was holding another grapefruit and apple.

He just shrugged, not taking the fruit.

The target offered to put these items on the curb, and he'd simply shrugged again.

"Okay?" the target asked, coming back toward the car, and he must have said something back, probably a *Yeah, all set*, or *Thanks, buddy*, but he wouldn't swear to it, intent on getting to the sidewalk, the crumpled shopping bag and some retrieved contents clasped against his chest, and he almost forgot to swing-gait his right leg with the crutch, hopping a bit in his delay.

Now, waiting and watching here in the approaching dusk's dimming light, he just has to wait for the tracking alert. It is possible the target won't even be coming to his deep woods retreat today, but he can repeat this plan for a couple more Fridays if he has to. It will mean again pushing the mountain bike through the woods, a bike he had simply walked off with somewhere near Indianapolis, a suburb he doesn't even know the name of, although he still feels bad about that crime because it hurt some kid, probably. He doesn't have a problem going after targets who deserve what they get, but he doesn't like doing bad things to people who in no way deserve it.

He had acted on impulse, grabbing the bike off the lawn of a residential neighborhood.

And here I am, he thinks, *putting the bike to use.*

He'd come on to the target's property far from the cameras that covered the driveway's start and the second set of cameras he'd discovered that extended coverage quite some way along the road frontage, bracketing the modest looking but quite effective gate. But the security setup seems to him a deterrent only for lazy people, and he had simply walked in from through the woods from the clearing where his Transit remains at the ready, just shy of two miles from where he waits.

Still, a bit of a haul, pushing the bike and carrying the duffel bag on his back, but now he's out in the target's woods, waiting in the first darkling of the summer sky, light enough, but the sun will soon fully set.

He's not sure how early the target might head out.

Or if he will head out, he reminds himself.

But in the growing gloom, the tracker pings, which means the Land Rover has just passed the activator a half mile or so down the road off the interstate the target uses to get to the road that passes the driveway gate, which means the Land Rover is about sixteen or seventeen minutes out.

He moves closer toward the private driveway to get to his deployment position, but halfway there he is startled by headlights coming from the cabin end of the way, the occasional flash and bob of headlight through the foliage. Still, he's been assuming there would be some sort of staff, and one of the outbuildings he'd looked at with the drone looked like housing, and a pickup truck had been parked in front of that building in the video feed.

He lies down in the undergrowth, sure of remaining unseen.

The passing pickup truck could well be the same one on drone feed, he thinks, as he tracks the vehicle as it disappears around the driveway's curve.

He rises and continues to move toward the driveway edge, crossing it, picking up a large branch he's already prepared. He's got about ten minutes to get the set-up right. This spot provides opportunity, although there are any number of spots along the road that are also black in terms of cameras. He'd picked up no Wi-Fi activity in this middle stretch with the signal scanner he uses whenever he approaches.

Unless they are hard-wired and I missed them, he nags himself.

It would be easy to step out on one or two spots with tight turns and just start shooting, but hard to guarantee good hits. He is standing just past one of those spots, the branch now dragged onto the driveway. He had made sure to find a deadfall that isn't too big, which might have the target call for help. He's sure there is a property manager locally, although that could have been him in the pickup.

The branch is big enough that it's unlikely the target would try to drive right over it.

And only now it occurs to him that someone with so many billions of dollars might not think twice about chancing damage, especially since the target's car is a Land Rover, which might embolden the target to go over the obstacle.

Wait and see, he says to calm himself. It won't be the last time he might have to call off a plan after realizing he still has to figure out some previously unforeseen challenge or trouble.

He waits in the darkened gloom, not bothering to use the night vision yet, not needing it yet, but he knows he'll use it to navigate the woods in the full dark, after.

He knows where the target's car is, more or less, maybe two minutes out.

The tougher problem he has worried long and hard is the companion, if there is one, and there could be more than one, or maybe friends are visiting, but he doubts they'd not have cars themselves.

If there is more than one car, or more than one other in the Land Rover, he'll have to abort.

Unless they see me, he suddenly considers.

He's not sure why he's only now thinking about these possibilities. He's getting upset that he hadn't mounted a camera of his own toward the road.

Maybe I'm not that good at this, he finds himself thinking, but then he dismisses such doubt and focuses. If there is another person with the target, an escort girl, presumably, he has the plan that will do all he can to avoid collaterally hurting her. He's in the best spot, a tight turn, good cover, and the good-sized branch he's dragged across the narrow way is in place. The target will stop to drag it off, and *pop, pop.*

The bigger problem to solve is the woman. He wrestled with one idea after another, and then it hit him. He wasn't a particularly tall person, and he'd dropped his middle-age weight over the last months on mission.

He'd be disguised as a woman. Time for the world to see KTR for the army it is.

He thinks this is subtle with the long blond wig poking out from the bottom cuff of the balaclava he's just now donned after strategically placing rolled-up socks that he settles into place in a makeshift bra before zipping up the dark windbreaker. His new pants are some knock-off of lululemon yoga leggings.

A bit of lipstick, very heavy perfume.

Who wears lipstick to an assassination?

He is only now asking himself this, but he shrugs and drops the tube back into the duffel bag. His mouth is covered by the balaclava, and now the lipstick idea is making him wonder again just how well thought out the plan really is.

He looks up, trying to find the approaching Land Rover through the trees, and then he lies down in his special spot.

The vehicle approaches, the headlights on, even though the post-dusk sky provides enough light for his own needs.

The Land Rover stops in front of the fallen branch.

He's puzzled for an instant until he realizes the target is having a woman get out from the passenger side. She's walking toward the branch, reaching to pull it aside, and he's now getting up, the Glock in his gloved hand. He's moving, raising the pistol, and shoots three quick shots, the first and third make a mash out of the target's head behind the crazed glass.

The woman is still holding the branch, halfway pulled off the driveway, frozen.

McPherson sees she's about to run, but she steps backward and falls, and as he comes around the front of the Land Rover, he notices she is wearing only one very high-heeled shoe, the other is pinned in the ground through the leaf litter.

The gun is pointed at her. She looks up, face filled with terror.

"Honey. it's this," he says in a weird falsetto he's been practicing, waving the plastic Ziploc bag in his other hand, just pulled out of his pocket, the bag holds a face mask with a small bottle taped to it. "Just a little nap?"

He's not expecting an answer.

"Or this." He waves the gun.

He walks behind her as he squeezes the ether into the mask's cloth fiber, then reaches to put the mask over her nose and mouth.

"Breathe, sister," he says, all girl.

She does and slumps, unconscious.

He keeps the mask on her for another two breaths, being cautious not to overdo it.

He polices the area until he's satisfied he leaves nothing

behind, the jury-rigged knock-out mask and small bottle back in his windbreaker's pocket, back sealed in the plastic bag.

It has gotten dark. He has a moment of panic trying to find the tracker, knees growing damp in his low kneeling position, but then his hand slides on to it.

He collects the duffel bag and pulls the night vison headset out. He then pulls off the balaclava and the wig in one motion, grateful for the cool air, and then pulls on the goggles.

He makes his way toward the bicycle, the woods alive in the green surreal light of the night vision, trees as negatives. Then he pulls the gun back out, holds it in front of him, both hands, and he's back in time, it's him and his brother, teenagers, on the old couch, playing first person shooters on PlayStation, looking for imagined targets among the ghost-green trees.

Chapter 19: Best to Think Tanks

Greene just sits at his desk and looks at the trappings of his office.

He comes together with senators and representatives and their aides and with judges, lobbyists, and other think tank folk. He's mixed and mingled, delivering messages, campaign money, advice, guidance, threats.

Personal networks, he tells himself. *Something of a mailman, a courier of real-politick, a quartermaster.*

He can marvel at the effectiveness of such informal systems of communication he works within. Everyone can know his Institute has a mission, but there is the official mission, and then there are the unofficial ones. A look at his board of directors over the time the Institute has existed might suggest funders, but with the big donors masked by PACs and 501(c)(3)s and 501(c)(4)s, there's no certainty about the real sources of the Institute's money. Efforts to pierce the money given and connect to the actions taken and the results expected, well, these connections can be suggested, but such efforts can still just be claimed as personal connections or common beliefs. The only way this informal system can ever break is if the connections are confessed, and only if the string of confessed connections is long enough. Such a trajectory is improbable with documentary collaboration absent, and so it is all code, all beliefs.

And money, he knows. *Of course, always money.*

The high-water mark for climate denial think tanks like

his, and the related advocacy organizations, industry associations, and particular PACs, is well in the past, the zenith having occurred a couple of years into the second decade, by the count he made back then. He discovered this when he was researching career prospects, after his divorce from his first wife, after years of frustrated academic adjunct slavery and then a stint of some very unsatisfying years with a national health insurance company, heading up the East Coast customer relations department, the sharp edge where misery met business resistance, a thankless job that involved far too many hard stories despite his best efforts to insulate himself from the frontline work.

What he had discovered is that by 2014, just shy of a billion dollars was being spent annually by the fossil fuel industry on countering threats from global warming claims, and that sum was only what was publicly noted. But Citizens United in 2010 was resulting in a giant shift and he had thrown himself into research on the climate change denial universe and quickly saw the opportunities.

He read the reports, followed the climate denial efforts, and tracked and named the organizations in play, many well-known and considered legitimate — Brookings Institute, Council on Foreign Relations, Cato Institute, the Heritage Foundation, American Enterprise Institute, Atlantic Council, Aspen Institute, Bipartisan Policy Center, The US Chamber of Commerce. He saw the fascinating roll call of participants, including a former vice president and a number of senators and other species of major figures. On the other hand, the individuals behind these participants and behind the PACs that controlled the political lives of many were modest in number, although immodest in the resources they controlled. This group — *The Gang* — included the biggest fossil fuel corporations, the Koch Brothers and Koch Industries, a Chairman of the Carlyle Group, some board members of hedge funds and holding companies, owners of capital management companies, the odd outlier or two from the tech monopolies, and partners in law firms that operated on a global scale.

A *Who's Who* of unimaginable fortunes, a group that understood how the world works. And he too had come to understand in detail how the system of influence and control works.

I have a doctorate in anthropology, for chrissake, he laughs.

Much of what he'd done early on could be directly traced to the tobacco industry's model for preventing, delaying, and suppressing the validity of health consequences of smoking, and for decades.

For a third of a century, he admiringly thinks of those accomplishments, although he's long been against smoking, personally.

Greene loves being executive director of the Kehoe Institute, he loves the frills, the status, the money, but he loves most that he has a useful place within the foundational mechanisms of the world. He knows how the world works and how this reflects his strongest belief that power and money rule because money is the direct reflection of the *Market* at work.

And not the so-called "Free Market," he is always quick to clarify, although it took him a long time to understand the irony of the term since it is the most common name for the belief system of which he's part. *Free Market,* like *Roman Catholicism*, like *Socialism*, like *Shamanism*, is just a catch-all moniker, a bumper sticker, a lapel pin most think little about, but just believe.

But the *Market*, or sometimes the *Marketplace*, if he's feeling folksy, he has no doubt there is no better way, that the Market, cruel as it can be, is what best drives progress, and progress moves forward, that's a fact. People live longer, diseases collapse in the face of human achievement, markets thrive.

Even the *Market* is inefficient, but that's unavoidable with anything involving humans, but he unwaveringly believes the *Market* is the least inefficient of all systems. Those who use moral arguments are simply making their own power play, and they fail because there's no mechanisms bigger than the *Market*, and their ideologies are more wish-seeking than reality. He is all about reality, and he understands the issue of climate change is important, *maybe the most important issue*, but unfortunately for climate, he thinks the solutions offered by most activists, and those allied public officials, organizations, and environmental entities, are all based on a faulty view of mankind. Their plans and hopes are unrealizable. There will be no replacing fossil fuels, not any time soon, not until wealth has richer options.

That hurricane was terrible, but the timing couldn't have been better. The Sea Wall Act is now one of the hot potential bills and the various Congressional committees are more likely to prioritize the work in the committees.

At his desk, he shrugs his shoulders, then rolls them, trying to loosen things up. His head makes a slow orbit of his shoulders, his neck still tight, but the movement helps.

He's been hard at it all morning, working at the position paper he's been assembling, and he gets back to it, scanning the partial draft he'd printed out that is already covered with his highlighter markings, margin notes, and Post-it flags. He's also been jotting down more notes on a legal pad.

What he has outlined is essentially an attack plan for fixing two impending problems many of *The Gang* are particularly worried about, one of which is how to keep the knives away from the fossil fuel subsidies and beneficial tax and regulatory breaks. The other is how best to capture control of the likely huge pool of allocations potential from the Sea Wall Act. With the latter, the greatest value to them may prove to be that adaptation against sea rise undercuts pressure toward fossil fuel reductions, shifting to remediation and adaptation as the next frontier in the fight to keep fossil fuels burning. He will be proposing this as a no-lose scenario—climate change means rising seas that demand remediation and offer big profit opportunities through projects that address the problems caused by climate change.

Greene knows what causes climate change, but he's got a job to do.

Hey, everyone, yeah, sure there are problems, but we can fix them, that is the message, and by extension arguing that these problems can be fixed without upending the foundations of the economy or the American way of life. The Can-do Nation will stop the seas, capture the carbon, and all else that is good for business-as-usual. Carbon capture is still getting a lot of money thrown at it, even if the furthest along of carbon capture and sequestration projects remain, at best, small capture and/or large financial losses, and, anyway, still mostly pilot projects. But the message about CCS is useful and still holds its value.

Fossil fuels? We need 'em to get things done. Climate change? We're on the front lines.

He smiles. The argument is shaping up.

He looks back at the marked-up paper, now feeling a bit less overwhelmed about the task at hand, which is to boil down the game plan in plain language and breaking out the steps and money needed into logical stages, using euphemisms only when needed. As straightforward as can be but avoiding the smoking-gun terms and plain giveaways on substance.

He already has some *sub rosa* steps in play, with his operator on the kill, and with that, like magic, there's another individual in the way of the big plan taken off the board. He's also inclined to go after a particular senator who looks to be on the wrong side of the play with the Sea Wall Act. He'll either get someone to buy this individual's re-allegiance, or use blackmail.

Well, I guess that would be re-buying. The problem with politicians is that they don't always stay bought.

He has drafted an appendix of sorts, a table breaking out officeholders and upcoming candidates in useful positions, some noted as already on board, some marked as problems and others ranked by opposition probabilities. He sees some holes in the list, and he will bring in a political consultant he's worked with to fill the gaps and supplement his list.

The overall play looks solid, though.

And then there's that group behind the recent textual analysis that has kneecapped some of his favorite climate denier rhetoricians with that big data AI analysis, although, really, this is looking more and more like nothing worse than a passing embarrassment. Still, he's had the people behind that effort checked out, and there are quite a few academics from the climate crisis side, plus a smattering of other professionals, journalists, and hard-science types, along with some public figures. The report he's received says there's no formal structure to the group, but there is one identified prime mover of this group known informally as *The Laundry*.

He has set up some protection should this group continue as a problem, just in case.

Lobinski is getting set for that action, just in case.

These extracurricular actions are not the sort of steps and details *The Gang* needs to know about, not in any detail.

Yeah, I don't think so, Greene contemplates.

They know what he does for them, but not details, no facts of the actions. He can make the dirty work barely inferable, unnamed, hidden and budgeted within the legislation research and one or two other departmental spendings.

It's surprising how expensive this kind of work can be.

He understands his plan is ambitious and that various parts will have to get passed to other entities, but these interorganizational assignments will add to his position, even though there will never be anything formal about the pie-splitting. There won't be a paper trail, no specific connections with different parts of the program going through different contractors and professional staff. All it takes are quiet conversations and proposal suggestions and meetings for drinks. All it takes is speaking in select and informal language, and then these people bring it to the other organizations, taking credit as they wish.

Dark money is always available with the right requests.

Chapter 20: Davin Takes a Poop

Josephine is not the last hurricane of the season, by any means, only the first, but the two hurricanes that followed within three weeks seem like gentle rains in comparison, and Davin knows that even now the Atlantic Tropic Zone is cooking up yet another storm.

The first hurricane after Josephine skipped across the Gulf of Mexico before petering out against the dry Mexican coastline. The second had hit far closer to home just six days after the Gulf storm. That Category 1 hurricane, Leona, had tracked inland, coming up the Hudson, feeding off New York's bays and river warmth from the early summer heat.

This is what Davin is thinking about, sitting on the john in his bathroom, up on the third floor of his house. It is Post-Josephine, Day 41, and Davin has been weaning himself from his near-constant attention to the news of hurricanes, not really needing or wanting to absorb any further images of destruction or follow the relief effort scorecards. The news these days is about the efforts related to Josephine relief falling short, but it seems to be improving. He knows his efforts to avoid getting caught up with such news is still falling short, but this too is improving

The weather in Housatonic has been better than most recent summers, and the sunscreens over the garden, put in by him and Marsha a week ago, could well be superfluous this season. Of course, there's a lot left of the growing season, and to the hurricane season as well. November is months away, so the growing season is still very much wait and see.

He turns to his right where there's a small shelf-like top of the toilet paper roll fixture. This is where he puts his coffee mug. He grabs it, taking a sizable gulp of tepid coffee before placing it back.

He tries to relax.

When did taking a crap become so hard? he asks himself.

These sorts of questions are becoming disturbingly frequent since hitting his seventh decade.

Pee more, shit less, and never trust a fart after forty, he wonders. *Back when I was young enough to think it was a joke.*

He uses that line a lot or at least thinks of it more and more. He remembers coming across the line in a Stephen Dobyns novel, one in a series about an older private detective working out of Saratoga Springs, Charlie somebody, but the speaker of the line was the main guy's pal.

He remembers that character's name, *Victor Plotz.*

Jesus, he thinks, impressed by his recollection. *All that fucking useless knowledge I retain.*

A year back, in one moment or other of idleness, he had Googled the phrase *Never trust a fart after forty.* He can even now recall his surprise that the first result was a video clip of a Jack Nicholson film, *The Bucket List.* The full line was, he is pretty sure, *Three things to remember when you get older: never pass up a bathroom, never waste a hard-on, and never trust a fart.*

Wisdom to live by, Davin thinks, reaching back to his right for another mouthful from the mug of now cold coffee.

The Bucket List result was followed by many others, including promotional coffee mugs and sweatshirts, and a bunch of Etsy listings he hadn't bothered clicking on. One odd result was a link to a forum on mixedmartialarts.com. He's pretty sure this was it, although he'd not bothered at the time to click on the link and certainly hadn't bookmarked it.

Because why would I? he asks himself, sitting on the toilet. It was just one of those weird Internet things, the quote showing up in a martial arts site.

And now he wonders why he's meditating on this topic.

He remembers wasting more time that day after adding Stephen Dobyns to the search string, but he never found any reference to the line or characters of the Saratoga Springs series he recalled as the first instance of his coming across the line.

He tries to dismiss such nonsense thoughts, although he is well aware this is typical for how his mind works. He closes his eyes, seeking to relax, but notices his right leg is a bit tingly and on its way to becoming numb, so he shifts his posture a bit.

His thoughts flow back to Josephine. In his mind he sees, again, the photograph of a shell-shocked Mickey Mouse, an image that has become iconic, reprinted often. The image, captured by an amateur photographer, was of a teenager in the Mickey Mouse costume, head and ears removed and held against his thigh as he blankly stared at the crowds of Josephine victims, the trucks and buses disgorging storm refugees at Disney World.

He sits on the toilet, waiting, straining a bit now and then, but mostly he's losing himself in his thoughts. He doesn't want those thoughts to be of the storm, or those images, or the endless news articles and talking heads.

What he does allow is that things are actually going well on the local front, workwise and otherwise. The *Berkshire Interactive* work is interesting, mostly, and Alicia seems to want him to take on yet more, although he remains wary of being consumed by it.

On the other hand, the credit line debt is shrinking, he acknowledges, even if he's always feeling pressed for time.

I don't even have time to take a shit, he tells himself, trying to clear his mind of distractions.

Ah, sitting meditation, he thinks and then snorts, *shitting meditation*.

As he sits there on the toilet up in the third-floor bathroom, just trying to relax in a house empty of others for the moment, his thoughts continue to race and rev. He's now thinking about the piece he's working on in the studio, even as he works on the finishing touches of another piece, the one with all those keys. The new piece is something of a folly, maybe, or maybe it is a real sculpture, or might be, when he's finished. He's taken an old wood box, and outside of cleaning the exterior a bit, he's done little to it. The interior, however, is upholstered, with a bit of batting behind the odd cloth he's had around since who knows when, and that cloth may indeed be upholstery material, and old-fashioned in some ways, with silver threading that runs in tapestry pattern throughout. The box sits vertically on short Queen Anne maple legs he's fastened on with clever skirt framing. He's mounted an old sort of nineteenth century engraving of a lady to the upholstered back of the box, or maybe it's some more modern facsimile, but the image is strange and compelling in its black ink on darkened paper. The frame is a bit ornate, and there's traces of old mildew under the glass, but that just adds to the antique effect. He's mounted on the ceiling of the box a few fragments of old circuit boards from one or another of the old computers he's kept around for some reason.

Like, for this, he reminds himself.

There is wiring carefully tacked to the back outside corner of the box, which feeds through into the top interior, but he's still figuring out what sort of illumination he wants to put in place. He's got more work to do, including putting a clear finish on the curved legs and figuring out how he wants to handle the top surface, whether simply using plate glass with a collage of some sort as yet unconceived, or maybe he'll pick up a scrap of marble from a local countertop fabricator.

He's not sure if he likes the piece yet, but he thinks he's leaning positive.

He has no confidence when exactly he'll next get to work on the piece, and that gets his mind darting among the many demands and decisions pressing down on him, those choices and possibilities and all the myriad details blinking to attention. He's caught up not only in these thoughts, but there are also fragments of regrets flashing too, most too fast for him to follow well enough to identify with any conscious certainty. But he certainly feels it all, a sensation like the exhaust of diesel as a bus or truck blasts by, leaving a residue of some phantom that passes through his chest, his lungs, and bumping into his heart as if neutrinos, some sort of substance only partly existing in the human dimensions and partly beyond.

Shit, Davin thinks, *I should write a novel*, Davin Takes a Poop.

And then he is moving his bowels.

Business done, Davin stands and before he reaches to pull up his underwear and pants, turns to look down at the now darker bowl. *Good poop*, he says to himself, wondering, hardly for the first time, just how many people look regularly at their shit.

He briefly wonders too, if there is some art piece in the question before moving on with his day.

Chapter 21: Smooth Operator

Joey Lobinski has looked over the material he's gotten from Greene, and it's not much, only a thin sheaf of cheap paper, just text, names, addresses, some early surveil notes. Not much, no masthead or other markings.

Kinda like this room, he considers.

He's in a hotel room, up past Dumphries, in Maryland, right off the interstate, close enough to Quantico, but not too close.

The television is on, muted, and every time he glances at the screen, there's some aerial tracking shots over destroyed houses, blue tarps spotting the occasional structure, and a lot of standing water.

He squints at the screen and sees the crawler placing the shot in Wilmington Beach, which he recognizes as the stormfall with heavy rain and wind of the most recent storm that, unlike Josephine, hugged the coast westward, swinging northeast to brush Cape Cod.

Muriel? Maddy?

He tries to remember the name, but he hasn't paid that much attention.

He clicks off the television.

It's been unpleasant enough up in Washington, DC, with the rain from Muriel's edges. The rain had still been heavy on his drive down here, but the storm is now past New England, petering out somewhere east of the Maritimes.

He turns back to the material he got from Greene.

This initial surveillance information is hardly sufficient

but a good enough start for his acquiring the depth and detail he'll need. He's been eager to get to work, but after getting this packet from Greene, he's had to cool his heels while the next package is acquired. He's not wasted his time as he waits though and has already largely worked out the operational stages, even if he can't execute yet, not without better background on *Kill the Rich*.

He's also waiting on the porn insertion package, but he is not expecting that for another week or two.

He thinks about what he does for work these days, the work a far cry from what he did in the service as a technical specialist, an operator, and typically in the middle of the most demanding action. Not that he didn't kill people, but what he did then was different, at least situationally. He has no illusions about what he now does, which includes killing for those people who hire him. Those who hire him, he is certain, are often much bigger assholes than the people he kills or otherwise destroys, but then, nice guys don't need his services.

The service is killing, mostly, and the reasons he's hired may vary, but mostly, he figures, it's for money reasons, despite the bullshit clients so often want to hide behind.

For the good of the country-type shit, Thank you for your service.

At least Greene isn't one of those clients.

Greene is an asshole though, no doubt. He's done enough operations for him—in fact, Greene was his entre into this business. He's put his name out at the few specialist employment agencies that cater to his sort of skillset, mainly security gigs and sometimes private placements. But one of these agencies, and he has no certain knowledge which one, seems to have some sort of side work, work on the dark side of security and force projects, which is how he got to meet Greene in the first place, getting an appointment notice not associated with any of the agencies he'd signed up with.

After checking out Greene and the Kehoe Institute, he'd taken the meeting. It had been a doozy, but then pretty much any meeting with Greene is like that, a lot of vague talk combined with rather specific — *and attractive, dare I say* — money amounts being bandied about. Maybe that was why he hadn't been all that bothered with the dance Greene performed with his coded language, his implications, innuendos, hints. He even found himself entertained and certainly intrigued by the idea of getting the sort of remuneration Greene kept talking about, even if it was obvious people like Joey Lobinski don't get paid those sorts of amounts for the typical security assignments.

But in that first meeting, this dance had gotten tiresome.

"Who do you want killed?" he had asked, interrupting Greene's ongoing cloud of words. He'd asked mainly to see Greene react, and it had been worth it just to see Greene flail, but of course it was like that, even if it turned out to be petty. Some asshole who was fucking this asshole's wife, who was probably an asshole too.

It had been an easy assignment, and the payout was cash, and Greene then wanted him on board for more.

The next job came quickly, and as Greene had roughly outlined it, it was a basic B&E to retrieve some files and leave some files on the subject's home computer.

"You basically want me to deliver a package," Lobinski asked. At that point Greene had another man join them, who, as best Lobinski figured, was Greene's main security on staff, another former technical operator from the telltales, although older, so probably First Gulf War or even possibly from *Spooksville*. The dossier the man carried about him certainly suggested deep access. There were documents from Lobinski's service records that shouldn't have been in any sort of folder outside secure sites. There'd been operation after-reports that were eyes-only.

The security guy took things over from that point, and the rest of that afternoon was the briefing and operational protocols, but these were like most any other he'd sat through over the years. The cut-out procedures and setup were different, of course, but then he wasn't a service member any longer, and the US Armed Forces, for whatever faults it has, didn't talk much about reasonable deniability, burner phone communication procedures, and self-destructing computer intrusion packages. The security guy — Lobinski has yet to know his name even today — was sure to make the point that if anything were to go sideways, he was on his own, and that traceback to the Institute simply wasn't going to be actionable.

Deniable to the extreme, as the man put it.

That first official assignment, the B&E, was straightforward and the one after that, too.

The current prep package on the bed looks solid, if light, and everything seems completely independent of anything traceable, just like the other prep packages, and he has no illusions about leverage should things go wrong. As far as he's concerned, the only procedural off-point is Greene always introducing the job at hand, when he could — *should*, thinks Lobinski — hand it off to his security head to do the assigning. He figures Greene is the type of guy who likes to show himself in charge, and that's a potentially dangerous illusion.

He once had illusions. He once thought service to country was a noble calling, and joining the elite was the best way he could serve.

But he'd been in Syria, and that forced open his eyes.

Tricks and betrayals and lies.

That's what he finally came to learn, that money is power and power is what those with money use to get more money and more power. He came late to realize he should be making money and might as well put his god-given talents to use.

He uses some of these talents to try his best to cover himself, whether with Greene or the two other clients he's been working for. He is building the best protection for himself he can, although it has taken a while to system that out, creating drop boxes and action plans that could help him influence any sort of prosecution should things go wrong. He's pretty sure his clients have no idea of his precautions, although likewise he has no certainty that trading off higher-ups for immunity, if it ever comes to that, isn't itself just another comforting illusion. He hopes not, but he also knows his clients tend to be smart about not leaving traces. He has no interest in any sort of fantasy, not on his part anyway, and he's happy to let those who need the illusions and delusions have their false comforts.

And let them pay well for that, he tells himself.

But he will not lie to himself. He's done with false comforts. He's done with pretending honor has a place in this world, that duty is an obligation.

Not the way it works, he tells himself.

No, he has seen with his own eyes how duty is pliable, honor simply a currency. He's seen information go up the chain of command, mutating on the way, until like some cheap card trick, what the powerful want to see is what they see. The facts on the ground be damned as are commitments and promises and vows made on the ground. The frontline subject for these people, this higher command and the people they want to please, is the bottom line, and there is no problem changing the intel to serve the needs of the adding machine.

The withdraw order, in Cizire, for instance.

He knew what would happen, and it happened.

Duty is just shit-paste, and honor, the cracker, he reminds himself.

There was that brief moment of the idea of Kurdistan as something within reach, a real homeland for those he fought alongside and not just the training camp on the Euphrates, and not just the Kurds he helped and fought beside, but also for their families. He had been helping toward this end. He had felt good doing so.

But in Cizire all his effort turned out to be nothing more than an inconvenience. Everything good he and his brothers did turned out to be just another item on the balance sheet. He had seen after-action images. He was glad he hadn't recognized anyone among the Kurdish dead, although he knew who they were and that they were dead, just the same, even if he hadn't pulled the trigger. It was betrayal by inaction and just the same.

He had been ordered to stand down, as he again reminds himself, a reminder repeated many times over the years, but he knows the particulars of the standing orders then were not much help in avoiding the feelings he's carried ever since or his unbidden and recurring memories of the aftermath of the Turkish forces descending upon and decimating his comrades and their families. All while he— *the Americans* – stood by, serving up the deal made by others that collapsed the hope and existence of Kurdistan, the briefest of candle flame snuffed out in an instant. In Syria, it was just another self-serving twist in another proxy war the armchair warriors played at. Russia still held some so-called annexed regions taken from Ukraine, and the play had been to nudge Turkey back into a hardline position with the West, and there were larger forces at work.

He had cared, back then. He had made promises. He had believed, but he's long since rooted out such tendencies. Things changed that day, and he learned a hard lesson about the nature of the world.

But then he shakes his head, ridding himself of the ghost images.

He pauses, picks up the paper, the assignment list.
Just business.

He has to laugh. Greene has his security, an elaborate counter-electronic surveillance suite, including alerts to his guys, *fucking domestics*. They would immediately know about any digital device brought into any meeting with him, phones handed over to assure Greene that nothing would be overheard or recorded, but as it turns out, this was nothing an analog mini-recorder couldn't solve. When there were no longer any pat downs, just the magic box for digital signals, he realized the opportunity of the old tech micro-recorder in the pocket. The only challenge was the capacity limit of the micro-cassettes, but he's never once mistimed things so an embarrassing clicking off might give the game away.

The recording of the latest meeting, with Greene's preening telltale phrases, is already in his safe stash. This little sheaf of paper, so carefully anonymous, will join the cache, literal fingerprints a possibility. He isn't out to screw anyone over, and it is his fervent hope he'll never need any of it because if he ever really does, then he is no doubt royally screwed anyway.

But you never know, he reminds himself. He's seen things go away. He's seen things fixed that he would have bet couldn't be done, so better safe than sorry.

This current assignment is hardly the first murder assignment, not even counting the first from Greene, although he doesn't know for sure that infidelity had been the actual situation and he still suspects that initial assignment was little more than a test, but he made sure he didn't care. Either way, the main point for him was that it led to another test — *a well-paid test* — and he passed that, and the work keeps coming. He knows what he does is murder, and he isn't the type that uses alternative words to hide the fact, no *terminate with extreme prejudice,* no *take care of him,* no *hit,* no *dispatch,* no *waste him, rub out, finish, put away, knock off, bump off.*

It is *kill* for Lobinski, and killing means murder these days since he is no longer a soldier, no longer at war killing the enemy if so required. Now what he does is just murder, plain and simple.

But even as a soldier, he came to think this, dropping all illusion about what he was doing.

I murder people.

He has his eyes open. He likes the money, and he lives well enough, but what he uses the money for, much of it, is to take good care of his nephew, his younger sister's kid, her ex-husband someone he wouldn't mind killing for free. His threat, that one time, driving the asshole back from having a few beers with this then-brother-in-law, pulling over to the side of the road and looking at him square, telling him he would divorce his wife, never touch her again, would provide child support payments.

That had proved effective. The asshole hasn't missed a payment. He's just a piss-poor earner.

But Lobinski does this—*murder*—for the money. He does this kind of work because he is good at it, but he doesn't take any pleasure except for a job well done, proud of his competence and the application of his very impressive skill set. It's a job, not an adventure.

He knows the people he murders have loved ones, most, anyway, and that what he does destroys lives, but he knows anything and everything in this world will destroy lives. That is just a fact and that is just a matter of time.

He is looking over the list of targets and the sparse notes. As meager as they are, each specifies how these targets are to be handled. There aren't that many on the kill list, but the *Kill the Rich* claim statements are a new angle that will take some additional planning on his part to get the deflection right.

It's the other targets that bother him more, the work less clean, although not lethal, at least not directly. These two on the target list are just to be sidelined. He doesn't like to infiltrate residences or offices to load a child porn package to implicate the mark, but he has no question about the efficacy of such action.

He can feel bad about how what he does hurts others, but this is an old feeling for him. He feels this every time he pictures the young Sunni boy, the look on that four- or five-year-old's face, the turning of the young boy from regarding his mother, her slumped bloodied burka, her lower jaw missing, his face turning to look up at Lobinski, was impassive, ancient, knowing.

Lobinski and his three-man squad had been on an operation for a high-value target, the intelligence strong. They were pumped as they rushed the adjoining house, the door just blown, directed fire coming from it. His squad was pouring fire back along with a grenade tossed in, and the firing from within stopped with the blast, but a microsecond past the detonation, the civilian woman had drawn his fire stepping out of a nearby doorway, and he had reacted. The child must have been behind her, and as she stepped out near where he was standing, the frenzy of action was still taking hold, those micro-moments of intense heightened attention and alert when the senses are a jumble. He hadn't even consciously processed the flow of black, but just the movement, his shooting automatic.

Right, even, for the circumstance, he knows.

People die, he thinks.

This became his calming mantra from that day on, leaving the service just weeks later, months after Cizire, when he realized staying on was one of the things that bothered him.

People die.

Someone is going to do it, killing, and if he does it, then the job is clean, the job hurts the minimum number of people possible.

That's the theory, he tells himself, shaking his head to dismiss the image of the young boy's face that often swims back before him, the boy's placid gaze that seemed a direct line into Lobinski, concrete in the connection.

He gets up to pace in the cheap hotel room of some business bargain chain he can't for the life of him recall at the moment, so he ends up over the end table, looking at the hotel's guest package.

"Ah yeah, Holiday Inn Express," he says out loud.

He's waiting, which is not his favorite thing, but it comes with the work.

He is waiting for the delivery of an FBI dossier. Someone will drop it at his door. There will be a brief knock and no contact otherwise, although Lobinski knows this sort of thing is still a risk. Someone could be watching, although he thinks that seems unlikely as he'd spot at least something of it.

He's under one of his assumed names for the hotel and for the car rental. He's got a couple of burn bags with other identities and money, and these are prepositioned and moved around as needed, but so far, no need.

That the material he is waiting for is from the FBI, a copy, anyway, makes him anxious. *Playing close*, he thinks, always a bit worried when one of the agencies is involved, even tangentially.

The knock, soft, and the softer footsteps away.

Lobinski waits a couple of breaths, slow and steady, and then opens the door just enough to snatch the manila envelope, pulling it in without opening the door any more than needed.

The envelope is surprisingly thick.

He rips the package open and starts in.

This is what they have on *Kill the Rich*, the so-called terrorist group that's been getting into headlines.

Within minutes, having thumbed through the pages, he sits back. It's a lot of shit, he concludes. They have almost nothing.

But there's enough for me to use.

Chapter 22: A Soul Adrift in the Ether

McPherson feels crazy. He can't get out of his pushed-back recliner, and his head is a pounding drum. He has managed to throw off part of his fleece blanket, pushed over the side to pool on the dense tight carpet that covers the van's floor.

He's feeling cold, although some part of him understands it is warm, maybe even hot in the van. The air conditioner unit that sits on the high top of the van has gone off sometime during the night when he must have managed to sleep, and the unit has a timer to keep from drawing too much on the bank of three batteries. Either that, or he turned it off in some dully conscious moment in the middle of the night, but that doesn't seem likely. It also doesn't seem likely that he is staying in the recliner, awake but inert, but the fact is that he hasn't moved. He is immobile and he feels like he is barely breathing. He feels the heat, but he feels cold too, and he realizes this is some species of flop sweat, just one feeling he is caught up in along so many other unidentifiable confusions.

He's deluged by a raft of odd sensations, but he can't seem to name any of these feelings.

Someone turned up the gravity, is what he tells himself.

He experimentally picks up his head from its resting place, but he lets it fall back against the top of the recliner immediately.

It occurs to him he doesn't want to move and he doesn't want to breathe, and now even having his eyes open seems dangerous, so he closes them.

He opens them though because behind his eyelids, even with the light coming through the window to paint his closed eyelids red, he sees the escort woman's terror-crazed face.

He sees the high heel spiking into the ground, the other one still on her right foot, and he can hear her moan, which is what opens his eyes, and he's on the recliner, pushed all the way back, making a sound something like moaning, and he's sweating and he's wondering if he may have killed her, by accident, too much chlorophyll. When he'd done the research there were all sorts of warnings.

Chloroform, moron, he tells himself. He'd researched it, looked up and read about all the safety issues, but trying to get to sleep last night, here, a day and three states away from Minnesota, he may have become convinced he messed up and put too much chloroform onto the cloth, or held it over her mouth and nose for too long, or maybe he did everything wrong.

She's dead. He feels certain. He feels sick.

He can't see her face clearly, just her terror, her animal instinct to run that had quivered throughout her body had been a visceral impression.

He remembers the target, and he can see perfectly well the high contrast of the crazed glass and the destroyed head of the man, the dashboard lights and overhead light still on from the woman having left the front passenger door open, and the car's headlights on. That image doesn't bother him.

But maybe, he wonders, another rush of panic cresting, he accidently killed the woman. He tries his best to recall her image after she passed out, her lower legs catching the side-scattering light from the headlights, her two feet, one still shod with that absurd high heel, slumped, passed out.

Or dead!

He can't bring this into focus, as if that night in the woods in Minnesota swallowed everything in blackness but her lower legs, akimbo.

He had read up on usage and safety protocols and there

are many sources for this information and he cross-referenced enough to be confident he understood.

Buying the chloroform was far easier than he had assumed, and just moments into the web search he had dozens of companies to choose from, companies mostly with names like Lab Alley, Safeco Dental Supply, CP Lab Safety, The Science Company. He'd spent more time than he planned checking out a number of sites, and then he was checking on shipping policies, but these were lax, only requiring ground delivery and an address.

No flying with highly flammable liquid was his guess for the shipping choice.

He ordered a 500mL bottle of 99% Lab Grade, and it cost about $50, including shipping, although he had added a 2.5kg bottle of Potassium Nitrate, the total coming to just over $110. He used his credit card and took a private P.O. Box and figured that waiting around for a week for delivery might be dangerous but he had judged this an acceptable risk.

Everything had gone well. There were no FBI waiting for him at the mailbox. No eyebrows raised. He had used his own credit card for purchase and for the mailbox rental, and he's been only mildly anxious, but it all happened as he expected and then he resumed his trip up to Minnesota.

And now it feels like he can't move, his heart alternating between unsettlingly low calm and frantic racing. He's trying to remember what he did last night as he manages to pull at the blanket to move it off completely in hopes of getting up. He's hit with the faint ghost of smell and realizes the smell emanates from a small white folded cloth on the floor that's half under his pushed-off blanket and he remembers.

Worried about that woman, what happened to her, he tested the chlorophyll on himself.

Chloroform, he corrects himself. He still feels fuzzy in the brain.

He sits up, a bit dizzy from the effort, but he's looking

at the tiny dining table that is in its raised position and sees the 500mL bottle.

Idiot! he tells himself.

He had administered the chloroform to himself, a test, and he may have put too much on the cloth, or maybe kept it on his face for too long, or maybe, and he thinks this is most likely, misjudged the time and passed out with the cloth on his face.

He understands he could easily enough have killed himself.

Idiot! he tells himself.

His head is clearing. The cloth had fallen off, maybe when he passed out, maybe when moving his head dislodged it when he slumped unconscious, but the cloth fell to the floor, but the space was enclosed so he was kept under, or out of it, at least, for hours.

Explains this fucking headache, he tells himself. It feels like his head is splitting open from the top.

He stumbles up from the recliner, his strength returning slowly, and he unlatches the door, pushing it open. Cooler air comes into the van.

He steadies himself against the tiny fold-up table, his hand near the bottle.

Maybe he was unconsciously trying to kill himself, it occurs to him.

He shakes his head, picks up the folded cloth from the floor with two fingers, gingerly, and tosses it out through the open door.

He has to get to a library to check if the woman is all right, and the news story should be easy to find since he's sent off the KTR claim one state away from where he is now.

He is pretty sure she's fine.

Knowing that is the only tonic he needs.

He takes a few more deep breaths.

Idiot, he tells himself.

Chapter 23: Post Paterfamilia Prevarication

Recently for Davin, the *Berkshire Interactive* work is increasingly interesting, and Alicia seems to want him to take on yet more. He is at his desk in his second-floor office, and he's looking through his music streaming service trying to find a particular Dexter Gordon album he's been wanting to hear again. He finds bebop well suits the work he's doing, preparing yet another ads-to-sales monthly report. He's got Wi-Fi in his studio too, and he wants to be working there, but at this moment he'll resist the temptation of working on a sculpture he remains excited about.

Still, he's frustrated he's barely made any progress with a new piece, one he's been tinkering with, the one with the hundreds of broken wristwatches and the several clock dial faces he's been collecting over the years, his own and from flea markets. His frustration is tempered by the fact it's more likely his lack of studio time these days has as much or more to do with seeing Gloria, and he's not inclined to cut back on that. He's not a fan of the hour-plus drive to get up to North County, but he's a big fan of the time he spends with the gal, and a lot of that time is in bed.

Nope, time well spent, he thinks adamantly.

He may still feel confused about what or where the relationship might head but seeing her is fun.

Well, looking and touching, too, he tells himself.

On the other hand, the additional *BI* work means his

credit line debt is shrinking faster, and he keeps planning on getting a replacement house sharer for Deidre's old bedroom up on the north side of the house at the other end of the library room that separates his office on the south side. He's recently realized, though, he hadn't really thought this out nearly clearly enough. Only yesterday had it occurred to him to take this second-floor bedroom for himself and have his third-floor bedroom be for the new house sharer, since the idea of moving his office up into the south half of the finished attic space is unappealing. One reason is the sound isn't all that well blocked by the dividing wall from where Marsha has more or less colonized the other half of the attic space that is accessed from the stairs in her bedroom. If her sounds can bother him, his sounds would be no less welcome to her.

He swivels slowly around to look at his office he'd made larger by combining two smaller rooms. There are plenty of windows and light, and the whole length of the west side of the second floor, which includes the office, the library, the second floor bedroom, can be closed off from the long living room on the east side, either by keeping the door to the office shut, or by closing the living room door on the other side of the landing, or both. There are also two other entries into the library from the living room, including the original double doors nearer the southern end and the big sliding door at the northern end, so he could have the whole west side of the second floor to himself.

He likes this plan.

His office and the bedroom are well separated by the library room and the small bathroom in the middle of the long adjoining space, the bathroom bumping out to create the sense of two distinct parts of the long library room. He won't have to move his office, which makes a nice bonus, although he's concerned Deidre's old bedroom is smaller than his current bedroom on the third floor, but then his current bedroom doesn't have its own outside door that opens onto a small deck. Another advantage is that the second-floor bedroom is above the Airbnb apartment's main bedroom, and there have been one or two noise complaints across all the seasons the Airbnb has operated, and he'd be in control of the noise level from his end.

Of course, the apartment below isn't going to be available if he pulls the trigger on the Americabnb commitment.

When, not if, he reminds himself. He is going to do the Americabnb deal.

Unfortunately, no more squeezing in an occasional friend or family visit in between reservations. On the other hand, this change will mean the three bedrooms on the third floor will be entirely house sharers, which has its own benefits, including having the second-floor bathroom to himself.

Thinking of family visits has him pull up the recent text he's received from Gwen late in the evening before, at least late enough by her standards, not that he actually knows what hours Gwen keeps these days. But she'd always been the early-to-bed sort, so the hour the text arrived was itself something of a surprise, even if the bigger surprise is to get a text at all. His contact with Gwen is light, and has been ever since she moved out.

Her text suggested he call his daughter. *Chat with Merri, she's upset, she'll like that.*

The text itself is strange, considering he has been thinking a lot about his daughter, and her husband, of course, since he really likes the fellow and they do share some important common interests, like making cocktails. The other thing he has in common with Marco is that only the two of them call Merri Skip. She doesn't mind and even seems to like it, although he and Marco are the only ones that call her this anymore, or at least he still often calls her that, a childhood nickname with no discernable connection with her given name, Merri, at least nothing he can actually recall, but she'll always be his little Skippy.

But while he and Merri don't email with any great

frequency, when they do it's more like an old-fashioned letter and always at some length, and her most recent one had struck him as sounding down, which is why he's been thinking of her, and Gwen's odd text pushes him to action.

It's late morning now, which means he can catch Skip at the end of her workday, if graduate students have such a schedule. With the six-hour difference, he figures he'll find her in, although she can always answer anywhere with her phone, but he's never liked that sort of semi-public video chat.

He is using a new video-call app, but he's old enough to usually call any such video conversation platform activity Skyping. He sometimes gets grief about that, but he will typically respond by saying something about *Kleenex* or *Frigidaire*, and at least that gives him some comfort in having confused the person busting his chops.

As for his daughter, the previous time they connected in a video call, she claimed she was currently majoring in word processing, making a joke out of being knee-deep in the writing of her own dissertation. It had been disturbing to him to glimpse Gwen passing by in the background in their Barcelona apartment, still there, although leaving in a day or two according to his daughter, who informed him that her mother was getting ready to head back home, her leave of absence over.

Skip had seemed bothered, even terse, in that last video conversation he'd had with her, that thought had crossed his mind. He hasn't seen her or her husband since they moved to Spain for the graduate work, and though there are regular video chats, those are not great replacements for real contact. There are plenty of reasons why he hasn't yet seen where they live, and one big one—one he doesn't like to admit—is that he's reluctant to pay the airfare. Flying has become so expensive.

Proportionally costly, relative to the growth in the discomfort, he can't help thinking. There's something, too, about the carbon tax provision for aviation that will further boost the price of an airline ticket.

Marco is working in the Computational Linguistics and Theory Research Group at *Universitat Pompeu Fabra*, in Barcelona, although Davin believes that Marco is now involved in the university's Artificial Intelligence and Machine Learning Research Group, somehow. He remains generally confused about what is, exactly, Marco's area of focus, although he's been reluctant to ask since he has still not tackled Marco's dissertation a year out from receiving it, and he's pretty sure the post-doc work is something else anyway.

Whatever, he thinks.

The video call had confused him with learning of Gwen's long visit, but what was more important was that Skip had seemed off. He'd figured she was just busy with her dissertation work or otherwise distracted by the life she's living as a doctoral candidate and with her Spanish husband, living in the center of Barcelona in what looks like a rather chic area from what he could best determine checking out her neighborhood on Google Street View, a bit of well-intentioned fatherly online stalking.

He still feels a mixture of envy and shame for begrudging Gwen this time with their daughter. He had been surprised at his reaction to seeing just a momentary whirl of Gwen coming into the frame and out again, and it had felt hallucinogenic in some way, or like a haunting. Even years after the final decree, he still has waves of feelings when he has any kind of contact with Gwen, contact that can include, it would appear, a brief background digital video image. Or even, often, simply when her name comes up in conversation.

His thoughts are interrupted by Skip answering his call, the blackening sky of the advanced time zone adding a halo-like glare on the window reflection behind her.

"Not *la hora del vermut* yet?" is the first thing he says, just kidding, continuing to tease the two of them this way after Marco waxed so enthusiastically when they'd first gotten to Barcelona, so grateful to be back where vermouth bars are still a thing. The first minute or two of their video conversation are the usual *how are yous* and *anything new*, but she looks tired and he asks if something is wrong.

Skip is silent for a beat, and then she asks, "Did Mom call you?"

"What's going on?" he asks, ignoring her question.

She's silent again for a moment, and then looks at him, or at the video representation of him, anyway, and says, "I don't know. We're, Marco and I are going through this thing right now, about having kids."

He assumes she is announcing she's pregnant, and a grin is forming, but she adds, "Well, about not having children, actually."

"Huh," Davin says.

Skip doesn't add anything.

"Well, are you okay, is Marco saying he doesn't want children? Are you upset, what's going on?" he asks in a rush.

"No, Dad, it's more me than him, he's still trying to figure out how he feels."

Davin is beginning to understand what he's hearing from his daughter is pretty much the opposite of a pregnancy heads-up.

"Well," he says, and then pauses, having no idea what he's trying to say.

Skip sighs audibly. "Yeah, I figured you'd be disappointed," and he can see, he thinks, a shadow of hurt on her face.

"Hey, hey, hey," he says. "No, I'm not. I mean that is always going to be up to you, I'm just surprised a bit, that's all."

"Okay," she says.

"Just, uh, what is your thinking around this, is it just a feeling, or, well, are there reasons?" Now he's getting worried something is going badly wrong in the marriage, and a ghost of anger starts pushing up toward Marco.

Apparently, Skip can read his thoughts because she tells him Marco has been great about her decision, although she knows he's disappointed.

"We started talking about starting a family as soon as my oral defense gets done, but that got me thinking, I mean, I'd already been thinking about bringing a child into the world, but, well, this all started to feel real, suddenly, then, and —"

"—so you're closing in on the final dissertation submission," Davin interrupts. "Well, that must feel good."

"Um, sure?" she says, making Davin feel like a complete idiot.

"No, sorry, I didn't mean it that way. It's just that we haven't talked about how all that is going, not for a while, and I'm glad, but, yeah, I'd like to stay on topic."

She nods.

"So tell me what you are thinking," he adds.

She's still nodding.

"I just think it isn't a good time to have a child, not with the way things are going."

Now it's his turn to nod into his laptop camera. He steals a quick glance at the tiny screen of his own image, and even he can't tell anything about his expression. His face feels frozen.

"I know there's progress," she says, "but it's coming slow, too slow, all the best analyses I can find, they're saying things are going to be even rougher, for like decades."

"The climate," he says.

She nods. "Yes, and all the other related things, the economy, the collapse of all these ecologies, you know, I study this, I get to see the science, half of my fieldwork had to keep getting rescheduled and some just dropped because of the heat wave last year."

Davin knows Barcelona has been caught in cycles of heat waves, just about every year, with some summers far worse than others. Last year his daughter and Marco had to stay on campus, in cooling shelters, for almost three weeks.

"I mean, it's nothing for you or Mom to worry about, we're in a good situation here," she adds, "but that is just one example, and I know you read the papers, the news."

"Yeah," he says. "But there's progress, right? We might be behind the Paris Agreement benchmarks, sure, things take more time, always do..." but he trails off. He has a pretty good sense of where the climate crisis is at the moment, and that it doesn't look great. He thinks he has a pretty good idea about what's coming.

Skip just looks at him.

"Look," he says. "I know you are super smart, you know how to think about things, that, well..." and he trails off again, but Skip jumps in.

"A lot of us are thinking this way, Daddy," she tells him.

He notices her use of her favorite thing to call him, *Daddy*, or sometimes just plain *Dee*. He hasn't heard that for quite a while, and it almost breaks him down.

She starts talking about BirthStrike, an organization he recognizes has been around for a decade or more, but he's still surprised Skip is part of it.

She's talking about what she's seeing from her field work on microplastics and all the new research on anoxia events, and he knows she knows what she's talking about.

"It's astonishing, awful, what's going on here in the Mediterranean, and of course the problems are everywhere."

Davin wants to close his eyes, but he doesn't, thinking Skip may take this as something, a judgement, something in his reaction she can misinterpret. For a moment he is self-conscious about holding his expression, but then he's nodding his head, and then tells her he knows this, but still, choosing not to have kids, that's a big deal, but she interrupts him.

"No, really, that's one of the problems, this expectation. I'll send you some links if you'd like. There's a great site by Conceivable Future, explains what I'm saying better than I am here about how much carbon load each new child is every year, about sixty tons of carbon for each child being raised in the nations of the developed world."

He's heard the figure cited, and what he recalls is the figure 57.2 tons, from some recently read article, but there's no reason to point out this number is trending down. Because, really, it isn't, not in any significant way. He remains quiet.

She's citing a few other sites and organizations, but what catches his attention is her claim that well over one-third of young people in the developed nations are concerned enough about climate to have fewer kids or none at all. He's heard something along these lines, but only now, talking with his anguished, determined daughter, does it become real.

"Oh Skippy," he says, quietly, his heart filling with a confusion of feelings.

"It's okay, Dee," she says, that well-known grin of hers appearing, or maybe it's just a touch of relief. "It's okay," she repeats. "I love you too."

Chapter 24: Externally Yours

Everyone brings something to the game, and his operative certainly has high value, but Greene can't stop himself wondering about the progress of Lobinski's assignments. He won't call him for a status report, of course, since minimizing contact just makes sense, even if it would be his security man making the actual contact, and on the new burners at that. The trouble with conspiracies is people can really never keep their mouths shut and nothing is ever really hidden, so it's always best to reduce exposure up the chain. He knows Lobinski is good at operational security and good at getting those above him to know he's good at that, but the bigger the play the more nervous Greene feels.

He's pacing in his office, which is how he best works out complex problems, and the Sea Wall Act strategy is one of the most complex he's ever undertaken.

And the most risky, he tells himself, thinking about all the secret actions he's instigating to shape things his way. Lobinsky should be getting to his list now that he has the KTR material, and that means a couple of Greene's problems will be solved. This is a big play, trying to engineer the shift toward an independent agency for the Sea Wall Act and in a manner that will make the agency advantageous to his patrons. It depends on having this act designate the agency as independent so that it becomes more likely his secret funders can use the allocations to capture contracts.

There a few key players in the way.

Still, the larger part of the strategy, though, is guarding

fossil fuel subsidies. These subsidies, or *That Which Must Not Be Named*, as Greene likes to think of them, have always been too important not to protect, and for *The Gang* there is the growing anxiety about the money at risk. The subsidies are growing vulnerable, moving closer to being front and center in climate debates. It's likely to become harder dealing with these kinds of growing political pressures despite all the influence money being thrown around, so his argument is to keep externalities from being seriously addressed. He must avoid and shift toward factoring in pollution and global warming as part of the intrinsic cost of goods and production of fossil fuels would drop hundreds of billions of dollars in costs each year squarely on the big oil companies.

Shit tax is how he thinks of the so-called indirect subsidies going away. His people suddenly having to pay to clean up their own mess, and that's a game changer. His clients know this, and they know that it isn't just the big additional costs that hurt the bottom line. Having to address the real cost of fossil fuel would make fossil fuels seen as even less competitive against renewable energy.

That's all she wrote, over and out, all bets are off, Katie bar the door, he recites, an old habit when noting a bad turn or a likely fatal turn of events. He tells himself that he's not that worried. The subject of externalities is difficult to understand, but that's a good thing since that means it's difficult for most people to grasp, even legislators.

Especially legislators, he tells himself.

A lot of the external costs that are currently passed along are hard to quantify, although he knows a consensus exists that underpricing fossil fuels by ignoring local air pollution is a big chunk of it, and he'd once seen the complex formula the IMF uses to determine the contribution of air pollution to fossil fuel's cost. The formula had been blown up to poster-size and framed like a piece of art and hung up on the wall of an outgoing legislature director's tiny office in Rayburn. Greene had claimed it as a prize, having been the one to deliver the news that the legislature director was getting shit-canned, and there and then at that.

His pacing brings him past his desk, and he stops at the mantle behind it, looking at the newly placed image, now out of storage, leaning on the mantle. The enlarged photostat of the five-line stack of sets and operations makes the sort of statistical analysis he'd done in his fieldwork back in his doctoral research days look like simple arithmetic, but he can follow along well enough to see the legitimacy of the argument. A similar process set, but longer and even more complex, has been printed out and taped to the bottom of the frame, the formula for figuring the cost contribution of fossil fuel climate change consequences. Over the past decade, climate change has been the much bigger externality cost factor to indemnify.

The office visit when he'd taken this framed work was shortly after the LNG export fight a half dozen years earlier. Pressure had been brought to bear for the legislature director's dismissal, post-defeat, and Greene, early in his tenure at Kehoe, was asked by a board member to deliver a message from them. He's put the framed photostat up to keep him focused what is important.

The Gang plays rough, he reminds himself.

These days, the other side is playing pretty damn rough too, he considers as he turns to pace some more.

The trick, he's arguing, will be to concede some of the defined subsidies that are in the form of direct government aid or fee forgiveness or some sort of tax or accounting advantage, both federal and state. The biggest attacks on subsidies over the last several years have focused on the direct subsidies and focused on these mainly because the direct subsidies are easy to identify and to understand as a matter of tax codes and specific legislative rulings. This looks like big money, but their totals pale in comparison to what the fossil fuel industry would face in added costs for addressing the pollution and global warming.

But we will use that, he tells himself, stepping back

toward his desk to scribble down some notes, a flush of excitement rolling over him as he considers the strategy in play. They can highlight all the renewable energy subsidies, like those provided through the IRA, and that contrast will be helpful in pushing the idea of renewables' reliance on subsidies.

Not that Trump could get much satisfaction in his fight to take back some of those billions, he well knows. The new administration is already frantic with new programs and proposals that will add billions more in support for climate programs. Big Oil's grudging acceptance of the end of some of these legislated or executive action fossil fuel subsidies will effectively counter the opposition's still-confused calls to consider the much larger potential real costs. This willingness to surrender some of the direct subsidies might even make the oil industry as a whole look fiscally responsible.

And we'll be the fucking heroes, Greene thinks, quite happy to take a hit to avoid the larger hit.

Take a hit, collect the kitty, he tells himself, but knowing the judo moves he's considering may well end up with him flat on his back if he plays this wrong.

Standing at his desk, he adds a note to identify all the direct subsidies and quantify the monetary impact. He knows there is really no doubt that at least some of the pre-tax subsidies are going away anyway, despite all the American Petroleum Institute's bravado. API has been a weak sister the last few years, notwithstanding all the money still being thrown at them. He thinks there are good reasons to hope some of that money could come Kehoe Institute's way.

The intercom buzzes, and he stretches across the desk to snag the phone.

"Yeah," he says, and after a brief moment he tells his assistant to reschedule the call.

"Jesus," he says. "Yeah, reschedule the fucking call. I know he's a senator, jesus," and he tosses the receiver back into its cradle.

His young assistant can drive him crazy. The kid keeps getting confused about his job, always slipping in advice as if he has every right and obligation to do so.

Greene is fine with putting the senator's call off. This particular senator is one of the ones he is worried about, despite the guy's steady support on all the right issues in the past, but the guy's state has had some trouble with bad weather, including a big flood last fall, and then, in the eastern part of the state there are still some wildfires going, although these seem likely to be fully contained soon enough.

If the weather brings rain, anyway, he admits and he reminds himself to check on the current conditions before he calls the senator back.

Greene jabs at the intercom.

"Espresso, double, sugar on the side," he tells his assistant, and his assistant is answering with a simple *Yup* that is cut off with Greene's jab breaking the connection. He settles himself on the front edge of the desk, arms crossed.

The real work is to protect indirect subsidies because the difference between consumers' fuel prices today and how much consumers would have to pay, is not good for his people. If prices fully reflect exact. By keeping supply costs plus the money needed to remediate environmental costs that the production and use of fossil fuels out of the pricing equation, he knows consumers pay less and use more and fossil fuel companies spend less and make more profits on volume. The loss of some pre-tax and legislated subsidies is nearly nothing comparatively to the potential externalities' cost consequences. Even the fossil fuel industry's hit from the recent Carbon Tax Bill is peanuts, relatively speaking, with those modest costs getting passed on to consumers.

The loss on the Carbon Tax Bill still irks him, but everyone on his side of the issue knows it is going to keep getting harder.

It isn't like climate change isn't real, he tells himself.

He laughs out loud at this thought, but there's a quick knock on the door and his assistant is coming through with the tray with his espresso, and Greene feels a bit embarrassed to be caught laughing, but he covers this by snapping at the young man to put the tray on the coffee table.

After the assistant retreats, Greene sits on the couch, leaning forward over the tray, spooning some sugar into the brimming espresso cup. He carefully brings the cup to his lips to take a small sip.

At least the kid makes a good espresso, he's willing to admit.

How best to protect these so-called indirect subsidies is the question at hand. He hates the term, but the more accurate descriptor is *costs*, and he hates that more. He knows he'll have more sympathetic legislators than the makeup of this Congress would otherwise suggest, because low fuel pricing keeps voters happy and current gas prices are already polling as a negative.

He also knows that he's more than happy to let his opponents argue that the true cost of gas and other fossil fuel products should be much higher. That is an argument he will never wish to be associated with in the public arena.

Still, with more voters supporting climate laws, the price argument is getting muddier, and some of the pre-tax subsidies have been around for a century in the States. Cheap oil has long driven economic growth, but such subsidies are no longer needed with oil both long mature as an industry and profitable.

It's all enough to make him miss the Peak Oil days, back to the 1990s and early aughts when his predecessors championed oil reserve scarcity to get more concessions and subsidy support for exploration and drilling. He'd just been getting established, working at the Heartland Institute as a newly minted program director, and by then that message's value was already on the wane, the victim of the industry's own success, especially with fracking.

It's now a game of giving as little ground as possible, he

knows.

He goes back to the coffee table and picks up the tiny cup.

At least the kid makes a good cup of espresso, he thinks.

Chapter 25: RE: CC

Jeannie Louise has been busy. The model for the articles for which Alicia Soares signed her could easily enough be applied to any area in the world and so this work will likely lead to more writing assignments in other markets if she wants. She knows this sort of local climate change speculation could easily become something of a cottage industry, but so far she hasn't had the opportunity to actually write more than a couple of articles for *BI*.

If I can find the time, she reminds herself

She's in her kitchen, waiting for the electric kettle to boil, the small teapot at the ready.

The projections for expected climate shifts are getting better and better, and that makes her own work that much better.

Well, worse, she reconsiders, having just been looking over updates and new models and seeing more and more dire news.

More accurate news, she corrects herself.

She knows pretty much front to back such resources as the 2014 IPCC Report, an effort spearheaded by the UN, called *Climate Change 2014: Impacts, Adaptions, and Vulnerability, from Working Group II of the IPCC*. She keeps up with all of the updates published every five years, too. The report title is a real mouthful and typical Geneva-based bureaucratese, but she has no doubt it's one of those seminal efforts to describe, in brass tack terms, the short-, mid-, and long-term expectations for the climate. The latest report is over a thousand pages long, and even the summary — which

Jeannie Louise insists to most every person she talks to that they read — is almost 200 pages. Maybe that's what happens when you have 309 lead authors, another 436 contributing authors, and 1,729 expert and government reviewers, she considers. And that was just for the first time around, in 2014. The number of contributors in subsequent reports has only grown larger.

She knows part of her value as a writer on climate change is the great job she does tracking what has become an ever-growing number of climate change reports and other content from the UN, and research universities, think tanks, and the various and many governmental and non-government organizations. The bad news for her, she knows, is that comprehensive tracking is growing increasingly difficult and steadily more time-consuming as climate change research expands seemingly exponentially. The effort takes a lot of her time, but in one way, at least, that too is good news as far as she's concerned, since the barrier to entry in the scale of effort is that much harder to overcome for those coming late to the game.

What a game, she thinks.

For as long as she's been writing, the enormous amounts of time she puts in makes for unimpressive earnings on a per hour basis, she's sure. The tracking of core information has improved since the early days, before the emergence of the UN Framework Convention on Climate Change helped coalesce resources. These days, her articles still have scientific and forecasting conditions playing a supporting role, but over time her writing has focused more and more on politics, quite different from those early days of simple extrapolation of climate effects. These days, her articles tackle more complexity in *RE: CC*.

She is quite proud of the blog name: *Concerning Climate Change*.

But if only I can find the time, she thinks. She reflexively checks the kitchen windowsill, grabbing the bottle of Adderall and is relieved to see that, yes, as she thought, this is the unopened bottle, and that is a comfort, although she can get worried she goes through the pills at a faster and faster clip.

She pours the boiling water into the small teapot. It's the afternoon, and there are three teabags in the small pot, but since her conversation with Davin yesterday, it feels like she needs all the caffeine she can get.

She ran into him when dropping by *BI* for a quick hello with Alicia, and Davin had asked her out for a coffee, wanting to talk with her, he said, "About where we can take this stuff," waving his arm vaguely about, indicating, she had momentarily mistakenly assumed, the *BI* office.

The resulting talk was strange, but in the end, interesting, if a bit too wandering.

He first talked about his early career and how he got into digital content infrastructure, after they'd settled into their seats at Fuel, a Main Street coffeehouse a short walk from the new *Berkshire Interactive* office.

"Used to cover the rise of electronic publishing, back in the days of the emergence of multimedia, then later doing the content management and consulting thing," Davin had told her.

"Okay," had been her reply. She knew much of that already and found herself wondering if Davin didn't remember some of their earlier conversations.

And then he set off on what he was doing at *Berkshire Interactive*, and his remuneration model, and how this was the best content management gig he'd ever had, even if some of the payout was likely still mostly in the future, if anything, and then he was rambling—she thought, especially at one particularly explosive moment, that he was kind of scat-singing—and then he took a dramatically deep breath and made a face, his eyebrows shooting up. He said in a normal voice, "Sorry. I'm kind of hyped up at the moment," and then he ordered a coffee.

He's actually entertaining, she'd found herself realizing midway or so through the conversation, but now it occurs to her the conversations might be better described as monologues. He started in on yet another exhaustingly fast roundup about his and his wife's move out here, and then mentioned his divorce, and then he caught himself again.

Jeannie could see it right in his face, a bit of a blush.

"Sorry," he then said, and then with a bit of a soft grunt or laugh, "I don't get out much."

She hadn't anything to say to that.

"Your articles are great, by the way," he said. "I was known as 'Long-form Caine' in the business, always only interested in really tackling a subject, like you."

Then he blinked. "Not like you as a subject, but you're getting into the substance, really helping people understand context and details, so they're able to go on their own from there."

She had nodded.

"Like you do, just about the best stuff I've read on climate change, ever," he continued. "So thanks."

She then found herself wondering if the conversation was over, but before she figured that out conclusively, he was back at it, talking about new models for trying to make some money publishing online and how creating content digitally provided a lot of opportunities previously unavailable for authors, including building articles that offer different levels of depth.

She had held up her hand to interrupt.

He stopped.

"I've got some deadlines," she said, but it only took a moment for her to realize she should have spelled this out more clearly, as Davin simply continued.

"Even though you have only started in *Berkshire Interactive*, your jump in the number of views is really strong, you should look at getting a sliding rate depending on the analytics."

She had thought she was understanding his point. "You mean, get a higher fee if the articles, my stuff, get a lot of traffic?" was how she put it.

"Exactly. Not just eyeballs," he answered. "The good news about the publishing platform we're on is that the analytics engine is really detailed, so you can see if people are reading the whole piece or clicking through on the notes and links to other stuff you've done, you know, that you've added, included, or other references, and track the actions of the visitors, the readers, of the article in terms of whether they click through an ad, even down to, sort of, how well they click through, which we can track to some degree, especially when the advertiser fully opts into our system."

He stopped to take a sip of his new coffee, finally.

"Anyway," he said.

She told him it sounded interesting.

"I think so," he said. "There's even stuff we can do with syndication, which your stuff would be really good for, I think." He paused for a moment, possibly to take a breath. "Your piece in *South County*, sorry, *Berkshire Interactive*, on the potential carbon reduction from using the Housatonic and the old dams and old sites for hydro is a good example."

Well, she had thought, *it better be since you gave me that assignment*.

He kept right on talking. "Do versions for the Northwest, other New England states, that sort of thing, use some of the same reference material and link back to our serving the ads, that could amount to something, and there's the whatever fees you'd get for the versions too," he went on before taking another breath. "Obviously not much for the hydro piece for the Southwest, or Midwest, I'd guess, but just an example.

"And anytime you use a government-published report or whatever," Davin then said, "that's public domain, and we can just bring in those links inside, but for the copyrighted stuff, we can always do a window in our tab and still track out-link action, and those out-link metrics have plenty of possibilities to track, which, in turn, may further contribute to your remuneration."

"Always a good thing," she replied.

"Of course," he nodded.

"Not to blow smoke," he continued, "there's not all that much action yet for me to grab a piece, but it is growing. Doing things like getting contributors involved, like I've been saying to you, helps potentially grow the action, which means we're talking about more revenue coming in. Of course, the local soft stuff, like restaurant reviews, theater or art coverage, whatever, generate links or at least encourage advertisers, but your stuff," and then Davin paused, looking right across at her, "I'm pushing as an experiment really, but looking at the kind of work you like to do, I think you will want to be part of, so…" And then he had simply stopped.

"Here's my email address," he then said, taking out a pen and what looked to her to be the back of a Big Y receipt, but then he stopped, and mentioned she had the contact information. "I have yours, too, obviously," he then remarked, although it took Jeannie Louise a moment to realize he probably was the one who set up her *Berkshire Interactive* email in the first place.

Chapter 26: Hey, Gang, Let's Put on a Show!

Greene is sitting behind his desk, leaning back for a moment. He knows he's got a compelling argument that supports the defensive play he's positioning. The angle is to give up as many pre-tax subsidies as necessary to keep the indirect subsidies arguments off the table.

It's always just an ROI argument.

The Gang, as best he figures, collectively spends $600 million-plus a year on the institutes, the PACs, the lobbying, the campaign contributions, but retaining the indirect subsidies pays back much more. The latest value assessment from IMF for fossil fuel companies not addressing externalities is $6.2 trillion per annum, worldwide.

There's no harm showing the stakes. He's got a copy of that latest IMF report somewhere around, and after rummaging through the second drawer he recovers it and starts skimming the text until he finds what he's looking for. *Efficient fossil fuel pricing in 2029 would have lowered global carbon emissions by 28 percent and fossil fuel air pollution deaths by 46 percent, and increased government revenue by 3.8 percent of GDP*, he reads.

Well, fuck me, he says to himself, wondering how best to counter this, but he is thinking the whole statistical assessment assumptions are easily enough questioned, *so, there*. The Carbon Tax Bill has taken some of the fossil fuel industry's costs advantages away over the year, but the bill is largely based on the pass-along costs approach, so if carbon costs increase everyone pays, not just the fossil fuel companies.

And Joe Blow increasingly will be unhappy.

He'll need to really think through both the value and defensibility of the specific direct subsidies he's arguing could be horse-traded as needed, so he picks up the information he's printed out earlier. He figures he'll start with reexamining the *Intangible Drilling Costs Deduction (26 US Code § 263)*, but he quickly scans the list and puts a tick next to *Percentage Depletion (26 US Code § 613), Credit for Clean Coal Investment Internal Revenue Code § 48A and 48V,* and *Nonconventional Fuels Tax Credit Internal Revenue Code § 45* because each of the IRS codes ring faint bells.

He takes a moment to look these acts up and sees two of them sunsetted in 2014.

The Foreign Tax Credit can be protected, he's pretty sure, since there are other industries that want this to remain, but even if that changes, not a big hit, relatively speaking. He sees that *Master Limited Partnerships* is on the list, and he's always loved MLPs because this gives publicly traded corporations, and mostly fossil fuel companies, the tax benefits of partnerships, exempting the corporations from some corporate income taxes. He also loves the MLP code because the provision is specifically not available to renewable energy companies.

"All right, going on since the Revenue Act of 1987," he says out loud, sitting back, looking away from the monitor up to the ceiling, arms clasped behind his head. He can see that with the long-running and still-growing outcry about corporations not paying taxes, this one should be very useful as a bargaining chip, but he'll need a more accurate assessment of potential monetary value before any legislative wrangling starts.

He sits forward again, looking through more of the marked-up position paper, now rereading the section titled "Fossil Fuel Research, Development, and Deployment," which sketches the history of various funds out of DOE and other Federal R&D programs, but his own marginal notes remain unchanged. *A fight here is just not worth it*, he had written. Any of these programs could be sacrificed, and he's identifying some inevitable compromises he can trade on toward control of the Sea Wall Act pool of monies. Not pursuing the proposals for changes in The Carbon Tax Bill might offer a lot of cover. The in-place step-down schedule on that bill's tax credit limits he considers a mixed bag, but a case can be made that any bill that increases gas prices has a tactical benefit in driving price anxiety.

The only DOE funding that is big money is on the carbon capture side, and there's been some wins there for some of the corporations, although only in securing grants and tax credits, not so much in succeeding in making direct carbon capture efficient and economically scalable.

He confidently believes giving up fossil fuels' direct subsidies — *as few as possible, of course* — will be useful to gain support for an independent Sea Wall Agency.

Help make the corporations look like they're in the fight against climate change, too, is how he thinks of the argument.

The most important thing is to keep the externalities out of cost considerations. That's the point he needs to drive home. That's the ROI hit against which all other givebacks, cost-savings, and direct subsidies pale.

And that's trillions, with a "t," my friends.

Chapter 27: The File Folder
is Getting Older

Lobinski looks at the closed file folder lying near his thigh as he sits on the bed in a small motel room. The motel is old-style and the front desk is light on questions. The motel is close enough to the interstate to provide the steady strumming of long-haul trucks. From the few days he has been in residence, his suspicion has been growing that the motel is used more for trysts than solid slumber, given what he hears through the walls across the late afternoons and evenings.

He has been getting up by 4:00 a.m. all this week, off to his assignment's neighborhood in one of the suburban areas of Bethesda.

The FBI file he received was plenty good enough to build a convincing facsimile of a KTR claim statement, but it's even easier now that a few more KTR claims have emerged to build up numbers beyond the three brief statements included in the file. The FBI hasn't been able to keep the claim notes from the public, a near-impossible task since the postings typically get copied to a number of online news sites and they always want the scoop. The FBI file includes a report on the claims posting methodologies, all different except for a group of KTR posts all similarly stripped of the metadata and obscured in their online posting routes shrouded by bounce-back servers and anonymity servers.

There have been several more KTR claims since the file

was compiled, including two KTR claim assignments of his own, the most recent a simple enough kill using one of his rifles, the Remington 700 with a nice scope, but nothing fancy. That assignment was a Washington lawyer, a partner in a firm well-known as a top fixer, but otherwise not widely known by the public.

Although, of course, the killing has gained the firm plenty of attention.

Well, the first one did too, he reminds himself. *And every one since, mine and all the others.* Kill the Rich claims are all front-page news these days.

His own assignments using KTR cover had more than sufficient financial assets not to stand out as outliers, although the first three KTR victims in the news were from a different and highest class of wealth, with billions of dollars of assets. His most recent assignment had wealth, but only some tens of millions of dollars' worth, and that included the firm's partner share value. The first of his assignments had been richer, according to the news reports, although still short of the billionaire class.

Lobinsky feels bad about the man — *the collateral damage* — who had been there with the first assignment.

Well, nothing to do about it.

He is confident he handled that situation exactly right. The other man had simply been in the wrong place at the wrong time, but the kill assignment he's working on now is going to be a lot more complicated. The plan is to make this look like death by natural causes, and a KTR claim is fallback only if it goes wrong.

He frowns, knowing this objective is a major pain in the ass, but he also knows that the level of difficulty tends to average out. The most recent assignment completed is a case in point, taking only modest planning that didn't go far beyond finding the best vantage on the assignment's home and simply waiting for the exposure opportunity. With the nice weather, the assignment's habit of taking breakfast on the back patio made the shot easy from up on the wooded slope less than 400 yards distance. After, he had only to walk back through the woods to the change vehicle he'd parked tucked behind a commercial building for lease.

The woman, undoubtedly the assignment's wife, didn't start screaming immediately, at least that had been his sense as he was still breaking down the rifle. He feels bad about the woman having to see the head shot, but he knows it's best to keep these things as simple as possible.

There are two KTR incidents in the recent news that have suspects in custody. He is convinced these incidents are not in the same class of accomplishments as described in the FBI file. The methodologies are very different, too, both basically walk-up shootings, in public settings.

Still, that doesn't explain the female suspect's arrest, nor does it answer the question of whether there is an actual KTR group or simply copycatting by people with some grievance or another who somehow thought to emulate KTR for cover.

Oh, wait, that's what I'm doing, Lobinski tells himself, the thought making him scoff.

If the woman turns out to be part of some KTR group, then as far as he's concerned it looks like KTR is having difficulty with quality enrollments. In this case, the female suspect remained free less than half a day, but her posted claim was traced back within minutes of the email's receipt by a local newspaper, with the arrest following soon after.

Certainly not the sophisticated stealth routing of earlier KTR claims.

The other so-called KTR arrest was even worse. The man who shot another man on the street had a KTR claim printout in his jacket pocket, and it's possible he meant to drop it next to his victim, but he never got around to doing that, getting tackled by people on the street.

That's the trouble with not getting trained, he tells himself. The man fired all five rounds from a revolver, if the papers got that detail right, and then dropped the gun and then stared at the man he had shot as that man, dead or dying, lay sprawled on the sidewalk.

And then the man was summarily grabbed by bystanders, who held him until the police arrived.

He is sure the man had never shot anyone before, had never killed before, and had reacted in an entirely predictable manner, entirely botching the effort.

Well, not botched from the dead man's perspective, I guess, he considers for a moment.

It's his sense that the two arrested are would-be copycats with some level of ineptitude and fantasy at play, although perhaps each of them really believed they would hide behind KTR and get away with the killings.

Amateurs.

Although his very first KTR assignment on the face of it looked a lot like the arrested man's effort in that it was a public street assassination, there were a few key differences. This first of his assignments was in the habit of dining on Tuesdays at the same restaurant and liked to dine on the sidewalk patio. This was known to Lobinski because he had done the surveillance.

He had simply walked close and shot the man, but with a suppressor. Suppressed pistols, when fired, are still loud, but the sound is different and usually confuses people not in the know.

The only problem was the man was not alone.

The only problem was that the other man's eyes and his met, and so identification would be more likely. It didn't take him any noticeable amount of time to shoot this man too.

And then he had simply walked away, moving at a reasonable city sidewalk pace, the pistol down along the side of his leg.

Don't dawdle, walk right, and know where you are going.

He had walked to the closest corner, pulling off his tie while placing the pistol in his leather messenger bag. As he rounded the corner, he unslung the messenger bag as the commotion behind him rose. But he kept focused, taking off the suit jacket he had been wearing, stuffing the suit jacket in the bag, and swapping the jacket for a colorful windbreaker. He rounded another corner as he made these moves, the plan of route clear, and next he pulled a ball cap from the windbreaker pocket and donned it without ceremony. Then on the second to last corner, he thrust his hand back into the bag for a different hat, pulled off the ballcap and with it the wig he had been wearing, swapping in the new hat, a hipster straw fedora. The windbreaker also came off and he rounded the last corner in shirtsleeves and walked two car lengths to his pickup car and then drove off.

He tossed the messenger bag with the gun and the clothing at the first safe moment, stopping on the bridge he knew he would be crossing, scanning for people who might be in view. He hadn't even waited for the splash before he was on his way toward his legitimate rental car.

That's how you don't get caught.

There have been two more unsolved KTR murders that look much more like the first several killings. Like the first ones, these later ones showed signs of smart planning and left nothing in the way of solid leads, but then he checks his thoughts on this, trying to avoid conclusions since he can't be sure he has the complete files on those cases. Still, he would guess plenty of care had been taken by the perpetrator, considering the latest press announcements by the FBI equivocate any clear sense of a suspect for those cases. In fact, they seem inclined to think it's likely different suspects are involved, touting the investigations with the arrested individuals in custody.

He's not buying it. He suspects there's an original KTR, although his own walk-up hit helps push the multiple-KTR-participants theory, since it was closely coincident with the San Diego claim. His study of the file and his reading of news articles on the more recent unsolved incidents all indicate deep planning and complicated setups, including the latest, in San Diego, with the exploding boat. The killings without suspects in custody suggest an almost absurd amount of surveillance and planning and are just plain odd in the executions, with a mix of professional and amateur that suggests to him there may be only one real KTR actor. But he'll admit he doesn't really have any more to support his theory than the FBI task force might have to support their theories.

He shrugs and picks up the folder, tapping edges straight and then putting it back down on the bed.

What he does know is the capture of the two newest would-be KTR claimants will make his work easier since he is now freer in the form and content of any claims he might make. Still, he has studied the person in the FBI file, and he thinks of that person as the real KTR actor, so he'll continue to cleave closer to that style because that person seems smart and he likes smart.

Smart enough, anyway, he thinks.

He stands up and grabs a bottle of water, twisting off the cap. He starts drinking it down while standing in front of the drawn blinds, looking out through the gaps.

He sees two cars pull into the far side parking. A man gets out of one and a woman out of the other. They lock each of their cars, arms out pressing the key fobs in almost synchronized time before walking together toward the same motel room.

A couple without luggage.

He puts his speculation about what they may be up to out of his mind, thinking instead about the challenges in email tracking. He knows the email claim posting routes can be reconstituted, but it will take warrants in some cases, and then only once the originator IP is identified. By the time one or another of the posting Internet providers is found, it's likely to be a public network, so any fieldwork and interviewing will be cold and unlikely to produce specific and actionable leads.

I'd use disguises, Lobinski considers, appreciating KTR's obvious yet effective moves, but of course that could be a wrong assumption, and the investigation could break faster if that person's presence can be established at any of the relevant IP origination sites, not that it matters.

It doesn't matter that he appreciates the work of the KTR person, and it doesn't matter how many might be part of the group. He knows with any group, it is communication between and among the participants that is most likely to produce leads. At the time of his receipt of the file, the FBI and NSA seem to have nothing of that sort of intel, although he knows the file he's been given is probably not comprehensive, and he knows the file is now hardly up to date.

He tosses the empty water bottle into the small trash can next to what passes as a side table of some sort. He starts in on his stretches. He always takes time to stay loose.

He's not really a bithead, but he's smart and knows a lot of the basics, and especially cyber security protocols, so that when he released his first and second statements as KTR, he'd done them from different public computers. He'd used disguises. He'd managed the trace trail drop to look like the sort of anonymizer block noted in the file. He had also copied a couple of key phrases from the previous relevant claim announcements.

He holds his hamstring stretches for a long count.

He turns back to his planning, trying to ignore something that bothers him, something that he can't help picking at, which is his assignments' identities. Lobinski knows enough about each of them to be surprised Greene wants them killed. That holds true for the next assignment, too, something of a political player or someone who had been before he went private sector as a lobbyist for some biggest players in the construction industry, including one of the ten top US-based companies with work that spans the globe. He'd looked it up and read that receivables were close to a hundred billion. This next assignment is, like his previous ones, right wing, and it's proving something of an act of will on his part to keep himself from being too interested. By all appearances, the assignments have something of the look of the masters eating their young. He isn't going to be digging deeper into the background of the lawyer or the man from the giant construction company or the lobbyist who is his next assignment. He's not that interested, other than some species of intellectual itch he really doesn't need to scratch.

What he needed was more surveillance specifics about the next assignment and the last week has given him this.

The assignment lives in the Kenwood neighborhood of Bethesda. He has learned that the assignment likes to drive. He has learned, from a public records search, the assignment is a bit of a lead foot, as an impressive collection of speeding tickets show. He knows the guy has a regular schedule of leaving the house every day around 5:00 a.m., timed, no doubt, to beat the traffic as he drives into town and the K Street office. What cements Lobinski's plan is the specifics of the assignment's home location because the options the assignment has for exiting his neighborhood are constrained. In fact, there is only one route choice that will make the hit staged close to the assignment's neighborhood.

Well, just outside the neighborhood, he clarifies. He'll want to wait until the target gets to the first big street, Dorset Avenue, a stretch where two traffic tickets for speeding were issued in a two-year span.

Apparently to no effect, he concludes. And he has seen this with his own eyes. He's been surveilling the last four workdays, dressed in different business suits, a briefcase in hand alternating with a shoulder bag, just another cog heading off to the train station, a forty-minute walk from the target's neighborhood. He's kept himself from a nodding basis with one other early riser, who is an actual regular walker heading into the train station, he's sure.

He goes into the bathroom to brush his teeth, and from the bathroom he can hear next door what sounds to him like shower sex.

He rolls his eyes.

Early to bed for him. He has an early morning schedule to keep.

Chapter 28: Follow the Money, Honey

Jeannie Louise, lying on her couch, has just read through the group email sent to each member of *The Laundry*, from Jersey, her old acquaintance since her *The Economist* days. She'd first met Jersey at one of the early conferences she'd been sent to as she was shifting beyond her analyst role into writer for *The Economist*. Not that she can remember the particulars of that long-ago program, but she sure remembers meeting Jersey. She had immediately liked him, especially because he insisted she call him Jersey, even though his name tag had his full real name, albeit crossed out with a Sharpie and replaced by his nearly indecipherable handwriting displaying his preferred name.

She had known of him because he had already made quite an impression on the national stage through YouTube clips of his congressional testimony that still gets views all these years later, although he also has plenty of newer clips too. Anytime he appeared with one or another of the late-night hosts, there was another boost in those numbers.

The famous Dr. Robert Penworth.

Meeting him had been a wonderful but surreal experience. Back then she was excited about her nascent professional prospects and still disbelieving, in a breathless sort of way, that she was meeting and listening to and breathing the same air as these others, these academics and writers and researchers who operated in the nexus of climate change, policy, politics, and finance. These vanguard proponents of the message that economics is central to the issue of climate change were a family she hadn't known she was missing until that moment, and only then had she understood this was something she had been longing for. There were other important issues beyond melting ice and rising temperatures, and there she was, grateful to find herself among those pioneering key adherents of the holistic approach to doing something about the world in crisis.

The biggest trigger for greening the world is money, Jersey had said, sitting among a small group of attendees in the hotel bar on the final night of that conference. This moment is what she still thinks of as the moment of the birth of *The Laundry*.

Follow the money, honey, Jersey repeated that night and repeated it enough times that it became annoying, but his excitement and his analysis of the reinsurance sector's risk management of climate change had been more than enough compensation. His explanation helped her better understand the issue and led to her first significant freelance article, although the small online publication in which her article appeared seemed in effect without readers, as she remembers it.

But Jersey had read it, and liked it, and sent out his positive comments to her and to several others, in what she believes might well have been *The Laundry*'s first group email.

He had thought her a good writer, someone able to take complex topics and render them in ways that made them understandable for any intelligent reader. He confessed in that first email that such a skill was completely beyond his abilities, and even though he was good for a piquant phrase or intriguing quote, he couldn't put together two sentences that made sense, not on paper.

Well, that's an economist for you, she thinks, glancing back at the latest email from *The Laundry*.

But Jersey's real talent is in understanding the big picture, seeing trends and futures that don't occur to most others. The year after her first and mostly ignored article on reinsurers appeared, her articles that followed grew more substantial, not least because of the input of some of *The Laundry*'s academics and researchers. Having access to richer data and analysis from these others allowed her to fill in the facts in ways that made the issues more real.

The facts, as she discovered, were there for the finding, a rich trove. Some of *The Laundry* were academics who pursued such collections and aggregations, then presenting critiques of those reports for the advancement of their academic standings. From her own brush with academia, she already knew this approach meant such articles for academic journals would have almost no presence in the real world, and so she set herself to take these efforts and make them over into something compelling for the public.

A nice idea, she thinks, and hardly for the first time.

The payment for such work proved rather less nice, although she admits to herself in the past year or two this has been changing. In those first few years she had worked with *The Laundry*, and much of the work she often took involved editing and rewriting others' manuscripts rather than publishing only her own work. But increasingly she became involved with contract reports and analyses for companies and think tanks, and that helped pay the bills as her public writing slowly grew an audience.

Slowly? she thinks. *How about glacially?*

A lot started changing during the Obama Administration and the establishment of the climate-change-savvy Financial Stability Board, a G20 successor to the Financial Stability Forum that emerged from the 2008 housing crisis and subsequent systemic financial disasters. The International Monetary Fund too had begun expanding its climate change-related activities at that time, and that was helpful to her still nascent endeavors, and by the time of the Biden Administration, she'd become well-established.

In fact, it was an IMF report on fossil fuel subsidies, *Global Fossil Fuel Subsidies Remain Large: An Update Based on Country-Level Estimates*, that helped her blog gain wider readership when she wrote a popularized analysis of the work. The report had data through 2017, although published in full form in 2019, and she still keeps current with the work, which has repeated annually since. The topic of fossil fuel subsidies sometimes was a presentation topic at one or another conference, although she knows she'd have to look up the conference to figure out which one and how many years back, since those times are mostly a blur now.

Far more clear are the years of the last Trump Administration, when his absurd giveaways to Big Oil had almost caused her to be so demoralized to seriously consider give up her climate work. Her long post on the subject was titled *Thank You for Letting Us Pay for Our Demise*, and over time Jeannie Louise came to think the subject of fossil fuel subsidies was key. Still, during Trump's disastrous tenure, public discussion of fossil fuel subsidies went missing despite the enormous sums provided to the fossil fuel industry worldwide. Of course, once any discussion got into billions of dollars, people can't comprehend, she's long believed, even as she built her business on efforts to explain such numbers.

She keeps updating her annual IMF copies, and she's back to reviewing these subsidies in the last few months because Jersey is asking *The Laundry* members to help revive the subject. She likes the goal, but she can't help feeling pessimistic, especially since any effort to do so will suffer from the one difficult-to-explain factor.

My old bugaboo, externalities, she thinks.

She still gets frustrated by the challenge of describing how such matters as air pollution and particulates and their health costs that result from fossil fuel use should be factored into any economic analysis of real cost. The complexity of the issue of the real costs of fossil fuels when one adds in increased property damage and rising sea levels and floods, heat waves, crop failures, and other pick-your-favorite climate catastrophes. The dollar amount is staggering. The numbers out of the Josephine event alone could add a trillion dollars or more to the 2029 ledger according to some estimates, if full restoration was the aim. But even now carbon mostly gets a free ride. A price on carbon would do the trick, and she's always liked the carbon fee and dividend approach as the mechanism for resolving the fossil fuel cost externalities, but the recent carbon tax is far too modest.

Despite her background, even she has difficulty mastering the big picture. For the United States alone, the total fossil fuel subsidies, direct and indirect, add up to a sum matching that of the annual defense budget, or nearly so.

War and oil, the business of America.

She continues to be shocked by how her fellow citizens don't think of their own country as a petrostate. Saudi Arabia, sure, and even Venezuela, and Russia of course. She's tried to edit Wikipedia several times to add the United States of America to the list, but the editors keep rejecting the changes, their argument that fossil fuels are a smaller percentage of GDP for America relative to GDP percentages for petrostates. Her frustrated point, of course, is that by volume the United States is at the top of the oil production list and has been for some time.

She glances back at the email and sighs. Jersey is right, she knows. With the big climate remediation infrastructure projects already in place—*back in place!*—and those currently being considered, including the Sea Wall Act, the fight for funding reallocation will be the real action to follow. She knows that solutions aren't ever going to be simple, but things are made more complicated by the systemic integration of fossil fuels into the macroeconomic framework, and with defense spending a part of that web of interdependence, extrication of the fossil fuel economy from the overall economy is difficult.

Jeannie Louise laughs, although her tone is merciless. *Difficult*, she repeats to herself. *How about impossible, more likely.*

This challenge is one of the reasons why she's excited about accessing the new AI analytics platform at Rutgers that Jersey is encouraging her to use. She has little experience with the platform, and what experience she has is mostly secondary. So far, it has mainly consisted of her lending assistance to the big data analysis of climate denial messaging. She mainly helped out by significantly expanding the list of target sources involved in the mishmash of efforts going on for the past two decades to retard public awareness of the science community's consensus on climate change. She's thrilled to have been useful in any way with identifying the surprisingly few individual authors behind the climate delay messaging. The AI analysis has proved revelatory, and the number of writers so engaged in climate misinformation had been barely dozens in number.

She and others had given the final roll call of those entities identified the sardonic name, *The Bad Dream Factory.*

This newest effort will hardly be the first to look at who is behind the decades-long funding to deny or minimize the role of man and greenhouse gases on the changing climate. She knows there have been plenty of investigative reports, articles, and even a few books on the topic of organized climate denial. Even Congressional committees have had hearings on the matter, but nothing much has come of such efforts. Now that the real producers have been identified in detail along with the commissioning associations and institutions, there is finally some talk in Congress about subpoena and money trace-back investigations. The identification of dark money sources is very much her interest.

She'll be more than happy to work with others who know how to build new AI routines for tracing such funding, although she remains at a loss understanding just how dark money can be revealed. Up to now, piercing the veil of the lobbying firms and their clients and PACs and think tanks and fossil fuel dark money has always been a fool's errand. The hope is that using Big Data and AI will make the difference. The potential of accessing Rutgers's computational resources sounds intriguing, and Jeannie Louise appreciates being asked to help. She's eager to move from guesswork and reasonable assumption to determine, in unassailable detail, where the money comes from and where it leads.

Follow the money, honey.

Chapter 29: Bottoms Up

Davin is throwing his second cocktail party in as many months, and Alicia, of course, is invited, and he'd made clear the invitation includes a plus one, but there is no plus one, it turns out, when Alicia shows up a bit late. There being no Deidre is surprising. Alicia's tardiness is not.

From what he can tell, Alicia seems to be living a quiet life apart from *BI*. "My early late husband died before he could become my ex," he once heard her joke about her marriage and widowhood, but otherwise she almost never talks about the marriage or her past. She also doesn't talk about her relationship with Deidre, which is a bit surprising to him, given that Deidre has moved from his Housatonic house into her house in Sheffield, although official the move was made only recently. In fact, Deidre has been living with Alicia for the better part of the past year and often there for a long time before that.

Not that he talks to Alicia much about his personal life, and these days it's mainly the video session with his old therapist where that subject comes up. He's back up to weekly frequency just recently, the same frequency he'd gone with the last several months before the decree and those first several months post-divorce.

He tries not to go on and on about the divorce with Gloria, who he sees is coming up from the kitchen with the lemon juice he squeezed just an hour before. He's glad to have her here, although he's feeling oddly a bit nervous, too. This is the first time any of his friends and acquaintances are meeting her, other than the two current house sharers. He's already introduced her to the early arrivals, Tim and Wanda and Tiff, but only now, with Alicia now here, does he use the term *girlfriend*. He finds the term a bit anomalous, considering their age. He's rehearsed *lover*, but each time he thinks of using *lover* it seems all too strangely serious.

He can simply call her his *friend*, he just now realizes, which makes him laugh.

He winks at her as she hands him a tall slim bottle filled with the juice.

"You having fun?" he asks.

She smiles and winks back. "If not now, then later," she says, and he's a bit self-conscious about his blushing, but the arrival of Marion Fletcher-Gray and her husband at the living room's exterior French doors gets him refocused.

Fletch, as he learned she likes to be called the very first time they met, is the still-new town manager. Her husband goes by Robby. Davin knows Fletch a bit, but he's pretty sure she accepted the invitation because she knows Alicia is likely to be here, and she likely wants to cultivate the press. Of course, Alicia had suggested the invitation to Davin, so maybe some mutual cultivation is at play.

Tim and Wanda, his friends from Alford, and Tiff, a mutual acquaintance who owns a small art gallery on Front Street, are chatting at the other end of the living room, and Gloria moves to join them, a tall ice-filled glass of seltzer with a chunky lime wedge in hand. It isn't that she doesn't drink, but he's never seen her drink much or ever be tipsy.

He turns around and tells Alicia, Fletch, and Robby that the terrace area outside the living room is set up with chairs and some small tables, but he suggests they stay inside because of the mosquitoes. But he's not even finished explaining his reasoning when Robby loudly smacks his own forehead. The offending hand is held forward, displaying the squashed insect, Robby's other hand idly wiping the area of forehead where the bite is already slightly swelling and the brow reddening from the self-delivered blow.

"Yeah, well, there you go," Davin says, more impressed, he's pretty sure, with how proud of the kill Robby seems.

"Yikes," Davin adds. "Hopefully that's the only gate crasher."

He gestures to the table with the liquor and glasses and asks what he might get them. He's only met Robby once before, and briefly at that, and he's still struck by Fletch's husband's good looks, an unusually impressive handsomeness, almost pretty, really, he thinks, although he also realizes the image of the forceful mosquito annihilation a moment before takes any sense of glamor down a notch. Robby looks younger than Fletch, who is in her early forties, close to Alicia's age, Davin guesses.

He introduces the couple to Tim and Wanda, who have drifted back to the drinks table, leaving Tiff talking to Gloria, and Davin makes introductions all around and queries drink preferences of the new arrivals, and then is busy with their orders.

Classic jazz plays in the background there in the living room, some Sonny Stitt at the moment, and the screened windows are thrown wide open. A floor stand fan is set low and oscillating to keep the large, long room quite comfortable. The weather has been pleasant, although the earlier string of hot days followed by long stretches of rain seems to have turbo-charged the mosquitoes.

Wanda is chatting with Alicia and Fletch, but Tim remains by the bar table set up, and Robby wanders back over too, the delivery of Fletch's drink complete. *Nothing like a nice lineup of liquor bottles and cocktail glasses to attract a man crowd*, Davin thinks. He doesn't even bother asking Tim what he'd like to drink because he knows quite well that another scotch and soda will be requested. He's already stuffing ice into a highball glass and pouring in some mid-shelf blended scotch, then the club soda.

He's just handed over Tim's glass when Professor

Jackson pushes open one of the narrow French doors from the back terrace.

The terrace.

Davin loves this particular affectation of his, somehow so easily satisfied by naming, as *terrace*, the flagstone area level with the second floor here on the back side of the house.

He waves his neighbor over toward him. Professor Jackson is the oldest person here. He lives in the house adjacent to Davin's place, and he has cut through the side property, as is his wont. Professor Jackson, still teaching American literature at UMass Boston, lives in Cambridge — not that Davin knew him there — and has his second home right next door. Jackson, who Davin always calls Professor, is a tall black man who typically dresses in suits, and tonight is no different, with Jackson in a slightly worn but comfortable-looking seersucker.

When Davin looks back into the room, he sees Tim stepping carefully around the low table in front of the couch that has the tray with all the hors d'oeuvres, and then Davin looks back to the approaching Professor. "Always great to see seersucker," Davin tells him as he lumbers over to the drink table.

"The usual?" Davin then asks.

"Yes, please," Professor answers with a smile. "You bet."

Professor is a fervent convert to an older style of Martini Davin champions, which uses orange bitters and is garnished with a long lemon twist, and of course great gin, and plenty of very good and very fresh vermouth. Davin, an apostate, likes to shake this up in a stainless-steel cobbler shaker, intentionally breaking up little bits of ice that pour through the strainer and float on the surface of the cocktail. The professor bows before taking possession of the drink.

Davin hasn't seen much of Professor Jackson this summer, knowing he'd been traveling somewhere in Europe. "What's the retirement status?" he asks him, wondering if there's been any action on the regularly threatened stepping away from academia.

"No," Professor answers, "no action." He pauses to take a sip, clucking appreciation. "I'm thinking these days I'm in no rush, although I've cut back on the number of classes I teach per semester."

Davin nods and tells him he's listening while pulling other bottles out to make some other drinks, having heard two other guests arriving, their voices rising as they climb up the stairs. The two are who he suspects they'd be, the man a musician friend of Tim's who Davin has sometimes gone to hear perform and the man's younger girlfriend, a staff organizer with The Third Way, one of McKibben's big climate organizations.

He's glad they've come. The musician, Rodney, is a saxophonist and a welcome fellow jazz fan, rare in these parts. Davin's only once before socialized with the two of them, although he's met them several other times at one or another venue. He finds them to be good company, and, well, the woman is a pleasure to look at, and smart, and funny.

Rodney waves to him but stops to talk to Alicia and Fletch. The woman—*Ainsee, Aine, something Irish,* Davin's pretty sure—looks over and makes the gesture of downing a drink, eyebrows arching.

"I realized," Professor says after a pause, watching Davin as he gets back to work, "that if I stay in, then I'm an old professor man. If I retire, I'm just an old man."

"There's some hard wisdom," Davin replies with an obliging laugh, and then he realizes Robby, who is listening to him, needs to be introduced, which Davin then does with the appropriate level of apologies. Once Robby is engaged with Professor, Davin gets on with finishing the drinks.

Tim comes back with an appetizer-filled napkin, and Davin asks him how his social media contract work is going, but he's mostly paying attention to the drinks he's now garnishing. The drink he's making, the Aviation, is an old gin-based sour recipe that carries Maraschino liqueur for sweetness to offset the lemon juice, along with a small measure of Crème de Violette that makes the drink a pale violet and gives the cocktail its name. The cocktail is garnished with a Luxardo cherry, of course, which brings the pale lavender color cast by the violet liqueur into sharper relief.

He picks up the two glasses, tells Tim he'll be right back, and makes his way toward Rodney and his girlfriend, with Robby right behind him. "Hey," he says with a nod to Rodney and the young woman, holding a glass up to one and then the other. "My promise is fulfilled. Here's the Aviation, the way it is supposed to be."

Robby slips past to stand near his wife.

Davin waits for each of the two new arrivals to sip and studies their reactions. Neither of them let him down.

"Oh man," Aine says, or at least he hopes he's got the name right, not that he says it out loud.

"Yeah," Rodney adds.

"My debt is paid," Davin intones and then turns to Fletch and Alicia and tells them the last time he went out with these two, he suggested they might like an Aviation, but that bar had blown the drink quite badly with too much Crème de Violette making it sticky sweet and overpoweringly floral, so he feels obliged to make a good one for them to compensate for that awful experience. He is pretty sure the lemon juice that bartender used that night was old and stale too, but he's kept that to himself.

"Did you guys all introduce yourselves?" he asks. To his relief they all jump in with their own introductions and handshakes and nods, and Davin sees his take on pronouncing Aine's name is more than a little off the mark.

He admits as much to Aine, who grins.

"Keep people on their toes," she says, but Wanda has sidled up and asks what she's drinking.

"Aviator," Aine says, but Davin corrects her.

Wanda takes the taste she's offered, and Wanda says she'd love an Aviation too.

The three of them retreat to the bar table, and the two women watch as Davin mixes up the drinks. He's pouring four Aviations, since Aine has expeditiously downed much of her first, and because he's decided to join in, since his Martini is mostly done. He is making an Aviation for Gloria, too, not that she's asked for it, off busy talking to Tiff. As he's finishing shaking the cocktails, Robby again returns to the drinks table.

"Uh, Fletch would love another one of..." and he trails off at that point.

"Yeah," Davin tells him. "Du, Du bon, Dubonnet," which clearly means nothing to Robby, from his reaction.

Fletch had seen the Dubonnet Rouge on the bar table and asked for it, which Davin put on ice with a lemon half slice nestled in. He now produces another one and hands it to Robby, who turns around, off to deliver the drink.

"Hey, Tim told me your son's girlfriend works for Climate Progress," Aine says as he pours out the four drinks.

"Cynthia," he replies. "Yes. Another of those spin-offs, or whatever the arrangement is, a project, advocacy, whatever, around meat alternatives, regenerative farming, that sort of thing."

She nods.

Gloria has come back but stands at the other end of the bar table listening. He hands her the cocktail. Wanda mentions she and Tim are signed up with The Third Way, but then she makes a face and confesses they really haven't done anything yet. Aine asks Davin if she could get Cynthia's contact information, and he suggests he can email this to her. He tears a corner off the piece of paper he'd used to scrawl a couple of cocktail recipes notes, and he grabs a pen and hands it and the torn-off scrap of paper to her, and a moment later she's handing back the fragment, now with her email address on it.

He turns and asks Gloria how she likes the cocktail and is answered by her nodding as she takes a second sip, but

Davin hears a tentative *hello* coming up the stairs, and there's Jeannie Louise. He waves her over, watching her stop for a moment as she is greeted by Alicia, Fletch, Robby, and Rodney.

After she makes her way to the bar table, and after he's made introductions all around the drink table, he then asks her what he can get her.

"Um, bourbon?" she asks or tells him, and he tells her to go pick her preference, gesturing past the open connecting doors at his shelf of bottles in the library.

With a nod, she heads over to the bottles.

"That's Jeannie Louise Smith?" Aine asks.

He nods.

"No shit," Aine says. "Her stuff, the things she writes about, just fantastic, really..." but she trails off.

"Yup," Davin says. "Our resident climate guru."

"No shit," she says.

Wanda asks what they are talking about, but Jeannie Louise is back, a bottle of Knob Creek 12 Year in her hand, asking if the selection is okay. "I've never had this one, but I've heard great things," she adds.

"Excellent," he replies, and he hopes his tone is right. His reaction to her selection is mixed, knowing she'll love this bourbon but also knowing the bottle has gotten stupidly expensive. "Let me get you a big cube for that, but take a sip straight first if you want," and he's pouring the bourbon into a double rocks glass, a big pour, trying to make up for his miserly thoughts.

He runs down the stairs and is quickly back from his kitchen run with the silicon tray of two-inch ice cubes. Aine and Jeannie Louise are already talking, but he gets a nod from Jeannie Louise for the big cube. He sees Wanda is back with Tiff, and Gloria is there too, and the three of them drifting into the library, and it looks like Tiff is pointing at one of his art pieces, a wall hanging sculpture from among his earliest work.

Tim and Professor are over by the fireplace, looking

through a stack of CDs.

Davin sips his Aviation and is happy. He slides the cherry into his mouth and sets down the now empty glass.

He picks up the remnant of his Martini and finishes it up, glad to empty the glass to avoid a spill. The small amount of the drink he polishes off has grown warm.

His thought on this matter is, *Safety first!*

It's a warm night, but the fan is doing its job, and the alcohol seems to be kicking in, at least from the escalating sounds of the small gathering. He listens behind him, making out that Alicia and Fletch are talking about yet another proposed Town Warrant, but he doesn't catch which one. He turns and sees Robby's glass is empty. He gestures at it, but Robby places his hand over the top of his glass, but Alicia holds up her empty wine glass, and Davin grabs the bottle of white wine, stepping forward to refill her glass with another pour of the Sancerre. He can see Fletch still nurses the Dubonnet, so he nods and turns back and walks over to check on Professor, who is still looking over some of the CDs next to the small stereo unit. Tim slips away into the library. Professor's martini glass is empty but still in his hand. Davin knows that Professor likes to pace himself.

"Remediation does make sense," he hears Jeannie Louise say, from ten feet away. "Or resilience, or whatever you want to call it. It isn't a matter of letting the oil companies keep selling, either."

He can't make out Aine's reply, but he catches the tone well enough.

"No," Jeannie Louise answers. "It isn't capitulation, it isn't pandering," but she pauses for a moment. "Well, it could be, right, depending on what actually comes out, the details in the Act, and if it ever comes about, but you can't unilaterally declare a full stop to fossil fuels because there's not enough renewables to fully replace what we need, the transition to renewables is itself energy-intensive, and there are still plenty of parts of the economy that can't sub out fossil fuels."

Davin hears Aine talk about oil exploration continuing, the tone even angrier.

"You have to listen," Jeannie Louise is saying, and the age difference between the two women becomes evident, her response more like scolding, more like she's talking to a child, and Davin can see they are both growing upset.

"Hey," Davin says to the two of them, some feet away, the Professor at his side. "There'll be no fighting in the War Room," and they both look at him, surprised by his interjection, but then, almost like it's been rehearsed, one says *Dr. Strangelove* and the other *Strangelove* exactly at the same time.

The three of them laugh, and Jeannie Louise tells Aine she's impressed she knows the film, then looks at Davin, who nods.

"Top marks," he says, then he looks at Aine. "You give me hope for the younger generation."

Aine rolls her eyes.

"*Dagnabit,*" Davin recites, "*Grandpa's up the persimmon tree,*" which loses them, but the weird voice and accent with which he recites the line makes them smile, despite their confusion.

"No?" he says. "Not familiar with *The Real McCoys*?" and he glances at Professor, who also seems at a loss, but Davin just laughs and tells him he's not sure if he's ever even seen a clip, but he had an old friend back in his college days who'd often recite the line and it somehow grew on him. He turns back again, speaking to the two women.

"What are you guys talking about, so hot under the collar?"

Aine tells him she was just being an asshole, really, and she apologizes to Jeannie Louise, who shrugs.

"No worries," she says to Aine. "It's all complicated, and that is sort of my point. Simplistic, uh, simple solutions, messaging, does more harm than good is what I figure. I've been fighting that for a couple of decades, more or less."

She turns to Davin. "Aine is understandably frustrated,

and rightly so, and we all are with all the bullshit the oil companies keep pulling and have been pulling for far too long already. She's afraid the Sea Wall Act, should it pass, will just be another excuse for them to *drill baby drill*."

He sees Aine nodding.

Jeannie Louise looks back at Aine. "It is super frustrating, I know, believe me. I was at COP28, my first one, and if you remember, that was in Dubai, with Sultan Al Jaber as president."

"Oh, I remember," says Aine. "I was there," and this surprises Jeannie Louise, Davin can see.

It certainly surprises him.

"Well, not at COP28, but there in Dubai, for the actions."

"Huh," is what she gets from Jeannie Louise.

Davin now feels unschooled. "Uh, what?" he manages to say.

"You were part of the actions?" Jeannie Louise asks, and Davin sees this means something.

Then it dawns on him. "Jesus," he says to Aine. "Weren't those demonstrations put down hard?"

Aine nods.

"Were you, uh, were you arrested or…" but he lets his question fade.

"Yeah," Aine says. "Arrested and a few of the other *or's*." Jeannie Louise reaches out to her, placing a hand on her arm.

Davin doesn't know what to say, nor really, what exactly is being exchanged between the two women. "That was the year Gore came out so strongly against the oil companies' participation, right?" he finally says.

Jeannie Louise tells him he's correct. "It was great," she adds, "not that it made much difference, except maybe, the spike in radicalization—"

"—which is what I was arguing about," Aine says, interrupting. "I tend to trigger with anything that might help keep fossil fuels in the game, and the Sea Wall Act could play out that way, at least I'm afraid it might."

"We're a long way from defining what the Act might be, never mind passing the Act," Jeannie Louise tells her, and Davin sees Aine nod.

"But you're right, this getting co-opted by fossil fuels has to be monitored, but a lot of people, a lot of organizations, are paying attention."

Davin sees Aine nod again.

"There's even a new section being proposed, about housing, in the markup work going on."

Davin sees Aine nod again. He hasn't read anything about housing, but then he's not following the bill that closely.

"The gross metropolitan product of New York City alone is around three trillion dollars," Jeannie Louise continues, "and the population since the immigration law amendments last month is likely to run around twenty-seven million, even more, by the Standard Statistical Metropolitan Area count. The cost of relocation of assets alone is inconceivable, the economic fallout."

No one speaks for a moment.

"Or it's Standard Metropolitan Statistical Area," Jeannie Louise adds, with a shrug. "I can never keep that straight."

"You're working on, well, following, looking at the Sea Wall Act, right?" asks Davin.

Jeannie Louise looks at Davin, then Aine, and nods. "There's always the danger that any remediation work will give fossil fuels further excuse to continue, and there's been plenty of talk about this in climate circles. Big Oil can say that rising sea levels are being handled, so there's less pressure to go fast on the decarbonization," and she pauses to take a good pull of whiskey, the big ice cube clunking on the side of her glass.

She looks at Davin, eyebrows up. "Wow," she says, toasting him with her glass.

"There's that series *The Expanse*," says Professor,

jumping into the conversation. "I still think it may be one of the best television series, sci-fi series, back in late 2010s, early 2020s?"

Jeannie Louise and Aine both look at him, and their puzzled expressions makes him laugh.

"The reason I mention it is the opening credits have this quick glimpse of Manhattan from far above, and it's surrounded by a sea wall. I hadn't even noticed that detail until, like the third season maybe."

"Hmmm," is all Jeannie Louise has to say about it, turning back to talk with Aine, and Davin can make out something about the problem of radicalization and simplistic messaging. From Aine's expression, he wonders if she's working hard trying to be polite. He thinks her body language suggests she's biting her tongue and her lips are pursed, like she's making an effort to be patient. Jeannie Louise doesn't seem to notice.

Davin figures now might be a good time for him to check on the other guests.

He is without a drink. *Put the oxygen mask on yourself before helping others*, he thinks.

A quick walk around shows that no one else needs a drink, and so he makes up a new Martini for himself and a new one for Professor, and he grabs a drink in each hand and walks around the two women, close to knocking shoulders with Jeannie Lousie as he heads toward Professor. He hears Jeannie Louise saying something about how naïve talking points can hurt climate change efforts more than help.

Professor, back to looking through the CDs, is delighted to see Davin, or maybe it's the fresh Martini.

"Thank you, my son," Professor wisecracks as he takes the cocktail. He gestures to the scattered-about CDs. "What a bizarrely interesting collection," he says.

"Thank you, my good sir," Davin replies.

"This one," Professor says, holding the case up a fraction. "Nineteen-fifties recording, big band-like, but big bands were in their slide into history, bebop emerging." He looks at Davin, who nods. "I've long been fascinated with genre shifts and transitions and overlaps, and that era is really very interesting, especially in terms of music."

One of the things he likes about his neighbor is this very tendency to move into teacher mode. He nods and then takes a nice long sip of his own cocktail. Professor does the same, and they both smack their lips, which seems to delight the both of them tremendously.

"This one, Chris Connors," Professor says, "I'm not familiar with her."

"She took over, I forget the band, but it was Julie, no, June Christy she replaced, both great," answers Davin.

"Stan Kenton, the copy says," Professor notes, gazing at the back of the CD jewel case.

"Right."

Professor makes a comment about compact discs. "I'm not sure when the last time was, I saw any getting played."

Davin shrugs, and then grins, holding up a finger, waiting for the piece streaming through the Bluetooth link to the stereo receiver finish — one of the many versions of "Round Midnight" he likes — and then he switches over to the CD function. Taking the CD case from Professor, he removes the disc and opens and closes the tray, checks the case index, and cues up the track he wants.

"Excuse me," Davin says loudly enough, and those scattered about the living room and library turn toward him.

"I'm going to play one track from this 1953 recording of Chris Connors, called 'Mad Miser Man,' and then we'll be back to our regularly scheduled program." The others figure Davin's announcement is over and the talk picks up again, but Davin is not quite finished. "Sorry," he says, getting attention of the room back on him. "I'd like you to consider this song for the political fight song for the country," and with that, he presses *Play* and the song starts, the volume turned up, the lyrics clear. The music is jaunty, Connors's voice is great, but the lyrics in the refrain are a counting chorus, *one million, two million, three million, four*.

Of course, he figures with today's dollars and the absurd incomes of the super-rich, the lyric should change to use *billion*.

"It perfectly captures the excessive greed mentality," he says to Professor over the music, but Professor is listening intently to the song.

Davin looks through the north double doors into the library and sees Gloria looking at him.

She gives a little wave.

The song continues with another verse or two and then ends, but as it does, Tim enters from the library holding up his empty glass, shouting, "Fight, Fight, Fight!" which gets people laughing or shaking their heads, depending, and then Aine, her glass upraised, adds quietly, but loud enough for Davin to catch as he looks at her, "Kill the fucking rich."

Davin is a bit surprised and slightly unsettled by this, but he's getting the playlist back running, volume back down, and then stands straight, turns, and shouts, "Let's start drinking!"

Chapter 30: Golden Green Pastures

William McPherson, with seven kills, has been on the road for nearly four months and has put in a lot of miles, the most recent big batch the drive from the West Coast after he finished his San Diego target. He is finally back in Kentucky at his former CEO's horse farm, standing in the early morning light looking over a green grass field he needs to cross.

He jumps the white-painted wood-slatted fence, clumsily enough because he's in his late fifties and isn't an exercise person, but also because he's taking care to avoid the electric wire fence right up against it. He lands with a gust of escaping breath, the knapsack bouncing on his shoulders, and then he walks toward the dark woods on the other side, being quick about it as he looks around to check for anybody who might spot him. He's not that worried about being seen unless it's one of the actual farm staff spying him. Otherwise, he'll come across as just some guy walking across the field.

A bit of a ramble, old chap, he tells himself, but his amusement cools. This isn't Britain where land access for walking is expansive, but Kentucky where guns and private property are sacred. When he was here before, he'd heard gunshots now and then, mostly distant, but always on those previous surveillance days, part of the background ambience.

He'd meant to get an earlier start today, before full light, but his preparations took longer than expected. Still, he's early enough to minimize traffic and the potential for being seen. Nice to have some light too, he thinks, and before it's likely to get really hot, sticky.

He feels he already knows the place well, between his drone surveys and Google Satellite studies and his earlier observations. Halfway across the field he starts cutting right, heading near the woods. He climbs another fence up close to spare clumps of trees, and sets off to where the trees grow denser, aiming for a small, paved road a bit beyond this field through the woods. A short walk up this road will bring him nearest to the network of riding trials that may be part of an old dirt road from when the farm was first built many decades back, he suspects.

After reaching the paved road and walking along it, he spies the place where the main riding trail dips close. He steps into the trees and walks to the spot he's previously chosen.

He settles down at the foot of one of the big trees, his eyes adjusting to the dimness under the canopy. He pulls out his sports bottle and drinks deeply. He's feeling fluttery, excited.

He takes from his knapsack an external battery power supply and a small Wi-Fi router, and he connects these together and powers up the router. He fishes a tablet from the knapsack and checks on the signal connections to several Wi-Fi-enabled Arlo Essential Video Doorbells which he has in previous days mounted high up in trees. The video cameras are a bit wider than his finger and about as long. These cameras provide good coverage of the trail, with one of the doorbell cameras on the edge of the tree line closest to the horse barn. The resolution of the cameras is HDR but given that last camera's distance from the barn, the image isn't great, but it should do.

He continues to be impressed by all the tech so easily available. The Arlo units needed little alteration other than covering LED telltales and painting over the surfaces to blend in to look like bark, a process he's repeated for the somewhat larger battery power packs, too. He remains a bit worried he will waste time hunting these hard-to-spot devices when it comes time to remove them afterward, but he figures that overall their blending so well and placed as they are, high enough, makes them very hard to spot. It could transpire, he assumes, that there won't be time to gather the equipment, but it shouldn't matter, because there is little danger in these devices being traced back to him anyway.

In predawn darkness two days before, it took him several hours to place the cameras and troubleshoot the Wi-Fi router, at times needing to work with his night vision goggles and at times risking the tablet screen's glow.

The cameras have now been up long enough to confirm his target's horse-riding habits.

He puts the tablet down, gets up, and cuts a few branches to put in front of his position behind the big tree near the horse trial. He checks on the nearby bicycle he dumped there the day before, already hidden under cover of brush. Pre-positioning the bicycle had been yet another risk, although not as fraught as the camera placements, but no one passed him the late afternoon before and he walked out unnoticed along the horse trail to where it crosses the state road, and by then he was just a guy walking in the country.

He checks his watch and notes he's got at least a half an hour before there's any chance the man will start his daily ride.

He settles against the tree.

Beautiful land, he thinks, looking through the trees and past the little paved road to the sun-bright green of the pastures, now glimpsed only in fragments through the darker green of the woods. He knows the private road provides access from the main residence to the back of the property, where there are the stables and a barn. A lot of money has been spent to repave this little private road, he's sure.

It's not that hot and not that humid this early in the

morning, but even with all shade from trees, the heat and humidity will grow oppressive as the day moves on. He'd checked the weather forecast earlier and hopes the forecast is accurate. The day is supposed to be less hot and humid than yesterday, although there is a big low-pressure system building in New England and the call is for some hard rain there in the next day or two. Either way the local forecast goes, there's no question this weather will ever be the dry and pleasantly warm air of San Diego.

And there's no ocean breezes here either, he notes.

It is a little before 7:00 in the morning, and he's here this early because of the target's habit of riding his horse farm's trails early. He's learned, across two stints of observation— *recon*, as he calls it—of the horse-riding schedule of *The Fucking Business Genius.*

He's been holding off on this target, because it is personal, and he wants to do what he can to throw off suspicion.

He can be patient.

He's not worried that the target isn't one of the Forbes 400 he uses as a starting point for target selection because the *asshole* is rich enough, valued in the hundreds of millions, and with all the others' killings so far attributed to KTR, he's confident this target won't raise any particular flag about him.

Very rich being very rich, is how he thinks of it.

Not all the KTR claims in the news are of those from the top tier of wealth. He remains surprised—a happy, hopeful surprise—by the number of copycat claims. There's been the claim with the woman in custody, and her victim was hardly rich. The others not his doing aren't Forbes 400 level either, but that can only help the perception of KTR running across a big organization. He's proud of his misdirection efforts to make it look like there are others with him in the shadows, and those efforts are made easier, of course, because he has managed to inspire others. There have been several *Kill the Rich* copycat claims to date, one where the man was caught, and just two weeks back there was another where a woman had been arrested, and another more recent, just a week ago, even less. This latest one bothers him some, it taking place geographically close to his present target, and that killing remains unsolved, along with a few others. He's undecided if this latest killing poses any additional danger to him. One could drive from there to here in plenty of time, after all.

Maryland and Kentucky aren't that close, really, he tells himself.

That target was some sort of big-wig lawyer, shot— *sniped!* —while eating breakfast outside his home, wife right there. He had found himself feeling a bit envious, since the use of a rifle would make things so much easier, but he neither has practice shooting long range, nor does he have a rifle any longer.

Some of the other Kill the Rich claims make him feel he is so much better than the two captured copycat individuals and the one shot dead, but there are others like him, good at the work.

Good enough, anyway, he tells himself. He knows, at least on some theoretical level, he will be caught, that this is inevitable. He doesn't let himself dwell on this certainty, at least most of the time. The copycats should help confuse investigations, and that thought can be helpful in easing this gut-burning worry from his thoughts.

Some of these other copycats seem smart, and any and all participation is welcome, especially since he has no plans to stop anytime soon. It helps there are so many targets, so many who have gathered far too much treasure onto themselves, and that even in the face of the desperate need that runs rampant in the world. Most people are facing difficult challenges while these *filthy rich assholes* pretty much ignore basic obligations.

The rich are letting the world burn.

He smiles because that thought makes him think about his most recent target. He'd come up with this tagline for that claim. That target had been someone just short of making the Forbes list, and something of a sailor with several large boats, but that target mostly liked to used one or another solo sailboats. He'd learned early in his researching that the target was a frequent participant in the Wild Wear SailingWorld Regatta Series, and as he learned more, the choice of regattas made sense, given the target's apparent love of sailing and given that the target's international apparels conglomerate owned, among the many dozens of companies, the Wild Wear Company, a maker of outdoor apparels and equipment.

The on-site recon in San Diego had been pleasant. The opportunity he had settled on was a regatta hosted by the San Diego Yacht Club and the Coronado Yacht Club, and the planning had gone well, and he had even gotten something of a tan. He also enjoyed the several restaurants close by the Coronado Yacht Club that were good for scene observation. He always paid cash, of course, although using cash itself seems notable enough in some places.

One San Diego surprise was the large number of bicyclists, so he had decided to leave the Ford Transit in one or another public parking lots that were plentiful on the south end of downtown. On the bike it typically took him fifteen or twenty minutes to cross the Coronado Convention Center Bridge and then take B Avenue.

The route over the bay had been stunning.

On the other hand, there were other aspects of the implementation of action that had proved challenging, entailing, as it did, a lot of swimming.

This morning's work requires the deployment of what he thinks of as a garrote wire, although he knows the actual point is to knock the target off his horse. This morning's work will be more hands-on than the San Diego action.

He is still using the mountain bike he'd stolen for one of his early target efforts, and he's glad that he'd kept it, despite worry he was holding on to potential evidence. But pedaling over San Diego Bay, looking back with sideway glances at the downtown towers across the sun-dancing blue-green water, he'd realized he'd been over-thinking things again. It isn't that cops would try to trace ownership of the run-of-the-mill mountain bike back to some town a half dozen states away and somehow connect him to his target out in the Minnesota woods or San Diego or here.

Still, he feels bad about stealing some kid's bike.

He also still feels bad about chloroforming the woman who was with the Minnesota target, but it all worked out fine. Better than just fine, even, since subsequent stories about that *Kill the Rich* claim speculated that at least one other member of the terrorist group might be a woman, with one of three subsequent copycat arrests being is a woman, another bonus.

It's a beautiful morning, and the target will be riding by soon enough. Still, best not have the garrote wire up any longer than it needs to be, he reminds himself.

He checks his tablet, but the first camera shows a quiet stable, but he catches movement on the road behind him and his heart leaps. The target, he's sure, driving up to the stable.

The brush blind he has set up is not any more sophisticated than a few cut branches, but it's behind a sizable tree, and there is a convenient depression on the back side of the tree away from the trail. He is wearing a camo sweatshirt and his pants are dark and the sweatshirt is a bit warm in the rising day. The bike is a couple of dozen feet away, invisible under its heavier cover of cut brush.

He's glad he has dropped the silly DNA protective efforts he so assiduously used in his first few targets. Such precautions are practically impossible and impossibly impractical and too uncomfortable.

He looks through the thin lines and copse of trees and can barely make out the emerald-green pasture, but sudden movement shows at least one of the target's horses is out grazing. He's disturbed to find any horse there since it means he's missed some barn and stable activity, and he quickly checks the camera feeds, calming down when no activity is visible.

From his lengthy study of Google Maps satellite images, he knows the horse trail farther down goes through a wide stretch of forest southward to the state road that's interrupted with a few unpaved driveways leading to houses situated deep in, but the closest one of these is quite some distance. His plan for afterward is to bicycle down the horse trail until it hits the road, and he will be just one more cyclist out and about. Still, if need be, he can head through the woods instead and bike down one or another of those dirt driveways.

Now he's keeping a constant eye on the tablet feeds, but he's also thinking about his list and that the guy, *today's target, this asshole,* is the inspiration for the list and for those irresistible steps from becoming unemployed to losing everything he always thought was rock solid, including his wife, his house, and after the divorce, his friends. His comfortable life had collapsed seemingly in the blink of an eye, and then he somehow became caretaker for his brother, and that last year, as his brother wasted away from his cancer and then was taken by the screwed-up treatment. Somewhere along the way he had become obsessed by the One-Percenters and the fundamental unfairness of it all, and the sense of worthlessness these people hold for all others.

The class action suit had been an object lesson too, a master class, in fact. He loves the irony of the windfall from the settlement providing the funding for his KTR project, and at least in this way the money is significant to him, but the pharmaceutical giant had merely written off the expense as the cost of doing business.

Fucking business.

No one has rights and justice anymore, not unless a person is rich enough to buy rights and justice, or lucky enough, that's the conclusion he has come to. The pharmaceutical company's lawyers were vicious, prepared to outspend, outwait, and outlive the plaintiffs, but with the internal memos discovery they were quick to cut their losses.

It had been as simple as that, an accidental reference in material supplied in the trial's discovery phase, and then, the memos themselves.

During this time his fixation on this target, his last CEO, had taken root.

Kill the Rich is important to him in and of itself and he understands his current target is a personal indulgence, but every time he wrestles with this as a potential problem, he keeps concluding it doesn't matter that it's a personal indulgence.

It's personal, not business.

What matters is that what he is doing will inspire others, and it has. The FBI seems inclined to see domestic terrorist conspiracies, so his efforts have helped make it look like the various targets are claimed by different people, and some actually are now accomplished by the hands of others. He can't be sure he'll really fool anyone, not in the long run, despite the news stories he eagerly devours, especially any of those articles reporting on the FBI's multiple-conspirators theory. He tries to keep in mind the FBI might engage in misinformation, perhaps to throw him off guard, but his best guess is that what he reads is an accurate enough assessment of the state of the FBI's investigation.

He pulls the Samsung Galaxy pad close to his face to check the video feeds again. He's spent a small fortune on Wi-Fi routers and relays, digital cameras, and drones too, and all sorts of other kinds of electronic doodads, but he has only recently begun to worry about budgeting.

It's expensive to kill people, he thinks, *if you want to get away with it.*

He wants to get away with it. He has a lot more work to do, and until four or five weeks ago, he'd been resigned to having to do it all himself, but then a KTR claim appeared that he had had nothing to do with it, and then another, and then another.

And ever thus, amen, he intones.

He doesn't know why some of those targets were selected, but if he hopes to have people participate, he can't control the rules.

He takes a deep breath and looks up into the filtered light of the morning sun through leaves. He's enjoying resting at the base of the big tree. It's an oak, he sees when he takes a moment to study the leaves above him.

One of the targets by another copycat was the head of one of the largest construction corporations, an arch conservative judging by the obit, and he hadn't bothered looking up net worth, with a second person also shot dead. The other person is what interests him, some friend of the intended target who had joined the construction executive at the same restaurant on that particular Tuesday, when, the articles he'd read had made clear, the executive always had lunch.

Who's more careful? he asks himself, as he thinks about the double shooting. *I'm more careful.* He's still thinking about the escort, pleased with how he handled that problem. Still, KTR will be seen as expanding its target criteria, and this may be helpful cover for his target today.

He sits up, seeing on screen the horse being led out of the barn, and he gets up, brushes off his pants, and looks to see if he's left any marks. Scraping at a partial boot print, he starts back toward the trail over thick leaf litter, knapsack in hand.

He walks to his pre-selected anchor trees, one on each side of the trail. He drops the knapsack and pulls out the thin wire and a pair of lineman pliers along with some rawhide work gloves and a tape measure. He sets to work attaching one end of the high-tensile wire to one trunk, taking care to measure the height up the tree. He has to stretch his reach a bit, and then he carefully puts the spool of wire down, not wanting kinks or tangles to measure the same height on the opposite tree where he will affix the other end of the wire. He then unspools the wire across the trail to this tree, pulling as tightly as he can.

He steps back with a critical eye.

He pulls out the tablet to check again and sees through the forward placement camera that his target is just starting to saddle the horse. This camera is a long view, but he's confident the man saddling the horse is the target.

He puts the tablet down and pulls out four hard plastic wedges and a three-pound sledgehammer.

He has worried the three-camera setup could well be the riskiest part of this undertaking, with the bigger danger of a Wi-Fi signal being discovered. He is literally broadcasting his presence, but the risk, he's figured, is acceptable since almost no one looks at available Wi-Fi connections when the active network is long-standing.

Well, it dawns on him now, if there are new employees or guests, they might notice when they try to connect, but he calms himself, thinking that even then, the likelihood of additional Wi-Fi routers wouldn't likely even get a mention. At worst, any attempted connection or disruption of his temporary network would signal an abort, and he would simply leave.

No harm, no foul.

Chapter 31: Greta Dabba Do Ya

*N*othing like an unprecedented disaster to stir up *Congress*, is what Jeannie Louise thinks as she reviews the latest speeches and statements in the *Congressional Record* out of the House Committee on Ways and Means in their work on Josephine relief funds.

She's being her usual ironic self. It's almost six weeks since the devastating storm and Congress, as far as she's concerned, is still fumbling. She wishes the still young Democratic Administration would act faster.

The Congressional committees remain caught up in posturing, as best she can figure, but there are signs positions have been shifting. The bigger problem is that Congress is still finalizing the Josephine-relief appropriations, and she would like to cut them some slack, but the partisan bullshit that has long shaped the country's politics is still far too much in evidence, and the relief appropriations are as good an example of this as any. Even a wonk can see how stupidly inappropriate the Republicans' last-minute effort is, a bald play to tie the emergency funding to the shaping of the Sea Wall Act in the form of a stupid, pointless tussle in the Rules Committee.

Greta dabba do ya, motherfuckers, as one particularly popular social media meme has put it as the Josephine relief funding fight has dragged on. She's not a big fan of cursing, but the line seems fitting.

Something she's finding of great interest from The House Committee on Appropriations is there an emerging sense that the new act requires a baseline budget figure at almost three trillion dollars. The fight will soon transfer to Ways and Means, where the budget, even spread across twenty years, will be a major revenue problem. One of the most interesting options being floated among the policy mills is to draw down or even eliminate various fossil fuel subsidies, including the still absurdly low public land exploration fees. More surprising and satisfying for her is that indirect subsidies, the externalized costs, have managed to get some attention.

And you are welcome, she thinks, pleased to have done her small part in resurrecting the matter of fossil fuel subsidies. She is hardly the only one to do so, of course, and her own work is part of *The Laundry*'s latest effort. The size of federal and state oil subsidies adds up to huge numbers, especially picking up the externality costs of fossil fuels goods and services, where the real payers are members of the general public.

The social costs of carbon, Jeannie Louise recalls from an early post of hers, a phrase she's come to appreciate more and more. A recent analysis she's looked over extrapolates that over the next two decades, keeping fossil fuel externalities out of pricing will likely result in using an additional seventeen billion barrels of oil, and that means six billion more tons of CO_2 that will be dumped into the atmosphere.

She squints up at the ceiling, musing. The first challenge is that fossil fuel corporations have been spending money for decades and that still shapes public perception. The second is that the fossil fuel industry's level of control in government is staggering, even if getting a detailed and accurate picture remains an ongoing problem. There are nearly one hundred PACs, think tanks, and nonprofit research organizations that are or were fronts for fossil fuel, always busy at controlling the message and peddling influence. The list of such organizations is one of her proudest possessions, although that first year she'd spent researching this was one of her worst in terms of income because she'd spent far too much time on this unremunerated undertaking. She still spends too much time trying to keep it all up to date.

She leans forward, pulling the keyboard toward her. She pulls up Word and opens a new document.

She loves a blank screen just slightly more than she hates it, but as usual the excitement of putting thought into writing prevails. In the back of her mind, she thinks that writing another *RE:CC* post is the last thing she should be doing, but that worry is kept quiet.

She begins with the title. *The Unforgiving Cost of Keeping Gas Prices Low.*

She is still mystified that business-driven manipulation of markets is such a rarely told story, considering the massive scope of it.

The effective political ploy of costs kept low, she types.

She'd studied this very concept in her economics graduate program, reading up on the Department of Agriculture changes during the Nixon Administration and how the real price increases for milk and other diary products had been checked through subsidies and that had helped check voter anger. She can't recall which professor taught that particular course, but she remembers the informal name of that course she and her fellow students used was *Yellow Cheese.*

Governments and Markets, that's the actual course name, she remembers. There was some tedious subtitle too, but everyone in the class, barring the professor, called it *Yellow Cheese.*

She barely remembers anything else from the course, but there was some coverage of wage policy and the minimum wage as well. The last rise of minimum wage goes back to 2009, but finally, as part of the Democrat gains, this year will see the national rate up to fifteen dollars an hour. By the time this bill was signed, unfortunately, most economists understood that rate was already badly outdated. Depending on the study looking at benchmark purchasing power, revised living-wage sums now range from twenty-eight to forty-one dollars per hour, yet the latest effort to change the minimum wage to fifteen dollars had nevertheless proved a difficult political struggle.

She types, *Election Financing Reform*. Without election financing reform, any progress at the national level on just about any central issue will remain modest, slower than slow. The system is rigged, bought and paid for, and she has no doubt many of the legislators, even among the Democrats, are little more than whores, likewise bought and paid.

And with apologies to sex workers, she mentally adds.

She types up some other bullet points, trying to capture enough of the salient arguments to give her a head start when she finally tackles the writing. She saves the outline and closes the document.

She intends to get to work on another of her pending articles, but instead brings up her browser, checks the local weather, and sees the forecast is holding for some heavy rains moving east, the potential for flooding still at watch stage, not warning. The street elevation of her house where she rents the second-floor apartment should be fine, even though the Housatonic River is just a block away. Typically, the river shows rocks and an old dam remnant, the water running over and around the rubble bottom. The old dam was part of William Stanley's alternator factory, some time back in the late 1800s, or a rubber factory that had then been taken over by Stanley, a converted use, when he was working for Westinghouse. This whole area is thick with energy history, but hardly any local knows much of it.

The banks of the river near her are steep, and she's never heard of any overflow, but she's still anxious about the forecast and the flash flood watch.

Her phone rings, and she sees it's Davin calling. She's tempted to let the call go to voice mail, but impulsively she swipes *Accept*.

"Yes, Davin," is her greeting.

She listens and then tells him, "No, I haven't started in on the potential floods crises from climate change," trying and failing to recall the actual name of the organization that studies the Housatonic and their study she is supposed to be writing about. "Got something of a dam here myself, like I told you earlier, backed up with a lot of previously committed assignments—"

She gives his interruption a pass.

This once, she tells herself.

She listens, concerned by the tone of low-lying panic, perhaps, or maybe its anxiety, anyway, hidden insufficiently by Davin's jocular manner.

She rolls her eyes.

"Yes," she says.

"Uh-huh," she says.

"I'm just being clear about the when of this work," she tells him. "I do want to do the local climate forecasts, I love the concept, that is not the problem, I just—"

She gets cut off again.

"Wait, wait, wait," she says to him. "Don't interrupt, please."

She nods, listening to his apology.

"Okay, thanks," she responds. "It's basically that I have to do this work when it fits into times, opportunities my other work allows, it's a simple economic calculus in addition to these being prior commitments."

He is talking about remuneration, asking her, or maybe he is telling her that this is a problem he understands.

"I'm sure you do," she tells him and then reiterates her workload challenges. She doesn't bother mentioning again that she's overcommitted and Jersey and *The Laundry* have just roped her into another big project. She tells Davin yet again she loves the local angle, but there's a lot to do before those pieces can really get going.

She sits back and lets out a long breath, not caring if he can hear. "Just tell her that it's likely weeks, but she should know I'm on board, not to worry," and she hopes that's clear enough, but then she decides she needs to be clearer.

"These calls, the check-in emails, I need a break from these for a while, it's going to be a while until I can really start in," she adds.

He is talking, but she's glad his tone has relaxed.

"Thanks," she says after he tells her he hears her. "By the way," she adds, "that was a fun party and that was some good bourbon." Before the party was over, she got to taste two other bourbons he'd suggested she try.

"Don't worry about me dropping out of touch, anyone who knows good whiskey is never getting ghosted by me," she tells him before she stabs the connection.

She puts down her phone and shrugs her shoulders and does those neck exercises she has trouble taking seriously because it always makes her think of being a turtle, her head moved backward and then all the way forward.

She checks her water bottle and finds there's some left, then she reaches to her right and snags a bottle of Adderall and shakes out another pill.

She is swamped but doesn't want to drop anything.

It is all interesting to her.

She pops the pill and swallows it with a mouthful of tepid water.

She rolls her shoulders a bit more, then turns back to her keyboard.

Chapter 32: Wretched Act

William McPherson knows the placement is tricky for the battery-powered Wi-Fi router carrying the camera feeds, in part because he had to figure out how to climb a tree high enough to get good signal lines between and among the cameras and router. Fortunately, the trail winds back and forth, especially at the start, making straight line distances modest.

He checks the tablet once again and sees that everything seems to be working right.

He needs to finish with the wire setup across the horse trail and needs to use the tree spikes and belt to get enough height up the two trees to effectively tap the top wedges to bring the wire tight.

Taking more time, more time! he worries.

He takes another quick glance at the tablet feed and relaxes. The target hasn't finished the harness work yet.

He straps on the spikes, pulling the buckles tight. He's learned the hard way these have to be tight, otherwise the feet can't keep a stable base. With the gloves back on he climbs the near tree, the three-pounder hanging heavy from his wrist by a woven nylon strap. He takes two of the wedges and wiggles them between tree and wire loop. With the three-pound sledge he taps the wedges as far down as he can, which tightens the wire. He scurries down, checks the tablet screen again, and then quickly scrambles up the opposing tree far enough to work the wedges into that end's loop of wire. Three steps up brings him above the wire and he snuggles the first wedge in between the wire and the trunk, then manages to double wedge the second one from underneath, and leans back on the tree belt and gently taps first the bottom wedge and then the top one, back and forth until he's able to pluck the wire and hears it sing.

He climbs down and walks back to the big tree, not yet removing the tree spikes and belt, instead worrying about his calculations about horse heights and rider heights, knowing the horse gait will rise and fall, but he's pretty sure the wire is at the right height to catch the target.

He doesn't want to hurt the horse, but he understands that may happen.

He takes off the tree belt but leaves the tree spikes be.

Even if the wire height is off and it catches the horse, this too will likely produce an acceptable result, the horse reacting, halting, shying, possibly dumping the rider. Even if the target sees the wire, he's likely to stop to check it out, and that too will be a good opportunity.

He pulls the tablet toward him and looks at it, seeing the target is heading out.

A fucking cowboy hat, he sniffs, shaking his head.

Don't get distracted, buddy boy, he tells himself.

The second camera is on the trail itself, right past a fork where it's possible the target might go left, but from previous reconnaissance, he is confident the odds are in his favor, and sure enough, the camera shows the horse and rider taking the right trail.

He slips a pistol out of the knapsack to nestle it behind his belt at the small of his back, making sure the sweatshirt bottom cuff is tucked behind the pistol.

The rider should be only minutes away. McPherson crouches down behind the big tree.

He isn't going to use the pistol. His plan is to use the three-pounder. It's still looped around his wrist. He figures with the target knocked off the horse, he will be on the target and a quick blow will be more than enough.

A part of him, at this moment, wonders if the hammer is too chancy, but his plan works best if he can keep from shooting, giving himself a few more minutes to disappear.

With another glance at the tablet, he sees the target is going past the third camera, which means he's less than two minutes out. Switching through the other two cameras, he doesn't see anyone else, so he puts the tablet down and crouches behind the tree, his stomach doing what it always does anticipating the moments ahead. It makes him feel like he's got to take a shit.

He concentrates on his breathing.

He concentrates on the task at hand.

They all fucking deserve to die, he thinks, his pulse rate climbing, his hands under the hide gloves sweating. *I'm a goddamn fucking culture hero*, he tells himself, trying calm. But his thoughts are racing and there's a whisper of cold fear and apprehension about doing any of this, and there's a bout of anxiety about getting caught, and then he hears the horse and then realizes he can hear the target singing. A moment later he recognizes a recent pop song that has been wildly overplayed in his opinion, and over-promoted, but catchy in a mass produced sort of way.

He ducks involuntarily, although the dark leaves are good cover. The horse and target are cantering, a good bounce as they go past him. Through the leaves he makes out a grunt, a gusting half shout, and sees the cowboy hat tumble on the trail, and he's flushing full on with panic, sure the situation has gone sideways and he is in *serious fucking shit*, but when he emerges from his blind the target is flat on his back, the horse is still walking forward, slowing.

He is up, the small sledge raised as he moves toward the target. He sees the wire caught right under the brim, the front hair is scalped back, the wound bleeding, a sheet of blood down the target's forehead and flooding one of the man's already sodden sideburns, and the target is looking at him, a look of mild puzzlement, and he brings the sledge down on the middle of the brow. The man coughs and his right eye is out of the socket, the forehead become misshaped. The other eye is open too, still in its socket, but there's a bulge to it. The man coughs, shudders, and exhales, long, rattling.

The man is still.

McPherson looks at the head, the face, and it all seems a long distance away, although a part of him knows he's standing right over the man. He steps back and sees movement from the corner of his eye that makes his heart jolt, but it's only the horse that has stopped and turned around, looking back toward the rider.

He stands up completely, shakily breathes out. "Hey, hey, hey," he says to the horse then takes a moment to swallow.

He finds it very hard to swallow.

"Hey buddy, I'm glad you're okay, that's great," he manages. The horse takes a step toward him. He steps back and his right heel is on the man's hand, the man's left arm and hand flung outward, and somehow he can feel the tree spike is cutting into fingers under his arch.

"Sorry," he says, a reflex, jerking his boot free.

"Huh," he says.

The horse is looking at him.

"All right, all right," he says, although he's confused whether he's speaking to the horse or to himself.

"All right," he says to himself.

He is still holding the three-pounder.

He lets the sledge drop to the trail, hitting with a thud.

The horse is looking at the dead man and he turns to look too.

The sight is disturbing, he'll admit that to himself. He feels like he barely hit with the hammer, yet the head is clearly crushed. He can see the sledge head's impact, the bone pushed down, a mold of the sledge face made of skin and skull, but the skull also looks like it's in two pieces, a lot of the right side, front, seems out of line with the rest of the man's head.

"Jesus fuck," he says quietly.

He sees the horse looking at him.

He tries to calm himself, get back to the plan, the next steps, but nothing comes clearly.

He is looking at the horse, he sees the horse toss its head, a whinny, and hears behind him the sound of a horse, a man shouting something.

What the fuck? McPherson is pretty sure the man he's turning around to see has said.

There's a second man and horse coming up behind the first. McPherson looks down at the man on the ground, the man with the broken head, and sees what he thinks might be brain pushing out from the side of the hammer mold depression. He sees one of the men dismounting, the other, the second, drawing a rifle from a scabbard. McPherson fumbles for the gun caught up behind him, yanks it free. The gun is in his hands. He lines the sites up on the man working to loose the rifle and fires, one, twice, and then he shifts to the first man, still halfway on his horse as he tries to reverse his dismount to put the horse between them.

McPherson fires blind, panic clenching the trigger. He stops when the magazine empties and the slide locks back, then starts toward where the first man's horse is down, two wounds across the horse's front flank with air gasping from the horse's bloody foaming nostrils and air and blood gusting through both gun wounds.

The first man is pinned under the gasping horse, a bullet through his left eye.

McPherson turns toward a sound of movement and sees the second man reaching for the rifle close to his outstretched arm. He moves toward this man, and as he does, he blankly pulls a second clip from his left front pocket, fumbling to release the empty clip. Then he manages to shove in the new one and re-rack the pistol. He fires two shots into the man's head from a step away, and the man's head is half exploded out the back of his skull, a mess heavy with brain splayed over the leaf litter.

McPherson's sight constricts to a blank darkness and he throws up over the dead man, sees that he gets puke on the man's legs, and he can't help saying what comes next, a reflex of politeness. "Sorry," he says to the dead man's legs or to no one.

"Huh," he says.

Chapter 33: Davin Gets Depressed

Davin, in his office, is pulling up the previous month's ad sales report to use as template, but he is having trouble putting aside his reaction to Gwen's latest text and her upset over Skip's decision to not have kids, this latest flare-up sparked by the news Marco is going in for a vasectomy. Her anxiety about Skip and Marco's decision not to have children has produced more contact between her and him than any other time post-divorce, including those couple of months when Jimmy was back living at the Housatonic house.

The dating he's been doing, seeing Gloria up in North County, carving out time to do things with her once or twice a week, is good, even great, but he sometimes catches himself wishing the divorce never happened, and this has been more pronounced of late with these recent texts about grandchildren.

Or lack thereof, he corrects himself.

He has a long history of talking with Skip about big issues and the fundamental questions of life. Not surprisingly, this habit had faded after she'd married Marco and, of course, even more so with her living in Spain. But now she appears to need some parental acceptance about her decision and her not wanting children has put Gwen on her back foot, or that's what he wonders, and now it seems like he's the parent Skip needs. This feels like a turnaround, especially after Gwen's recent long visit, when his own interactions with his daughter had by then felt unreal, a shadow.

It just feels strange. He hasn't seen Skip or Marco since they moved to Barcelona, not in the flesh as it were. The reasons for this are understandable, with Covid shutting down air travel, and then the divorce, and the economic consequences of that in his keeping the house, and all that making things difficult, but even emails and video chats had faded in their frequency. He wonders yet again why he doesn't understand this more clearly, and he has begrudgingly come to admit his isolation post-Covid and post-divorce. Quite a few of his old friends have made this exact argument, and often enough.

He has turned inward.

Instead of thinking about this uncomfortable truth further, he allows himself a distracted glance at his Google news feed and sees the economy is the top headline, some new report or Congressional panel on the cycles of pseudo-recessions. The up and down economy is due to structural problems, the coverage notes, including some connection to climate change, and some of that to the abortive tariffs. One item in the report is that the energy infrastructure spending should have a more positive impact on the economy, but the political infighting and Trump's attempts to rollback spending on renewables has made the impact weak. And there's been the typical annual debt ceiling hostage-taking that keeps roiling the markets. Just last year, this had happened twice, with a full-on federal shutdown the first time, and the markets tumbled and a lot of the spending temporarily shut down too.

No shit, Sherlock, he tells himself.

He hopes the coming elections will see a stronger shift in Congress, but somehow enough Republicans still have been getting reelected, and he doesn't know if this gridlock will ever change.

He is angry that the Democrats haven't done much more than minor tweaks of the income tax code, and the minimum corporate tax from the early Biden period has proven too easily circumvented to make much of a difference, while Trump getting many of his tax cuts extended had further tightened purse strings. It drives him crazy that the rich are so far from paying anything close to their fair share. It upsets him that the prospect for more aggressive progressive income tax rates remains a third-rail issue. He doesn't understand why this isn't a big lever for the Democrats, but the argument about taxing the rich is too easily turned into the argument about everyone getting taxed, never mind the facts.

Maybe those Kill the Rich assholes should form a political party, he jokes, but then immediately feels bad about his dark jest.

He starts back on putting the new data into the report template. He sees the month looks good. It looks like his higher schedule payout numbers should be triggered, finally. This won't make a big difference in his total income, unfortunately, which gets him thinking about his money worries.

Who knew you can't make money making art? he asks himself, repeating a frequent joke, such self-deprecation a regular guest in his thoughts. He was productive in the studio that year before the divorce, enjoyed some commissions, had been close to nailing down a show in a Hudson gallery, but the world had turned upside down.

Who knew plagues are bad for artists' incomes?

He and Gwen had been doing okay financially, and her institutional job remained a safe income during the shutdown. He even had some solid subcontracting from one of his longtime colleagues who happened to have been having a good year. But during the shutdown the marriage was coming apart, and he'd gotten caught up in the *strum und drang* and his work in the studio suffered and fell off. A few months later his marriage was declared done, and he had gone deeper into his own private shutdown after that.

He keeps thinking about family and that he misses family. His son, Jimmy, is doing great, still with Cynthia, and it was great seeing them recently, even if they had found themselves in the middle of a *terrorist event*. This was how the story has been covered and he's taken aback by how readily and widely this new organization, No One is Safe, has been labelled *terrorist*. Sure, blowing up cars in a parking garage in the middle of a major American city is certainly on the spectrum, he'd admit, but no one was hurt, just property.

These days, the most terrifying act imaginable, I guess, he tells himself, *is the attack on property*.

This organization is already mostly referred to by its initials, NOS, and he thinks this works to the group's advantage since NOS brings up SOS in the mind's ear.

Good branding, anyway, he tells himself.

There have been some arrests, but he has the sense from the news articles he reads that NOS may have some kind of decentralized and virtual structure that makes it hard to identify the group's members. The investigation into the hack into the city's public alert network has come to nothing, too, although he knows there may be more to the investigation than what gets reported. Still, something of a black eye, the hijacking of Wireless Emergency Alerts, something in operation since 2023, he's read somewhere, some congressional act, he thinks.

Jimmy probably understands this better than I ever will, he supposes, making a note to ask him next time they talk.

The current administration was wailing on the terrorism angle, showing that the Democrats are tough, too, promises from the Justice Department and the FBI and DHS still part of the daily caterwauling. There'd been injuries, of course, and even he has a battle scar to show, except it is not a scar but a mostly faded bruise he can still feel when he twists his torso into certain positions. He was luckier than the hundreds who got medical treatment, but there were few long hospitalizations, nothing beyond three days, and that for just one bystander.

Just a lot of bumps and bruises, and some bones broken and bad sprains.

Despite the drama of that day, the visit was great, and even that night, back at Jimmy and Cynthia's apartment, they'd been jazzed and stayed up late making cocktails, he proud that Jimmy had the necessary bar equipment on hand.

The conversation was interesting. Cynthia was incensed by NOS, repeatedly arguing how such action would only hurt all the legitimate and already hard-pressed efforts underway toward climate progress. He had tried to play devil's advocate but quickly stopped, since it was clear she seemed intent on taking no prisoners.

To Davin, when he thinks back to the visit, the best gift from that day was the image of Jimmy protecting Cynthia as the crowd panicked, but there is something bittersweet about it, too. The empty nest feeling had again flared on his way back to the Berkshires the next morning, the train westward crowded with other marchers on their way home, including a few people from town he had recognized but done no more than nod their way. On the ride back he'd emotionally crashed, overwhelmed by the same feeling he had after his son went off to his new job in Boston, and then with Chaplin leaving, and then with Deidre leaving, and all of it seems to have set off echoes of his sense of isolation.

Jimmy's great with him, Davin knows that. But Jimmy's not one to reach out often, and Davin's not so practiced at that himself, that having been Gwen's initiative back when. And Skip away in Spain. He understands he can be easily triggered thinking about his family, and learning about Skip's decision is simply the latest pull. What he does not know, to his disappointment, is what he's supposed to do about it. All too often he has the uncomfortable sense that in some way he's lost his children in the divorce.

His feeling of loneliness strikes him as odd, or oddly strong, at any rate, considering he's been seeing Gloria for weeks, typically including one or two nights getting together, usually with him staying overnight.

Still, the last time he was with her he had tried to talk

about his loneliness, and she'd been polite and listened, but had little to say. He suspects the truth is his desire for emotional connection with her is inappropriately strong considering they haven't known each other that long or that well.

Except biblically, he tells himself. *Thank god*. He's been shocked by how great the sex is, and that continues.

He still hasn't acted on the third house-share opening post-Deidre. He knows he will be better off if he acts sooner than later. The addition revenue could help him not be so constrained and worried about the expense of the airfare he's now obsessing about for a trip to Spain.

He tries to clear his mind and get back to work. He'll make sure he meditates today, maybe before he calls Jimmy, or maybe after.

He should call his old friend Dominic, too. A mutual friend had recently texted, mentioning Dominic, something about prostate problems.

Fuck, he thinks. Dennis is the second of his old friends now dealing with this cancer.

He'd been meditating more with Gwen the last year they did much of anything together, and recently he's been trying to get back to sitting. He'll always be less steady in practice than he'd like, but the whole Josephine thing has forced him back to it, if only for the moments of calm that meditation can offer. Sitting also influences his thinking, freeing it up, and nowadays he keeps a notebook by his side, because his meditation sessions often conclude with rich sculpture concepts and art ideas, although any bright ideas for how he might clear time for the studio remain far more elusive. He figures that maybe he needs to get back to more therapy, maybe going back to a weekly session instead of the once-a-month check in.

Now that's depressing, he jokes, but he also knows deflection through humor only goes so far.

He should email his therapist and ask about more sessions.

Well, I'll meditate on it, he jokes.

He pulls out the external keyboard he uses with his laptop when he's at his desk and starts an email to Skip.

He doesn't know if he has anything new to say about what she's been struggling with, but he figures he can start out by telling her how much he loves her.

Chapter 34: Accidents Happen

Today, in addition to the business briefcase, Lobinski also carries a small white shoebox. *Maybe a bit weird*, he thinks but shrugs off the concern since very few others are out and about this early, which is good. On the other hand, the neighborhood is mostly devoid of sidewalks, and that includes Fairfax Road where the assignment lives. He remains a little unsettled by this since it means he walks along the sides of streets, but the two or three early morning joggers he has seen do it too.

He has gone back and forth about again dressing as a jogger, but he needs to carry materials for the setup, so the briefcase and the shoebox puts him in the suit and tie.

He's a bit early and has left the car parked a few streets away, having switched license plates for good measure. He tries to look the part of a businessman, again wearing a suit for camouflage, although the very early hour puts that to the test. The predawn glow is just starting to build and the hint of heat and humidity declares a typical Washington day is in store, although the weather report has the capitol region likely on the edge of a big low-pressure system that is reported likely to soak New England. He looks north by northwest, and sees what may be dark banks of clouds, but it's too early in the morning to be sure he's not simply looking at the darker western skies before dawn.

He heard the newspaper delivery car making its rounds, and then he spots it turning at the next block up from the one where he's keeping watch. This morning the driver is also on the early side, his vehicle an old station wagon, something he doesn't see much anymore, but his own dad had one, a Ford Taurus wagon, and that car was old enough even back then it hadn't survived to his driving lessons age. The newspaper delivery station wagon, as he's seen in a close pass-by, looks too rusted to even pass inspection.

He loves the driver's delivery technique, though, having seen him in action at various spots over the course of the week he's been gathering a sense of the area, jogging the streets of the neighborhood and beyond. The newspapers, rolled and bagged, shoot out from a device in the station wagon's front passenger seat. He would like to check that out closer, but he's only had the one quick glance as the station wagon passed close by him his second morning surveilling. That had been enough though to make out something that looked like a mortar tube sticking out of the front passenger-side window. The man has some sort of newspaper cannon, probably spring-based, and likely a motorized pullback since having to manually reset the spring so frequently would be too much. *The guy would have one arm that looks like Popeye's*, he'd thought as he watched the station wagon disappear past the intersection turn.

What he's witnessed is when it's a single paper house, the guy doesn't even stop but has the timing right when the paper snaps and sails away, almost always hitting the walk to the front door. So far, he's observed only one bad miss, with a paper landing in shrubs to the side of a front entrance of a house, this observation made from his temporary stop two days ago, standing with one arm against a tree doing jogger-like stretching.

He takes a look at his watch, hoping to mime a person waiting by the street edge for a ride. He knows the time, but he won't move to the setup area for several minutes yet. Just minutes ago the assignment's house lights have been going on, first on the second floor and then a couple of rooms on the first.

At the other end of the block, he sees the paper delivery vehicle pass through a more distant intersection, no doubt following a well-set grid. He's pretty sure there are stacks of the different papers on the back seat of the station wagon from which, he figures, the driver reaches back for the reload, selecting from what he guesses might be some sort of rack, something to keep the different papers in order. He has only once seen the vehicle stopped, the headliner light on and the man reaching into the back. From the wrappers he has seen of the flying newspapers, he concludes the papers are mostly *The Washington Post* and some *The New York Times*, mixed in with some *The Washington Examiner* and *The Wall Street Journal.*

He saw that one house gets four papers. That was the most fun to witness, but he had to alter his jogging route and timing for the surveilling over the days, so missed a repeat of the station wagon stopping perpendicular to the home's front walkway and the man feeding one paper after another, *ping, ping, ping, ping,* before moving on to the next house.

He can just make out the station wagon's rumble and the stuttered shots as the car moves slowly one street up. He takes a moment to wonder how the launch system might work with grenades before shaking his thoughts back to the task at hand.

Which, of course, is to murder this guy, Lobinski tells himself, glancing toward the assignment's house.

The outside driveway light has switched on, which means he needs to get back into operational focus.

The timing is critical. The setup is a bit baroque, but he can't see any major faults and believes this may help sell the KTR claim, if he needs it, but he hopes he won't have to send in the claim, considering this murder is supposed to come off as a natural death.

Sweet and low, Lobinski thinks, aiming to keep his exposure minimal. The death is supposed to look natural, that is the key. He looks at his watch, pulling up the suit jacket's sleeve to reveal it.

Showtime.

The morning light is brightening as he starts walking

up to his spot on Little Falls Parkway, which is divided by a median in this long section of road just three blocks and two short turns away from the assignment's house. The parkway does have sidewalks, and he gets himself set, the newspaper out, standing on the concrete sidewalk near the curb, looking up the street every now and then, just a guy waiting to get picked up by the carpool.

He keeps an eye on the Fairfax Road turn onto this street, up about 300 feet where another car is just now whizzing past. The speed limit is thirty-five miles per hour, but this early he has seen many cars race down the stretch.

Where the assignment will turn onto Little Falls Parkway is far enough up to provide plenty of time for the car to pick up speed.

He knows he can't put the tire buster out too early since another car could come first.

Well, so try again later, he thinks. He knows there's nothing wrong with an abort, there will always be other chances, other approaches, and he's once again wondering if this setup has too many pieces to it, but he's pretty sure he can get the car stopped with the tire damage, maybe even cause it to swerve into one of the trees that line the length of the landscaped divider. There is the possibility the assignment keeps driving on the blown tire, driving too far for the next part of the plan to be plausible.

And then he pushes such thoughts from his mind. These thoughts are just pre-action jitters and second-guesses. He relaxes himself and then tenses when he spots the assignment's car approaching the intersection of Fairfax and the parkway. A quick glance finds no other cars coming behind, although a car goes in the other direction on the other side of the divide.

He opens the briefcase and puts on a pair of black nitrile gloves then puts the needle ring on, takes out the tire buster, holding it along his right leg, briefcase and shoebox in his other hand.

The assignment's car turns onto the parkway, and as

anticipated, starts accelerating. Lobinski steps on to the road, the half-crumbled shoebox dropping where he wants it, and as he bends down toward it, he slides the rusted metal length with the sharp edge up in one smooth motion then scurries back toward the sidewalk, the white box left in place.

The car is still picking up speed.

Speed Racer, Lobinski thinks as the car gets closer. Then he steps toward the white box, reaching to pick it up, and the car swerves left to avoid him.

This is a dangerous moment for him, he knows, but he knows the assignment will have registered the white box and see him stepping back toward it and will react by swerving left, instead of plowing into him.

The car swerves toward the medium perfectly, the front left tire hitting the thin jagged metal with a satisfying *pop!* that sounds enough like a gunshot to flash him back to Syria for the merest of moments. But he's tracking the car, which is pulled hard on the blown left front tire and going fast enough to jump up the medium's curb. It clips one of the trees and settles to a stop. Lobinski runs toward the car, going around the back side. The target is bleeding from the nose from the airbag punch but looks undazed.

Lobinski tries the door, but it remains locked, the car still running. He shatters the glass with a small window break he's pulled from his side pocket, and he shouts at the target, asking *Are you okay?* and telling him help is coming, and *What's wrong?* as he leans in. The assignment is confused, is saying something about being fine. Lobinski is low, arm reaching around the target's head, saying something about concussions, saying, *It's okay, It's okay* as he presses the shallow needle of the ring injector into the back of the neck, above the hairline, and Lobinski sees the man's expression change, a sharp frown and an unasked question and a move of the man's arm toward the back of his neck, but by then, so fast, the potassium mix is doing its work, and the target grabs at the other arm, and then his chest, clawing at it as Lobinski steps back to make a quick survey. On the other side of the street he sees a woman walking her dog, so he steps farther back, shouting, calling out to her to dial 911. He steps around the back of the car as the car begins to creep forward as the assignment's foot slips off the brake pedal. He shouts he'll get help and crosses the street, kicking the piece of metal in front of him. It lands with a clang against the curb as he swoops up the box and then he's off to the next corner, slowing to a walk, and his quick glance back shows the woman is leaning into the still creeping car, and another car is stopping, and then he slowly walks toward the side street where he left his standby car, just another Washington lawyer, heading off for work.

He really likes his tire shredder, enjoyed working on it at the junkyard in Pennsylvania. He thinks it might well pass muster if anyone were to look at it, meant to look like nothing too identifiable, the sharp edge washed to rust, maybe a rusted frame fallen from some junk truck, its presence and origin unknowable.

If they really need to determine why the tire blew, it would likely suffice, but nobody looks closely at a guy in a car, crashed because of a heart attack.

Happens every day, Lobinski thinks, but then he's thinking about the KTR claim he could send, would send if needed, the notes for it already well along, the elaborate murder a good fit. The cops could look closer and see the tire buster for what it is or find the puncture mark and the telltale blood levels.

He gets to his standby car and climbs in. It's still early enough that he's passed no others.

This is not the last of the assignments, but the next one should be less difficult, just B&E, adding computer file folders to a laptop at that assignment's home.

The child porn packages.

The insert folders likely to be unnoticed until someone goes looking, so there's a link-up routine that will lead the law to the assignment as soon as his client wants it activated.

He heads for his motel, removing the wig and mustache for disposal somewhere before he gets back, but the long drive suddenly seems impossible. He is exhausted.

Shit, he realizes, noting his adrenaline shakes, the typical post-action reaction, and then he's at his drop car, thinking of the next task, the shakes gone.

Chapter 35: Flooding Emotions

Davin has spent most of the morning cleaning up the yard, having intended only to check things out post-storm, but he ended up at it for a solid three hours. Now he is finally sitting at his desk, either trying to write up notes from the latest Select Board meeting, or to rouse himself to get to the garden cleanup work, or to give himself permission to slip into the studio where, maybe, he'll have some time to sketch out what he's trying to do with this new piece, except it isn't all that new anymore, just still largely unfinished, the small box with some of the old and broken watches ready for the next time he can work on it.

There really isn't any time today, he sees, not with the storm just passed. He'd just as soon try to ignore the storm damage, but the ferocious system of thunderstorms that passed late in the night knocked down tree branches all over, and a lot of leaves and twigs still litter the lawns. Some of the plastic furniture on the north deck has ended up in the hydrangeas on the north property line, although all that happened with the furled patio umbrella was it getting knocked over.

A lot of young fruit on the apple and peach trees are on the ground. The sunscreens he and Marsha had strung up over the big garden survived pretty well except for one big seam that is badly ripped, but he thinks he can patch that back together. He'll have to spend time setting the whole thing back up, however, because the screens are mostly wrapped around the guide ropes and frames or bunched against the fences.

He hopes Marsha will help, but he's hard-pressed to see why she would.

At least if I don't pay her, anyway.

He's amazed they didn't lose power, but then the Housatonic Valley had gotten off easy.

Today he'd planned to work on getting a gallery show, although his discussions with the two galleries—one local, one in Hudson—will stubbornly stay in to-do list territory for longer now.

He feels he should be adding *Get some fucking energy* to his to-do list.

All in all, there's not a lot of serious damage from the winds, and in Berkshire County they've missed the heaviest storm-system deluge that dumped further east. Palmer, about an hour or so eastward on the Pike, has taken it hard and not only because of the heavy downpours themselves, in the form of some twelve inches of rain in less than three hours, but because the absurd amount of rainfall overtopped the Ware River Reservoir, which caused some flooding beyond the wetlands with the high water following the lower land around a small creek, flooding a couple of mixed business and residential neighborhoods. The bigger problem was that overtopping of the Ware reservoir dam led to the overtopping of the Hill Street reservoir down in Palmer, and that added water caused the failure of the dam up by the Thorndike Fire and Water District facilities. There has been a flush of swelling storm waters across the Three Rivers area, taking out several neighborhoods along that long portion of Main Street, including Country Corner and inundating all along the full length of Palmer Road, the water swallowing ancient floodplains with ease. Farther north on the Ware River there was more flooding that was less catastrophic, but the Chicopee River flood-management system put in to protect the Connecticut River plains from major floods after the 1935 disaster has held, and according to the news it's mostly just Chicopee River flood plains and farm fields and a few farmhouses that have flooded.

The Quaboag River southward in Palmer is still rising, last he checked, which was after his first coffee and before heading out to police the yard. Now he brings up his local news feeds and according to Channel 5 out of Boston, an ABC affiliate, eighteen people are dead in the Palmer area, and they haven't even started a list of the missing. Several small tornados have been reported across Monson and Brimfield to the south and southwest of Palmer, although official confirmation is still pending. From the images already showing up on social media that he's also looking at, there is significant wind destruction and the takedown of swaths of trees in Monson, and at least three houses are extensively damaged. There is an image of a car wind-pushed onto a front porch, the porch columns knocked out or broken and the porch roof resting on the sideways-leaning car.

It certainly looks like extensive damage to him.

Just back from the kitchen with a fresh cup of coffee, he looks again at a video he's already watched a couple of times. The video, post-storm, is shot from the Interstate 90 bridge high over Palmer's Quaboag River, except it doesn't look like the bridge is all that high over anymore, the now-fat river filled with parts of houses and some cars and trees and unidentifiable debris, and the National Guard is just starting to mobilize.

He has driven that part of the Pike countless times. The river was always hard to see from the long bridge span, the banks narrowed close in by trees, but now it looks like a lot of those trees are gone, swept down.

I've cleaned up some branches, he tells himself.

Davin, sitting at his desk, is feeling unsettled.

Any number of things might explain this feeling, including the just-passed storm and all the bother of it, even though he knows what he's dealing with is nothing, really, not in comparison to what's happened an hour east. But there are several things he's been obsessing about, can't help but obsessively think about, such as the all-too-modest pay from *Berkshire Interactive* for all the work he's been doing for Alicia and not getting into the studio to work on that one particular sculpture he keeps thinking about, but thinking is all that's happening, given that he can't rouse himself to take an hour here or there to fit in even just a bit of time. The problem isn't he can't steal an hour here and there from *Berkshire Interactive*, but then there is the household work, too, and the garden, and the Airbnb apartment that tends to attract the two-day minimum guests so he or Marsha is always changing bedding, cleaning, and doing laundry. The problem is working on his art in little fits and starts strikes him as ineffective and downright frustrating.

Boo hoo hoo, he says to himself.

At least he's not in Palmer, he tells himself.

To be honest, one of his assignments for *BI* is an interesting one, tracking developments from the statehouse about a new permitting change that could help move the latest municipal solar project ahead, but there is yet another *not-in-my-backyard* pushback that could be a problem.

He finds NIMBY particularly galling. He finds he has to make great effort to control himself when present at meetings when this comes up, and it comes up again and again. But he was at such meeting wearing his press hat, so shouting at people about being selfish and entitled assholes had to be left to other attendees.

He does take a certain relish in reporting on such exchanges, though.

And then he is back to thinking again about the sculpture, still rough, still sitting on a workbench in his studio so close by, but then that's again subsumed by a sense of dread concerning what Alicia is expecting from him these days, pushing for more of his involvement.

I could say no, he reminds himself.

One problem with saying no to Alicia's assignments is he usually likes what has turned into his town hall beat, even though much of it can be just too damn boring and time-consuming for the modest pay. What he does like is the connection it provides him in the town, not that he hasn't run into his share of kooks, bores, and people so self-centered it stuns him. He assumes, anyway, that this has been helping him counter his propensity for isolation.

He knows, though, there are other of his assumptions that are more suspect.

Like being an artist, he is now telling himself, and now he is slipping into a session of sighs, a sign of his feeling state getting worse.

He puts his head in his hands.

It's always fucking like this, he tells himself, but even as he says it, he recognizes the cognitive trap in it.

No, it is not always like this, he corrects himself, straightening up in his office chair, pulling himself closer to the desk, but his mental correction also carries a vitriolic tone so that he might as well still be beating himself. So, he tries again, looking for the positive, trying to put his feelings in check.

I have made progress, he tells himself, but a hint of negation still washes over him, but fortunately, he's gotten to the point where he can acknowledge and articulate his negative perceptions.

Ah, yes, goodness gracious, he says to himself, *The Complex is back.*

Davin has always been hard-pressed to describe *The Complex*, although not for any lack of trying. The best he's ever come up with is that *The Complex* is a matrix of feeling states and memories of feeling states that carry long-established but entirely unhelpful and adverse suppositions, cross-referenced to childhood perceptions of his family's behavioral history long hardwired as a bad coping habit. He thinks of this as a decision tree and flow process that culminates in *The Complex* and its associated negative feelings. At the time he had articulated this, some years and several therapists back, that therapist had clapped and shouted, *Bravo!*

He still remains tempted, when he is caught up in these

negative feelings, to plot out *The Complex* using a software architecture build program he owns that does process flow diagramming, but he is usually feeling better by the time such temptation emerges and he's always got better things to do, like remembering his kids and his friends and that good mental health is all a matter of connections with others. He acknowledges his tendency to detach himself and most typically and unhelpfully in times of stress, like today, and he is well aware this is a stupid way to react and very much not helpful.

But there you go, he tells himself, but he's already feeling calmer, despite the anxiety his agreeing to Aine and Cynthia's scheme to hold a local program at his house that benefits their two organizations. It is cleverly titled *MMEAT and Greet* and will be a cocktail-party affair featuring meat alternatives and a talk by Aine about The Third Way and with a fundraiser component, assuming anyway, they get enough participants to cover his costs. They haven't set a date yet, and the whole thing is early days, but at least he's been having more conversations with Cynthia, which means with Jimmy too, and that's been nice.

About the only thing accomplished so far, though, is walking the grounds with Aine, figuring out parking and where the Porta Potties might go and working out some rough sense of costs. He hasn't mentioned anything about the event yet to his two boarders and he reminds himself there is still the whole third-boarder search he hasn't gotten to, despite his worry about creeping expenses, and there's the recent concern about next tax year's reduction in the Carbon Tax Earned Income Credit even while the heating oil for the house and the gasoline for the old car are up yet again, so now he'll be paying more income tax because of the tax credit pullback.

He's been looking at electric cars, since the Hyundai is not just old but ancient and decrepit. The differential between electric and gasoline is compelling, and there are still good tax credits for buying electric with Congress reasserting and clarifying IRA funds. There's the state's rebates on top of that, too. Still, it means a loan, and he'll need to install a home charging port. The expenses that are involved remain significant despite all the credits and rebates available.

He's well aware that his income problems aren't addressed through his artwork, and that would still hold true, he also knows, even if he were more productive in the studio. On the other hand, the garden helps lower food costs, or will help, eventually, in theory anyway. Even now, after years in production, the big vegetable garden seems to be better at supporting the outflow of money rather than saving money on groceries. And then there is the actual season transitioning into full summer with July half done, which means the garden is demanding more and more time, so thank goodness for Marsha, and thank goodness she has worked out well, all things considered, and especially with her garden involvement.

Finally got the serf I always wanted, Davin thinks. He makes the mental note not to try this joke out loud, ever.

The income making the real difference is the Airbnb apartment that takes up one-half of the first floor and is set up as two bedrooms, one with a queen bed and the other, rather tiny, with a twin bed. Except for a nice bathroom with original clawfoot tub and all, there is only one other room which is the kitchen/dining room/living room all-in-one. Still, the apartment is a comfortable space, and attractive after his big renovation, if he does say so himself, and the three-season front porch is a nice place for the guests to hang out. The short-term rental gig is working out well, and he is now almost eight years into it. Post-Covid and post-divorce, the bookings have been pretty constant, although he doesn't take bookings for December through April despite Great Barrington having one ski facility within its borders and another one, in Hillsdale, New York, that is twenty minutes away. These slopes simply aren't big enough to attract many non-locals, and don't really help drive wintertime rentals, and the lack of good snow is another increasingly common problem. Considering the challenge of his steep long driveway, too, he doesn't want to put winter renting to the test anyway. The apartment booking starts slow each year, with April known as mud season in the Berkshires, but the apartment is usually rented half the time coming into June, and by the start of July there are typically a series of the two-day minimums with a smattering of week-to-week rentals that last pretty much through Labor Day. The rentals start dropping off after that, though there is a bump in October through Indigenous People's Day, that holiday he still too often reflexively calls Columbus Day, which is when the foliage is largely peak color. It doesn't seem to matter the foliage colors are more muted, for years now, and apparently, according to Cynthia, another result of climate change.

But now Airbnb has proposed a new program that extends to any and all participating listings the opportunity to aid Josephine-displaced people, something that remains a crisis, despite FEMA going full tilt and nonstop. Too many of the tent cities remain full, but he doesn't see any blame on par with what happened in the Katrina fiasco because there isn't a fair basis for comparison. There are much larger differences in the sheer number of displaced, near enough five times the Katrina count. He's not sure of final numbers, but somewhere between four and five million people uprooted by the storm are now being rehoused. Many of these remain in temporary housing and tent cities or other forms of shelter provided nearby. Cities as far away as Denver, Wichita, and Milwaukie, and even Battle Creek, Michigan, have even gotten involved.

The main characteristic of those remaining unhoused is that they are disproportionately black and Hispanic, and these people are the visible manifestation of institutional racism as far as he's concerned. But now Airbnb is putting the liberal in him to the test by allowing hosts to clear their calendars of scheduled guests penalty-free and take in the

Gold Coast unhoused with good stipends from the brand new federal program.

He knows he has to do what's right, despite all the little misgivings that keep coming up. Though he can still surprise himself with the places his thoughts go, dark and fearful, he will likely sign up.

Even at the pain of making more money, he confesses to himself. The Americabnb stipends are below normal rates, but he can carry the apartment well past his typical seasonal close date at full occupancy.

At the moment, the program is still unfunded, waiting for congressional authorization, but he can't see how he can say no when that time comes, not that this resolves his doubts and worries about participation.

He's even having doubts about the woman he's dating, or whatever one should call it, with the relationship with Gloria feeling static, or stuck, and he is bothered by the odd lack of emotional connection on her part. On the other hand, he's got no complaints about the sex, and just last week he learned she loves to be entered from behind, which certainly works for him. He'd always thought of this as *doggy style*, but in the course of that particular conversation, he discovered this is what an old English term, *rogering*, means. At least he's pretty sure this is what she told him.

Getting Rogered? Rogering?

He'll have to look this up.

He goes back to YouTube and watches the Palmer flood clip again, but he also opens a side tab and looks up *rogering*.

Chapter 36: To the Benefit of All

Gerald Greene is not happy. He is supposed to be on a teleconference call in a couple of minutes, speaking with the general counsel of the second-largest global construction corporation in the world, along with the Institute's ex-board member, who has been chairman of this very corporation for almost two decades. They are supposed to be discussing the candidates and incumbents who he's recommending to the chairman's PAC, *America Works*, so campaign funding can get underway. The candidates and incumbents to be backed are those most likely to support the sort of Sea Wall Act *The Gang* wants to see.

The day's schedule is full of such calls, following up on the position paper he's circulated a few days ago.

Just an hour or two ago, he'd been riding high on the positive reaction to the position paper now in the hands of his patrons. The responses coming back have been glowingly positive.

Glowingly positive until a couple of hours ago, he adds angrily, because he now feels anything but positive.

Someone has talked, leaked.

Or maybe someone got hacked, he wonders. He makes a note to call in his cyber security service to run a full analysis. The idea that somehow there's been a hack or leak from the Institute keeps poking at his attention, but he keeps a clamp on it. He'll wait for facts and his secret hope is that the leak happened through one or another of the many recipients.

All he knows is the position paper — *my position paper!* — is now available in full across the Web for anyone to see. It has only been out for a few hours at most, but it must have been leaked early, because the posted version has been explicated, annotated, and otherwise analyzed. This he had discovered this morning by way of *The New York Times.*

He is not happy, although he's calming down and starting to see how this can be handled, and maybe even turned to advantage.

Yeah, good luck with that, he tells himself, but his anger is fading and a plan is forming.

It isn't that there is any acute issue with the position paper being public. Greene long ago learned one doesn't put out such things with too specific instructions or baldly obvious action-benefit arguments, ROI claims, or detailed strategy. Still, he knows, the strategy is there for anyone who wants to see.

He hears his administrative assistant through his closed office doors, hints of hysteria and frustration seeping through with the occasional word or phrase as the young man frantically follows up with all those so carefully scheduled conference calls. The assistant arranged all these calls in the days before, and now they're shot.

He steps toward the dark panel doors that lead into the outer office and waiting room.

Yes sir, yes, I'm making a note of the time. I'll have him call, yes sir, Greene can just make out. He turns abruptly, heading back for his desk, his office doors left shut.

He settles himself down in his office chair. Before him on the large desk are several newspapers cast across the surface, including *The New York Times* and *The Washington Post.* He can't look these over any further, still feeling too sick to read about this public turn, so he turns to his monitor, pulls up a cable network on his browser for a financial show he often follows, and unmutes the streaming video.

"... widely released this morning to a storm of reactions. The Kehoe Institute's executive director, Dr. Gerald Greene, has not issued a statement about what some analysts describe as a blueprint for political manipulation of the Sea Wall Act, still in committee. In the words of a spokesman for the House Speaker, 'A callous play by special interests to potentially control and direct many billions of dollars of infrastructure spending over the next decades.'"

He shuts that tab, but the one under it is another cable network, a talking head mid-speech, mouth frozen in the pause, silent.

Fucking Speaker, Greene says to himself, letting himself ease back against the chair, eyes closed.

He begrudgingly notes the Speaker's synopsis is spot on.

His eyes open and he sighs. "Well," he says out loud to the empty room, "we were going to come up against you anyway."

Just not so soon, is his added thought.

It isn't even so much the issue of the paper being public, but the real hit is the analysis of the paper's import, which slants negative in devastating ways, compellingly translating his guarded phrases into buying politicians and naked assessments of voting blocs. The other problem is the renewed interest on the Institute and a number of PACs and the large campaign funders. Worst of all, though, all the unwanted coverage includes discussion about fossil fuel subsidies. He had hoped to play the issue better with the media and the public when it came time. He hadn't planned on public messaging as yet—in fact had only roughed-out some talking points as a courtesy to the recipients. The cover email with those talking points hadn't been part of the leak, but the inference was there in the position paper, nevertheless. What seems strange to him is the uniformity of the analysis across the media reports and talking heads, especially since the paper could not have been available for that long, unless, of course, the leak was earlier, and this thought again gets him worried about internal problems. But most unsettling, he fears, is the damning analysis, which is sophisticated and thorough, and yet there is no mention or reference or credit for any analysts.

No attributions have been mentioned at all, as far as he can tell.

"Who the fuck is behind this?" he asks the empty room.

Greene is going to be speaking about this problem with some very pissed-off people later today, and these are people he'd really rather not piss off.

Greene pushes away from the desk and walks to the doors, flinging one of them open, only to see his assistant gesturing with his finger to let him finish the call he's trying to wrap up.

I fucking hate that finger thing, Greene tells himself, feeling an explosion of anger coming on, but he controls himself.

The assistant is off the phone and his look has an apology pantomimed across the young face, up into the hairline.

"Sorry, sorry, sorry," the assistant says to Greene.

"Denkel," Greene says. "Get me Denkel on the phone and right now." Denkel is one of his smartest directors and should be a big help with the work ahead. The three other program directors of the institute, not so much.

"You got it," the assistant says, dropping back in front of the keyboard and multiple monitors that surround the desk's edges. He punches the phone's keypad and talks into it, but Greene is already heading back into his office.

"Five minutes," Greene shouts through the door as he pulls it shut. He thinks he hears his assistant say, *Yup,* which annoys Greene. *Sounds like a kid,* he thinks to himself as he settles back behind his desk.

He pulls a legal pad toward him, pushing the newspapers aside, one slipping off to settle in a heap on the rug.

About jobs, he writes. He adds, *Government can't be trusted, boondoggles, Big Dig, find more recent examples.*

Climate remediation too important to leave to public sector, too pressing. He stops at that phrase, rereads it.

Oh, nice positioning.

He continues to scribble away.

No time for politics as usual, climate work is too important, we support elected officials who can get things done, this is part of the political process, corporations have rights to participate.

Greene decides the last phrase needs work.

Professional politicians get in the way, make everything, he scratches that last word out, adding in *every decision about themselves, but climate change is too important.*

That seems key.

American Jobs for American Climate Change Solutions.

Greene is not sure why he's using all initial capitals, but this does look like the beginning of a slogan, maybe.

American Companies Built This Land, and American Companies Build America's Future.

He stops again. *Mr. Fucking Slogan,* he says to himself, but he's calming down.

Good jobs, good American jobs for good American work. America's businesses care about climate change. It makes good business sense.

He pauses, not happy about going around in circles already.

Get to the subsidy shit, he tells himself.

We're not politicians sitting around talking. America's businesses mean business. We get it done!

He thinks, *Yeah, well, maybe.*

Subsidies should be rolled back, but rollbacks need to be done right. Don't crash the economy.

He likes *crashing.*

Cutting subsidies shouldn't cut jobs. America's businesses aren't looking back, aren't interested in old, outdated laws.

Greene stops because he knows his afternoon calls are going to want to know how this *hullabaloo, brouhaha, ruckus,* this *shitstorm* will affect the new tax breaks effort, and he knows he'll have to think this through better.

We are about the business of the future.

If the worst happens, Greene thinks they'll need the right talking points and attacks on the statistics behind externalities cost figures. They will definitely need to raise the prospect for and fear of potential price hikes and paint it all as antibusiness, anti-jobs.

Keep the eyes on the prize, he tells himself.

Greene is exhausted, and it's not even lunchtime yet.

He pushes the intercom. "Coffee, Justin, coffee. Please."

"Yup," Justin replies, but before Greene can become more annoyed, the assistant says, "Denkel, line one, sir."

Greene picks up the handset, pushes the button.

"I need your ass in here ASAP. We need to brainstorm responses to this clusterfuck," Greene tells him.

Greene listens to Denkel's reply.

"Yes, yes, right," Greene then says. "So, big deal, you're taking a few days off. Well, not anymore. I'm in the middle of a shitshow, and I need someone else with a brain too."

Greene listens, then laughs.

"Right," he says. "But also, listen, we need to know who is behind this, the analysis—"

Denkel says something.

Greene alertly listens, not making a sound until he hears a name.

"Penworth?" he asks, shaking his head.

Denkel tells him about Penworth and a group called *The Laundry*. Greene realizes he knows all this, but hasn't, somehow, been worried about Penworth. He stopped thinking of this man and his group as a problem because he'd already planned an effective counter to these *sons of bitches*.

Lobinski delivered the packet three days ago, but Greene had thought to wait until it was needed, or if it even would ever be needed.

He wants to kick himself for being *Mr. Nice Guy*, but he's realizing the timing may be the best of all possibilities to undermine the analyses of the position paper.

Fuck 'em, he thinks, barely hearing anything Denkel says.

"All right," he says to Denkel, but Denkel's still talking, going on about repositioning.

"All right," Greene repeats.

"Reposition the context, right," Greene says into the phone, repeating what Denkel has just said to him. He rolls his eyes, not hearing anything different than the thoughts he'd been wrestling with, and he wants to get going, but then Denkel is complaining about having to reschedule other work.

"All right, who cares?" he says to Denkel. "Just get your ass in here, get together with Mitch, bring in who you want." Mitch, the Institute's director of communications, isn't a favorite of Denkel's, but there's no time for that sort of bullshit, and Greene figures Denkel knows that.

"Yeah, yeah, it's a job effort, getting the money away from Congress, from their slow inefficient wasteful ways. America's companies care about climate change," Greene tells Denkel. "I got notes for you."

He's annoyed at having to call his people in when he should just buzz them on the intercom, but *every fucking one wants to work remotely.* Times like this it's just a pain in the ass.

He focuses back to the task at hand.

Yes, the reposition, go on attack, make this America versus Congress, private sector versus government, he tells himself. He'll write out a talking-points script, but he's having trouble really focusing, but now it is because he's getting excited about the conference calls that have been rescheduled, no longer dreading them because he has a plan.

Yes, all for the best, he tells himself. *Always was going to be an attack, so why wait.*

Yes, he thinks, nodding his head.

He reaches into his desk's side drawer, pulling out the current burner he uses for Lobinski. He dials and Lobinski picks up, the sound of a restaurant, Greene wonders, in the background.

"Penworth," Greene says. "Deploy." He clips the flip phone closed, tossing it back into the drawer.

They'll make sure everyone knows it was Penworth. Not quite yet, though, since the child smut will take a day or so to play out.

Fucking Penworth and his fucking gang of geeks.

Chapter 37: Captain America AirBnB

The Americabnb offer is pretty good, Davin would admit if anyone ever asks, although of course he'll more likely emphasize the altruistic and patriotic aspects of his motivation.

The funding for the program has come through in the newest emergency funding, and the deal actually seems good for all concerned. He won't take much of a hit from the tourist rates. The arrangement means full occupancy and having longer-term guests means he'll be free from having to turn the apartment and enjoy a break from all the cleaning, laundry, correspondence, and scheduling, which means the demands on his time are a bit freer.

All good, he says to himself. Well, except for those guests who already reserved the listing, he knows, but Airbnb has waived cancellation penalties for participating hosts, and his Super Host status won't be affected.

The operating concept behind Americabnb is that in this time of national emergency, vacations are a secondary priority, and would-be travelers still have the option of using hotels and motels and Airbnbs that aren't participating in the Josephine Emergency Act. Still, he knows occupancy availability will be tight, especially in some areas of the country, including the Berkshires.

Tanglewood gate numbers will probably be down, he assumes, although he considers maybe the evacuees might fill some of the gap.

Lose Everything, Gain Beethoven, he thinks.

I'm such an asshole, he thinks.

But with still almost two million homeless and the enormous efforts to repair or replace housing carries a long timeframe, so relocation of many of the storm-made homeless is pressing and the return for many of these displaced will be a long time coming. The extensive infrastructure damage from Josephine swamping the high-population metropolitan area of Miami and South Beach means the housing problem is acute and there's more talk that some Gold Coast areas won't be rebuilt.

He likes that he is in a position to help and is even begrudgingly proud of Airbnb for its creative solution, countering his long-growing dislike of the company, now public and trading shares and hardly the sharing economy star with the heart of gold it still likes to insist it is. For years now, he has seriously considered leaving to Airbnb, but like other kinds of social network businesses, the alternatives are at best modest and so he remains part of the monopoly that is Airbnb.

Unfortunately, he signed on to Americabnb before all the details were complete and he finds himself questioning why he didn't really think through some of the economics of the situation. The answer, he's pretty sure, is he is simply trying to help out in some small way. After all, these displaced people from Florida have lost just about everything.

I'm a saint, I tell ya.

In his locale, Airbnb has partnered up with Berkshires Cares, an ad hoc organization formed from a number of social aid groups seeking ways to lend a hand, and even as the Americabnb program is coming up to speed, his main worry is that the small apartment will be home for the next several months or more to a Haitian family of five — a grandmother, two parents, a daughter, and her three-year-old. It is a bit crowded, Davin thinks, and he is worried about wear and tear. He has gone so far as to look for a couch on FreeCycle, and he has already swapped out the two small recliners in the apartment's main room for the newly acquired used pullout sleeper couch. He has also gotten a secondhand dining table to replace the much smaller table that was perfectly fine for the typical one or two guests of the short-term rental.

He figures the main thing he'll have to watch for is how hot the Devreauxs want the heat to be set considering they're not used to winters in New England. He thinks he can adequately explain how the thermostat should be set, and that it's on a schedule, being a Nest thermostat. What he suspects he won't bother to mention is he can track the settings on his computer and phone and so nip any overheating in the bud remotely.

Don't want to confuse them, he rationalizes.

You are a fucking cheapskate, he adds.

While their English is limited, they did seem grateful and happy in the one video chat set up by Americabnb, and their smiles were not in short supply.

He figures the Americabnb fee may be almost as good as what he would likely have made continuing with the normal short-term rentals, although he is entering peak season in the Berkshires, but that doesn't last all that long. The biggest sacrifice will be not having the apartment to use for family for Christmas or other holidays, but he doesn't think his daughter and Marco will be heading across the ocean anytime soon. Jimmy — *and Cynthia*, he reminds himself – could stay in the second-floor rooms he uses as his office if he has a third house sharer in place. Marsha has already taken his third-floor bedroom for herself, now that he's moved to the second-floor bedroom, so it's possible if there's isn't a new third house sharer Jimmy could have his old room back.

If they're likely to come at all. Maybe they'll split the time with Gwen, he wonders.

He expects Gloria, if they are still together by the holidays, might want to stay here, but his growing dissatisfaction with the relationship has him thinking about getting back to online dating. Still, he isn't keen on acting too quickly.

Alicia is something of a surrogate family these days, but he's worried about Deidre and Alicia, not that it's any of his business. Early on, Alicia seemed very happy about the relationship, if circumspect, but he senses growing uneasiness between the couple, although he doesn't know for sure whether it's just everything that is going on at the business.

He knows that while he remains ambivalent about his growing involvement in what Alicia is trying to do, he's not ambivalent about the regular paychecks he's just recently started getting from having taken on the day-to-day editorial responsibilities of *Berkshire Interactive*. He's certainly gratified that the editorial he'd recently written, "Zero Degrees of Separation," seemed to help others. He knows writing it was as much an effort to help himself understand his own feelings, but he was glad for the editorial's reception.

And it helped make clear he should do something to help, hence Americabnb and the Haitians.

Ain't I a saint, he thinks.

Chapter 38: Tough Fall

Jeannie Louise is busier than ever, summer fast slipping away. She's too busy, and for the worst of reasons, although good for her, she can admit. The market for disaster coverage has increasingly grown to include the very sort of climate change causation analyses she has become well-known for, at least among magazine editors and conference program directors. Her work has been evolving into something of a specialty shop, somewhat to her annoyance, with her producing more sidebars supporting articles written by others rather than writing the main articles herself. She's been busy cranking out sidebars and companion pieces that focus on the climate change consequences to the human-interest articles on the misery and disaster of drought, famine, and other climate catastrophes.

Climate change disaster sidebar factory, she can't help thinking, and she's finds herself thinking this more and more. She also can't help suspecting she's directly contributing to and making a living from a sort of disaster entertainment industrial complex.

Climate porn.

This phrase surprises her, but then she realizes it shouldn't, considering the past several days have been fixated on the child pornography charges against Jersey. She finds it all hard to shake, even after getting the most recent email from Jersey passed on by his lawyer out to the full list, letting everyone know the files found on his computer have been flagged with telltale markers, and he'll be working on a press release shortly to report definitive proof of these anomalous traces of a plant. His lawyer is still getting the details and anything and everything is on hold for at least a couple more days until his lawyer can get the specifics from the law agencies involved.

The best news is that charges will be dropped, or so his lawyer has assured him, but Jersey added there could also be actionable information on the developing situation.

Actionable against others, not him, it had taken her a moment to parse. Someone planted the porn files, that is his position, although Jersey has said nothing about knowing who might be behind this awful thing.

Jersey ended the email with a thanks to all for standing by him, although Jeannie knows Jersey must be aware quite a few in the group were scrambling to distance themselves or openly assuming his guilt. And for now, the papers and social media, of course, are still having a field day, and Jersey is lying low, out on bail, at a location he isn't sharing.

She knows him well enough, and she can't believe the charges would have any merit, but she also knows that she can't really know, and she hates she's had these nagging seeds of doubt. This situation is awful in any number of ways, and she knows the worst way is what the arrest could do to Jersey and she's been feeling plenty awful about it.

She had also noticed that she felt a growing impatience to get back to her bread-and-butter analytic work of showing connections between climate change threats and political activity focused on climate change, including the Kehoe Institute position paper analysis she'd helped with recently. There's been a lot of other work that sometimes comes through one or another of her *The Laundry* contacts, but any and all such has all but disappeared since the child pornography scandal had broken. There's been panic within the group, and some of the accusations flying about among them will be hard to come back from. She hopes Jersey's latest email will help, but some things, once uttered, are too hard to pull back, and she thinks it's likely the group will be diminished even with charges cleared.

But there's a silver lining, too, even if it's due to this awful business. She is still swamped, but now less so now without any new *The Laundry* projects. She's finding herself very grateful for the work contacts she's built up with trade media over the last couple of years, and these connections have been unaffected by the Jersey scandal. And the money's been good with the latest rush of assignments.

She knows, of course, that getting back to her core work isn't going to make a lot of sense income-wise at least, not when she assigns herself the stories she most wants to write, which are her in-depth blog posts. This work has value for her, but she doesn't really get much out of it in terms of income, not in terms of billable invoices anyway. After all her time and effort spent with *RE: CC* she understands all too clearly it's these posts and $6.50 in her pocket that will get her a cup of coffee.

She is well aware coffee prices are demonstrably tied to climate change and the resultant rising temperatures and shifts in rainfall patterns that continue to reduce coffee plant habitats. Still, at least she is better buffered these days from any personal economic disaster. She is still able to afford the ever more expensive cup of joe, she acknowledges.

There are already far too many examples of climate-distressed situations. She knows she can have all the writing work she wants, at least as long as she doesn't get tainted by Jersey's child pornography scandal. Given his email today, it seems like that disaster has been averted. Emails in her inbox this morning included two new assignment requests, one from the editor of *The Boston Globe Sunday Magazine* and one from some staffer at *Woman's Day*. Being associated with an alleged child pornographer would not produce such offers, she is sure.

Her real problem with these requests is they are both looking more or less for the same thing, in a thousand words or less, which is *more goddamn sidebars* supporting the article file attached in each of the assignment offers.

She has already looked over the attached *Woman's Day* draft. The article is titled "Natural Foods and Green Cosmetics: What Today's Woman Can't Afford!" and she's being asked for a sidebar that looks "seriously" — the staffer's word in the email — at how climate change is affecting production of botanicals and quinoa and a number of other items provided in a nice, neat list.

She's sure she'll be mentally rolling her eyes as she works on this, but she wants the billables. She is also sure she won't dwell on the drought-related famine going on through the spine of Central America and down into parts of Columbia and Ecuador, even though the very same drought system is affecting the quinoa growing areas in the Andean regions of Bolivia, Ecuador, Chile, and Peru. She shouldn't mention in any detail how the drought, which is part of the Amazon watershed, is made even worse by the ongoing sugarcane production in Brazil and the continuing deforestation of the Amazon region, both of which are direct contributors to Brazil's drought that has been an issue for a decade and half. The last year that saw reservoir levels so low was 2024, but even since quite a number of Brazil's hydro-electric generating stations are online only sporadically. The irony of the biofuel production efforts Brazil continues to pursue is not lost on her. With the dropping rainfall levels, sugarcane production has been using large-scale irrigation of these vast plantations, and this, along with the rainfall reduction, is a major factor in the emptying of reservoirs and the reduction in hydroelectricity.

We are morons, she tells herself. The whole point of Brazil's biofuel efforts has been to capitalize on sufficient natural watering through plentiful rain that sugarcane requires. But as the rainfall patterns change and the Amazon Basin's rain forest declines, no one seems to act, and the sugarcane keeps getting grown. She does enjoy a perverted pleasure in noting sugarcane thrives in the hotter temperatures being delivered through the greenhouse gas buildup.

Assuming available water!

There being available water these days in many parts of South America makes for a poor assumption. There also remains the companion problem of unchecked deforestation in the Amazon and parts of South and Central America to supply McDonald's with beef patties.

She has half an impulse to see if McDonald's advertises in *Woman's Day*, but she wants the money, and the money keeps getting better as she is seen more and more as a name, as the go-to person, as a value add. There are certain subjects that would be a little *too* serious for *Woman's Day*, Jeannie Louise completely understands. Fortunately, a maximum cap of one thousand words doesn't allow for much detail, she tells herself.

The billable is nice, she reminds herself.

Maybe I'll slip in something about Sugar Pops, she tells herself, but that thought doesn't make her smile, not even a little.

And then she thinks yet again, and with growing bitterness, how Jersey's arrest could still blow things up for her. She hopes his insistence there are grounds to prove the content on his home computer has been planted is more than wishful thinking, and she realizes she wants someone to blame.

She wants to go after them with a vengeance.

Or, she reminds herself, *I could just pour myself a nice glass of Widow Jane Bourbon.*

Writing crap for big publications does indeed have its perks, including being able to afford good bourbon.

Chapter 39: Davin and the Devreauxs

From the open window in his office Davin can hear the Devreauxs out in the front yard talking, not that he can follow what they're saying.

It was past Labor Day by the time Americabnb finally got around to sending Davin his guests, or as he finds himself thinking of them, his charges. He's upset with the program because the Family Devreaux is late to take up residence and late by more than a month and being out a full month's worth of high season income is a financial hit. He had used the week he thought it would take to bring the Devreauxs to Housatonic to set the place up for them and was unbegrudging about the loss of a week's income, but a full month's loss is another matter.

But now Davin has the Devreauxs in place and the first month paid in advance. And they are the nicest people, he is pleased to see.

Of course, right from the first day, the man, Eugene, has been politely pestering him about work possibilities in the area, and both the grandmother and the wife—*Delmay? Delmerre?*—have gone into high gear on the apartment. They've been going to thrift stores, and even Marsha is helping by using her mother's car to shuttle them back and forth. The apartment, he knows, is less well-provisioned for an extended stay than for the short-termers who mainly dine out or picnic at Tanglewood. The thrift store trips were numerous that first week they took up residence.

Marsha's told him the car is in effect hers since her mother no longer can drive, if he's got that right, so now there is this car, plus Turk's crappy one, plus his own crappy one, the now seventeen-year-old Kia that has been on emissions exemption for the last two inspections and the maintenance and repair costs piling up are enough to have him finally ready to get an EV, another budget worry even with the rebates.

Plus her motorbike, he thinks, hoping that with her car, Marsha will not be using the motorbike much as the weather gets colder. He makes a note to suggest she could store the bike in the garden shed out back. He's never been a fan of the small motorcycle parked and covered on the back terrace.

He's already shown the Devreauxs how to silence the Nest Protect and had to do so twice the first day, the second time including pantomiming the use of the exhaust fan and the open window to keep the smoke detector from going off when cooking. He figures to dig out the old Weber for their use outside, even though the grill's legs are rusted out, but it can sit on top of a small metal trash can with some rocks in the base to keep the jerry-rigged arrangement from being top heavy.

He thinks about how he'll pantomime that the grill must be used only outdoors.

The grandmother has already discovered the garden out back, and Marsha has gotten her going. He's happy about sharing some of the bounty from the garden, not that Marsha has bothered to ask him. He is relieved to see the Devreauxs and Marsha connecting, especially because he's always had a hard time reading his house sharer and had worried that the loss of the Airbnb fees would upset her and negatively mark her attitude toward them. From his kitchen, a couple of days ago, he caught a few snatches of conversation among the three older Devreauxs adults and Marsha on the front porch, their speaking with heavily accented French or a patois or creole, except for Eugene's limited English, but the biggest surprise is that Marsha speaks French. Davin's foreign language skills go back to his high school days, which is to say, completely gone, but he'd taken Spanish anyway. He's thrilled that she'll take some of what he has been assuming would be yet another demand on his time.

He's mostly been working with and for Alicia, and with the investors seeming more and more likely to be coming on board, a part of Davin's attention has been taken up with platform transition tasks that anticipate the change to a site license, which means he has to review best options. He is mostly supervising the IT contractor he's had Alicia hire for the task, but a lot of small yet crucial questions keep popping up, and it's up to him to figure out the answers. What should be the last of the planning duties is in front of him, both on the screen and in hard copy since his review of the transition is fraught with all manner of details all too easily missed on screen.

It's one of those gorgeous days today when the suggestion of fall makes being outside perfect.

Not much fun, he reminds himself. *Stuck inside.*

At least he's getting to spend some time in the garden and the greens are piling up, despite Marsha furious cooking up and freezing gallon bags of them, typically in a collard/kale mix with garlic, a minced beet or two, and vinegar. The tomatoes are at their tail end of frenzy-stage, and a huge stock pot filled with in-process sauce is a near-constant presence on the stovetop. The sweet corn has proved once again an elusive crop despite the additional rows they've planted, and he'd spent half a day at the start of August setting up motion floodlights and a digital camera to help him figure out what was taking the ears, often breaking the stalks in the process. He had suspected raccoons, and the image feeds when reviewed the first few mornings confirmed it. The lights snapping on seem to have no effect, and in one image sequence he's watched, he would swear one of the raccoons was looking directly into the camera, eyes retina-blazed, giving him the finger.

He keeps intending to take up position with his twenty-two-caliber air rifle one of these nights, maybe behind the shed not far from the garden, or maybe up on a ladder to the shed's roof, to wait for the motion detectors to trigger the lights and give him the chance to plink some of the bastards. But at sixty-four years of age, the idea may be attractive but acting on it not so much. He has already tried a large Have-a-Heart trap, but there are plenty of food options and it took some date bars to get the raccoons' interest. Even here he was frustrated as three nights running the raccoons knocked the trap around, which not only triggered the catch closed without them inside but also brought the treats within easy reach through the cage's wire walls.

News of Josephine has faded into background noise, and these days mentions are mainly focused on various governmental recovery bills and the ongoing problems of the remaining many thousands of internally displaced persons. Of course, any and all other hurricane activity this season has received more attention than normal, but he figures that's not surprising, considering. The strongest hurricane post-Josephine had topped out at Category 4, which now seems *ho-hum*.

Much of the news is far from *ho-hum* however. The political news has been wild on the national level, reaching new rhetorical extremes, although as soon as he thinks this, he remembers the Trump years when the rhetoric had little or no basis in reality, at least on the Republican side of the aisle. He can't recall too many instances of the mainstream Democratic National Committee and leading lights in House and Senate shining all too brightly either, unfortunately.

Politics has settled down a bit since those dark days, with progressives doing better. He suspects this is mainly in response to the long-continuing money problems most of the nation's citizens experience that now contrasts more and more starkly with the ever-aggrandizing multi-billionaire class. But still there may be something to the old saw that America is a centrist state since the Republicans haven't been entirely trounced and in the 2028 have started to approach parity again in the House, offsetting Democratic gains in the previous mid-terms.

He sometimes wonders why the state of public protest is so anemic and having been at the Boston march following years of no marches, he knows his own record in showing his discontent is hardly brilliant. Marches and demonstrations are nowhere close to what he remembers from his own youth, although he personally missed a lot of those, too, to be able to confidently claim that legacy, and he'd been a bit too young for the Vietnam War demonstrations. The big one for him was the NYC Anti-Nuclear march in the early 1980s that may well be his personal high-water mark.

Nearly fifty fucking years, he tells himself, and this just makes him grumpier.

For someone who has grown increasingly concerned about climate change these last few years, and with Jeannie Louise Smith added to the writers' pool at *BI*, his awareness and understanding of climate change is being further boosted right along with his own shortcomings. He's periodically embarrassed about how inactive he is. Cynthia seems always happy to criticize him for this.

He is glad that Aine followed through after the cocktail party, contacting Cynthia, with *MMEAT and Greet* finally is trying to settle on a date. He might even get Alicia involved in some way, maybe with *BI* as a sponsor or publishing some climate change content that would be relevant.

These thoughts are interrupted by sounds coming in through the open office window. He can hear the little Devreaux girl out front, low murmurs and singing she's making at play. He stands up and leans toward the front yard-facing window.

He sees her on the lawn, twirling round the crab apple tree.

He smiles, feeling good about having a young kid on the premises, but then he sits himself back down, picks up a printed checklist sheet, but immediately puts it back on the desk and opens his Google Calendar instead. Cynthia has asked him to suggest a couple of dates, and they've talked about these being before November or not too far into that month because whatever the program, it will be an outside event.

As he looks over the November calendar, he finds himself wondering about the last time he'd been involved with anything related to climate change, apart from the Boston march, now nearly two months ago.

Maybe the People's Climate March in 2014, he considers. That gathering might still hold the participation record officially, although he had only gone to Pittsfield for the local action at Park Square. The 2026 climate turnout was strong too, and some claimed the total number of participants was quite a bit higher than 2014, but he's got no opinion about this, having sat that one out. While he sees protests and demonstrations as important in theory, he's not much for demonstrations in practice.

It'll be fun, he tells himself, now back to thinking about the meet and greet thing, but he's also trying to think through the tasks he'll have to get done. One such item is applying for a one-day liquor license, and probably event insurance, and he's never worked as a real bartender, so there will be all that to figure out.

Have a drink, save the world, he tells himself.

He hears quite clearly a burst of laughter from the little girl and soft French sounds he figures must be her mother. He gets up and leans toward the window, looks down and sees he's right.

What he sees makes him feel good, but strangely, he also feels a bit like crying, too.

Save the world, he repeats.

Chapter 40: Smile,
You're on Candid Camera

William McPherson is in an isolation cell. It's not too small, bigger than the back of the Transit, but hardly as nicely appointed. The room contains a double bunk and a stainless-steel sink and toilet, and a solid door with a peek hole and a food port.

The surfaces are all one color, a green-toned gray, graffiti scratches here and there over the concrete blocks, but the cell has been recently repainted, the paint new enough to still contribute a chemical reek to all the other, odder odors.

He sits on the lower bunk, back tucked against the wall.

He is at the moment in the Ada County Jail, but he assumes this is temporary, although he admits to himself he really has no idea how this sort of thing gets handled. He's been told he is being held for the FBI.

It doesn't matter, he keeps telling himself.

The phrase *like a deer caught in headlights* keeps occurring to him, although each time he thinks of the phrase he feels surprised, as if he keeps thinking of it for the first time, every time.

His sense of time itself is off, as is his sense of place, of circumstance. His sense of his life itself is off, something out of phase. Everything feels entirely unreal.

He's always known he would get caught, of course, but he figures that some part of him must have assumed this would never really happen, or at least that is all he can think might explain his ongoing state of surprise. There is a part of him that finds this interesting, even amusing, but that sense is ephemeral, fleeting.

I'm of two minds, he jokes in an odd manic moment that crashes immediately.

They finally found him in Boise where he was studying up on his next target, someone from the actual Forbes list and a worthy selection on paper, but he can admit to himself he'd been growing increasingly removed from the whole undertaking, more and more caught up in the habit of it all, on automatic, unmotivated. This whole endeavor has been feeling more and more like a job.

The Boise target's security began to look insurmountable, and he had been thinking about choosing a different target, although he doesn't have any sense of clear thinking about that, then or now.

Behind his now shut eyes he sees the deformed skull of his last target kill, and this is just one of the many reoccurring images he compulsorily cycles through, the crushed and staved forehead of the man who killed his brother, but he also knows this is not the factual case. It was the pharmaceutical company that killed his brother with their sloppy QA, but in his mind, the blame goes to the man who caused his layoff, who acquired the company he'd been working for, had caused the divorce too, and the caretaking of his brother, and his brother's illness and death. It often seems all of a piece with the purpose he has taken on, with *Kill the Rich*.

Sitting in his cell, *Kill the Rich* feels like a dream. He can't seem to really think he had done any of it, not really. There are moments when he does feel pride of accomplishment, and in other moments, he feels only confusion about his actions. The worse moments of all is when he feels embarrassment. Surprise, too, keeps cropping up and his not quite believing he has been this person who has killed others, the person who carried out elaborate campaigns and careful planning. He doesn't have access to newspapers or online searching, but the last count he took was that there were twelve KTR claims he knows are not his doing, but this just another of the thoughts that come and go, thoughts that are simple gossamer threads compared to the images that revisit him over and over, the deformed skull of his last target, of that man, the crushed and broken forehead, and he hears again and again and again the thud of the three-pound hand sledgehammer dropping to the dirt of the horse trail.

He sees the two other men he shot, the two who surprised him on the trail.

He sees the horse he accidentally shot with the bullets he'd let fly, the horse down, gasping for breath, one bullet striking the rear of the horse's left shoulder into the barrel of the body. The horse had dropped on top of the man who had been halfway dismounting, the burbling bullet wound in the lung-shot horse pushing out and pulling in foaming blood with every gasping breath.

Killing the two additional men hadn't been part of the plan, but he had seen no other choice.

At least one had a rifle.

And they had seen him, of course.

And he panicked, of course.

He should have put the horse down, and of course he knows that, but at the time he was removed from such conscious thinking, any clarity of thought pushed out by the ascendancy of panic and fear.

He also thinks, at different moments, he should have had a different plan. He knows his plans had been growing increasingly elaborate and unattached from any sensible judgment, but he remains unresolved as to cause. Maybe, he finds himself sometimes wondering, it was simply a matter of growing pride or maybe some subconscious wish to fail, although he suspects the answer is more complicated.

It doesn't matter. These questions are irrelevant.

He finds himself slipping into other thoughts, and one that keeps returning is driving his Transit, relaxed in his travels across country roads and secondary highways, his mind free to simply enjoy the views.

He's seen a lot of the country. There is that, and he's visited several presidential libraries too, there is that.

And now, among the multitude of the other images and thoughts, he sees the man in San Diego, a moving form alight, the flames burst at the push of a button on a cheap flip phone turning into a burning shifting chimera of dark moving limbs and bright orange and yellow flames climbing out of the companionway to collapse in the tiller pushpit, and moments after, the boat fully engulfed by the final gust of flame bursting out from the berth below.

That death was observed by means of binoculars from his vantage 300 yards away. He was standing near the dumpster outside of the restaurant near the marina, the spot providing clear line of sight, his bike resting against the metal side.

Afterward he had bicycled back across the bay bridge and had some trouble remembering which of the downtown public garages he'd left his van.

He is spending his days awash in the images that come and go, images pulsing without his intent, but the one image from the trail cam that captured his face seems indelible, his unintended self-portrait.

He thinks about the irony. He took great care to camouflage the reconnaissance cameras at the Kentucky horse farm, the one with the long view toward the stables, the other two along the horse trail itself. He hadn't retrieved them, hadn't even thought to after everything that had happened, and there was little traceback that could be gleamed anyway, no telltale serial number that would lead back to him, no fingerprints, digital or physical, because he was always careful.

Huh!

That wasn't entirely true though. He hadn't noticed the trail camera he must have passed on his long exodus from the horse trail. That had been careless of him, although he hadn't intended to go through the neighboring woods, that was only a fallback option, but he had found himself pushing his bicycle through the woods until he came to the county road, foregoing his plan to bike down the paved access road that ran near the trail.

He wonders if he unconsciously followed a deer trail to make pushing the bike easier.

He lets out a long sigh.

He tries to think of something else beside the images resurfacing yet again of the two other men he shot.

And the horse.

He pulls himself up and out of the bunk and starts pacing.

The plan succeeded, despite the two extra kills and the lung-shot horse. He was pedaling away on the side of the county road, passed by the warbling police vehicles, and moments after, the wailing ambulances. He got back to the Transit and drove away. Three weeks passed and all seemed fine, the headlines on his KTR kill plentiful, news he had checked repeatedly over time, and in the stories there were no suggestions of any real threats to him, but of course he knows that means little, really.

They had known who he was within a day of getting the trail camera image from the target's neighbor, his identity, he's been told, made by his driver's license photo once they ran nationwide face recognition routines using the trail camera capture. That had taken some time after the target and the other killings, because the authorities didn't get the image for almost a week. The trail camera, being an older type, not networked, was the sort that had to be downloaded physically, probably using an old-style SD card.

Not that the investigators who interviewed him spoke in any detail about the methodology of his identification, but they did show him the trail camera image. To him, his face, despite the day light, looks like a death mask in the mediocre resolution black and white. He couldn't have been more than a dozen feet away, and one of the several images triggered by his motion looked as if he was staring right at the device, but he hadn't seen it of course.

His court-appointed lawyer has prevailed upon him to remain silent, but the prosecutors from the US Attorney's office are happy to describe their slate of evidence pulled from the Transit. A lot of what they claim is from all the content of his laptop and the USB stick he always uses to download his public Internet work. There are the files on the targets and more on the potential targets, including the Boise target, that location close by to where he was picked up. There was the bicycle tire match from a muddy patch near the trail camera, and of course he had kept the bike. Other physical forensic matches are likely enough. They eventually found all the cameras and power packs among the horse trail trees.

The investigators have been eager to share other information too, including the geolocation data they'd sifted through, and there is plenty of that despite his care to avoid the obvious toll cameras and logs. Once they knew his name they knew his Transit registration, and the license plate turned up on video camera logs in enough places coinciding in time and place with at least some of his targets. But he also had not destroyed or discarded some of the burners, including the one he'd used in San Diego.

There is at least one eyewitness they claim. Probably it was the dishwasher from that restaurant who came out to the dumpster while he watched the sailboat burn.

"There's a boat on fire," he had said to the young man.

There were probably others that might identify him, if the FBI had enough geolocation data and would do the work, or if anyone remembered him at the right place and time. There would be more likely coming forward, no doubt, from all the information in the news he assumes is being posted.

It doesn't matter.

He keeps cycling a mix of high anxiety, panic, and relief.

The image capture they showed him keeps floating into his mind.

The black-and-white poor-contrast image had been enlarged and looked disembodied, the stark infrared black and white, the eyes flat.

It looks like his dead brother's face.

Chapter 41: Kill the Entertainment

Davin spends a lot of time following the news, even if he too often doesn't read past headlines. He's developed a bit of a habit looking for stories about all those weird murders, despite his low-grade embarrassment about the fixation. He's got a Google Alert set for the topic. He can spend far too much time reading about *Kill the Rich*, some sort of terrorist cell that has murdered at least nineteen rich people.

The FBI seems confused in their KTR investigations taking place all over the country pretty much, but recently investigators are proposing that some of the killings are by "emulators." That's the word they use, and he thinks it's odd that they don't seem to use *copycat* anymore. The most recently arrested KTR suspect included something of a manifesto about climate change in his claim. That claim contributed to his apprehension because the FBI used their database of extremist climate organizations and groups as a filter, and the man arrested, a twenty-two-year-old, is a member of Earth First, an organization with roots in Earth Liberation Front from back in the 1990s.

The biggest story, though, is the break in the case with a suspect brought in from Boise five days back, with the FBI claiming that this perpetrator is behind multiple killings across many locations. The man's name is William McPherson, formerly from Wrentham, in the eastern part of Massachusetts, some sort of IT professional, laid off, divorced. Yesterday and today's news articles recount a long string of attacks all around the country, the last killing of a somewhat famous CEO, along with two of his employees. The guy doesn't ring any bells, but then Davin's not one to follow the business pages much.

In the last couple of days, he's a bit concerned a part of him may be feeling disappointed this McPherson character has been caught, and this bothers him some. As far as he's concerned, the KTR sentiment is not entirely wrong, even though he knows killing leads nowhere good. He figures he'll keep this inclination to root for the assholes running around killing billionaires to himself, even while suspecting he's not much of an outlier on this score.

On balance though, he knows he'd rather see protests against income inequality than these killings, although he is confused that it's been years since income inequality has been a rallying cry, going back to the 2016 elections. In the most recent elections that brought more progressives into Congress, there'd been the argument for closing of certain tax code advantages and sunsetting of some of Trump's big tax cuts that had been extended in 2025. Although the Congress is still young, there's finally a financial transactions tax, although at a rate set much lower than what many progressives would have liked. So far, the best accomplishment has been the Carbon Credits Act. He finds it makes sense, as does the means testing for credits qualification, although he worries this next year's scale-down credits are likely to be more regressive in effect. He is also upset that Medicare for All remains just a slogan, especially with healthcare costs pushing ever higher. He can't help but count the days until he can get rid of his private health insurance, anxious as he is about stretching his resources for one more year.

At least Medicare coverage still starts at sixty-five years of age, and he will hit that early next year. Social Security won't trigger for him until sixty-eight years and four months of age, thanks to a recent tweak in the eligibility timelines.

He doesn't have a lot of sympathy for the very rich, he

knows that. Still, he wishes he wasn't so pleased whenever a new *Kill the Rich* story appears. His guiltiest pleasure to date is the coverage of the financial services guy in Minnesota, the one where a woman, who claims to be a fashion model but who has been identified in some news pieces as a high-priced escort, was present during the killing. There is a lot of evidence, according to some of these articles, that points to McPherson. The woman had originally described the assailant as a woman but subsequently has stated the attacker could possibly have been a man. If it was indeed McPherson, at least he did right by the young woman, using some knock-out drug for his escape instead of simply killing her.

He closes the Alert list tab. He pokes at the small pile of printouts to the right of his monitor.

"Fuck me," he says to himself. "I really don't want to review this shit." He pushes the printout pages further to the side and rubs his face with both hands. His hand reaches toward the mouse, poised to click on another KTR alert result, but he manages to resist the pull.

He hauls the printouts back in front of him and gets to work.

Chapter 42: Hey Ho for Kehoe

Jeannie Louise is doing some office housekeeping, sitting at her desk organizing her email and putting the right emails into the right email folders, including, at this moment, one labelled *Press Queries*. She sends out a half dozen such queries each week, and she is happy to get a better rate of replies than she used to, although big assignments still lag. She remains frustrated by the overall lack of focus by the various news media on policy battles, but she knows what's really needed is to follow the money and to reveal the self-serving motives and self-embraced delusions of those who gain from doing little about climate and those who actively work to keep fossil fuels burning.

The leaked position paper from the Kehoe Institute that's been kicking around and the explication of the document by several members of *The Laundry* brings dark money into high relief. She's thrilled to have played some small part in the too-rare feat of revealing those who move invisibly and under cover of plausible-sounding misdirection and intentional clouding of the issues, but that did little more than weakly tug the curtain. Even efforts like Climate Trace, an Al Gore–promoted project that was up and running by 2023, couldn't, or at least didn't, connect the dots of dark money spent, but instead satisfied itself with identifying high polluters by specific location, naming companies, and as the satellite technologies have become better and better, quantifying to an intoxicating degree the levels and type of greenhouse gases produced by these entities. The organization Open Secrets, along with a few other such efforts, are good attempts to expose campaign financing and dark money, but none have been linking such money directly to policy and legislation, and so the behind scene actors — the ones with direct benefit — remain obscure, even if inference is nominally easier. The PACs and think tanks and institutes and industry trade groups are shadow makers with dark money washing over politicians and bureaucrats alike in hard-to-trace ways, and the maze of fictitious names and pseudo-organizations continually proliferates.

She realizes that it's been almost three months since *The Laundry* had revealed that the climate denial sector was tied to a small cadre of writers of bullshit research papers, posts on social media, and speeches delivered through the mouths of others. She had found the use of AI natural language processing fascinating and had been delighted with the results. Now *The Laundry* is kicking around a new project that may provide a clearer sense of dark money funding sources and mechanisms. AI, some of her colleagues are saying, could perform iterative cross-referencing of publicly identifiable remunerations found in annual reports of the various anti-climate PACs and 501(c)s and other dark money conduits, and this approach could help further reveal the entities and individuals engaging misinformation efforts and influence peddling. Identifying all the dark money feeding anti-climate efforts would be a coup, but she knows that there are a lot of moving parts to such work, and it will take time to get everything going.

Fortunately, the most recent triumph by *The Laundry* with the analysis of the recent Kehoe position paper helps her impatience. The teardown of that content into plain unambiguous English starkly highlighted the plan to bring significant resources to redirect the Sea Wall Act implementation into an independent agency outside of and apart from any federal cabinet departments and the Executive Office of the President, and the papers had energetically picked up on this. It's been better than a week, and the work she'd provided some help is still causing trouble for the Kehoe Institute.

Jersey is proposing more trouble yet with the dark money analysis and she, for one, would love to know the specific sources of funds behind the recent Kehoe Institute position paper. Kehoe Institute has at least one mega-construction giant on its board, or used to anyway. It isn't that most individuals and corporations behind entities like Kehoe are unknown, exactly, but revealing how much such entities give, for what specific ends, and toward which particular outcomes is the essential aim of the new research project she is trying to help establish. Influence and funding attribution is likely to weaken those individuals' and corporations' hold over politics and the mechanisms of change.

From my lips to God's ear, she tells herself.

She clicks away from filing email to the spreadsheet she uses for tracking her work. She has recently finished a piece on population migrations that focuses on the southern Mexico border and the refugee pressures that keep building as the drought in Central America and parts of Columbia worsens. The proximal climate causes of the drought, she'd reported citing some science sources, have direct ties to the warmer water of the mid-Pacific and *El Niño* cycles coming around more often. She's also sold an article, but still to write it, on the West Coast drought that is also caused, as much as anything, by the same changing *El Niño* cycle that is affecting parts of the South and Central America countries. Unfortunately, as for the border immigration surges, the much-ballyhooed immigration reform compromise of 2026 is proving to be ineffective, and the resulting increase in asylum seekers remains insufficiently funded. The pressure on the southern border continues and even many Democrats are desperate to distance themselves from the failed reform, especially as Josephine and the other storms have ratcheted up the need for assistance to the domestic displaced.

She checks the status of a pitch on the sub-Saharan disasters occurring across several countries, but it is too soon to send out a follow-up to her query. There is a note about file location for the notes she's put together for that pitch, but she doesn't have to check because she well remembers angle she wants to explore is the UNHCR policy efforts that are a new attempt to address the resulting refugee problems. She'd also cover the proposal that the International Organization for Migration has brought to the UN to strengthen policy changes, with IOM battling above its weight but possibly pulling off a win.

There are other proposals to several magazines for an article about the major drought and high temperatures in the Middle East that have some very dramatic consequences for several million people—including the hapless Syrian Kurdish refugees—as they move across national borders and across religious and ethnic demarcations where the only flush resource seems to be weapons. In parts of the Middle East the number of dead from starvation, heat exposure, or violent assault is increasing and she has a great contact at Climate Refugees.org who wants to coauthor, although Jeannie Louise's categorization of Israel as a walled camp is something the two of them will have to work out before going forward.

Disaster Roulette, that's how she thinks of this category of article queries, although there is no such heading on the spreadsheet.

She's less interested these days about articles on the failure of recent COPs, especially after COP29 came and went with little recollection of the COP27 pledges, perhaps because COP28 was deemed generally ineffective.

Unless talking is action, she tells herself. *One hell of a lot of talk, that one.*

The fluctuating recession-inflation economic cycles are generally blamed for making COP29 through COP 33 timid and forgettable. COP34 was originally planned to be held in Pakistan, but when that country's latest heat wave began to take its toll, COP34 got relocated to Quebec City instead. She knows real progress does happen, but when there is some advance, it always seems too little, too late.

Maybe lucky number COP35 will do the trick, she tells herself.

She pushes back from the spreadsheet, having noticed the deadline for her next article for *Berkshire Interactive* is coming up fast. By request of Alicia, this article is on connecting climate change to increased population locally and the serious consequences that have already occurred. *Serious consequences* is a relative term of course, and to Jeannie Louise the local changes are subtle and remain at small and manageable levels. She's been managing to get a piece done for *Berkshire Interactive* here and there, but of late that it mainly more an exercise in whack-a-mole as much as actual writing.

She is feeling jittery. She wants to do everything, and she's sure she can do it all, except at times it all seems hopeless. She's got to get out of here, cooped up the whole day and having accomplished far too little.

At the moment, she's got little on her whiskey shelf, and she's not so desperate that she'll drink the Jack Daniels some well-intentioned visitor has recently given her. That would be backsliding, in her opinion.

Quit complaining. Go buy yourself some Widow Jane, Jeannie Louise tells herself.

She rises from her office chair and grabs the shoulder cling she uses for her phone and keys when she goes out walking. She unzips the middle-sized pocket and stuffs her phone in and then grabs her keys, securing them in a smaller pocket after she locks her apartment door, and then she's stepping down the front stairway and out through the front door, stopping, blinking into the light.

She hasn't brought her sunglasses and considers for a moment scurrying back up to get them. She looks up and sees it's partly cloudy, and her eyes start adjusting to real light, despite being trained for such long periods of time on the ghost cast of her monitors. She rolls her shoulders, stretches her back, and squints at the sky again.

She sees her hands are trembling once again.

She'll try Domaney's first. It's the closest liquor store, just down Cottage and then two blocks up Main, right near the Brown Bridge. If there's nothing in the way of interesting bottles, Package Plaza is just another four minutes on foot and the walk back to the apartment is easy, right up East Street.

Two whiskey museums five minutes away, she kids herself. She does love looking through the shelves though.

She's halfway across Cottage Street when her phone rings. She fumbles it out from her holster bag, thinking it might be Davin looking for a schedule on her next assignment, but she doesn't recognize the caller ID.

"Yeah?" she says.

She stops, stands stock still.

It's her younger brother calling from yet another rehab clinic.

She shuts her eyes and listens.

Chapter 43: Rain, Rain
Come Away with Me

Deidre is halfway done putting some of her clothes into her old duffel bag, emptying the small bureau Alicia bought for her. The duffel bag is one she's had since her community college days and it's been long enough for her to no longer remember what the now faded logo on the nylon sides is supposed to be or what it refers to. It had been a secondhand purchase from the thrift store up in Pittsfield, now closed, but one of the stores she and her mother often scoured for nice clothes, kitchen appliances, even furniture.

She looks back at her bureau, the two top drawers still half-pulled open. This bureau is on the opposite side of the room from Alicia's bureau, in what Deidre can't think of as anything other than her own side. Her side of the big bed. Her side, toward the door.

It's strange thinking that way, the raw assumption behind the thinking, the thoughts of possession and position.

It seems a strange thing to think, especially at this moment, all things considered.

I can't stay here, she tells herself, a repeating line from her decision.

Her side, her bureau, her shelf in the bathroom *en suite*, although it has only been in the last year she stopped using the other bathroom off the upstairs hall across from her official bedroom a good twenty feet down from the bedroom where they sleep.

Together.

Deidre is tired of crying.

It's been almost three years since she moved in, in effect anyway, and since then she hadn't spent much time at Davin's house. Her keeping that room there had been silly, except now, she wishes she still had that room. She'll spend tonight and maybe tomorrow at a friend's place and then a few days with her mom or however long she needs to figure out what she should do.

Hoping, she admits to herself, but that only makes her sigh.

She looks around the bedroom, turning slowly. Alicia's side, Alicia's bureau, Alicia's bathroom vanity drawers and shelves, Alicia's cosmetics, soaps, and brushes on the vanity top except for one small ceramic vase, wide and short, where Deidre keeps her hairbrush, her toothbrush, tweezers, mascara, and some hair clips clipped around the squat vase's top lip. The only other thing of hers is the unopened soap she got as a gift years ago.

She had thought this special soap was glamorous.

Well, she used to think it was glamorous, but living with Alicia and with all the nice things, the big house, and the amount of clothes she's been given by Alicia, despite her wishing she wouldn't, all these things have changed her view of what is or isn't glamorous.

Soap glamor, she thinks. *God help me*.

She sits on Alicia's bed and starts pulling some clothes back out of the duffel bag, placing them on the bed, neatly sorted. She is aware, looking at what she's doing, that she does like tidy.

Deidre doesn't like that she doesn't know what she should be doing.

Coming and going, coming or going, she says to herself.

She should leave some of the clothes, she thinks.

She is tired of crying.

Alicia's bureau is a nice piece of furniture, more than

nice, although she can't say exactly why she knows this. Maybe it's the dark wood, the curve of the drawer fronts, the large mirror fixed into a swivel frame capturing a large part of the bedroom in reflection.

Everything is nice in Alicia's house.

Except Alicia and Deidre, Deidre thinks.

She doesn't know what she should do. Alicia is no longer interested in her, that's what it feels like. They are barely touching and haven't had sex for weeks, haven't had any time together to speak of. It seems like they see each other only in passing. Deidre knows Alicia is *busy busy busy* with the online newspaper and with the expansion business, the meetings, the worries, the second-guessing. She knows all this.

But it's more than *Berkshire Interactive*, it has to be.

She's done with me, she thinks, letting herself think this yet again, the ache of it rising in her chest, but she is tired of crying.

Grow up! Alicia had yelled when Deidre tried to talk to her the night before about the way they were being with each other, distant, although she feels it's Alicia who is the distant one, that she was trying to tell Alicia she misses her, wants to be with her, wants to be loved by her, and to love her.

That's not how it went, oh no, she thinks, still trying to figure out how it went so bad so quickly.

Not that things were going well, she knows, not for a long time, but they had both been busy with their lives, she working more at Farm Table, now with a couple of the busy shifts, now one of the senior servers, and she still has her day job at the store, the manager in most ways but still short of acknowledgment, title, and pay-wise too.

Alicia had gotten them memberships to Kilpatrick, the gym for Simon's Rock at Bard, the small early-admission college, just a ten-minute walk from downtown Great Barrington. The school allowed residents to sign up to use the athletic facilities and the pool and take yoga or other exercise classes.

Deidre's been going there by herself, especially since the *BI* expansion effort really got underway.

But really, before that too.

There are so many things that hurt, and Alicia calling her immature is particular in its sharpness since Alicia knew right from the start how she feels about their age difference, that she would prove to be too young for Alicia.

And too different too, she thinks.

There are big differences, of course, in addition to the ten — *nearly eleven* — year age gap, including the education gap she can't help but think about, her Berkshire Community College associate degree up against Alicia's Princeton BA and her New York University master's in journalism. Alicia has long insisted the difference in education experience, like the difference in their ages, has no bearing, and Deidre knows she is smart enough and enjoys deep conversations with Alicia on many topics, but she also knows she's not interested in some of the things that drive Alicia, and this knowledge is more certain now as Alicia has focused on investments for expanding *Berkshire Interactive,* something Deidre considers to be something akin to obsession.

Deidre has her own interests. Her poetry, especially, is important to her, and her modest but growing list of publications that have published some of her work. Alicia seemed proud of this or said that sort of thing once, although Deidre knows the small literary journals where she's placed some pieces aren't a big deal. Alicia used to seem excited and loved to have her read her work to her, but she can barely remember the last time that happened.

It's like Alicia doesn't know what to do with me, she thinks, and she's confused by Alicia drawing back, work the excuse, at least when Alicia is present enough to offer an excuse, but that itself has stopped these last few months. So much has stopped, including going to bed at the same time. Alicia is either out late at the office, or out of town for meetings with the investment group, or on some sales call, or at home but still in front of her laptop and monitors, a dim blue light through the open office door off the upstairs hall.

She looks around Alicia's bedroom and down at the piles of clothes next to her old duffel, and she begins repacking and then done, brings the duffel to her own bedroom that she's been re-inhabiting more often of late. She gets out an old garment bag, a hand-me-down from Alicia, and she pulls clothes from the closet, careful to lay these few dresses, some blouses, and a couple of jackets flat, tucking shoulders and hems into the corners of the bag, adding two pairs of shoes into the bottom pockets.

She still travels light, and she is glad she's long resisted Alicia's impulse toward buying her things, but then, she has never been a fan of ordering clothes online, still liking the visceral sense of the chase she and her mother embraced in their secondhand clothing store expeditions, an activity in which she never could get Alicia to show any interest. Like other activities involving being in public, whether shopping, or going to the movies, or going out to listen to music — pretty much any of the many activities a place like the Berkshires offers.

Being in public.

Deidre knows Alicia loves her, and she has every reason to think Alicia loves sex with her, although Deidre has been the one to initiate it for a couple of years now, but Alicia remains passionate, though it's been a while, and Alicia simply hasn't wanted to talk about that.

Grow up!

The echo of Alicia's shout keeps returning.

Deidre knows what to do. She knows she has to leave. Not because she doesn't love Alicia, or Alicia her, but because over time it has become undeniably clear to her that Alicia remains uncomfortable about being in love with a woman, with her. Deidre long assumed Alicia's ambivalence would resolve, that as they built a life together Alicia's hesitancy and discomfort would fade, her discomfort would be seen as the absurdity it is, that she would be proud to love so well.

Discomfort, shame, or whatever it is.

Deidre is down the stairs and packing her things in the car, but each time she comes back up for the next load, she can't help looking around. *Better than the apartments I shared with Mom*, she can't help admitting to herself. She'd liked her room at Davin's place when she was one of the two first house sharers he'd taken in. Her bedroom there had been a small room but with its own deck, its own entrance. Her bedroom there was where she was living when she first met Alicia, and the thought of this makes her smile, but the swell of heartache quickly ends it.

No, not the first time they met exactly, Deidre corrects herself, but the first time they had said more than hello. The moment when everything changed had been at a cocktail party at Davin's house, and he had invited Alicia, had been working for her in some capacity even back then, although she still has only a vague idea about the particulars of what he does. Cindy had just showed up, that whole thing about her being on the run, her boss getting murdered, and a killer after her, not that Deidre was aware then, not specifically. She wasn't involved and spent little time with Cyn. She had learned, mostly afterward, how strange a time it had been, then, at Davin's house, but that is not what she thinks of when she thinks back to that time.

She thinks of Alicia, meeting over a cocktail.

Old Pal, she still remembers. She still remembers how Alicia looked at her, how she looked at Alicia, the flirting subtle until it wasn't subtle, her showing Alicia her room, the door closing, that first kiss, then their leaving by the door off the deck, the world having contracted into themselves alone during that drive to Alicia's house.

The house I'm leaving now, she thinks.

Now she is in her own car, plenty of her stuff still back inside the house. She's taking only what she thinks she'll need, her work clothes, her outfits, sundries.

She's not asking Alicia to give up her work.

She's not trying to make Alicia angry.

She doesn't want to go.

This is what she knows, but when she thinks this, sitting in the car, the engine running, she can't help but miss the place already, the comfort, the style. She's aware of how different her friend's apartment is, a dump, really, but she would never have thought that, not until she moved in with Alicia, and she doesn't want to go, but she puts the car in gear and slowly backs up, turning the car around, heading out toward Great Barrington, her heart racing.

I can't stay here, she tells herself.

She doesn't want to cry, she doesn't want to be angry, to feel hurt.

She wants Alicia to be comfortable loving her.

She sighs, wiping at her wet eyes, and she half looks for the box of Kleenex she keeps on the passenger seat until her hand goes to it, fumbles out a tissue.

It's starting to rain, her wipers first on intermittent and then full-on as the sky opens up.

She wipes her nose, one-handed, and then with that hand pushes on the radio.

Come away with me, Norah Jones is singing.

Chapter 44: Greene Turns Green

Greene clearly understands more than ever the disadvantage of getting one's position paper leaked is that one's opponents get more time to work on a counterstrategy. He understands that *The Gang* is not happy.

His brilliant play of getting them to accept that some fossil fuel subsidies would have to be surrendered, serving as an incentive for favorable Sea Wall Act deal making, while also keeping the advantage of ignoring cost externalities, the so-called indirect subsidies, off the table. That's the big money. He has been battling for years various schemes like revenue neutral carbon fees, and while there've been some defeats, Congress is still incapable of acting in any effective way, and that suits him just fine. Despite gains among climate-change-focused Democratic Party candidates, there are still enough Republicans and Democrats enjoying *The Gang*'s largess.

He doesn't like even to use the term *subsidies* because these are mostly not subsidies, but that is the vocabulary in use in the press these days, and the term is showing up more and more these days. But *moral hazard* is even worse, if more accurate. He knows Big Tobacco played with fire when they decided to repress the facts about the health effects of smoking, but that worked out pretty well, even with those huge settlements against the industry's liabilities, but there's been extra decades for profit taking and the industry is still going, even after all the state and federal settlements.

What he's part of is far bigger than the tobacco business, and the stakes are much higher. His new strategy's whole point is to give up some small direct subsidies for political advantage and in doing so, also gain more cover to keep the concept alive that fossil fuel companies avoid the full cost of their industry. Nothing would change, nothing too important. Fossil fuel companies would still sell their products and everyone else still gets to clean up the mess.

Fortunately, he can still console himself that the concept of externalities remains a challenge to most people. He is coming to understand, and with trepidation he'd rather ignore, that the issue of indirect subsidies seems to be becoming less of a challenge for more and more people these days.

The Gang is not happy, not with the position paper's leak and not about the resulting growing public awareness about externalities. He's not happy either, but there are additional reasons for his unhappiness and some of these reasons he's disinclined to share with his putative bosses. The kid porn angle he'd played to keep *The Laundry* out of effective action looks like a Grade A failure. He's getting more detail about where this case stands through his security head's friend in the Justice Department, and the reality is worse than what the papers have been reporting. What they've been reporting is that Penworth has been cleared of any child pornography charges, which is bad enough, but Justice Department contact had mentioned that the files are thought to have been planted.

Not thought to have been planted, he corrects himself, *but known to have been planted.*

Not only are all charges dismissed, but there is now an active investigation into the planted files. The same Justice Department source mentioned that the files had raised so many flags, and so quickly, that the dismissal of charges was guaranteed within a few days of Penworth's arraignment. Greene supposes he should be grateful that getting this conclusion signed off took a while longer because confirmation of the forensic work behind the early conclusion required effort and time. He'd feel a lot more confident if this had worked as designed, with everything going on in the subsidies debate and the concomitant uproar about political influencing. But any delay with Penworth was better than nothing, if hardly good enough.

Lots of leads, the source had said about the new investigations.

Greene knows he himself could be found at the end of that particular thread's unraveling, but he has further increased his plausible deniability, even though Lobinski assures him there is no chance of blowback.

The newest headache is the scuttlebutt tied to Penworth's group, something about AI use for tracing money.

He has scrambled, and the Rutgers AI platform is now unavailable, thanks to a huge donation to the Rutgers Artificial Intelligence Research Center newly named *The Koch Research Center for AI in Business*. The change includes immediate and sweeping facility and computation platform improvements that keep the old platform offline. Penworth and his people had used the Rutgers facility in the textual analysis that had exposed his own institute and many others to be behind so much of the climate denial and delay disinformation.

For the first time in years, Greene is thinking it may be time for a career move.

Chapter 45: Upsey-Daisy
Goes the Price of Juice

Jeannie Louise sighs. She's trying to read *The New York Times* on her tablet, stretched out on the old sofa that sits in front of the big table she uses as her desk. She has some extra pillows stuffed behind her against the upholstered arm. She sighs because she just got the update from the new rehab facility where her brother is now.

Along with the invoice, she scoffs. This makes the third time Jerry has been admitted, the first following an OD that was Narcan-revived by EMS. That had been years ago, back when their mother was still alive, and that bill had been covered by funds raised at her mother's church. The second time was three years ago, and their mother had been dead for a decade, and somehow, Jeannie Louise scraped up the money.

Third time's the charm, she tells herself. At least she has money saved and her income looks good through the rest of the year. She's pretty sure anyway.

She had thought he was doing well, finally, with a full-time job and subsidized housing.

He'll lose the housing, she realizes.

She hadn't really been keeping close track of how he was doing, and now she wonders how much that might have been wishful thinking on her part.

No news is very much certainly not good news, she considers.

He's not available for a conversation until the first two

weeks are done, and she is grateful for that rule because she'll have time to think through what she should be doing to help. Already she feels the idea of his moving in trying to poke through her resistance, and she's struggling to convince herself that wouldn't make sense. She's feeling swamped with all her work and projects, after all, and she'll need to remain swamped now that she has the new bill and all the follow-on bills she knows will be on their way. She does the math and realizes he's still two years away from Social Security, although it then occurs to her that with his spotty employment history, he might not be eligible for all that much in his monthly check.

She doesn't need this.

She doesn't want this.

She can't see much of any way around this.

The light is dimming again, despite the morning hour. It's been raining heavily on and off, a more common occurrence these days whenever a cooler high-pressure system ambles into the Northeast, wringing the water out of warm moisture-laden air.

Tomorrow looks like a beautiful day, the clouds clearing overnight, according to her weather app. The drier air and blue skies will make for pleasant weather, something that has become rarer for autumn days that are more often more humid than she remembers.

She grabs her stylus and switches apps and gets back to work.

Energy price increases are not without costs, she writes, tapping away on her notepad app. This is a line she thinks is clever and certainly the line has something to say about the reality of dealing with climate change. She is trying to write a different sort of article than her normal technical analyses, more an essay, and she is far from sure she can pull it off. The topic is the cost of fixing climate change at the personal and household level.

She's been looking over the history of civil unrest stemming from fuel cost hikes. It's a long history, but by the time the second decade of the new century rolled around, various countries were trying to reduce their own budgets by reducing public fuel subsidies. The resulting incidents of protest and rioting became a regular feature of the frontpage headlines, and she knows there's nothing new about pocketbook issues getting people's close attention.

Chile is at it again. She's had to look for the earlier stories, although she thinks her earlier inattention is understandable because the Chilean government's rollback happened on the same day Josephine hit the Gold Coast. Chile's fierce public protests against the resulting price spikes followed in quick order, but Josephine's fierce destruction of the Miami area had been about the only news most any American paid attention to then, and she knows she was no different. She is only paying attention to Chile's unrest now since it is sparked by that country's fossil fuel subsidy rollback. The issue of fossil fuel subsidies is the hot domestic topic of the moment and on the verge of breaching in Congress.

Thar she blows, is the phrase the pops up in her mind.

The Chilean protests and riots are still a daily occurrence in late September, and the violence keeps escalating. She half-remembers that Chile has a long history of fuel cost–related civil discord, including in 2009. Back then, she'd easily confirmed, electric grid prices shot up due to a significant drought that reduced the hydroelectric generation and increased the use of oil and gas power generation, which spiked prices upward. This was made worse because the Chilean federal government had already raised fuel taxes in order to improve repayment on national debt. Almost exactly one decade later, there had again been trouble from the national budget efforts that called for reducing fuel subsidies, again with leaps in electricity and gasoline prices. Those protests lasted weeks, and were often violent, and stopped only after the government relented and restored the subsidies. Now another decade has passed, not even, and there is another quasi-revolution, this again tied to changes in fuel subsidies. The news is openly speculating on the possibility of the Chilean government falling.

But it isn't just Chile. The past two decades have seen fuel cost–related civil unrest, protests, and rioting in many countries in South America, the Caribbean, Middle East, and even Europe. Both Iran and Iraq suffer through recurring social upheavals sparked by energy costs, the former mostly due to embargoes and corruption, the latter mostly just corruption.

She is also aware it isn't just oil and gas. Last year Puerto Rico needed the National Guard called up, although that was related to the cascading collapse of the territory's electrical grid due to a series of strong storms. In both Spain and Italy, the year before that, there were energy cost rise convulsions, with price increases resulting from the transitioning from coal and natural gas to wind, solar, nuclear. One consequence has been an increase in national debt of these countries, and the EU continues to refuse any further monetary assistance.

She knows Spain, even more than Italy, has worked hard to shift toward renewables, where wind and solar now accounts for some thirty percent of the power the country needs and hydroelectric something on the order of fifteen percent. The rains have been good for the last five years, but the European drought of 2022 had meant a sharp decline in hydroelectric generation that had destabilized clean energy efforts. Despite two more nuclear plants that doubled a still-modest modest contribution to Spain's grid, and on paper the steady increase in clean power supply is impressive.

Except, as she knows, one has to account for increases in electricity usage too. One disturbing statistic for Spanish coal usage is that it has remained steady in the low double-digit range for a decade or so and only in the past year has fallen to 9.6% of the country's power generation. Spain's use of petroleum and natural gas too has barely budged downward, despite the gains in renewables and despite the market prices for natural gas remaining. There has been sourcing problems with North Africa and both the Maghreb-Europe gas pipeline and the Medgaz pipeline have seen trouble in the last half decade, one shut down for a period of time as part of an economic negotiations reset and the other because of damage that was intentional, although no individual parties or state sponsors have been publicly identified. There is a recurring rumor that radical Greens were behind the sabotage, and she hopes to high heaven this implausible theory never proves out. It is bad enough that some young idiots still throw soup at masterpieces.

She settles back against the couch arm, knees up to scribble more notes with her stylus, but then she's shaking her head. She hates it when her writing makes her feel hopeless. She hates it when she starts writing in circles.

She needs to focus on the public perception of costs as related to the shift to clean energy, how the message about price increases gets explained.

Drives me to distraction, she scoffs.

She pops up from the couch with a quiet *Jeeze Louise* and starts pacing.

The Republican minority leader in Washington is jabbering on about how the climate bills that have been getting passed in Congress and signed by the new president are the wrack and ruin of the country, although there's never much mention of the fossil fuel companies continuing to insist on their right to dump CO_2 into the atmosphere for free. Instead, the arguments are always couched in terms of job losses, never profits.

She's interested in too many subjects, always has been. After college, armed with her freshly minted economics degree, she'd worked at the Fed in St. Louis as a number-crunching cog. She had enjoyed the work, but over the few years of her tenure she grew increasingly impatient with the failure to explore the larger meanings of the numbers, especially as the climate change battle surged and her own interest had deepened. She moved on to *Harvard Business*

Review as an economic analyst, but when she had the opportunity, she took the editorial job at *The Economist*, at their Washington, DC, office, where she got to help with some of the research in the sister organization's Economic Intelligence Unit. Through some of her new colleagues who did political reporting, she started helping with analytic climate change pieces.

She'd enrolled in the NYU journalism masters program by then. Those first few articles of hers had been modest efforts, and there was nothing in remuneration, but she found she loved that work.

And then she met Jersey.

Your hobby, as her supervisor called the writing she was doing on her own time, but as her stories started showing up in periodicals that had actual readers, this work became increasingly problematic for the magazine.

Or at least to my manager, she thinks.

She stops for a moment, and she appears to be looking through the gauze curtains, but she remains lost in her thoughts.

She pivots and scurries to her desk, putting down the tablet and flipping open her laptop, bringing up her big monitor.

She sits.

Even today, all these years later, she still feels embarrassment with how things turned out at *The Economist*. For someone good at analyzing data, she'd seriously misread her manager's view on the outside work of hers, and she came too late to see that he, and then also the editorial chief of the Washington office, increasingly and more clearly signaled their dislike of her doing any of the freelance work. By the time she could see this, she had to scramble to build a pirate copy of her contact management database and a few log-in credentials to essential research databases. She doesn't like thinking about this, and whenever she does, she experiences the ghost of the burning weight in the pit of her stomach she had felt those last few days before she handed in her resignation, a resignation that had been requested.

She lets out a long breath.

"Get to work," she says.

She knows there have been plenty of reports and analyses that show, and for years now have shown, that climate remediation efforts in the energy sector create many more new jobs relative to the losses seen in old energy sector employment. The facts are readily available, but there are still far too many times when she reads something stupid, incomplete, or lazy, and that often makes her think of that old movie, *Idiocracy*.

Maybe we are getting stupider and stupider, she wonders.

Girls are from Venus, they don't have a penis, she suddenly brings forward from some corner of her elementary school memories, and she laughs. She tries to think of the next line and out pops, *Boys are from Jupiter, they get stupid and stupider.*

She pushes her tablet away from the desk edge and closes her eyes for a few moments, trying to clear her mind, listening to the rain that remains a steady low static beyond her windows above the air conditioner's sounds. The windows are closed because even though it's late September it is unseasonably warm.

Just the previous year, she'd finally broken down and installed two window unit air conditioners, putting one in the front room she uses for her office-slash-living room and the other in the kitchen window at the back where she typically had positioned a box fan. She still tries to use the fan as much as she can, but the mugginess of the last several days has the air conditioners back on duty.

It's the humidity not the heat, she says to herself.

Okay, also the heat, she adds.

So now she's just another energy hog, although both air conditioners are high efficiency models. She is also one hundred percent LED for lights. Her cooking is mostly microwave and coffee machine, but her refrigerator, part of the apartment furnishings, badly needs replacing with a newer model that uses the low-compression system that draws less current. There is a furnished electric washer and dryer too, and hardly new or efficient, and she's intentionally remains in the dark about heating, included in the rent. She hasn't even used a hairdryer since her college years, when in the 1980s she suffered through a delayed Farah Fawcett phase.

And the electric bill is still nigh-on staggering, she tells herself.

She received this month's statement alert just this morning and went online to check the amount due. The utility bill was high enough to have her then log into her bank to check balances. These days covering the bill is not in doubt, but old habits and anxieties die hard.

And here I am writing a piece on power costs.

She knows better than most that a part of the ongoing increases in electricity costs is tied to the Carbon Reduction Act passed at the start of the new administration, and this is before the tax credits for lower income people face the big drop in credits next year that will have more people paying more for the carbon tax on their electricity bill.

She knows better than most that the schedule of reductions in income tax credit levels included in the Act had been part of the compromise to make the Republican minority vote more palatable by including what some had called *Trojan Horse* provisions. It had been widely reported at the time that the minority leadership had worked with those few aisle-crossing senators to rig the schedule of EEIC credit step-downs to be timed for the minority's electoral advantage, although of course, any such machinations were and continue to be rigorously denied.

It remains to be seen whether this strategy will pay off, especially with the ongoing reconciliation fight with H.R.32 that includes what is called the Clean Tax Act, which, among other ends, will amend the Carbon Reduction Act's EEIC reduction schedule to be more progressive.

They Shoot Trojan Horses, Don't They? pops into her head, not that she is planning to write on the topic, because she'd already used the title a while back for a piece following up on her analysis of the original CRA compromises.

She stands back up, shrugs and rolls her shoulders, and sits down again.

The latest Kehoe strategy is to paint renewables and other climate mitigation efforts as additional taxes in every way but name. She knows public resistance is building in reaction to the scheduled drop of EEIC, and those anticipated increases in electricity bills are being attacked as a regressive tax increase. Unfortunately, she's not seeing much effective countering by the Democrats, at least not yet. Of course, if H.R.32 goes through, this all becomes moot.

What has surprised her in Kehoe paper are the proposals to cancel of a number of direct fossil fuel subsidies. On its face, this is shocking coming from that source, but it hadn't taken her long to determine there is no mention of the much more significant indirect *de facto* subsidies for Big Oil dumping pollution and greenhouse gases into the atmosphere, that treat the air like an open sewer.

The phrase *open sewer* rings a bell, and sure enough, after running a search for "climate change open sewer," right up top is Al Gore, from back in 2023, when he turned against any involvement of Big Oil in climate talks. He had finally called the fossil fuel industry out for its hypocrisy and their behind-the-scenes efforts to capture the process of climate mitigation even as the fossil fuel sector's leases and drilling and production was skyrocketing. This was the year of COP28, when the head of EUA's oil industry was the president of the proceedings, although she's hard-pressed to recall his name. *Another Al*, she recalls, and then, *Dr. Sultan Ahmed Al Jaber.*

The economic concept of externality remains difficult for people to grasp, she knows. *Even Saint Al can't help.*

She drags the keyboard back toward her. She starts typing, the keys rumbling as she captures her thoughts.

The main focus of this piece, she's decided, will be on the climate change activists' failure to talk about the real-world economic consequences of today's efforts to decarbonize and instead mostly talk about the cheap energy to come.

And tomorrow's and tomorrow's and tomorrow's energy transition benefits, she tells herself.

She knows the Berkshires, at least the southern part of the county, tends to lean left and progressive. She'll get the early version of this essay into *BI*, using this audience for test reaction to her argument, which is that real climate solutions will exact costs for years and probably decades, and the left and climate progress allies, by not acknowledging these necessary costs, will present themselves to many of their fellow citizens as liars, elitists, or hypocrites. Being open about the cost of climate progress is a strength for the climate change movement, she wants to argue. It isn't like the other side remains silent on costs, she'll point out, even if those attacks on costs are absent real solutions.

Climate activists have some good stories to tell, including that jobs creation is a real outcome of climate amelioration, and more and more people know someone or another who now works in new climate jobs. But the fear of further loss in economic status is a powerful lever to pull with those who have too little already. The real questions should be who pays and what is fair and necessary. These questions cannot be properly considered if the climate progress side lets the far-right scaremongering go unopposed about costs and taxes raised and jobs lost.

It's our own damn fault, she tells herself, again pushing back in her chair, and then she's back leaning forward, rereading what is already an outline with substance.

She scoots forward and starts typing again.

The climate movement habitually doesn't speak the truth

about climate change as reflected in peoples' everyday economic lives, and by not doing so undercuts public support. This is why the left generally has been so dependent on college-educated professionals. College-educated people have more resources to weather price increases for the good of the planet.

She also wants to show the role climate justice has in the larger movement to meet Paris emission drawdown targets.

Already missed targets, she thinks and sighs. It isn't that there hasn't been plenty of climate progress, and it's easy to list all of it, but even if the world went net zero today, she knows all too well the negative consequences of global warming will continue for many decades.

It is all a hard sell: *Take a hit so things don't get even worse, because things can get a whole lot worse.*

She looks over her notes and decides that she's still pulling punches. People are not stupid, although some part of her wonders for a moment if this is indeed a justified assumption, but she pushes this thought away.

She's well aware that most people are struggling with costs as part of their day-to-day reality, and climate organizations too often can be patronizing, afraid citizens can't handle facts about cost, or won't understand causation, or are confused by explanations. The left promotes its righteous causes but doesn't often mention higher costs are demanded.

We sell the better days of 2050 or 2100 without being clear about the price of getting there, she types.

We paint a picture of clean energy in abundance, and more comfort, better health, she types, and it is true, that future, if everyone works together, works hard enough, and invests enough.

Ya can't git there from here, she thinks of adding, but that old joke doesn't fit, not really. Progress is possible, and even underway, but the fits and starts still make it all seem tenuous. It remains unknown, too, if enough people understand the hard and costly work to fight climate change.

Pay now or pay later, she types. *The later you pay, the higher the costs.*

She finds herself sliding into an all-too-familiar discontent, and she fixates on the pervasive disconnect concerning electric vehicles in the climate progress's messaging efforts. She decides to use this as an example of her thesis.

Disconnect, she scoffs, but she'll forego that potential joke.

She believes talk about the growing percentage of electric cars is all fine and dandy, but this exacts a cost too, including raising demand for electricity, and even while electric vehicles are going mainstream, inching upward toward the fifty percent mark of new vehicles sold, there are many people who need to keep their internal combustion cars longer and longer because even with help, they can't afford to buy a new vehicle, electric or not.

She starts a new section of her outline notes, recounting the arguments that going EV means one spends less over time.

Unfortunately, she types, *the argument that EVs brings down expenses over time is a nonstarter if the pressing concern in a household is paying today's bills.*

And there is the continuing problem of EV incentives hitting their caps of course, and while the build-out of charging stations has had real gains after taking body blows from Trump, there remains the problem of proprietary charging stations, and home charging necessitates a home and driveway, if not a garage. And then she types out what she still hears from people who tell her they want to buy an EV but worry about range in the winter when up in the Northeast and other cold season regions, comfortably heating the car in cold weather can drain batteries more quickly and thus reduce range.

That's less and less an issue, she knows, with heat pumps now the heating system in EVs and all the advances with batteries. And, of course, no one mentions how internal combustion engines drop in efficiency too in the very cold, or are sometimes found dead, no cranking engine starts.

Thinking of cars in the cold has Jeannie Louise smile, recalling a moment in her childhood when she was eight or nine years old. She can't remember where they might have been heading, or the why of the rarely offered position of shotgun in the front seat of the old family Oldsmobile next to her dad. She hasn't thought about her father all that much for years, he dead for almost three decades. He was typically without much humor, but loving enough, not at all a bad fellow in her memories, but not known for jokes and quips.

What she is remembering now was that on a typically frigid winter morning she was sitting up front, and the car had quickly warmed, the heat set full blast with hot air blowing on her face. Driving down the road, her father had reached over to the fan controls, turned the fan off with a flourish, saying, *Flamethrower, off!*

"Flamethrower, off!" she says out loud, and her reminiscence has her think of her brother.

She'll need to check in.

She resumes her draft, noting that telling people solar and wind will bring cheap electricity is correct, but what is too often not mentioned are the complications and the timelines and the costs of transitioning major energy infrastructures. She wants to address the ongoing need to expand power generation to keep up with the power demands of universal electrification, and she mulls exploring using home heat pumps as an example the clear benefits, but how these don't magically appear and replace oil- or gas-fired furnaces in households and commercial buildings, nor does better weatherizing or air sealing one's old house occur without some cost and with plenty of disruption.

A key point she'll expand, she sees, is that making household budget decisions based on long payback ROI is something well-off people can do, but installing PV, even with incentives, is like taking on a mortgage for most people, just like air sealing one's house—if one even owns a house, that is—or adding insulation or replacing windows. Even with all the programs that can help financially, this still feels like debt to those who don't have money to spend. Without doubt, she tells herself, taking days off from one's job to watch the house while contractors deal with weatherization is a good example for many people of an everyday problem.

She pauses and takes a minute to straighten up one of the piles of reports on the desk.

She considers putting on some music and thinks Joni Mitchell would be a good choice.

She gets back to her writing.

She knows that transitioning to renewables is an argument almost everyone agrees with, pretty much, but climate change professionals and the legions of supporters don't often talk about upfront costs and ongoing costs and the home economics challenges this all presents. Or at least this isn't talked about nearly enough, and despite the efforts of organizations like Rewiring America and a few others, this failure produces an unavoidable takeaway for regular people that climate change professionals and the politicians who espouse the climate amelioration programs, incentives, and legislation don't get what it is like to be a regular person, or worse, that these professionals don't care. Even programs like Energy Earned Income Credit are clumsy for most households, with higher energy costs offset only at tax time, which is something only people with enough money in their bank accounts don't worry about. But people who live in week-by-week increments of seemingly ever-tightening budgets worry about bills constantly. And those energy efficiency programs that help the very poor do little for those many caught in the desperate economic middle, other than to add to the sense that no one is aware of the challenges they face.

She knows that any discussion of the cost of the energy transition has to note that there is a much bigger price to be paid if state and federal climate policies slip backward. The last four years should make this point more than obvious.

There will be a far greater cost if nothing is done, she types, *or if the Paris Agreement goals continue to slip*.

Slip worse, that is, she thinks. The 1.5-degree mark is already well past achieving, and the most positive analyses hope for a 1.7 C top limit, but she is hardly that positive.

The essay about energy costs she's attempting to write remains stubbornly abstract. She's been a belt tightener with the best of them, and especially in the last decade as she's built her freelancer business, but with her advanced degree and her variety of professional jobs, she even then walked among the so-called elites.

What was the old term? she finds herself wondering, and then it comes to her. *Knowledge worker*.

She laughs and shakes her head. She understands it makes all too much sense there is little love for elites, even while most people do understand the need for climate action. But for the pace of climate amelioration to improve, it will be because more politicians, and the analysts, and the academics, and all the assorted other professionals and mass media and everyday people all get it: *Climate progress comes at a cost*.

The question about such costs has long been absent from the perspective of most people who struggle economically. Most people working toward climate progress don't talk about the economic stress of it and aren't upfront with this obvious factor. There is no question that the extreme poor — whatever the race or religion or gender orientation or developing nation or whatever *ism*-of-the-day is considered — need help. But there is also no question that fundamental economic infrastructure improvements needed to reverse three centuries of carbon-dumping into the atmosphere are costly and long-term undertakings that require big spending.

Build, Baby, Build, not Drill, Baby, Drill, she types.

She pauses, scanning her notes, and then shakes her

head. She reaches out for the bottle of Adderall and gives it a shake.

She's between doctors. Her previous one had grown adamant about not extending her prescription without a satisfactory ADHD assessment on file, so another item on her to-do list is find a new primary care physician.

She needs to take a break.

She is up and pacing again.

She needs to think more about including the issue of tax reforms still falling short and the issue of the gamed system of laws and taxes and subsidies and other mechanisms that corporations use to buy advantages from governments. She knows she is taking on subject matter far more expansive than her usual focus, but the main thing she'll have to do is keep it real.

This shouldn't be beyond the capacity for an elite, she admonishes herself.

But she needs a bit of a pick me up.

She doesn't even have a title for what feels like is an ever-metastasizing piece.

But given how much more expensive Florida citrus is, post-Josephine, with winds that badly damaged so many of the groves, maybe she'll go with *Upsey-Daisey Goes the Price of Juice.*

Chapter 46: Boom Boom Boom

"W hat the fuck," Davin says out loud, not an exclamation, but maybe more a prayer. He's looking at the television positioned above the bar with Alicia and an old friend from his Cambridge days at his side. Alicia's agenda with this outing is to recruit his friend, and Davin and his friend's agenda is having a drink on *BI*'s tab while checking out a new place. The bar has only recently opened its doors, another in what has been a rash of tiny places, and this one's just big enough for the bar and a line of tight booths arrayed across the opposite wall. This bar on Railroad Street is a would-be classic cocktail bar, although Davin's already thumbs down on that, and this is what he'd been thinking about before the images on the television take his notice.

They'd been sitting in a booth, Davin and his friend squeezed close, but the three of them are now standing at the bar with a live news report that has their attention.

"Yeah, indeed, the fuck," his friend says.

Alicia shushes them, but they are fixated on the news as much as she is, the video of still fierce flames mostly obscuring the large house the fire is in the process of swallowing. The emergency response seems outmatched, and the firefighters, from the look of it, are mainly trying to keep neighboring properties from the flames. The houses are far enough apart the video camera can only catch the edge of one neighboring house getting water dumped on it, although there is a panning shot moments later.

Nice neighborhood, Davin finds himself thinking. He's

not sure he's ever heard of the town where this is happening, but the location may be somewhere along Philadelphia's Main Line.

The on-site reporter is back onscreen, and Davin now understands the video of the structure burning they'd just watched is not live because the reporter is standing with the same house behind him, but now the structure is a heap of smoking rubble, the firefighters pouring water on the remains of it.

The reporter is answering the in-studio anchor's question.

"That's right, Renee," the reporter says after that weird delay that's been ubiquitous forever, whether the in-field report is coming from down the street or halfway around the world. "We're told the house belongs to Alex Ecsialles, who is the chief of operations at Sunoco's Eagle Point refinery in nearby Westville, New Jersey. According to Merion Station town records, Ecsialles lives here with his wife and two daughters. There is no announcement about people in the house, but several of the neighbors have stated the family was at home and that they fear the worst."

The anchor comes on screen before handing off to a camera at another location, the scene a mix of officials, including the Merion Station Chief of Police who is first up at the podium. He describes in sober terms that any search for remains is waiting on clearance by the fire department, and then he talks about Alex Ecsialles, that he was a friend and active in the community and about the wife, Katherine. He stumbles when he tries to speak the names of the two girls, and the only audible words are "eight and ten" before his voice breaks and he covers his eyes with a broad hand, a woman coming to the podium and placing a hand on the chief's shoulder. Then a man approaches too, and it looks like they are there to help the chief from the podium, but the man is saying something to the chief. The next decipherable sound on the mic is "Jesus Christ," plaintive, uttered by the chief, and the man continues to speak to him, but the rest is all unintelligible.

The chief straightens up as the other man stands clear.

"We've just received word there has been an explosion at the Eagle Point Refinery," he says, and clearing his throat, he tells the assembled reporters the press conference is to be rescheduled, but what the chief is then saying is lost in the scramble of questions getting shouted toward him.

Now the anchor is back on the screen, recapping the aborted press conference and handing off to images of the burned house from above. The image twists as the camera drone moves, now pointing eastward over North Philadelphia and across the Delaware River toward a column of black smoke taking over the horizon.

"What the fuck," Davin says out loud, quietly.

Chapter 47: Operation Fuck Me

Joey Lobinski is furious with himself, furiously thinking about the sloppiness of his covert operations, his all-too-apparent ignorance about the surveillance culture that has screwed him royally.

He had followed good protocols, he had been careful, he had taken calculated risks, but what he hadn't done is think about the growing numbers of certain new types of video. An epidemic of this kind of video, as it turns out.

Fucked by a doorbell video.

Or maybe his protocols hadn't been that great, he wonders. Maybe he had simply gotten sloppy.

You plan for bad luck, he can hear his instructor say, clear as the day in Field Practice Procedures class when he was in AIT, at Benning, before it was called Fort Moore.

Thinking is your best weapon, he hears.

He has plenty of time to think now, sitting in this nondescript interrogation room, the inset ceiling fluorescents humming, one tube blinking off periodically, a stutter-step distraction as he waits for the agents to return. Although he would be fine if they simply forgot about him.

He knows he's fucked, majorly fucked.

He closes his eyes, then opens them abruptly, looking toward the ceiling-mounted video camera bubble, then turning around toward the other, off to his right behind him. The first bubble is above the room's one door, the other in an opposite corner, and it takes an uncomfortable twist to see it, given that his hands, handcuffed, are anchored to a tabletop loop of metal.

He really wants to do his stretch practice, his shoulders, neck tight and tense. He tries to sit up straight to bring his spine into a stretch, and then he almost laughs thinking about asking the agents to uncuff him so he can do his training stretches, the ones he does before sparring, from back in his hand-to-hand days, *just like half of these guys do*, he's thinking, but he quiets himself. He tries breathing deeper, surprised how high in his chest he's been breathing, tight little breaths a half pace away from gasping, but the main result of his effort is feeling like he needs to take a piss, maybe a dump, but he knows that's mostly a somatic reaction to feeling *completely fucked.*

It isn't that he doesn't know about home security video. He knows about Nest Hello, and Blink, and Ring, and all the other wireless security products of the Internet of Things. He even has a Google Hub system at both his apartment and his cottage. Being caught on video doesn't matter if no one knows what to look for or if there's no likely reason at all for anyone to look.

But he got sloppy, lazy, that's all there is to it. He's even not swapping burners faster. He likes to dump the phone right after the assignment, but it was such a string of assignments with Greene and Greene always wants to be able to contact him, and Greene or his security guy was simply too cheap to supply enough phones.

He'd love to blame them, but he knows he got sloppy. Blaming Greene doesn't make sense, other than the fact it's Greene's assignments that have gotten him in this fucked-up situation, but the blame really is on him, he is the professional and his assumptions and operating protocols were slovenly, period, full stop.

He's trying not to wonder if maybe he was hoping to get caught somehow, maybe that's why he's always taken care to cover his ass in case he's caught.

Don't think about that shit now, he tells himself.

Look, listen, learn, he says to himself, although what he's already learned from the first go-round is he is paddling up shit creek with his hands.

They have his operations laptop, to name one bad piece of news, although he'd run through his hygienic routines, deleting operation files and clearing the memory caches, but he hadn't wiped the porno package material since he hadn't yet used this on the next insert assignment.

There is still the current assignment list, but he keeps that working list on a thumb drive and that drive is currently sitting safely in one of his drop spots. What they do have is his burner and his personal phone, which means they can place him anywhere he's been when he's used either phone or even with just a tower ping, assuming the agents are interested enough to file the inter-agency requests. They'd have the streets among the cell locations and they might correlate names and start rebuilding a picture of his recent assignments and if they do, he is royally screwed anyway.

No fuck, asshole, he tells himself.

If they do, he thinks.

Which they will do, he thinks.

These agents may not look like they are smart, but then, that would be the smart way for them to play it, he can guess.

So far, the only charges have to do with the Penworth package, the child pornography frame, with B&E the charge. How that package should have even raised questions surprises him, but then, he's feeling surprised all around, he can admit. Someone must have done some forensic analysis of the assignment's laptop, that is his best guess, but it would have had to be a pretty damn deep analysis, and even then, he is pretty sure, any flags raised on the package plant would be hard to spot. Not impossible, probably, he has to wonder, but still.

He is plenty curious about how they might know the package is a plant, but then he thinks about the video angle, that he must have got caught on one or another private camera, maybe even at Penworth's home, although he thought he'd checked that carefully enough, but probably a neighbor's system or even several of the houses on the street here. The First World is full of surveillance, and he knows that in the abstract, but the question he wants answered is why the insert package got such strong analysis. The whole point of child pornography is to render the assignment *persona non grata*, with no effective friends, a tainted person. The beauty of child pornography is people so easily believe anyone is capable of such depravity.

Apparently, he considers, this guy Penworth must have different sorts of friends. Or the timing was too convenient, too suspicious, he wonders. He can't ask the agents, of course, since he's still playing it all silent, and asking the wrong questions is a great way to give them leverage.

But I'm fucked anyway, he tells himself again. The package is on my laptop, it's obvious this is the identical collection and identical false download dates and valid source sites.

Well, he reminds himself, he's got money for lawyers and other, deeper sources for help, if it comes to that. Some sort of plea deal, B&E, libelous intent, who knows? This is another of the things he's been wondering, knowing that whatever charges might be brought against him, he's done far worse.

He'll have to play it cool.

He starts, a body sweat pinpricking his torso, his armpits. He only now is realizing they have him on child pornography too, maybe even distribution.

Fuck!

He's trying to recall what the sentencing for child pornography might be, but he's not certain if he's ever paid attention to such things, and then the door clicks open, the two agents coming back in, the show of a large folder slap-tossed onto the table.

They are FBI, but he hasn't heard their names.

"Comfortable?" the taller one, the one with the blond crewcut, says, unbuttoning his tan suit coat, taking a seat. The other agent is darker and shorter and without a jacket, and he remains standing, leaning against the reclosed door.

Lobinski sits still, arms resting on the table as best they can, considering the placement of the table loop and the tightness of the cuffs.

A minute, maybe, passes with the two agents just looking at him until the standing agent says, "Hey, look, SERE training, right?"

The seated agent keeps his eyes on him. "A lot of good training time went into this piece of shit," this agent says, whether to him or the other agent.

"Well, you know," the short one says. "Thank you for your service." The comment seems to crack him up.

Lobinski keeps himself still.

"You must be curious how we found you," the short agent says, pushing off the door, a smile quirking his lips. They both are looking at Lobinski, watching for a reaction.

Lobinski ends up looking up toward the ceiling.

"Well, Frank," the seated agent says, "we got us a cool character here." And Frank sniffs, amused, or pretending anyway. The agents' behaviors are hard to read.

Just as it's supposed to be, he thinks.

"Got ourselves quite a royal asshole here," the seated agent then says.

Frank doesn't seem to need to acknowledge his partner's assessment, but starts in, stepping closer. "This guy Penworth seems to have some very loyal friends," he says to Lobinski. "Couldn't believe, wouldn't believe the porn story, and someone had some pretty smart friends too."

Lobinski glances back over to the agent seated opposite him but sees he is still just staring at him.

"You familiar with the National Child Victim Identification Program?" asks Frank.

"He doesn't give a shit about that," says the other agent.

"Now, James, James, I just want to know how smart our Mr. Lobinski is," says Frank, but he's also keeping his eyes on Lobinski. "That is the world's largest database of child pornography, maintained by the Child Exploitation and Obscenity Section of the United States Department of Justice," the shorter agent continues.

"That's got to be a job, huh," Frank says to James, who merely grunts.

"Well, kiddie porn gets sent to that very Section, a dupe, anyway, adds to the collection these days, typically hard drive dupes."

Lobinski now is irritated about how much this agent talks, but he also wants to hear what they have to say. That matters, but he knows he should keep his mouth shut, not ask anything, so he'll just have to wait them out.

"Well, guess what?" Frank says.

Lobinski remains silent.

"Don't want to guess?" Franks says, and this gets a chuckle from James.

"No? Okay, I'll tell you. Turns out it's an exact copy, file for file, the structure, everything down to every last bare bum."

Lobinski remains silent, but he's starting to guess where Frank is going.

"Not just a copy, but these guys already have two caches just like it, including the dates, the download dates, sites. The Section has been looking into those copies, and I'm guessing they were thrilled to get another one because they requested an interview with the local district attorney. Your victim's defense lawyer gets notified, and," Frank waves his hands, "yadda yadda, the game is afoot, lawyer raises a ruckus, and the rest is history, *ding dong* bell, face recognition, you're on file, probable cause for B&E. *Howdoyado*, bingo."

Lobinski is pretty sure his face is flush, reflecting the rage boiling up inside of him. *My fucking source for the package,* he thinks, screaming inside himself. *The fucker, the lazy fucker,* he shouts in his head, but James is snapping his finger at Lobinski, who realizes one or the other must have just said something.

"We got questions for you," James says. "We'd love to know where you got the package that still is on your laptop—"

"—you stupid fuck—" adds Frank.

"—could help you, give us what we want, help us with this, get some kind of break," James continues.

"We want to know who hired you to do this," James adds.

Lobinski would gladly give his source—*the fucker!*—to these guys, but he's not going to say anything until he lawyers up. As for Greene, Lobinski knows the smart play is silence, and he can always make something up, a blind drop for instructions, cash payments, that sort of thing.

He'll burn one of his blind drops if he has to, but so what.

His mind is racing.

Frank barks out a laugh, getting Lobinski's attention.

Frank is shaking his head, smiling. "Hey, James," he says, eyes never leaving Lobinski, "get this guy, you can see he's thinking he's working us."

"Sure as shit," James says, no smile, no laugh.

"This is priceless," Frank says. "I love my job."

Lobinski's palms start popping sweat. *Fuck*, he tells himself, *something's coming*. He can't keep his eyes off Frank's grin.

Frank's grin vanishes.

"You stupid fuck," he says and Lobinski hears him, all too loud and clear.

Chapter 48: An Act Underwater

A nother of Jeannie Louise's Google Alerts is for the Sea Wall Act, which is still being marked up in various committees in both chambers, and it's a big act, so likely months more in the making. But with Josephine and that storm's immense destruction of Florida's Gold Coast and the ongoing displacement of well more than a million people, public interest in the bill has exploded.

She lies back against the couch arm cushions, eyes closed, but then sits up, knowing there will be no time for a nap.

There is good public support for the potential bill's basic concept of federal largesse to help protect coastal cities, but she remains reluctant to read too much into it this early in the process. She will want to track how acceptable the final Act will be for residents of cities that don't qualify for such big infrastructure help, and how much managed retreat funds there will be. There's also the likely coasts-versus-midlands struggle ahead. The proposed funds to rework the Mississippi with a series of giant locks and dams up from the delta might help sway some of the midwestern states, but this is only blue-sky tinkering at present, according to some sources. She is especially focused on the list of potential metropolitan candidates for the major infrastructure grants. No such list is yet defined, but there is plenty of speculation among the talking heads and Washington wags about which cities may not make the list, and she's already tracking polls.

She can guess Miami is out, with its high level of

destruction and underlying vulnerabilities, and the widespread damage and destruction of infrastructure. Probably many other smaller cities in South Florida, too, with enough compelling projections that some bottom parts of Florida will be underwater by the time the next century rolls around. There are a number of proposals for New Orleans as part of various major Mississippi projects, but then there's a big question of the Mississippi River's long-term viability as a shipping infrastructure if the dry weather systems behind the recurring droughts along much of the watershed hold as a new climate pattern. There's a lot she doesn't know about, and there's plenty that nobody really knows, and she again reminds herself it's early days still, and Congress being Congress means she won't put money down on any outcome.

She's got to make a telephone call soon, but she figures she'll check her various other Google Alerts first. She remains on the couch but pulls her tablet to her.

Before checking the alerts, she pulls up one of the many interactive sea rise maps to be found online—she'd stopped counting at twenty-six. Even though she always takes herself to task for procrastinating, she finds these sea rise maps fascinating.

Or perhaps just distracting. Click on a one-foot rise and see whose feet get wet, she thinks.

She can already assume Washington, DC seems an obvious candidate for infrastructure buildout. Rightly so, in her opinion, since the control of the ocean's ingress into Chesapeake Bay would also address many other population centers, including Alexandria, Annapolis, and even Baltimore, although ten-foot rises over the next decades would only swamp Baltimore's waterfront, leaving most of the city still well above the extended ocean. Newport News, Norfolk, and Hampton could even gain protection since the bay's mouth narrows between Cape Charles and Virginia Beach. A sea wall and locks there would likely follow the Chesapeake Bay Bridge-Tunnel span.

And there's all that Navy infrastructure to worry about, it only now occurs to her.

One thing that she learned just yesterday is that a big part of the infrastructure isn't about keeping the sea out but dealing with water from the river systems so many cities have, with the biggest challenge likely to be the Hudson, for New York City, and the East River too, along with a few other smaller rivers, creeks, and streams. Gigantic pumps systems are one option and redirect tunnels and outflows another, but the problem of rising water in the upstream flow is massive and likely ever more so with more frequent heavier rainfall patterns in the Northeast. It hadn't occurred to her that a city can get drowned just as easily inside a seawall as from without.

Fortunately, there is likely time to build out water control infrastructure. Some of the newer projections are calling for a two-to-five-foot sea rise within another thirty or forty years or so, depending on the model, although there are a few models that include climate cascade factors like methane release from permafrost melt or ice cover collapse in Greenland, usually, or Antarctica's West Shelf, or both. There's been a lot of new research and modeling on sea rise, but the range and timelines remain wide open.

She knows at some point she will need to get back to work on the political maneuvering coming with the Sea Wall Act itself. She has to be careful not to waste too much time chasing down possibilities, the *what ifs and who knows*, as she calls such pointless activity. She understands any and all such speculation is absurdly premature, considering the Act isn't finalized, and even if passed, the early work will likely involve study and plan development for the next half decade or so before the real spending starts.

She scoots herself back up toward a sitting position.

While looking at how much land gets submerged in these interactive sea level maps is oddly addictive, her current compelling interest is the dark money hunt. The biggest barrier at present is lack of access to the Rutgers AI for big data set triangulations around money movement. She's already in several private forums where she and other members of *The Laundry* share or pass on tidbits and theories about tracking the flow of money in politics. She's been a good source for them regarding fossil fuel interests, although she's hardly alone in that focus, but then, *The Laundry* has also helped her a lot by providing access to other knowledge domains and practices and experts. One such area is artificial intelligence, including one strong lead from Jersey he claims is better than the Rutgers lab, and she decides there's no good reason not to make the call now.

Again.

She fishes her phone out from where it slid down between her thigh and the couch back cushion. She dials.

She is surprised the MIT professor, the AI lead she's been given, takes the call. "Yeah, thanks," she says to his greeting, but gratitude is not her prevailing tone. She has been pestering the man with unsuccessful calls, and she's been worried he was ghosting her.

She is listening.

"There's no way," Jeannie Louise says.

She starts in about how long she's known Jersey, but she gets interrupted by the man.

"Yes, yes, Penworth, of course." She had assumed the colleague would know the nickname, but it must be more of *The Laundry* thing.

"I've known Jersey for much of my adult life," she says, "and there is no way." She had thought about saying *no fucking way*, but as her father always used to tell her, bad language is a sign of a weak mind.

"The guy is something of a hound," she continues, "he likes women, been in a number of long relationships, beyond a bit of dogging around at conferences in between, but he's known, a good man, the way he treats women."

She glances away.

What the attorneys working with Jersey have been saying should answer this guy's pathetic worries, but she'll aim for patience.

"Some of his exes are good friends still," she adds.

The man says something that makes her laugh.

"No, never that kind of a relationship. Wasn't my type."

She rolls her eyes as she listens to his next questions.

"No, this is very likely. There's this case, back in 2003, about the condition of the pictures found on this guy's hard drive, Tompkins? Thomson? Doesn't matter," she says, shaking her head. "Folder structures, file dates, metadata, the case dismissed because of inconsistencies, the argument the files were intentionally placed on the hard drive, download times that corresponded with the guy being out of town on business, that sort of thing.

"One or two other such cases, something of a *cause célèbre*, there's the one from right after Covid, when there'd been a bunch of those sorts of prosecutions."

The man is saying something.

"Look," she says, her face dropping into a neutral expression. "If you don't want to hear me out, I know this is all weird enough."

She listens.

"Okay," she says. "You've read the findings from his lawyers?"

The man says something.

"Yeah, no kidding," she replies. "He was physically and digitally isolated. He hasn't been able to do much work, never mind keep in contact with everyone he'd like."

The man says something.

"I've been getting my information mostly through the lawyers, but now all such restrictions are lifted, so feel free to email or call." She pauses. She's not inclined to discuss recent phone calls she's had with Jersey, not with this guy who remains so skittish despite the expected exoneration.

Another question from the other end of the line.

"Yeah," she says. "Jersey would be a lot of help. I'm sure you understand he's still sorting out this whole mess."

The man says something.

"What I need is to get some access to the AI platform Jersey says you rock at—"

She is interrupted.

"—yeah, his words."

The man says something.

"Yes, we want to schedule some time on the platform, but first we need to Zoom—"

Another interruption.

"I know it isn't called that, I'll send you the meeting link, but I need to better understand the capabilities and how the variables are presented, terms control, iterative calendars—"

Another interruption.

"Yes, I do my homework," she answers the man, trying not to scream.

For a certifiable genius, the guy is a certified idiot, she can't stop herself from thinking.

"Yes, the forensic accountant is on board. He is a computational forensic, you know him," she says, telling the man that fellow's name.

Yeah yeah yeah yeah, she says to herself, listening. She decides there's not much use talking about who she'll be working with from the Brennen Center or the other participants from various 501(c)(4) frontline tracking efforts, including Reclaim, CLC, and Issue One. She doesn't want to complicate today's conversation any further.

The two agree on some times and dates for group planning sessions.

"Okay," she says, and the telephone call is over.

Like pulling teeth, she tells herself, but at least the project is moving to the next step, in theory anyway.

She lets out a long sigh.

Jersey had been taking the lead on the new project to identify money sources in relation to the Sea Wall lobbying, and the child pornography charge has been a big hit to Jersey's reputation, and she wonders how long and how strongly this will dog him. Even though his lawyers are confident and all charges are already dropped, and there is even the possibility of an apology from the DA's office. Nonetheless, the palling effects of the charges will continue for some time, of that she is sure.

There are plenty of times when she can feel she is not smart enough, and at the moment she is finding that the learning curve for the AI project is a killer, and she's not even a central part of the team, just providing various species of support. She has agreed to work with *The Laundry* colleagues on an article as they get clarity on the money sources, and if she needs to reach out to the political scientists for help, she will.

Not opinion, but fact, is the agreed-upon mantra of the project.

The Laundry seeks to demonstrate money sources with high confidence.

Before the floods of dark money can drown the project, she hopes. *Before the very seas themselves rise*, she adds.

Chapter 49: Tag, You're It

*A*ssholes, is what Lobinski thinks about Frank and James, the two FBI special agents, and the hell if he can remember which last name belongs to one or the other. They might be assholes, but he has no doubt they know what they are doing.

There are others in the big conference room on the fourth floor of the new offices in the FBI headquarters building he was shuffled into this morning. He is in the new headquarters that was formerly an office tower, at least from the look of it. He remembers the news about a long-term lease while the J. Edgar Hoover Federal Building undergoes repair and restoration after the bombing. Militia members had been caught, charged, and convicted, or at least those who hadn't been turned into paste in the second truck, the one that went off early, still in the industrial zone near Reagan International. The first truck, which started to target a couple of minutes earlier, must have been aware of the explosion, but the sons a bitches kept on mission. *Good on them*, he remembers thinking, simply as a professional nod. He didn't give two fucks about what those idiots believed in, but he admired the tenacity, *the balls.*

He's feeling particularly ball-less at the moment though, even if there's something of a plan in place with his lawyer.

Or at least the start for negotiating one, he mulls, trying for a bit of calm.

In addition to Frank and James, there is his own lawyer sitting to his right and busy with papers that he hopes is the plea deal they'd discussed. There are a couple of other lawyer-like people across the table, a man and a woman, both dressed better than his own lawyer, although that's not saying much. The woman is pulling documents out of her briefcase, and for a moment he thinks she's mimicking his lawyer's paper shuffling, but he clears that impression quickly. He's been having these sorts of perception problems for quite a while, mostly since the officers came by his motel room and took him in six days ago.

At any rate, there's been progress, at least in that he is no longer in the interrogation room *with that fucking tinking fluorescent*. He is happy to note the new room is well-appointed, and the view beyond the window across the conference table is of the Capitol. *A money shot*, he thinks, and then he's surprised to have had this idle thought come into mind.

He's not cuffed, but there are two armed uniforms, one behind him to the left, one behind to his right. Automatic pistols, holsters unsnapped, at rest and ready.

He is again second-guessing how well he's gamed out his situation, how smart his play really is, but there's a lot more factors in motion, a lot of concrete specifics, and he can't help feeling his thinking is falling woefully short. He wishes he was clearer on sentence lengths they're trying to bargain down, for one thing.

The best all-around play is to give them smoke, and to remain silent, and keep Greene out of it, but he can hand off any others he can.

The lazy fuck keeping old porn packages, for instance, he considers, still furious. He will be happy to pull that guy down with him, seeing this guy's bullshit package so easily raised flags. He has some contacts, dark web shit, and that should be a good bone to throw too, but rolling on Greene is too dangerous a game, and serving some time is looking like the best option. It's his understanding that this is what this meeting is for.

Six days of this shit, six days of the Frankie and Jimmy show.

He can't help but think they're not big fans, that they would just as soon piss on him as say hello, but today, in each their own way, they seem excited, puppy-like, vibrating.

Which makes him worry.

The other man across the table is now leaning into Frank, conferring with him and James, who is leaning in from the other side. What they are saying is completely unintelligible to him, despite the distance being less than seven feet.

As they talk, he finds himself sketching out how he would get to them, how much damage he might cause before the armed guards shoot him dead.

Probably not much, he thinks, although he figures his best bet would be his lawyer's pen, here at hand, maybe get one of them through the eye socket. He'd go for the older guy, he thinks. *Better angle of attack.* He figures that man is the most important person in the conference room, and one should always prioritize high-value targets. He isn't troubled by these sorts of thoughts. His training was thorough, and he's accepted that he enjoys these sorts of puzzles. What he's not enjoying is somehow really screwing up. He most definitely doesn't enjoy mission puzzles when the mission goes into the toilet.

Still, for a guy who is about to get his ass handed to him, and all the feelings that go with that, he realizes he's also feeling bored.

Of course, if Phillips, or at least the guy who calls himself that when working with him, hadn't gone retard-lazy with the child pornography package, there might not be any problem now. He's not concerned he might not know the guy's real name because he knows how to contact him anyway, and he has a pretty good idea of that guy's base of operations, which he believes is in a strip mall off 117, in Gaithersburg.

Pretty fucking sure. Might have relocated though, he considers.

He's going to trade Phillips for a reduced sentence if

things go right. The FBI seems to be very interested in the leads they think Phiilips might give them. He'd done his homework before ever saying hello to Phillips, checking the guy out, and he's confident he can deliver Phillips.

Yet here I sit, he thinks. *For someone who does his homework, you're not showing too well*, he is telling himself, but his internal dialogue is preempted by Frank standing up.

Frank is introducing himself and Lobinski sees that Frank is showing a solemn side today. Frank goes around the table, introducing James and then the lawyer guy, who turns out to be a deputy assistant attorney general, and the lady turns out to be with Homeland.

Frank stops as an older man enters the room, and Frank waits until the man stops at the head of the conference table to introduce him, and Frank sits back down.

The man is Special Agent in Charge, Washington, DC, office, and the name rings a bell, and then the face resolves. Special Agent in Charge, McMillian, something McMillian, head of the KTR Task Force.

Seamus McMillian, right, he recalls as this man walks around the table, now standing behind Frank.

What the fuck? KTR and a fucking deputy assistant attorney general?

Heavy guns for a plea deal arrangement. Homeland is less a surprise to him since they seem to like being everywhere, but KTR and a deputy assistant attorney general?

He finds himself sitting straighter, leaning forward.

He glances over to his lawyer whose own face remains a neutral mask.

"Umm," Lobinski says. He feels foolish for mewling like that, but he'll admit he's a bit flustered. "Uh," he starts again, "some heavy hitters for a plea deal," he says, feeling his lawyer's hand on his arm.

He sees Frank's sudden grin and something like a laugh escapes from the grin, but Frank goes quiet after a light touch on the shoulder, a quiet rebuke from McMillian.

His own lawyer pats Lobinski's arm once again and then leans forward to address the table.

"Excuse me," his lawyer says, "but we have a draft limited immunity agreement, and it is my expectation this meeting is simply to formalize, finalize this agreement, yes?"

Lobinski's mind is racing with what feels like a thousand thoughts and fragments of thoughts, all vying for his attention. One fragment is thinking his lawyer's speech has probably added to his bill, but his sense of dread is the thing that blossoms and fully takes over.

He sees McMillian tap Frank on the shoulder.

Frank stands and Lobinski thinks Frank is trying hard but can't quite suppress his grin.

Frank looks right at him.

"So, Mr. Lobinski, a surprising thing happened when the lab was going through your other laptop, dotting the i's and crossing the t's as it were." Frank looks like he wants to play to the audience, but instead he pulls some paper from an interoffice folder, sliding it across to Lobinski, and then pulls out another, for his lawyer.

Lobinski immediately realizes what he's looking at, and at the same time sees around the table the others already have a copy.

Fucking Microsoft.

He has good computer hygiene as a rule, and at the end of any project he cleans the hard drive by overwriting it, and he makes sure to clear RAM, he knows the drill.

He hadn't wiped the drive yet, but he had executed all his other precautions, deleting files always, ASAP. He knows how to flush the Trash, and he knows it isn't easy to do, but he takes the trouble.

Fucking Microsoft.

He is looking at a saved draft, automatically saved in its own special subfolder, under one of those many Microsoft Application partitions. He'd been working on the KTR claim document when the laptop blinked, a semi-crash, but not enough to reboot, just a glitch, really, and he had thought only that he might be in the market for a new laptop soon.

Not in the market for the fucking coup de grace.

But Word had gone ahead and put aside a backup copy anyway, in one of those weirdly numbered folders, ones you had to change the read hidden files setting even to see, and then must have concluded it needn't mention it, the program crash aborted.

He starts to laugh, or something close to a laugh, low, but with something of a skip in it.

Frank pulls out another paper, slides one toward Lobinski, another to his lawyer.

Lobinski knows what it is, doesn't even look at it closely since he's seen it on the front page of *The Washington Post* a few weeks past, the published KTR claim he sent out after his hit on Little Falls Parkway and the heart-attack potassium dose had been tox-screened.

It wasn't the outcome he had worked toward, but the KTR cover was a nice fallback with benefits.

Fuck.

He hears his lawyer make some grunt, half throat clearing, half something else.

"Look," Lobinski says, all eyes on him. "I'm not KTR, I'm not with him, it, or them."

McMillian is staring at him, waiting.

"I can prove that," he says. He can hear Frank scoff, but he keeps his eyes on the silent McMillian.

His lawyer's still making some sort of grunting, coughing sound.

"It's going to take a new deal though," he says, and then he is feeling suddenly light, now relieved in some important way, clear.

It's over.

Frank, he sees, is shaking his head again.

"You're going to want it," Lobinski says to McMillian, and then he starts talking about Greene, the Kehoe Institute, the other organizations he's done work for, what he's got to back it up, in a safe drop holding documents, tapes, files they'll never find without him, and everyone around the table seems to be talking, but then he is somewhere else, lost in the noise. He is caught up in wondering when he became so stupid, how he has ended up in such a mess, how he managed to convince himself what he was doing these past few years was neither right nor wrong, just business, just okay, somehow, and he's wondering when this happened to him, this change from the person he can still remember, the boy his folks had raised, the young man, the person who could see the value in others, in believing, in ideals, in service.

It's over.

He feels completely exhausted.

Exhausted by how long back he has to reach to get to this other life, another reality, now only a ghost of a life to him. It all seems like a long time ago, and he feels exhausted by the fury of his wondering. The exhaustion and the wondering are mixing and making him feel sick, and then he sees the young Syrian boy's face rise up to him, that ancient look, and the black burka and half-shot face of the boy's mother in the dust, the moments rise up like moments of time travel, and he is suddenly self-conscious, aware he is sitting in some non-descript conference room surrounded by others, afraid of the sob that wants to burst out of him.

He knows, knows it was then, that moment, when he signed up for all of it, the start of it, the additional training.

It started when he told some part of himself to be quiet.

And had kept it quiet.

Fuck me, he says to himself.

And then Lobinski hears his name and the room quieting, and he understands his lawyer is asking for a few moments to confer.

Chapter 50: Hurricane A'Comin!

Jeannie Louise is at her desk but feels too wired to prioritize what she should be doing. She is astonished with what is going on these days. Of course it doesn't hurt there's the newest political scandal.

She probably shouldn't be reading more about the Kehoe Institute implosion, but she doesn't feel the least bit guilty about rooting for the Institute's full and complete collapse. She's battled much of the Institute's climate denial and delay efforts over the years and knows the Institute is just one of dozens upon dozens of front organizations for the fossil fuel industry's increasingly desperate clasping for control.

Still, the coverage in the mainstream media has been satisfyingly harsh, including an op-ed piece in the *Times*, titled *Fuel for Dirty Deals*, a title that sparks some envy in her. The columnist, she was thrilled to read, had nicely laid out the argument for investigation and prosecution of those people Jeannie Louise most often calls *The Boogeymen*, but still she's torn between hope and pessimism. She hopes some of the big-name funders of this particular think tank are going to have a problem walking away unscathed.

But then she thinks, *don't bet on it.*

She checks the spreadsheet she's been working on, but it feels like a never-ending task tracking all the climate change actions in Congress that seem to be coming out of the woodwork, but part of her lack of motivation, she can admit, is her sense that the flurry of bills and hearings and claims and talking points are all tentative. She's reluctant to believe much of any of the sudden flush of the swelling climate bandwagon is real, having had her hopes frustrated time and time again.

But Big Money is out of favor, she argues to herself. She hopes these dark influencers will stay on the defensive, and the calls for investigations are heartening, but she's been disappointed too many times to let herself be too hopeful.

At least Jersey's good, she deems, now pawing through a sheath of diverse papers and printouts, looking for her handwritten notes so that she can add the very latest congressional committees' updates to the spreadsheet. She's glad the revelations about the operation that set Jersey up on child pornography charges has made him more popular than ever on the talk show circuit, but she is even happier to see he's been busy, back on the dark money AI project.

He is even talking more and more about this project in his latest rounds of interviews.

Early days yet, she thinks. The project meeting last week made this clear, but there is room for guarded optimism.

Something she's not that happy about is the modest number of indictments from all the Kehoe fallout, but at least there is an arrest warrant out for that guy, Greene, the executive director, but he seems to have managed to make himself scarce, unfortunately. The prevailing assumption is he's out of the country, and the disappearing act probably has something to do with the high bail being discussed for the small number of indicted Kehoe staffers, including the institute's security head, or chief, or whatever title the guy carried, and someone in accounting, if she remembers right. There is a lot of talk about obstruction charges, but the prosecutions are barely underway.

And then there is the unnamed person, referred to in articles and the AG's statements only as *Kehoe operative* and there is some sort of plea deal or immunity. She expects this person's name will come out when trials start and she hopes this guy serves time, considering he was the person responsible for the plant that made her friend Jersey out to be a child pornographer. There are rumors too about worse deeds, and all kinds of scuttlebutt online, including something about assassinations, but that's all talk and speculation.

She shudders, thinking about it all. Everything has happened so fast, the red flags the pornography files raised, all the panic among *The Laundry* members, the dark money project stumbling, some of her own work stopping, and all those painful repetitious conversations she'd had, and although she heard from Jersey early on about these file flags, the investigators kept poor Jersey in custody for a longer time than needed. Still, Jersey seems to be dining out on the story these days, and he's been mentioning how the delay in revealing the false charges against him was strategic. In the latest interview of his she's watched, he'd made it sound like he'd been happy to go along, in favor of the ruse. She's pretty sure this was not his actual attitude for most of his exile, but things can be remembered quite differently when circumstances change.

Much of the news about the Kehoe Institute is really still more guesses than facts, but it has been suggested the Kehoe operative could be ex-military. She feels it doesn't take a genius to think that. Just this morning, there are news reports alleging a connection between the unnamed operative with *Kill the Rich*, but this sounds unlikely to her. For one thing, there's already a KTR suspect heading to trial on federal terrorism charges, and the papers have been full of evidentiary content from the indictment phase for six or seven murders, if she remembers it right.

Six or seven, maybe eight?

She accepts there could be an organized group, but the other KTR claims seem mostly happenstance or acts of opportunity, and none of those seem capable of organizing a tag sale, never mind a nationwide conspiracy. Two claiming some KTR connection seem run-of-the-mill mass shooters with screeds on their social media pages mentioning *Kill the Rich*, but nothing in the victims' backgrounds suggest any similarity in argument. Of course, those mass shooters can't shed any further light on the matter, both being dead.

Just run-of-the-mill mass shooters, she thinks and then is shocked by her thinking such a thing. Many such people are really pursuing suicide-by-cops, and those two had followed that exact model. She has long thought about the need for a public service announcement that suggests such people shoot themselves dead first, and only then shoot others.

She sees that she is in a strange mood.

There's plenty of speculation online about the KTR killings and there are plenty of breakout lists about what are real KTR and which are copycats. The latest was a video of Jimmy Fallon playing a *Real or Not* game with a guest, but that had turned out to be an AI fake.

The real/copycat breakout tends along the lines of whether the victims were billionaires, although the dividing line that defines wealth makes for different guesses. The guy captured in Boise has all his alleged victims from the ultra-wealthy side of the ledger, and most of the KTR kills being attributed to or claimed by others are well-off, but not sickeningly rich.

Most, she thinks. There are two or three other may-be KTR attributions that were very wealthy.

Poor victims, she tells herself, thinking of those wealthy targets of KTR and the jokes making the rounds on social media, vehement sarcasm of *poor victims*.

Just three days back, the most recent mass shooting took place, this time in Topeka, at a bowling alley, which made the left-behind hand-written rantings about killing the rich pretty absurd. She'd considered cross-referencing Fortune 400 individuals and bowling, but she figures she already knows there isn't a lot of overlap. She also knows that she shouldn't be bothering about KTR or the mysterious operative or her giving her dark joke about a PSA the time of day, not when many of the news stories in the past week are about influence peddling.

It's about corruption, pure and simple, she thinks.

There are plenty of allegations being flung about, including quite a lot related to the still-committeed Sea Wall Act. Politicians and very powerful people are scrambling. She doesn't expect much in the way of legal action will come of any of it beyond the Kehoe Institute, but she can hope. That scandal has lifted dark things into the light, along with the names of some very wealthy people, any number of lobbyists, and numerous PACs, and it seems like everyone is now talking about the machinery of buying influence.

There's a development in the Dark Money AI Project, and, of course, there's yet another mysterious Jersey connection involved. The senator from Rhode Island is interested in *The Laundry*'s Dark Money AI project and has suggested the possibility of getting the project access to more government data sets, and that could make a big difference.

She's also being told that any useful outcomes are months, if not years, away. She's skeptical, even worried about the public's appetite for such stories when it takes so long to get them published. She's concerned that the story of buying special advantage through laws and regulations will be seen as old news by the time any of these new stories get out, but she's hoping that they'll have at least something by the next big news cycle, when the Kehoe cases go to court. Such prosecutions take a lot of time, and such cases often progress slowly enough that people forget their initial outrage. Trump's first term impeachments are case in point, where he'd managed, in what now seems entirely improbable, to get reelected four years later.

At times during that dark second term, she'd worried about the very existence of the country.

Thank god for those first mid-terms, she reminds herself. Even then, after the House and Senate swung against him, it had been chaotic, and the Judiciary had taken its sweet time shifting the country back to the law and the Constitution.

Even now there's plenty of damage still to fix.

Despite all that, she's still interested in trying to fix things. In one way, she's less interested in future news stories that may come out of the Kehoe Institute scandal and more interested in the more immediate effect this seems to be having on Capitol Hill. Lots of previously climate-neutral congressmen are suddenly lining up behind climate legislation, even if this is more a kind of *not-with-them* reflex rather than sincere change of heart, but now many congressional members who have long been funded by those immensely rich fossil fuel interests would rather not be seen that way. She knows the chances of real progress resulting from all the recent climate attention in Congress is anyone's guess, but the level of sudden activity, she concedes, is impressive.

She sighs, flipping through more of her pages of handwritten notes. There has also been a high volume of climate-related disasters in the news, so maybe it is more than just the Kehoe scandal that's getting people's attention. It does seem like the business world may be getting better at understanding losses due to climate change, although she knows all the analyses supporting such a conclusion have been around for years. Some years back, for example, there'd been that article in *Nature*, a report from Potsdam Institute for Climate Impact Research, which showed that the impact of global warming came in at $38 trillion, per year.

Per year.

That is what people have trouble getting their heads around. That report projected costs related to climate change could be as high as $59 trillion by 2050. Her economics background had been essential for pouring over the full report and its methodologies and she still wonders if there were all that many people who had read more than the abstract, but then, most people aren't math formulae crazy like her.

Yeah, no kidding, she thinks.

She knows that Josephine has clearly intensified the

debate about climate-related costs. The storm's massive destruction, the shocking death counts, the displaced residents of the Gold Coast scattered across the country and the almost 100,000 still in temporary camps after so many months, and all those images of the destruction and the endless piles and mountains of debris, all this continues to capture the public's attention.

And the images of all those dead bodies, she reminds herself.

A real Hanson Event, she thinks.

One of her news alert pings. She sees immediately it is from her alert string "Kehoe Institute Executive Director Gerald Greene."

The headline in the top spot of the alert results reads, *Kehoe Institute Director Dies in Jet Explosion*. The top story is only a news brief stating a small business jet has been brought down within minutes of taking off from Palo Alto Airport, one of the several small executive airports in Silicon Valley, and there are no survivors. According to the news brief, eyewitnesses described an explosion near the tail of the airplane. In addition to a two-man crew, the sole passenger was Gerald Greene, the executive director of Kehoe Institute, who had evaded legal warrants and congressional subpoena.

She doesn't even have time to fully register this when the alerts start pinging again, and she pages through more headlines. She is stopped by one particular headline: *Ka-Pow: Fugitive Kehoe Director Found… in Pieces*, and she is trying to puzzle out the strange headline, but an instant later regrets the effort. The odd and awful headline is formed by the fact that KPOA is the airport designation and the *found… in pieces*, is easy enough to parse, but she's not at all appreciative, and marks the news source as *Prohibited*, meaning she'll never again have to see anything in her Google News alerts from that particular news information service, some small market digital rag she is confident she'll never miss.

The alerts notification pinging continues, the list of headlines and decks growing longer by the moment. She keeps paging through and reads an update that a suspect is in custody, and that he had been restrained by airport staff after being earlier observed dressed as a technician and seen doing an air skin inspection. One witness claimed the suspect had attached a small blister to the Gulfstream G850's undercarriage.

Various social media posts are already getting into the alert list, and with a sigh she closes all the items. She'll let the reporters get the actual facts and come back to the story once more is known. At least the Feds now know where Greene is.

Was, I guess, she tells herself.

Another sigh, and she closes her eyes for a moment, but there's another alert ping, this one set up for stories about *Kill the Rich*, but she has to double check, because when she glances down the list she's seeing headlines she's just been looking at about Greene's demise, but when she goes back to the top the newest headline reads *Palo Alto Airport Bomber Claims Kill the Rich*, and then that story is pushed down, the growing list with newer ones coming fast.

"Jeeze Louise," she hears herself say.

She mutes this alert.

She takes a moment to close her eyes, trying to steady herself. She has to get some work done.

Before she takes an extra breath another of her alerts pings, this one for hurricanes. She starts clicking through the latest forecasting of the hurricane season, a season that normally starts in August, but then there's no such thing as normal weather these days. Hurricane season comes to an end in November, many weeks away, but she's not going to bet on it ending then. This year's season started with a bang that ripped a piece of Florida coast away, and that was close to two months ahead of the official season's start point. The indicators she is currently looking over show possible storm formation, although it's too early still to know what kind of storm might form, the power of it, or where the potential landfall might be. There have been an abnormally high number of these storms this year, no doubt in part due to the early start, but fortunately most of this season's hurricanes have been weak. There are weeks yet to go, but that is only if the storm systems to come are sticking to their official season end date.

But now she can't seem to get out of her head the *Hurricane 'a Coming!* call from Disney's *The Little Mermaid.*

Hurricane 'a Coming! again repeats in her thoughts, and again, and it is all a bit annoying. If she had known this insipid and damned refrain was going to reappear out of the depths of her past like some demented mental hiccup, then she would have just as soon excused herself from any exposure to the source material. But she was the young auntie back when her sister-in-law had her first child and she had helped watch her niece in those formative Disney DVD movie-watching years. Now at great remove, she is being punished for her acts of kindness, except, taking a moment to be honest, it occurs to her that she is simply being punished for relying on video too much to take up some useful chunk of her lovely but endlessly needy niece's preschool days.

Thinking about her late sister-in-law makes her think of her brother, who has completed rehab and is doing okay.

So he says, she can't help noting.

His wife died of breast cancer, and that could be a good enough excuse to turn to drugs some might think, but she knows her brother had problems with substance abuse long before any of his wife's medical problems revealed themselves. Her niece, now twenty or twenty-one, is in the Marines, of all places, but the few texts and emails she gets from her look like she's doing well.

She wonders how safe her niece is and will be, but then she sees the absurdity of such thinking. The Marines, she knows, are hardly known for being safe.

She also knows her niece is not to blame for what Disney

detritus is stuck in her head today. If anything, it is the alerts she keeps disappearing into as she works in fits and starts. This latest alert she's set up is easy enough to understand, since her article topic is the likely scope and timeframe for increased damage along the Eastern seaboard due to both sea rise and more frequent and stronger storms.

Hurricane 'a Coming!

For her, the rise in sea level is not a matter of conjecture, and while the Western Antarctic Ice Shelf remains in place, she knows its melt rate, like that of other main glacial repositories, continues to increase, and the effects of the higher sea levels are showing up on America's shores, albeit still modestly. The second New Orleans flood two years back has seen the storm surge over-topping the repaired and expanded levies with the water overwhelming the pumps, and that itself should have helped focus the public's attention, but it has taken the Josephine disaster to spur the drama in Washington over the Sea Wall Act.

Shifted the tide, as it were, a sea change, she tells herself, feeling only a slightly nagging embarrassment for thinking this.

The debates about addressing coastal city vulnerabilities are already brutally highlighting which areas possess enough political capital, and New Orleans is not on the list, not even for discussion. The Sea Wall Act is still being defined, but there are already other sea wall planning projects underway, and some cities, such as Boston, argue topographies and dense urban cores make their projects reasonable.

Whether or not any of those more modest efforts make a difference remains to be seen. Emerging models predict earlier hurricane seasons as the growing norm, and such storms have a greater chance to track north if the shifts in the jet stream happen, as other models suggest. One or more of these storms might hit with the tides, and if this happens sooner rather than later, the Boston sea wall work that is underway is unlikely to have the integrity to stop Boston's Back Bay and Fens from flooding, while the old hurricane walls and systems of dikes for some of the cities and harbors off Buzzards Bay are likely in danger too before the planned protection projects by Massachusetts are complete.

Numerous cities, especially on the Atlantic coast, could be subject to great flooding storm systems. The project for New York City may be the biggest target failure, since the New York State Assembly has suspended advancing the state's project to wait to see what Congress will do.

God help New York, she tells herself.

She chases a bookmark and now she is looking at a particularly terrifying climate model factoring in hurricane predictives. The screen shows various storm models looping in high speed with false colors of fronts and surges racing across next year's hurricane season, with a number of them tracking northward up the Atlantic coastline or crossing over land.

One of her recent *RE: CC* posts is about this very subject and had been entered into the Massachusetts legislative record as part of the deliberations on supplemental funding for the Charles River Dam rebuild, but she doesn't see any amount of funding is likely to get this flood protection section done in time, and it could be that luck is the only thing that will save Boston and other coastal towns along the Bay of Boston this next season and the next and the next.

Hurricane 'a Coming!

Chapter 51: Wait a Minute Mister Past Man

Davin is at the *Berkshire Interactive* office this morning, in for a presentation Alicia is making to the investor she is hoping to finally sign, and then it will just be a matter of getting the lawyers to draw up the appropriate documents and some signatures. Davin tries to pay attention to this whole process of choosing the right investor, but he doesn't really want to spend the time. He hasn't had interest, at least not for the learning curve required.

Alicia is still on her phone, and he's waiting to go over some of the new slides he's worked on for the presentation, but there's plenty of time since the presentation is slated for midafternoon.

Right around the time I'm most nap-prone, he points out to himself.

He checks email on his phone again, but there's still nothing from the Hudson gallery owner about a show of his work. He's leaning forward in the office chair in the big front room of the office, looking at the wide monitor, elbow on the front edge of the worktable, his chin in his hand, his slides up on the next slide, but he's not really thinking about the presentation.

He's thinking about a lot of different things, including the growing to-do list for *MMEAT and Greet*, now scheduled for the first week of December, and that's late enough that it looks like someone will have to check out tent rentals for the event Aine and Cynthia has been working on, if by *working on* one might mean making him run around like a crazy man. Just yesterday, he dropped by the town hall to check on the status of the one-day liquor license, but he'd learned he has to get an insurance rider before the license gets issued, and he will have to get TIPS certified too before the rider is issued. He's already looked at the online TIPS qualifying exam and knows that will represent little more than the challenge of keeping his temper about the poor design and boring quality of the certification course work.

He's been idly thumbing through the slide deck, but mainly what he's really trying to do is recover from Skip's video call earlier this morning, and his insides are still buzzing with the news. He'd enjoyed a good day in the studio yesterday and had intended to spend this morning there again before helping Marsha finish putting the garden to rest for the winter, a few things still left to do, including tipping the water barrels and turning the compost to be ready for spring. He'd just popped into his office for a quick email check with his coffee, only to read that the presentation had annoyingly been rescheduled for this afternoon.

And then Skip called.

And here he is, downtown, distractedly looking at the slides again, waiting on Alicia.

He also feels he should call Gloria. He hasn't touched base in days, but exactly what he wants to say remains confused. The last couple of times they'd gotten together, it didn't feel satisfying. The sex was fine, but something felt missing despite the physical intimacy. He'd like to talk to someone about Skip's call this morning, but he can't see this someone being Gloria.

He minimizes the presentation and checks the news.

He sits up straight.

The news story is about Kehoe and that guy, Greene, who'd been killed, and the most interesting stories are now about the man who killed Greene, along with a couple of aircrew as collateral damage, and that man is some middle-aged man named Jeremy Wenton, who immediately claimed to be a *Kill the Rich* person, but there are plenty of pieces of that puzzle that don't seem to fit. The reporters are having a field day adding new bits, and just yesterday another element to the story appeared, which is that Wenton has a prognosis for brain cancer, with his lawyer claiming Wenton likely has no more than a month or two to live. This news had come out of a petition to the court for a competency-to-testify assessment. Wenton's lawyer submitted that his client's cancer has made answering questions difficult, claiming that "Glioblastoma is a terrible disease that can rob its victims of memory and as we are seeing now, even speech."

So stipulated, he intones as he listens to the news anchors droning re-cap. The presiding judge is expected to rule on this petition in the next week, he learns. There's plenty of speculation about the disease progressing quickly, especially given Wenton had been plenty vocal about KTR after his arrest and had to have been physically quite able, back just a little more than two weeks before, when he'd planted the bomb in plain sight.

The competency assessment should answer all that, he figures, but the latest news has taken an even stranger turn. The first new item of interest is that little has been found in the way of prior involvement or interest in *Kill the Rich* before the arrest, nothing other than a couple of unsigned computer printouts found in Wenton's home. Another thing raising questions are financial statements showing several significant bank balance jumps in an account belonging to Wenton's wife in the last couple of weeks, with the first deposit dated before the airplane incident and then two more following Wenton's arrest. These deposits are from a friend of the family claiming to help with the medical bills and then giving more to help with legal fees. The family friend has been identified as Sjors van Gelder, director of communications for Energy Progress Research, a Stanford University-linked consultancy.

The San Jose Mercury story he's now skimming reports that Van Gelder feared Wenton's actions might be his fault because he had shared with Wenton his anxieties about threats to his own employment at the consultancy. "This Kehoe incident has been causing all sorts of problems for any and all outfits that have fossil fuel clients, and we're all being painted with the broad brush, and I'd been complaining about us getting slammed because of this one bad apple," he had stated. He also said, "I feel bad that I did talk about this. The poor guy had plenty of his own challenges. Jeremy was worried for his wife and their two-year-old twins."

Jack Ruby indeed, thinks Davin, but then he knows he's just looking at the news to distract himself, so he doesn't have to acknowledge his mixed reactions to Skip's video call early in his day, though it had been afternoon in Barcelona.

"Dad," she had started but quickly burst into tears, which had made it hard for him to make out what she was saying. After a moment of two of her struggling to speak, and with a breaking beaming smile, she announced that she is pregnant.

He was and is stunned by this news, although he is thrilled to pieces, too. He had worried about how she felt, and he had had to ask her directly, remembering the time, maybe two months back, when she declared, with a surprising fierceness, she'd decided not to have children.

"I know, I know," she'd replied to his query, her lopsided grin reappearing, followed by a shrug of her shoulders.

He has always loved that grin.

"We had decided, but, well," she said with another tiny shrug.

"Oh my god," he'd replied, deadpanning his comment. "You had sex?"

Skip simply shook her head, but smiled at the stupid joke, and just kept talking. "You know, when I found, we found out, all that thinking, all the rational considerations, they just…" but she stopped her words, substituting hand gestures to show such thoughts had vanished.

"Well," she then added, "it's not like these worries are gone, the facts haven't changed, but…" and then she again went quiet and again burst into tears.

Davin then again became confused, but she answered his next question clearly.

"I am very happy," she told him, and then Marco was behind her, stooping down to get into camera frame.

"Hey, *Abuelo*," he said to the screen, grinning. "*Abuelito*," he'd then added before straightening up to stand behind Skip, his upper chest and head cut from the video but both his hands on her shoulders.

Aboo had immediately struck Davin as the choice name he'd like the kid to call him.

They talked just a minute more, and there was no gender mentioned, which hadn't surprised him. Skip would keep that bit of information under wraps until the birth, he is sure.

And then Skip begged off, saying they still had to call Marco's folks, but that they'd talk soon.

Sitting here in the *BI* office, it feels like he has a million different reactions, sensations, and responses. He doesn't know who he should call about this, or even if there's much need, given his thrill with the announcement. But there's a lurking odd trepidation, too.

He pushes back in the chair, now reminding himself that he is supposed to call Gloria to see about their doing Thanksgiving together. Thanksgiving is just the day after tomorrow, which is why Alicia has rescheduled today's presentation, because the investor will be heading out early to go home for the holiday.

He thinks he'll call Jimmy, who will be spending the holiday itself up in Dover, New Hampshire, where the family tradition has long been to congregate at Gwen's older sister's home. Jimmy and Cynthia are heading over early Thursday morning and then back to Boston that evening, at least if the plan Jimmy texted him is holding, although Jimmy hasn't mentioned whether Cynthia would come back with him. She could well be heading to the tiny Middlebury apartment she's kept for the three years she's worked on-site at MMEAT, the climate change organization focused on agriculture reformation where she is now the associate director.

Meat, Methane Emissions, and Agricultural Transformations Center. He is pretty sure that is the full name. Meat alternatives are her focus, and he briefly wonders if the Dover Thanksgiving will see a subbing for turkey. *Tofurky*, is what he thinks, but he knows there are actual turkey-like alternatives now, including some of the recently fully approved FDA meat culture products.

So, he'll call Jimmy to see if he and Cynthia can come down for a second Thanksgiving, either Friday or Saturday. It would be like old-home week with Deidre back living at the house. It would be nice to have the whole house and Jimmy and Cynthia for a big dinner, but he hasn't mentioned the possibility to any of the house sharers yet.

If there is a dinner, he tells himself. He's feeling conflicted, especially about Gloria coming over. He could say last minute that Jimmy and Cynthia are visiting and he wants quality time, especially with the news about Skip being pregnant.

Quality time, jesus, he scolds himself.

And if there is a dinner, he won't ask Alicia, as much as he'd like to, not if Deidre is attending.

Alicia is finally cutting back on asking after Deidre, but that doesn't mean she's done with her inquiries, only that she is no longer asking after Deidre each and every time she sees or talks to him, which for a while in the past weeks seemed about every day. It's none of his business, nor would he ever want it to be, but he is curious about what's happened between the two of them. As best he can see, it isn't as if there's anything other than gentle concern between the two, judging from the requests made of him to relay that, with one or the other asking after one or the other. They both claim to be fine, but he can see it's hard, whatever exactly is going on. On the other hand, he doesn't have to advertise for another house share, and he is personally thrilled to have Deidre back. She may be less thrilled she's up in Jimmy's old third-floor bedroom though, instead of her old room.

House-sharer floor, he can't help thinking. *Ghetto*.

He rolls his eyes at this thought.

He has commandeered the whole second floor's long front half of the house that spans his big office at the south end to his bedroom with an exterior door and deck at the other end, with the big library room and the small bathroom in the middle. The two entries off the living room into the library he mostly keeps shut.

He's now got three house sharers contributing, plus the Devreaux family in the small apartment, paid through Americabnb. Marsha still has a lower monthly rent because of the work she does on the property, and he hasn't raised her rent back up any even though she is no longer helping with the Airbnb now that it's rented long-term.

I'm a bit afraid to adjust her rent back upward, he laughs at himself.

A quick glance out the downtown office windows shows a dimming of the light. He checks his weather app and sees a storm coming in this afternoon. There's nothing special about it, just some rain that will put the kibosh on the garden work today. Tomorrow looks like a nice day, even a bit warm, so he'll text Marsha to see if she can help out then.

Although Josephine-related news still often makes the front pages, and there's now the never-ending Kehoe pieces, there is plenty of world news to take in, too. One such is Chile's third uprising against poorly managed and increasingly higher public transit fare prices. He's afraid something like this can happen here, despite the rise of the political fortunes of progressives across much of the United States.

Or maybe because, he finds himself wondering.

There are still many states that are holdouts, redoubts

of MAGA conservatism, and even, he knows, places in this country that have significant nationalist and fascist supporters. Federal policy toward immigration has grown more sensible, especially in the rollbacks of the Trump-era decisions and the recent reforms, but there remains plenty of fearmongering and unease.

As far as he's concerned, the immigration improvements don't go far enough. He's doubtful there will be any further progress, though, not with the stories and speeches about the country needing to take care of its own or other such calls to action, and then there are the statements made by some politicians claiming illegal aliens are keeping hurricane victims from getting housing or throwing out homeless Americans from limited shelter space. He figures this may be true in some instances but only because the issue of homelessness remains under-addressed.

Well, I'm doing my part, he tells himself, although he can't ignore that this is bullshit on his part, really. Americabnb has been a nice bonus since the Devreauxs are likely staying in place for months more through the off-season. On top of the extended season's income, Eugene has been doing some much-needed window trim paint scraping and sanding and some of the yard work. He's getting paid in a rent reduction, although this is more in the form of a kickback since he still gets the full rate from Americabnb. He's been building up his savings, more modestly than he'd like, but steady, and he feels like he's finally getting something of a buffer.

The economy keeps getting worse for many people though, and there are all the Wall Street panic stories these days in response to the climate change legislation in Congress. Retirement accounts for many have taken another tumble with stocks for fossil fuel companies leading the way downward. Not his IRAs though, at least in any big way. A couple years ago, back when Jimmy and Cynthia's relationship firmed up, she'd insisted he get his investment and retirement funds reviewed and had hounded him enough about the new assistance programs available through Carbon's End that he had done it. He'd been surprised to learn that so many equities related to fossil fuel businesses remained in his various mutual funds. He would have bet he'd selected funds because they hadn't been oil-heavy, but as he learned, he would have lost that bet.

The rain starts, though the fall is gentle. He considers taking a quick nap on the office couch under the street windows, but then he hears someone coming in and sees its Stephanie, *BI*'s Gallery editor, and he tells her Alicia is still on the phone.

"Crazy times," she says, not bothering with a greeting. "That refinery attack, that poor family, and that group, the eco-terrorists," she says, and he can't disagree with anything she is saying.

Pre-attack images of the Merion Station home for before/after effect have been ubiquitous since the story broke. It seems like anytime the story is raised, it is as if the crime of destroying a beautiful house makes the murdering of its inhabitants that much worse.

"I mean, that drone attack, they think a special thing was dropped on the refinery," she says. "And they rigged that big gasoline tanker truck to roll down the lawn and everything," she adds, shaking her head.

She doesn't seem to be a close reader, he thinks. The fuel truck was nothing special, just getting it going after it turned off the road and crushing a decorative wrought iron fence. The driver, identity still unknown, put a brick on the gas pedal and jumped clear. According to reports, the truck had come close to missing the house but had managed to clip a corner.

He shrugs and tells Stephanie the truck wasn't anything sophisticated. "The detonator used an infrared signal and could easily have failed," is what he says, but her expression makes him wish he'd remained silent.

"I mean, it did go off, and that was terrible," he adds.

She nods, but he can't shake the sense she's disappointed

he's offered any alternative that the perpetrators, a group calling themselves *No One's Safe*, might be anything other than highly trained fifth columnists or foreign terrorists.

The oil farm attack was interesting though, and there's been a steady stream of updates on what the officials have determined. It isn't so much the use of a drone, those are a dime a dozen these days, but what's been reported recently is the nature of the devices dropped by the drone. The investigators' drawings of the device released two days ago reveal an impressive understanding of how one would light an oil storage tank ablaze, first dropping a shaped charge designed to crush in the top of the tank and produce holes, and then a second release of a device filled with magnesium shavings or road flare filling, the particular ingredient choice dependent on the article read. This second device was weighted, pointed, and finned to fall true, with three simple prongs attached to redundant igniters that were nothing more than Bic lighters.

"Do you think it was employee revenge?" she asks, and he manages not to roll his eyes. He's sure she's referring to the recent discovery that McPherson, that KTR asshole, had personal animosity toward his last victim. He's trying to think up a joke about his assassinating Alicia because she's rescheduled the presentation, but thinks better of it. Then Alicia saves the day by coming out from her office, but now he's waiting for her to finish up with Stephanie.

His phone rings.

"Hey, Daddo," Jimmy says. "Got a minute?"

Davin jumps right in about their coming by for a second Thanksgiving, and Jimmy tells him they are planning to visit, but dinner isn't necessary. They've got something they need to talk about.

That gets him wondering if maybe they're pregnant, or getting married, and maybe because of the call from Skip just this morning he's still thinking this is what the call must be about, but Jimmy tells him Cynthia wants to talk to him about something. That, of course, just makes him flash more on the idea of pregnancy.

Gwen must be head over heels, he thinks.

"Davin," Cynthia says, having taken Jimmy's phone, "don't do anything with Aine, there's not going to be any event."

He asks her why, and her answer is not something he would have ever guessed.

"Climate Progress is one of the sponsors," she tells him, although he knows she knows he knows this, although it is MMEAT they've talked about as a sponsor, but there's no significant difference.

"Yeah," is his reply.

"There's a problem with Aine, you can't say anything to her, anyone," she says.

He's got no idea what is being said.

"This is on the QT, super absolutely, but Climate Progress's intelligence department just reached out. They've flagged Aine, a security flag," she tells him.

"Uh," he says. What he thinks is, *Climate Progress has an intelligence department?* This is what he's finding himself fixing on, but he tries to keep himself on topic.

"There's a problem with The Third Act?" he asks.

Cynthia laughs. "Jesus, no," she says. "McKibben isn't flagging as an associate to known violence groups," but at least she's not sounding exasperated by his question.

"So," he says.

"Aine's comes up, flagged a possible *NOS*, that's what they're saying."

It takes him a moment to process what Cynthia is saying.

"You mean *No One's Safe*?" he asks after a long pause on his part.

He's got a couple more questions, but Cynthia promises they'll talk more about it when they visit on the day after Thanksgiving. He's fine with not taking Aine's calls, if she does call. He thinks that there's renewed hope to get garden work done, then studio time.

And then he thinks, *so apparently that's two women I'm not taking calls from.*

The problem with Gloria, he is more clearly understanding, is he's been feeling there's not much emotional connection, and what he wants, he's more and more convinced, is a fuller relationship.

He's also wondering what Aine could possibly be up to, what trouble she may have gotten herself in, and he feels concern for her. He likes her and thinks she's funny, a too-rare trait these days.

He shakes his head, trying to rid the unease he's experiencing.

And then he thinks, *well, no one is safe.*

And then Stephanie is leaving and Alicia's calling out to him from her office, asking him to set up the presentation for a last quick review.

But what he's now mainly thinking is that he doesn't have to worry about renting a tent anymore.

Chapter 52: No One is Safehouse

We gotta move, gotta split," the young man is telling his girlfriend, but the sparsely bearded man doesn't give her a chance to ask why or what he's talking about, because he just barrels on.

"The soup can's been thrown," is what he adds.

The woman with the straight blond hair, who's a few years older than the man, just looks at him, waiting for him to tell her what he means.

He looks at her. They are in a bedroom that is neither big nor small and indistinct in other ways, too, and in an indistinct house in an indistinct part of Lockwood, a suburb, of sorts, of Buffalo, NY. The walls in the dim light of the bedside lamp are beige. The bed is rumpled. They'd been making love when the text notification had sounded and the man had simply rolled off her and fished a phone out of his jean front left pocket.

He sits up, peering closely at the text.

"It's the code," he adds, still peering closely at the phone screen in the dim light, but then he tosses the phone on the bed, fully rising, pulling on underwear and his pants, and she can't help notice his movements are telegraphing something like panic as he roots about for his other clothes. She also notices, even as her surprise and annoyance grows, that this is not his phone lying on the rumpled sheets, not the phone she has seen him use for the four months they'd been together, the four months she'd called or texted him and from which she'd gotten calls and texts from him.

"Code," she says. "What the fuck are you on about?"

She too is fishing her underwear from the rug by the bed, where the rest of her clothes lay in a heap. She has a faint accent, something out of Britain, but she's never told him much in the way of details of where she's from.

"Jesus Christ," she adds, as she steps into her panties, pulling them on.

The young man sniffs.

"Code, that's right," he says, nodding down at the phone on the bed. Jeans on, he is now rebuttoning his shirt, fixing the first attempt, now getting the right buttons and buttonholes right.

"Fuck," he now says, less to her than simply into the room, in a quiet voice that carries disappointment. "It was looking like a nice evening in the making," turning to look as she fastens her bra and then watches as she snags a pull-over blouse over her head.

She looks up at him, waiting.

He leers at her, but it's cartoonish, she thinks, exaggerated and mixed with some anxiety, she thinks, and it is an unattractive and uncomfortable attempt, his effort to joke.

"Well, instead of us fucking, it looks like something got fucked," he says.

A threat to the cell?" she asks. She quietly finishes dressing, her annoyance now getting replaced by her own growing anxiety.

"Yup," he says, then sitting on the bed. He sits there long enough for the woman to grow irritated.

"Jesus," she says, gesturing the question with her hands, her face, *So?*

He looks up at her.

Sorry," he says. I'm just," and he pauses, and then gestures with his hand, a finger up, "just going over the protocols, but I know we have to move, that it is possible this location will be compromised."

"Well, a shitty place, really," she says, attempting to calm him, seeing that he's growing more agitated, his mind racing, scrambling, that's what it seems to be going on. She's not bothered much with learning the protocols, hadn't been particularly interested, not like he had been, anyway.

The second of his phones, the surprise one, tones again and he snatches it up off the bed.

"An address, probably," he says, and she knows he means their next destination, although the text, which he shows her, is a block of numbers.

She recognizes from her brief orientation that this is an encoded message.

"The book is on the coffee table," he tells her, but he is getting up, swipes his sock off the small wooden chair where he'd dropped it, and he's struggling, halfway hopping as he pulls one on, then the other, then goes into the other room. He's back a moment later and tosses the book on the bed, the orange and white cover of *How to Blow Up a Pipeline*, by Andreas Malm, landing without a sound.

He sits again and pulls on his shoes.

"I'll do it," she tells him, holding out her hand for the phone, then picking up the book. She's better, faster at decoding the cipher. *How come I never got a second phone?* she thinks to ask, but she's already heading to the living room where there's a notebook and some pencils. She's good at this kind of puzzle, that's how she thinks of the cypher number sets, the key a specific book, specific edition, and they've been using Malm's book for a short time now.

She hasn't otherwise read it.

In the dim living room, with its one stingy floor lamp barely bright enough for her to see the page numbers and letters that follow the numbered sequence, she parses the code.

From the sound of it, the man is busy in the bedroom pulling their clothes and things together, stuffed with no thought, no doubt, into their backpacks.

He's still at it when she comes in, a page torn from the notebook in hand.

He stops what he's doing and looks up.

"Duluth of all god forsaken places," she says, not at all happy. "And our insider says several NOS have been flagged, six actually, but no one's yet got nicked."

He keeps his eyes on her.

"Two have connections to Beta," she continues, "which is why, I assume, we're on the move." She does recall from her few glances at protocol that anyone compromised with potential identifying knowledge of a cell triggers the move.

"Beta move then, right?" he says, but she's not amused, thinking that it is likely that one of the two with some connection to the Beta cell, which is made up of just the two of them at this moment, is his old high school girlfriend, the one who'd gotten raped, or something like it anyway, at COP 28, in the Emirates. She's heard the stories, but always just intimations.

She looks at her transcription of the code. "Two more things. Next book is Power's *The Overstory*," she adds. "I've read that one, its good, and huge, so we'll probably stick with it for a while."

She's decoded the right ISBN, easy once she'd figured the dashes, since the numbers were in the clear.

"The paperback," she adds.

"Whatever," the man says, his attention on the room, checking to see if there's anything he's missed. The cyphering is not his favorite thing, and quite low, actually, in his queue of interests.

She can't think of anything potentially incriminating here. They've been in place for about a month and building fast food profiles isn't that useful in America, she's pretty sure.

They'd been a transfer stop for some cardboard boxes, that's the only material activity they'd had over this time, but those cartons had remained plastic wrapped and unopened the two days they had been on premises. They'd spent most of their time having sex or going for walks or getting on each other's nerves.

"What's the other thing?" he remembers to ask.

"I'm sorry to say, Peaches, but the next action is on hold, at any rate," but she's sure he's already assumed this.

"There's a good used bookstore two blocks from the bus station," is all he says, hefting his backpack on, and holding hers out for her.

She shrugs hers up on one shoulder and turns back to look at the place they've been living. Her expression is neutral, but what she utters before she pivots out the door is clear.

"Good riddance, a dog's dinner," she says, and then as she closes shut the door, muttering low, "Rambles, shambles, and happy trails."

Next up in The Steep Climes Quartet, *Over Brooklyn Hills*

Chapter 1: Happy Trails

Davin Caine sees his first backpacker of 2035 traipsing down Main Street, although he's heard from others about their own sightings for a couple of weeks now, often excitedly reported as if these hikers were red-winged blackbirds or one or another of the migrating birds in the early waves of northward-bound birds, as if the scraggly and too often musty-smelling would-be backwoods men and women are the new herald of spring.

These are the sort of thoughts drifting through his mind as he sits alone at a tiny café table on the sidewalk on Main Street, the minuscule tabletop wobbling as he replaces the cup in the saucer after another sip of coffee. His chair's cast iron seat is even smaller than the white-painted iron tabletop, and overall, the diminutive size of this café set and the four others in a scattered line alongside the curb make him think of dollhouse furniture. It seems improbable that anyone would consciously choose to sit there, but he knows that he's lucky to have found an open table, with the set's other chair holding his side bag with his laptop.

It is early in April, and the day is sunny and still on the cool side, although tomorrow will bring the first early season hot spell. He can't help wondering as he watches the backpacker advance up the sidewalk just how miserable it must be to start from the northern terminus so early in the season. He thinks that the guy certainly looks miserable enough, even when the sun is shining and the temperature is a very nice 56 degrees and not yet ten o'clock in the morning.

But then again, Davin will always assume the connection between hiking the Appalachian Trail and misery, and that is based on his own now ancient experience backpacking. Still, he has always liked that name for the Appalachian Trail, *The Green Tunnel*, a simple but accurate enough description as he himself had learned. As for the actual name, the only thing he would change would be to misspell the second part of the name as *trial*. The summer before heading off to college, he had hiked the very northern start of the trail from Katahdin, along a stretch he had belatedly learned was named, colloquially, the Hundred Mile Wilderness. The experience had pretty much cured him of any further backpacking despite all his preparatory research and anticipation, but then he's always been inquisitive, even, as it had turned out, when he was young enough and foolish enough to lace up a Sears & Roebuck pair of hiking boots and set off to hike the Appalachian Trail.

Sears & Roebucks, he thinks, *the Amazon.com of my youth.*

The hills and mountains of the Berkshires where he lives now are part of the Northeast Appalachians, as he'd discovered back then, in his preparations and research all those years ago. He is sure most people don't know this but rather think of the various geologic structures along the length of the trail as distinct elements apart from the others. All these decades past that time he'd found himself struggling up and down mud-encased tree roots and wilting in swelteringly humid and oppressive greenery, he still vividly remembers the geologic revelations back in his pre-hike planning, which is that all the multitude of mountains and ranges are part of the Appalachian Range, starting with the Mahoosucs, those mountains at the northern start of the trail midway up the large state of Maine, and then New

Hampshire's White Mountains, which themselves are a close range over from Vermont's Green Mountains. The very same Green Mountains are themselves an extension of the Berkshire Mountains that range from southern Vermont through Massachusetts and into northwest Connecticut, and all of these are part of the larger geological structure known as the Appalachian Mountains all the way down to the southern start of the trail in Georgia.

When he was reading up on all this, his biggest surprise had been that the Appalachians were once part of the geologic structure of the Scottish Highlands, but if that hadn't been interesting enough, the Appalachians too had once been geologically joined with the Atlas Mountains of North Africa that span Morocco through Algeria and Tunisia. Of course, all connected eons back when most land was all part of the Earth's giant landmass called Pangaea. He has no clue this morning just when this supercontinent existed, since any numbers above seven-figures mostly become static in his mind, although he knows that it has to be at least hundreds of millions of years ago.

He considers looking it up, the number of millennia and the name of the era now lost in his memory, and he hates to lose track of any and all facts and figures he thinks may have once been in his possession, but he decides not to bother. In his seventy-first year he's slowly accepting such gaps and now more often than not doesn't bother querying Google. He's not even sure if he is remembering the right name of the supercontinent, but he is certain that he lacks any confidence in how one spells Pangaea.

His attention comes back to the lone backpacker, now stopped and saying something to the first table in the line fronting Beannies, the latest coffee house iteration to inhabit the storefront that has seen near-countless versions of a coffee establishment. Seeing this interaction his thinking shifts to active defense. As best he can tell from the backpacker's posture and the responding physical reaction of the two young people sitting at the table a dozen feet away, there may be some panhandling he'll want to cut short if the disheveled and trail weary young man decides to request some tithe from each and every table.

The young couple at the first table hand the hiker something and with a nod the hiker moves to the next table and now Davin can hear him clearly enough to know that a donation request is being made of the single occupant of that table, and when that man turns enough toward the standing hiker, Davin realizes that he knows him. The man is one of his Housatonic neighbors, up from his house a couple of houses, and hardly more than a waving sort of acquaintance, although that may be as much Davin's failure as his. The man has always struck Davin as a bit of a jerk, and especially all the more so after the guy's uncalled complaint to him about Davin's poor trash barrel securing technique after a bear had spread the content of ripped bags across the road.

Donny, that's all Davin can think of his neighbor's name.

He is sure that he must know the guy's last name, since they've been sort of neighbors for years, but this fact is beyond recall at the moment. The man hadn't bothered to use his own name when he'd been stopped from proceeding in his electric Equinox by the clean up action because Davin was in the middle of the road with a push broom corralling the trailing rivers and smears of trash. But then why would he use his name? They'd been waving neighbors only, with the occasional *how are you* if they'd gotten their mail from the Post Office at the same time.

He remembers with a jolt that some years back this neighbor had tried to NIMBY against the carrying capacity upgrades of the power lines that run a quarter mile or more from their respective backyards.

That hadn't been fun, he reminds himself, recalling some of the details of the arguing that had been generated by that permitting fight.

I'm the winner, he tells himself, but he can guess his

grasping tightly to that victory may well be the biggest reason for the two of them being little more than waving neighbors. He knows that he is still considered a newcomer by most of those who grew up here, although he'd moved from Cambridge to Housatonic sixteen years ago.

Seventeen, he realizes.

Donny says something sharp and the young man steps back with a nod, and then both the backpacker and Donny look toward him, and both, almost synchronized, nod at him.

He nods back at Donny, with what he hopes is a friendly enough smile, although he's wondering if this is seen as encouragement for the backpacker, who is stepping toward him.

My turn, Davin thinks.

Sure enough, there's that wave of sweat and body musk that advances as the backpacker steps toward him, and then there's the request for any extra change and don't you know, he's telling Davin, he's on his way to resupply and Davin stops him with a hand raised.

"You started out from Katahdin?" he asks the young man, who sems delighted by the question, perhaps thinking it bodes well for his immediate future's finances.

"Yeah, sure, started end of March, went through that cold stretch," he is saying, apparently glad for an attentive audience. "Had to hunker in a motel for three days."

"Tell you what," Davin says to the young man. "Tell me the name of the mountain range Katahdin's part of, I'll contribute to your travel fund."

The young man no longer looks expectant, but then he's rummaging inside his Gor Tex jacket and pulls out an obvious pair of smart glasses.

"I'll call that a cheat," , Davin says, but even as he utters this the young man is saying into the air "Mount Katahdin is in what mountain range," and his gaze is that inward one that Davin still finds weird as the fellow reads off the information from his heads-up display.

"Mahoosucs," the young guy says, looking back at Davin.

Davin is shaking his head, but he's amused by the kid's fast thinking. "You know that before you started hiking, before just now?"

The backpacker, who Davin sees now must be in his early twenties, grins. "No."

Davin reaches into his jacket and pulls out his wallet, selecting a five-dollar bill, handing it over.

"For your honesty," he tells the youngster, who grins more, nods, and steps to the next table, leaving his trail of odor, and then on to the next, and then is gone.

Donny is up from his table and steps closer to tell Davin that he shouldn't give handouts, and Davin can't even manage a *how are ya* before Donny steps away.

Davin looks at his coffee, but it has grown too cold and he will abandon it, and while he is thinking this he turns to look down the street toward a big timber truck and its gurgling diesel engine unpleasantly announcing its approach towards him. With more EVs on the road, outdoor dining can be more pleasant, but Route 7, which is also Main Street in town, still has plenty of noisy vehicles.

He pulls out his phone and sees that his meeting with Alcia Soares is getting close. She owns the digital newspaper he still sometimes works for, but then again, the office is just two doors down, so he still has a couple of minutes to kill.

He wonders at the glasses the backpacker carries. He knows that the prices for these AR rigs have fallen, although these remain twice or more the cost of a good phone, and he knows that you still need the right phone, most times, to use the glasses. And then he laughs, knowing that almost all of the Appalachian Trail has good signal coverage these days. He's heard that drone delivery on the AT is common, and for some time now.

We live in a well-connected age, he mulls, and certainly Great Barrington, with open 6G Wi Fi all around, is a good example. These days are so different from his own experience and preparation for his ten-day hike decades earlier.

He laughs again, imagining backpackers wearing AR glasses while hiking, and as absurd as the image is, he suspects that it must happen, at least on occasion. He can hope that if he were there, he'd avoid using glasses, although this isn't an issue, really, since he doesn't own a pair, happy enough with his laptop and his phone.

He pulls his phone out again and sees that he needs to get going, but as he picks up his bag and starts toward the office, he finds himself still dragged back by his long-ago time on the trail.

Those boots of his had been a poor choice, even though he'd followed the best advice about breaking them in, even to the point of repeatedly applying mink oil, although the boots remained stiff and easily water soaked. The biggest problem with the boots though was how the eyelets for the laces had been made, a loop of metal with edges that tended to saw through the laces with alarming regularity. He still often tells the story most any time any mention of backpacking comes forward, recounting in agonizing detail his frequent stops to repair his laces, and how that had felt a mortal threat, the mosquitos so thick on those northern late summer days on the trail that he feared, whenever he had necessarily stopped to affect the lace repairs, he might prove sufficiently drained of blood to continue on.

In his mind's eye he can still see — even feel — the cloud of voracious mosquitos and the ghost of panicked annoyance he'd increasingly experienced. He can also admit — and sometimes still will do so, although mostly as a self-deprecating joke — that he'd found himself while on the trail half-wishing that he'd break a leg or some other sort of injury that would require he be helicoptered out, rescued from the ordeal of backpacking. Those first four days had been agony, the pack heavy enough for him to be always on the lookout for imbalance, and the trail up there well-churned and well-soaked dirt and a seemingly endless series of steep climbs with only muddy roots for handholds. The last four days were actually something of a pleasure though, his 19-year-old body quickly adjusting to the physical demands even while the way grew more level and the pack lighter.

The Green Tunnel. He had heard that term was a common name for the Appalachian Trail, and when he had learned this years later, the name had stuck with him as the right description, given that vistas were surprisingly hard to come by. Two years ago, however, wildfires had solved that problem for a stretch of the trail within White Mountains National Forest, ripping through the eastern slopes of Mount Jefferson in the Presidential Range, and claiming some part of Franconia Notch State Park before traversing eastward as far Maine's Lake and Mountain region, stopped only by Keezer Lake and some luck in Lovell. An old friend's vacation house there had been spared.

He looks southward on Main Street, but the parade of cars and trucks seems infinite.

That summer two years back, with the fires up north, had been a rare dry spell for northern New England, but rare weather has become more common. In the southern part of Berkshire County they'd escaped the drought conditions and that summer had been a great one for his garden, fenced and hardened against the critters that otherwise had easy access from the woods that surround the back of his property past where he'd levelled off a good parcel of land. For some reason, his house in Housatonic, the odd village that is part of Great Barrington, Massachusetts, was built on a slope, and that part of the valley constricted. This part of the river run had made for good waterpower and in the mid-nineteenth century the big textile mill complex buildings had been built, and that had offered prosperity to the region for many decades.

Days long gone, he thinks, and now the vehicles heading north are thinning, although the southbound lane remains unrelenting.

Both to the south and to the north of the village the valley widens out again. The Appalachian Trail runs through Great Barrington on its southern border, crossing Route 7 heading north coming up from Sheffield across the Housatonic flood plains that run for miles in the broad section of the Housatonic Valley, well below where the valley rapidly narrows between the geological structure of Monument Mountain and its companion small mountains and hills on the eastern side of the valley, while on the western side of this constricted run, there are gentler hills that rise toward Alford and build into the Taconic Range. This range straddles the border of Massachusetts and New York, and farther to the west is the much larger and longer Hudson River Valley, with the Catskills westward in the distance.

After crossing Route 7, heading north, the Appalachian Trail picks a meandering way across the flood plain and starts climbing again, a steep rise up the west face of June Mountain and then dips down before going up the southwest ridge of East Mountain to follow the ridge around south of Butternut Basin, where Butternut Ski Resort runs its slopes down northwards. Past that, there's a stretch of the trail that lowers easily down into the small Konkapot Valley, until, crossing Route 23 at the border of Great Barrington and Monterey, the trail begins another steep ascent, this time toward Livermore Peak and then up Baldy Mountain in East Lee, before heading up toward Becket, crossing at the Appalachian Trail bridge over the Mass Pike. A short hike crosses Route 20, with hundreds of miles yet to go until the trail's terminus on the top of Mount Katahdin, in Maine.

Neither the trail's Route 7 crossing on the south side of Great Barrington, nor the Route 23 crossing to the east of the town is all that far from the town's Main Street, and it has long been a common to sight backpackers, lone or in two's or three's, carrying their gear down the sidewalks on Main Street, or toward one of the two big supermarkets, one about two miles north of town center on Route 7, toward the village of Housatonic, and one south on Route 7, halfway toward Sheffield. Another popular destination is the Berkshire Coop just off Main Street in the new location, having moved from its old quarters further east on Bridge Street and now that much closer to the center of Great Barrington, and now housed in a purpose-built mixed-use development completed some dozens of years back. There is an ice cream shop on Railroad Street that is popular with the backpackers, and restaurants, a laundromat, and the Barrington Outfitters store, are common visits for the hikers. Any or all of these destinations could be tempting for through hikers.

But he's has noticed over the last couple of years that there are more of these backpackers around Great Barrington, more of them and earlier in the season, often well before July and August when through hikers would have made their way up from Georgia's trail start.

The traffic pulses slower and faster, but he decides to stop being stupid and walks down to the crosswalk, pushing the button that brings the metal chorus of *Wait wait wait*.

It is not even May, and he knows that nights can still be quite cold and the weather generally messy, although, this Spring, it has been unusually warm.

Not that unusual, anymore, he corrects himself.

The ever-earlier influx of hikers is a solid topic in the two coffee houses downtown, or among acquaintances bumping into each other on the street, and especially standing in line at the Post Office, particularly when any number of the subjects of the conversation are standing nearby, all too often with the funk of trail life a far too noticeable miasma as they wait to collect their *poste restante*.

With a tone, the metallic voice changes to *Walk walk walk,* and he's stepping on to the crosswalk but jumps back, a rider and his electric bike whizzing by seemingly unaware of any right of way.

Visit Amazon or https://davidguenette.com/ for information on where to buy *Over Brooklyn Hills*, including the many places where you may purchase this book.

About The Steep Climes Quartet

The Steep Climes Quartet is a four-book literary climate fiction series that examines the near- and mid-future consequences of climate change as experienced in recurring characters' lives and through the lens of Berkshire County, Massachusetts.

The climate change science, technologies, and politics in the books are grounded in long-term and in-depth study, rejecting needlessly gratuitous exaggeration for realistic extrapolation designed to help readers identify with their own reality of near-and mid-term futures. This climate crisis is terrifying enough, but might this be a future that remains open to our own agency and the potential in working together toward solutions?

Book One: *Kill Well*

In *Kill Well,* it is 2026 and the nation is still reeling from second-term President Trump's oil-centric chaos, but the pro-Democrat mid-terms has helped rebalance the federal government. There are still plenty of climate activists working hard, too. Cynthia is a young woman on a trip with her boss, a V.P. at Carbon's End, a ClimateProgress.Org spin-off aimed at accelerating fossil fuel divestiture, but on the way to a meeting with an investment group near Mojave, Cynthia witnesses his murder, and someone is trying to pin it on her.

Panicked and terrified, Cynthia is on the run, moving

in and out of disassociated states echoing a childhood trauma re-triggered by what she's seen. She's obsessing to find a place she might be safe, and Great Barrington, in the Berkshires, has good memories for her. Meeting sixty-one-year-old Davin Caine's son, Jimmy, who is homeward bound on the North Shore Limited, Cynthia ends up at Davin's Housatonic house, and a great news story for the interactive newspaper Davin has helped start lands in his lap. On the other hand, a contract killer comes to the Berkshires, looking to finish the job of making it look like Cynthia is simply a suicide post-murder of her putative lover and boss.

Book Two: *Dear Josephine*

Dear Josephine finds now sixty-four-year-old Davin Caine frustrated by the constant game of financial catch-up he's forced to play keep his Berkshire County, Massachusetts, house. It's 2029 and the Republican Party is continuing its losing streak, and now new climate bills and regulations are passing in Congress and getting signed. Like many, Davin's also still struggling past the legacy of Trump and high energy prices and jumps in costs for insurance policies are just the latest challenges. He must take on more paying work at the online newspaper service he helped design and spend less time in his art studio, and with food prices that keep increasing, his vegetable garden is more important than ever.

And then Hurricane Josephine, the earliest and strongest on record, hits Florida's Gold Coast, and the devastation of South Beach and the Miami Metro area and the count of the dead and the displaced staggers the nation.

There are some victories with climate change actions, but not so welcome are the costs that come with the budding number of such legislative initiatives, and the pending The Sea Wall Act legislation is one such potential enormous budget. In national news there is the developing story of a series of murders and a possible terrorist organization calling itself *Kill the Rich*, but it just may be that fossil fuel-funded operatives are also using this as cover in the latest behind-the-scenes effort to influence and control key legislation. Meanwhile, Jeannie Louise Smith, a national climate change politics analyst who lives in Great Barrington, and her researcher- and professor-filled collective, *The Laundry*, is applying AI to uncover sources of dark money, triggering a level of pushback that is far from academic, even while a new and violent climate group, *No One is Safe*, is making the news.

Book Three: *Over Brooklyn Hills*

In *Over Brooklyn Hills*, it is 2035, and six years have passed since The Sea Wall Act was enacted, thanks in part to the exposure of The Kehoe Institute's criminal efforts to push the goals of an informal group of the extreme wealthy who hold vast fossil fuel interests. For Davin Caine, now seventy years old, the economy finally has some bright spots, including ongoing renewable energy infrastructure programs that are relieving unemployment and chipping away at the country's carbon footprint. But these efforts are expensive, and for many, including Davin, the cost of living remains expensive too. He's become more politically active, and is now a member of Climate Covenant, an organization that pushes climate change progress as the single-issue vote. The upcoming 2036 election may hinge on getting candidates high and low to sign the pledge to prioritize the renewable energy transition, but the fossil fuel industry has its own ideas and still possesses the means to carry its ideas to fruition.

On the international front, China has grown belligerent as it tries to recover domestically from the worldwide recession that has stunned it, and America's expanding efforts to build out renewable energy infrastructure in the Global South is part of the rising tensions between the two powers. Another point of contention is China's hundreds of additional domestic and exported coal plants, and the resulting economic sanctions against China are making that nation desperate to enlarge and strengthen its geo-political sphere of control by any means necessary, which means U.S. defense spending keeps rising and the National Debt is spiking yet again. Mass climate migration is adding fuel to the fire with border wars raging in a mix of allied nations and our very own escalating conflict on the southern border.

Even the Berkshires is having its own migration challenge with increasingly shocking numbers of young and economically marginal New York City residents trekking to the relatively cool hills of the Berkshires to escape the brutal summer heat of the city and power cost demands for vital air conditioning. Vagrancy laws are referenced, but many of these young adults work, and the plethora of smart glasses and VR headsets that let them work anywhere are one sure sign of rising conflicts. Great Barrington's attempts to deal with the wave of "free campers" and an out-of-control housing crisis and a spike in petty crime results in an "us versus them" reactionary response, and civility and basic rights hang in the balance.

Book Four: *Farm to Me*

In 2049, twelve years after the events of the previous book, *Farm to Me* sees eighty-two-year-old Davin Caine losing sight of his dreams, literally, as his worsening macular degeneration is making it difficult for him to continue his art. Climbing all those stairs in his house in Housatonic is getting hard, too, and he's having trouble believing he shouldn't sell the house and studio and move somewhere more sensible.

Costs are still high, even with clean energy infrastructure driving down energy costs. More and more extreme weather events demand costly responses and are starting to take noticeable bites out of the U.S. GDP and troubling markets.

Food costs — beyond what Davin needs out of his garden — are levelling off, at least locally, with more and more local farms in regenerative agricultural production as the movement toward local economies grows deeper and deeper roots.

But where there is business opportunity there is conflict, and *Tri-Interactive,* the expanded online news and information service Davin still occasionally works with, has been hearing rumors about a play for consolidating the local food distribution business, and it's looking more and more like extortion is becoming part of that play.

Davin's been mentoring some of the newly expanded *Tri-Interactive* staff of writers, and when the young reporter chasing a story about shifting affiliations among small food distribution companies dies in an unlikely accident, Davin finds himself caught up in a hometown conspiracy. It's complicated for him because he's long known Marion Fletcher-Gray from covering town politics over the years she's been the Great Barrington town manager, but it looks like the town may be choosing the wrong side.

Acknowledgements

Thanks to all those who have contributed to this book's existence, from casual conversers to the mix of specific editorial services. I am grateful for their help and patience.

Speaking of gratitude, a big shout of appreciation for my dear partner MAP, who has exercised plenty of patience herself, along with encouragement and the occasional gentle dope slap when I've let the anxiety of the publishing business in these odd days get to me.

Thanks go out to my old friends, of whom these days are correctly referenced as The Ancient Ones, and who have been tolerant—and even supportive—of all my talk about climate change and the long-running project that is The Steep Climes Quartet. These people include David Rivard, Dianne Cella, Nancy Silva, Mark Ouellette, Brian Moriarty, and my sister Elaine. A special tip o' the cap to my younger brother Michael who, even when my doubts about the work abound, has been especially heartening in his listening, reading, encouragement, and comments, and despite his knowing me for so long he has been one hell of a help getting the manuscript into shape.

As always, the connections to my daughter and son and their families are crucial touchstones in my life and work, and ever more so with my granddaughter, Magnificent Mae, and her recently emerged sister, Celeste Emma.

I fervently wish all of us grownups manage not to make too big of a mess of this precious world and that we do our part healing it.

About the Author

David Guenette is the author of the climate fiction series, The Steep Climes Quartet, a four-book literary climate fiction series with the first title, *Kill Well*, published in September 2023, and the second title, *Dear Josephine*, published in Spring 2025.

He worked in book publishing as a developmental and acquisitions editor before shifting his focus to digital publishing, long serving as a journalist and editor for electronic publishing trade periodicals, and as a consultant and electronic publishing business and technology analyst. While undertaking a deep energy retrofit of his house in Berkshire County, he combined his background in digital technologies and his growing understanding of building science and house renovation and retrofitting processes to found Retrosheath, a start-up that aimed to reduce cost for energy efficiency improvements in the built environment.

He still lives in the Berkshires and is part of Citizens' Climate Lobby (Berkshires Chapter) and 350Mass.Org. He posts about climate change frequently at davidguenette.com and gives talks on a range of climate change issues.

DavidGuenette.com

For information about the series, including synopsis of the four books of The Steep Climes Quartet, visit my website, davidguenette.com. You'll also find information about where the books in this series can be purchased, and there's my "About" information, a link to CMTI Publishing website, and a contact form. There is a sign-up form on the site if you'd like to receive notification of new posts.

There are three categories of posts:

1. **The Steep Climes Quartet**, which presents posts about the ongoing work on and aim of the series;
2. **Snips of Passing Interest**, where I note and react to content on climate change that catches my eye;
3. **Other Writing**, where I talk about climate fiction generally, and where I offer other of my own writing work.